The lift shook. Something had plumped down on its roof. Whatever she had heard was above her now, fumbling softly at the trapdoor.

It couldn't get in. She could hear that it couldn't, not before the lift reached the third floor. Then she could run for the fire escape.

The doors were only beginning to open as they reached the third when the lift continued downward without stopping. The trapdoor clanged back and something like a hand came reaching down toward her.

It was very large. If it found her, it would engulf her face. It was the color of ancient dough, and looked puffed up as if by decay; patches of the flesh were torn and ragged, but there seemed to be no blood, only grayness.

Look for these other TOR books by Ramsey Campbell

**INCARNATE**
**THE NAMELESS**

BY RAMSEY CAMPBELL
Dark Companions

TOR

A TOM DOHERTY ASSOCIATES BOOK

DARK COMPANIONS

Copyright © 1982 by Ramsey Campbell

Reprinted by arrangement with Macmillan Publishing Co., Inc.

A TOR Book

Published by Tom Doherty Associates
8-10 West 36 Street
New York, N.Y. 10018

Cover art by Jill Bauman

First TOR printing: June 1985

ISBN: 0-812-51652-4
CAN. ED.: 0-812-51653-2

Printed in the United States of America

*for Carol Smith,*
*for many reasons*

# ACKNOWLEDGMENTS

I should like to thank those editors who bought various of these stories:

Charlie Grant, for "Mackintosh Willy" (*Shadows 2*, Doubleday) and "The Little Voice" (*Shadows*, Doubleday)

the late August Derleth, for "Napier Court" (*Dark Things*, Arkham House)

Lin Carter, for "Down There" and "Calling Card" (*Weird Tales*, Zebra)

Stuart Schiff, for "Heading Home," "Out of Copyright" (*Whispers* Magazine), "The Chimney," and "Above the World" (*Whispers* and *Whispers II*, Doubleday)

Ed Ferman, for "The Proxy" (*Magazine of Fantasy & Science Fiction*)

Gerry Page, for "Drawing In" (*Year's Best Horror Stories VI*, DAW)

myself, for "The Pattern" (*Superhorror* alias *The Far Reaches of Fear*, W. H. Allen)

Hugh Lamb, for "Baby" (*Star Book of Horror No. 2*, Star) and "In the Bag" (*Cold Fear*, W. H. Allen)

Michel Parry, for "Conversion" (*The Rivals of Dracula*, Corgi)

Kirby McCauley, for "Call First" (*Night Chills*, Avon) and "The Companion" (*Frights*, St. Martin's Press)

# CONTENTS

# *INTRODUCTION*

To the interviewers' favorite question—why do you write horror stories?—there are many answers, all of them true. Here are some. My most vivid memories of my early childhood are of being frightened: by Hans Andersen and the girl cutting off her feet to rid herself of the dancing red shoes; by the deformed creatures that swarm out of the mine in *The Princess and the Goblin;* by (most unlikely of all) an edition of *The Rupert Annual*, a British children's book, in which a Christmas tree stalks home to its forest one night, creaking away in the dark and leaving a trail of earth through the house. The cinema got to me too: I spent most of Disney's *Snow White* in a state bordering on panic, and then there was the scene (meant as a joke) in Danny Kaye's *Knock on Wood* where a corpse is hung up like a hat and coat on the back of a door. I began to read adult horror fiction when I was eight or nine years old, but I'd already known for years that fiction could be terrifying.

So when I began to write stories, they had to be tales of

would-be terror. At the age of eleven I had finished a short book of ghost and horror stories, patched together like Frankenstein's monster from fragments of tales I had read. Most writers start by imitating their favorites. Mine, three years later, was H. P. Lovecraft, now that I'd found a complete book of his stories. Lovecraft's style seemed easy to imitate, and so did his monsters. I wrote half a dozen stories in the manner of Lovecraft, with titles such as "The Tower from Yuggoth," and sent them to August Derleth of Arkham House, Lovecraft's American publisher. Derleth liked them enough to tell me how to improve them—by describing fewer things as eldritch and unspeakable and cosmically alien, for a start, and by rereading the ghost stories of M. R. James to learn suggestiveness—and eventually he published a book of them. You can tell I was seventeen when I finished the book—one character thinks nothing of buying a house sight unseen—but all the same, it began my career.

Literary imitation is rather like ventriloquism—trying to say things in someone else's voice—and just about as limited a skill. My next book was a reaction against this, and sometimes so personal as to be willfully incomprehensible. By now I'd left school and was working in the tax office, where I wrote stories at my desk in the lunch hour, surrounded by bureaucratic activity and ringing phones. No wonder my surroundings began to appear in my stories, and so did my growing obsession with movies and the dying cinemas where I caught up with films of the previous thirty years. Since my first book was an imitation of Lovecraft's horrors, it had been a way of sidestepping my own fears—I sometimes think that is why so many amateur writers imitate Lovecraft today—but now I was beginning to write about them, perhaps because I was gaining enough confidence as a writer to be more honest about myself.

While the supernatural elements in these new tales weren't autobiographical, the feelings were—particularly the descriptions of how it felt to be afraid. During my schooldays

I'd often been terrified of going to the Catholic grammar school, where they were fond of using corporal punishment, but now that I was growing up I found that there were many other things to fear: women, and answering the office phone, and talking about myself, and going to parties where I knew almost nobody . . . Well, I needn't go on; most of it is in my stories somewhere. All the same, I'm convinced that good horror stories nourish the imagination, and so I hope these stories do.

I had four years of the tax office, and another seven of public libraries. It wasn't until my second collection was published that I decided to try to write full-time. I was growing bored with irrelevancies: at least everything you do as a writer is relevant to the job—no cramming yourself for examinations (a pet hate of mine) with facts you will never use again, no dressing up and looking servile at interviews. The first couple of years were hard; if my wife hadn't then been working, they would have been impossible. At least writing for a living persuaded me to make myself clearer, and so, I suppose, did reading my stories to audiences—for me, the most enjoyable part of my work. I use many of the stories in this book.

With the exception of "Napier Court," all the way from 1967, the stories here were written since that freelance plunge in July 1973. They can more or less speak for themselves, I hope. The very short stories ("Heading Home," "Out of Copyright," "Calling Card," "Conversion," and "Call First") are the best of a group of tales I wrote as a kind of tribute to the old EC horror comics such as *Tales from the Crypt* and *Vault of Horror,* which in fact I never read until my twenties. Horror and humor have much in common, and it was often difficult to see where the horror comics ended and EC's other comic, *Mad,* began; perhaps these tales of mine are black jokes. "Out of Copyright" is one of my attempts to be clearer, since another acrostic tale of mine ("The Words that Count," where the entire story was an acrostic) left many readers bewildered. "Calling Card" was written (as "First Foot") in response to a commission from the Liverpool *Daily Post* to write a ghost story for Christmas and the New Year, which the newspaper then refused to publish. "Drawing In" probably belongs with these stories, since I was trying to discover if there was still any terror to be had from the best-known (and most domesticated) horror character of all. Many of the stories grew out of their settings; the setting of "Mackintosh Willy" is real, and so is the graffito that gave me the idea for the story; the location of "Above the World" is real, down to the hotel, a favorite of mine; the cinema in "The Show Goes On" was real until they knocked it down—and so on, for almost all the settings. Of course, they may not look quite like that to anyone else but me.

Three of the stories have been given awards. "Mackintosh Willy" tied with Elizabeth Lynn's "Woman Who Loved the Moon" for the World Fantasy Award in 1980; "The Chimney" took the same award in 1978, again for best short story of the previous year. "In the Bag" was given the British Fantasy Award for best short story in 1978. (The story was published in November 1977. Up to that time the award had been based on the previous calendar year, but after that, for one year only, it was based on the period from July to June. Harlan Ellison's "Jeffty is Five" became eligible for a second time, and this time it won, all of which has caused some confusion in reference books.) All three stories are about childhood in some way; make of that what you will—perhaps that I often return to the theme that deep down, we are all still as vulnerable as we were in childhood; sometimes it takes very little to break through our defenses. It's a disturbing thought, but then I believe that horror fiction cannot be too frightening or too disturbing. Too much of it seeks to reassure, often by reinforcing prejudices.

And that's as good a way to end as any. Now you're alone with the stories and yourself.

*Wallasey, England*
*23 December 1980*

# *Mackintosh*
## *Willy*

TO START WITH, he wasn't called Mackintosh Willy. I
never knew who gave him that name. Was it one of those
nicknames that seem to proceed from a group subconscious,
names recognized by every member of the group yet apparently originated by none? One has to call one's fears
something, if only to gain the illusion of control. Still,
sometimes I wonder how much of his monstrousness we
created. Wondering helps me not to ponder my responsibility for what happened at the end.

When I was ten I thought his name was written inside
the shelter in the park. I saw it only from a distance; I
wasn't one of those who made a game of braving the
shelter. At ten I wasn't afraid to be timid—that came later,
with adolescence.

Yet if you had walked past Newsham Park you might
have wondered what there was to fear: why were children
advancing, bold but wary, on the red-brick shelter by the
twilit pool? Surely there could be no danger in the shallow
shed, which might have held a couple of dozen bicycles.

By now the fishermen and the model boats would have left the pool alone and still; lamps on the park road would have begun to dangle luminous tails in the water. The only sounds would be the whispering of children, the murmur of trees around the pool, perhaps a savage incomprehensible muttering whose source you would be unable to locate. Only a game, you might reassure yourself.

And of course it was: a game to conquer fear. If you had waited long enough you might have heard shapeless movement in the shelter, and a snarling. You might have glimpsed him as he came scuttling lopsidedly out of the shelter, like an injured spider from its lair. In the gathering darkness, how much of your glimpse would you believe? The unnerving swiftness of the obese limping shape? The head which seemed to belong to another, far smaller, body, and which was almost invisible within a gray balaclava cap, except for the small eyes which glared through the loose hole?

All of that made us hate him. We were too young for tolerance—and besides, he was intolerant of us. Ever since we could remember he had been there, guarding his territory and his bottle of red biddy. If anyone ventured too close he would start muttering. Sometimes you could hear some of the words: "Damn bastard prying interfering snooper . . . thieving bastard layabout . . . think you're clever, eh? . . . I'll give you something clever . . ."

We never saw him until it was growing dark: that was what made him into a monster. Perhaps during the day he joined his cronies elsewhere—on the steps of ruined churches in the center of Liverpool, or lying on the grass in St. John's Gardens, or crowding the benches opposite Edge Hill Public Library, whose stopped clock no doubt helped their draining of time. But if anything of this occurred to us, we dismissed it as irrelevant. He was a creature of the dark.

Shouldn't this have meant that the first time I saw him in daylight was the end? In fact, it was only the beginning.

It was a blazing day at the height of summer, my tenth. It was too hot to think of games to while away my school holidays. All I could do was walk errands for my parents, grumbling a little.

They owned a small newsagent's on West Derby Road. That day they were expecting promised copies of the *Tuebrook Bugle.* Even when he disagreed with them, my father always supported the independent newspapers—the *Bugle,* the *Liverpool Free Press:* at least they hadn't been swallowed or destroyed by a monopoly. The lateness of the *Bugle* worried him; had the paper given in? He sent me to find out.

I ran across West Derby Road just as the traffic lights at the top of the hill released a flood of cars. Only girls used the pedestrian subway so far as I was concerned; besides, it was flooded again. I strolled past the concrete police station into the park, to take the long way round. It was too hot to go anywhere quickly or even directly.

The park was crowded with games of football, parked prams, sunbathers draped over the greens. Patients sat outside the hospital on Orphan Drive beside the park. Around the lake, fishermen sat by transistor radios and whipped the air with hooks. Beyond the lake, model boats snarled across the shallow circular pool. I stopped to watch their patterns on the water, and caught sight of an object in the shelter.

At first I thought it was an old gray sack that someone had dumped on the bench. Perhaps it held rubbish—sticks which gave parts of it an angular look. Then I saw that the sack was an indeterminate stained garment, which might have been a mackintosh or raincoat of some kind. What I had vaguely assumed to be an ancient shopping bag, resting next to the sack, displayed a ragged patch of flesh and the dull gleam of an eye.

Exposed to daylight, he looked even more dismaying: so huge and still, less stupefied than dormant. The presence of the boatmen with their remote-control boxes reassured me. I ambled past the allotments to Pringle Street, where a terraced house was the editorial office of the *Bugle.*

Our copies were on the way, said Chrissie Maher the

editor, and insisted on making me a cup of tea. She seemed a little upset when, having gulped the tea, I hurried out into the sudden rain. Perhaps it was rude of me not to wait until the rain had stopped—but on this parched day I wanted to make the most of it, to bathe my face and my bare arms in the onslaught, gasping almost hysterically.

By the time I had passed the allotments, where cabbages rattled like toy machine-guns, the downpour was too heavy even for me. The park provided little cover; the trees let fall their own belated storms, miniature but drenching. The nearest shelter was by the pool, which had been abandoned to its web of ripples. I ran down the slippery tarmac hill, splashing through puddles, trying to blink away rain, hoping there would be room in the shelter.

There was plenty of room, both because the rain reached easily into the depths of the brick shed and because the shelter was not entirely empty. He lay as I had seen him, face upturned within the sodden balaclava. Had the boatmen avoided looking closely at him? Raindrops struck his unblinking eyes and trickled over the patch of flesh.

I hadn't seen death before. I stood shivering and fascinated in the rain. I needn't be scared of him now. He'd stuffed himself into the gray coat until it split in several places; through the rents I glimpsed what might have been dark cloth or discolored hairy flesh. Above him, on the shelter, were graffiti which at last I saw were not his name at all, but the names of three boys: MACK TOSH WILLY. They were partly erased, which no doubt was why one's mind tended to fill the gap.

I had to keep glancing at him. He grew more and more difficult to ignore; his presence was intensifying. His shapelessness, the rents in his coat, made me think of an old bag of washing, decayed and moldy. His hand lurked in his sleeve; beside it, amid a scattering of Coca-Cola caps, lay fragments of the bottle whose contents had perhaps killed him. Rain roared on the dull green roof of the shelter; his staring eyes glistened and dripped. Suddenly I was frightened. I ran blindly home.

"There's someone dead in the park," I gasped. "The man who chases everyone."

"Look at you!" my mother cried. "Do you want pneumonia? Just you get out of those wet things this instant!"

Eventually I had a chance to repeat my news. By this time the rain had stopped. "Well, don't be telling us," my father said. "Tell the police. They're just across the road."

Did he think I had exaggerated a drunk into a corpse? He looked surprised when I hurried to the police station. But I couldn't miss the chance to venture in there—I believed that elder brothers of some of my schoolmates had been taken into the station and hadn't come out for years.

Beside a window which might have belonged to a ticket office was a bell which you rang to make the window's partition slide back and display a policeman. He frowned down at me. What was my name? What had I been doing in the park? Who had I been with? When a second head appeared beside him he said reluctantly, "He thinks someone's passed out in the park."

A blue-and-white Mini called for me at the police station, like a taxi; on the roof a red sign said POLICE. People glanced in at me as though I were on the way to prison. Perhaps I was: suppose Mackintosh Willy had woken up and gone? How long a sentence did you get for lying? False diamonds sparkled on the grass and in the trees. I wished I'd persuaded my father to tell the police.

As the car halted, I saw the gray bulk in the shelter. The driver strode, stiff with dignity, to peer at it. "My God," I heard him say in disgust.

Did he know Mackintosh Willy? Perhaps, but that wasn't the point. "Look at this," he said to his colleague. "Ever see a corpse with pennies on the eyes? Just look at this, then. See what someone thought was a joke."

He looked shocked, sickened. He was blocking my view as he demanded, "Did you do this?"

His white-faced anger, and my incomprehension, made

me speechless. But his colleague said, "It wouldn't be him. He wouldn't come and tell us afterward, would he?"

As I tried to peer past them he said, "Go on home, now. Go on." His gentleness seemed threatening. Suddenly frightened, I ran home through the park.

For a while I avoided the shelter. I had no reason to go near, except on the way home from school. Sometimes I'd used to see schoolmates tormenting Mackintosh Willy; sometimes, at a distance, I had joined them. Now the shelter yawned emptily, baring its dim bench. The dark pool stirred, disturbing the green beards of the stone margin. My main reason for avoiding the park was that there was nobody with whom to go.

Living on a main road was the trouble. I belonged to none of the side streets, where they played football among parked cars or chased through the back alleys. I was never invited to street parties. I felt like an outsider, particularly when I had to pass the groups of teenagers who sat on the railings above the pedestrian subway, lazily swinging their legs, waiting to pounce. I stayed at home, in the flat above the newsagent's, when I could, and read everything in the shop. But I grew frustrated: I did enough reading at school. All this was why I welcomed Mark. He could save me from my isolation.

Not that we became friends immediately. He was my parents' latest paper boy. For several days we examined each other warily. He was taller than me, which was intimidating, but seemed unsure how to arrange his lankiness. Eventually he said, "What're you reading?"

He sounded as though reading was a waste of time. "A book," I retorted.

At last, when I'd let him see that it was Mickey Spillane, he said, "Can I read it after you?"

"It isn't mine. It's the shop's."

"All right, so I'll buy it." He did so at once, paying my father. He was certainly wealthier than me. When my resentment of his gesture had cooled somewhat, I realized that he was letting me finish what was now his book. I dawdled over it to make him complain, but he never did. Perhaps he might be worth knowing.

My instinct was accurate: he proved to be generous— not only with money, though his father made plenty of that in home improvements, but also in introducing me to his friends. Quite soon I had my place in the tribe at the top of the pedestrian subway, though secretly I was glad that we never exchanged more than ritual insults with the other gangs. Perhaps the police station, looming in the background, restrained hostilities.

Mark was generous too with his ideas. Although Ben, a burly lad, was nominal leader of the gang, it was Mark who suggested most of our activities. Had he taken to delivering papers to save himself from boredom—or, as I wondered afterward, to distract himself from his thoughts? It was Mark who brought his skates so that we could brave the slope of the pedestrian subway, who let us ride his bicycle around the side streets, who found ways into derelict houses, who brought his transistor radio so that we could hear the first Beatles records as the traffic passed unheeding on West Derby Road. But was all this a means of distracting us from the park?

No doubt it was inevitable that Ben resented his supremacy. Perhaps he deduced, in his slow and stolid way, that Mark disliked the park. Certainly he hit upon the ideal method to challenge him.

It was a hot summer evening. By then I was thirteen. Dust and fumes drifted in the wakes of cars; wagons clattered repetitively across the railway bridge. We lolled about the pavement, kicking Coca-Cola caps. Suddenly Ben said, "I know something we can do."

We trooped after him, dodging an aggressive gang of taxis, toward the police station. He might have meant us to play some trick there; when he swaggered past, I'm sure everyone was relieved—everyone except Mark, for Ben was leading us onto Orphan Drive.

Heat shivered above the tarmac. Beside us in the park, twilight gathered beneath the trees, which stirred stealthily.

The island in the lake creaked with ducks; swollen litter drifted sluggishly, or tried to climb the bank. I could sense Mark's nervousness. He had turned his radio louder; a misshapen Elvis Presley blundered out of the static, then sank back into incoherence as a neighboring wave band seeped into his voice. Why was Mark on edge? I could see only the dimming sky, trees on the far side of the lake diluted by haze, the gleam of bottle caps like eyes atop a floating mound of litter, the glittering of broken bottles in the lawns.

We passed the locked ice-cream kiosk. Ben was heading for the circular pool, whose margin was surrounded by a fluorescent orange tape tied between iron poles, a make-shift fence. I felt Mark's hesitation, as though he were a scared dog dragged by a lead. The lead was pride: he couldn't show fear, especially when none of us knew Ben's plan.

A new concrete path had been laid around the pool. "We'll write our names in that," Ben said.

The dark pool swayed, as though trying to douse reflected lights. Black clouds spread over the sky and loomed in the pool; the threat of a storm lurked behind us. The brick shelter was very dim, and looked cavernous. I strode to the orange fence, not wanting to be last, and poked the concrete with my toe. "We can't," I said; for some reason, I felt relieved. "It's set."

Someone had been there before us, before the concrete had hardened. Footprints led from the dark shelter toward us. As they advanced, they faded, no doubt because the concrete had been setting. They looked as though the man had suffered from a limp.

When I pointed them out, Mark flinched, for we heard the radio swing wide of comprehensibility. "What's up with you?" Ben demanded.

"Nothing."

"It's getting dark," I said, not as an answer but to coax everyone back toward the main road. But my remark inspired Ben; contempt grew in his eyes. "I know what it is," he said, gesturing at Mark. "This is where he used to be scared."

"Who was scared? I wasn't bloody scared."

"Not much you weren't. You didn't look it," Ben scoffed, and told us, "Old Willy used to chase him all round the pool. He used to hate him, did old Willy. Mark used to run away from him. I never. *I* wasn't scared."

"You watch who you're calling scared. If you'd seen what I did to that old bastard—"

Perhaps the movements around us silenced him. Our surroundings were crowded with dark shifting: the sky unfurled darkness, muddy shapes rushed at us in the pool, a shadow huddled restlessly in one corner of the shelter. But Ben wasn't impressed by the drooping boast. "Go on," he sneered. "You're scared now. Bet you wouldn't dare go in his shelter."

"Who wouldn't? You watch it, you!"

"Go on, then. Let's see you do it."

We must all have been aware of Mark's fear. His whole body was stiff as a puppet's. I was ready to intervene—to say, lying, that I thought the police were near—when he gave a shrug of despair and stepped forward. Climbing gingerly over the tape as though it were electrified, he advanced onto the concrete.

He strode toward the shelter. He had turned the radio full on; I could hear nothing else, only watch the shifting of dim shapes deep in the reflected sky, watch Mark stepping in the footprints for bravado. They swallowed his feet. He was nearly at the shelter when I saw him glance at the radio.

The song had slipped awry again; another wave band seeped in, a blurred muttering. I thought it must be Mark's infectious nervousness which made me hear it forming into words. "Come on, son. Let's have a look at you." But why shouldn't the words have been real, fragments of a radio play?

Mark was still walking, his gaze held by the radio. He seemed almost hypnotized; otherwise he would surely have flinched back from the huddled shadow which surged forward from the corner by the bench, even though it must have been the shadow of a cloud.

As his foot touched the shelter I called nervously, "Come on, Mark. Let's go and skate." I felt as though I'd saved him. But when he came hurrying back, he refused to look at me or at anyone else.

For the next few days he hardly spoke to me. Perhaps he thought of avoiding my parents' shop. Certainly he stayed away from the gang—which turned out to be all to the good, for Ben, robbed of Mark's ideas, could think only of shoplifting. They were soon caught, for they weren't very skillful. After that my father had doubts about Mark, but Mark had always been scrupulously honest in deliveries; after some reflection, my father kept him on. Eventually Mark began to talk to me again, though not about the park.

That was frustrating: I wanted to tell him how the shelter looked now. I still passed it on my way home, though from a different school. Someone had been scrawling on the shelter. That was hardly unusual—graffiti filled the pedestrian subway, and even claimed the ends of streets—but the words were odd, to say the least: like the scribbles on the walls of a psychotic's cell, or the gibberish of an invocation. DO THE BASTARD. BOTTLE UP HIS EYES. HOOK THEM OUT. PUSH HIS HEAD IN. Tangled amid them, like chewed bones, gleamed the eroded slashes of MACK TOSH WILLY.

I wasn't as frustrated by the conversational taboo as I might have been, for I'd met my first girl friend. Kim was her name; she lived in a flat on my block, and because of her parents' trade, seemed always to smell of fish and chips. She obviously looked up to me—for one thing, I'd begun to read for pleasure again, which few of her friends could be bothered attempting. She told me her secrets, which was a new experience for me, strange and rather exciting—as was being seen on West Derby Road with a girl on my arm, any girl. I was happy to ignore the jeers of Ben and cronies.

She loved the park. Often we strolled through, scattering charitable crumbs to ducks. Most of all she loved to watch the model yachts, when the snarling model motorboats left them alone to glide over the pool. I enjoyed watching too, while holding her warm, if rather clammy, hand. The breeze carried away her culinary scent. But I couldn't help noticing that the shelter now displayed screaming faces with red bursts for eyes. I have never seen drawings of violence on walls elsewhere.

My relationship with Kim was short-lived. Like most such teenage experiences, our parting was not romantic and poignant, if partings ever are, but harsh and hysterical. It happened one evening as we made our way to the fair which visited Newsham Park each summer.

Across the lake we could hear shrieks that mingled panic and delight as cars on metal poles swung girls into the air, and the blurred roaring of an ancient pop song, like the voice of an enormous radio. On the Ferris wheel, colored lights sailed up, painting airborne faces. The twilight shone like a Christmas tree; the lights swam in the pool. That was why Kim said, "Let's sit and look first."

The only bench was in the shelter. Tangles of letters dripped trails of dried paint, like blood; mutilated faces shrieked soundlessly. Still, I thought I could bear the shelter. Sitting with Kim gave me the chance to touch her breasts, such as they were, through the collapsing deceptively large cups of her bra. Tonight she smelled of newspapers, as though she had been wrapped in them for me to take out; she must have been serving at the counter. Nevertheless I kissed her, and ignored the fact that one corner of the shelter was dark as a spider's crevice.

But she had noticed; I felt her shrink away from the corner. Had she noticed more than I? Or was it her infectious wariness which made the dark beside us look more solid, about to shuffle toward us along the bench? I was uneasy, but the din and the lights of the fairground were reassuring. I determined to make the most of Kim's need for protection, but she pushed my hand away. "Don't," she said irritably, and made to stand up.

At that moment I heard a blurred voice. "Popeye," it muttered as if to itself; it sounded gleeful. "Popeye." Was it part of the fair? It might have been a stallholder's voice, distorted by the uproar, for it said, "I've got something for you."

The struggles of Kim's hand in mine excited me. "Let me go," she was wailing. Because I managed not to be afraid, I was more pleased than dismayed by her fear—and I was eager to let my imagination flourish, for it was better than reading a ghost story. I peered into the dark corner to see what horrors I could imagine.

Then Kim wrenched herself free and ran around the pool. Disappointed and angry, I pursued her. "Go away," she cried. "You're horrible. I never want to speak to you again." For a while I chased her along the dim paths, but once I began to plead I grew furious with myself. She wasn't worth the embarrassment. I let her go, and returned to the fair, to wander desultorily for a while. When I'd stayed long enough to prevent my parents from wondering why I was home early, I walked home.

I meant to sit in the shelter for a while, to see if anything happened, but someone was already there. I couldn't make out much about him, and didn't like to go closer. He must have been wearing spectacles, for his eyes seemed perfectly circular and gleamed like metal, not like eyes at all.

I quickly forgot that glimpse, for I discovered Kim hadn't been exaggerating: she refused to speak to me. I stalked off to buy fish and chips elsewhere. I decided that I hadn't liked her anyway. My one lingering disappointment, I found glumly, was that I had nobody with whom to go to the fairground. Eventually, when the fair and the school holidays were approaching their end, I said to Mark, "Shall we go to the fair tonight?"

He hesitated, but didn't seem especially wary. "All

right," he said with the indifference we were beginning to affect about everything.

At sunset the horizon looked like a furnace, and that was how the park felt. Couples rambled sluggishly along the paths; panting dogs splashed in the lake. Between the trees the lights of the fairground shimmered and twinkled, cheap multicolored stars. As we passed the pool, I noticed that the air was quivering above the footprints in the concrete, and looked darkened, perhaps by dust. Impulsively I said, "What did you do to old Willy?"

"Shut up." I'd never heard Mark so savage or withdrawn. "I wish I hadn't done it."

I might have retorted to his rudeness, but instead I let myself be captured by the fairground, by the glade of light amid the balding rutted green. Couples and gangs roamed, harangued a shade halfheartedly by stallholders. Young children hid their faces in pink candy floss. A siren thin as a Christmas party hooter set the Dodgems running. Mark and I rode a tilting bucket above the fuzzy clamor of music, the splashes of glaring light, the cramped crowd. Secretly I felt a little sick, but the ride seemed to help Mark regain his confidence. Shortly, as we were playing a pinball machine with senile flippers, he said, "Look, there's Lorna and what's-her-name."

It took me a while to be sure where he was pointing: at a tall, bosomy girl, who probably looked several years older than she was, and a girl of about my height and age, her small bright face sketched with makeup. By this time I was following him eagerly.

The tall girl was Lorna; her friend's name was Carol. We strolled for a while, picking our way over power cables, and Carol and I began to like each other; her scent was sweet, if rather overpowering. As the fair began to close, Mark easily won trinkets at a shooting gallery and presented them to the girls, which helped us persuade them to meet us on Saturday night. By now Mark never looked toward the shelter—I think not from wariness but because it had ceased to worry him, at least for the moment. I

glanced across, and could just distinguish someone pacing
unevenly round the pool, as if impatient for a delayed
meeting.

If Mark had noticed, would it have made any difference?
Not in the long run, I try to believe. But however I
rationalize, I know that some of the blame was mine.

We were to meet Lorna and Carol on our side of the
park in order to take them to the Carlton cinema, nearby.
We arrived late, having taken our time over sprucing
ourselves; we didn't want to seem too eager to meet them.
Beside the police station, at the entrance to the park, a
triangular island of pavement, large enough to contain a
spinney of trees, divided the road. The girls were meant to
be waiting at the nearest point of the triangle. But the
island was deserted except for the caged darkness beneath
the trees.

We waited. Shop windows on West Derby Road glared
fluorescent green. Behind us trees whispered, creaking.
We kept glancing into the park, but the only figure I could
distinguish on the dark paths was alone. Eventually, for
something to do, we strolled desultorily around the island.

It was I who saw the message first, large letters scrawled
on the corner nearest the park. Was it Lorna's or Carol's
handwriting? It rather shocked me, for it looked semiliterate.
But she must have had to use a stone as a pencil, which
couldn't have helped; indeed, some letters had had to be
dug out of the moss which coated stretches of the pavement.
MARK SEE YOU AT SHELTER, the message said.

I felt him withdraw a little. "Which shelter?" he muttered.

"I expect they mean the one near the kiosk," I said, to
reassure him.

We hurried along Orphan Drive. Above the lamps, patches
of foliage shone harshly. Before we reached the pool we
crossed the bridge, from which in daylight manna rained
down to the ducks, and entered the park. The fair had gone
into hibernation; the paths, and the mazes of tree trunks,
were silent and very dark. Occasional dim movements
made me think that we were passing the girls, but the

figure that was wandering a nearby path looked far too bulky.

The shelter was at the edge of the main green, near the football pitch. Beyond the green, tower blocks loomed in glaring auras. Each of the four sides of the shelter was an alcove housing a bench. As we peered into each, jeers or curses challenged us.

"I know where they'll be," Mark said. "In the one by the bowling green. That's near where they live."

But we were closer to the shelter by the pool. Nevertheless I followed him onto the park road. As we turned toward the bowling green I glanced toward the pool, but the streetlamps dazzled me. I followed him along a narrow path between hedges to the green, and almost tripped over his ankles as he stopped short. The shelter was empty, alone with its view of the decaying Georgian houses on the far side of the bowling green.

To my surprise and annoyance, he still didn't head for the pool. Instead, we made for the disused bandstand hidden in a ring of bushes. Its only tune now was the clink of broken bricks. I was sure that the girls wouldn't have called it a shelter, and of course it was deserted. Obese dim bushes hemmed us in. "Come on," I said, "or we'll miss them. They must be by the pool."

"They won't be there," he said—stupidly, I thought.

Did I realize how nervous he suddenly was? Perhaps, but it only annoyed me. After all, how else could I meet Carol again? I didn't know her address. "Oh, all right," I scoffed, "if you want us to miss them."

I saw him stiffen. Perhaps my contempt hurt him more than Ben's had; for one thing, he was older. Before I knew what he intended he was striding toward the pool, so rapidly that I would have had to run to keep up with him—which, given the hostility that had flared between us, I refused to do. I strolled after him rather disdainfully. That was how I came to glimpse movement in one of the islands of dimness between the lamps of the park road. I glanced toward it and saw, several hundred yards away, the girls.

After a pause they responded to my waving—somewhat timidly, I thought. "There they are," I called to Mark. He must have been at the pool by now, but I had difficulty in glimpsing him beyond the glare of the lamps. I was beckoning the girls to hurry when I heard his radio blur into speech.

At first I was reminded of a sailor's parrot. "Aye aye," it was croaking. The distorted voice sounded cracked, uneven, almost too old to speak. "You know what I mean, son?" it grated triumphantly. "Aye aye." I was growing uneasy, for my mind had begun to interpret the words as "Eye eye"—when suddenly, dreadfully, I realized Mark hadn't brought his radio.

There might be someone in the shelter with a radio. But I was terrified, I wasn't sure why. I ran toward the pool, calling, "Come on, Mark, they're here!" The lamps dazzled me; everything swayed with my running—which was why I couldn't be sure what I saw.

I know I saw Mark at the shelter. He stood just within, confronting darkness. Before I could discern whether anyone else was there, Mark staggered out blindly, hands covering his face, and collapsed into the pool.

Did he drag something with him? Certainly by the time I reached the margin of the light he appeared to be tangled in something, and to be struggling feebly. He was drifting, or being dragged, toward the center of the pool by a half-submerged heap of litter. At the end of the heap nearest Mark's face was a pale ragged patch in which gleamed two round objects—bottle caps? I could see all this because I was standing helpless, screaming at the girls, "Quick, for Christ's sake! He's drowning!" He was drowning, and I couldn't swim.

"Don't be stupid," I heard Lorna say. That enraged me so much that I turned from the pool. "What do you mean?" I cried. "What do you mean, you stupid bitch?"

"Oh, be like that," she said haughtily, and refused to

say more. But Carol took pity on my hysteria, and explained, "It's only three feet deep. He'll never drown in there."

I wasn't sure that she knew what she was talking about, but that was no excuse for me not to try to rescue him. When I turned to the pool I gasped miserably, for he had vanished—sunk. I could only wade into the muddy water, which engulfed my legs and closed around my waist like ice, ponderously hindering me.

The floor of the pool was fattened with slimy litter. I slithered, terrified of losing my balance. Intuition urged me to head for the center of the pool. And it was there I found him, as my sluggish kick collided with his ribs.

When I tried to raise him, I discovered that he was pinned down. I had to grope blindly over him in the chill water, feeling how still he was. Something like a swollen cloth bag, very large, lay over his face. I couldn't bear to touch it again, for its contents felt soft and fat. Instead I seized Mark's ankles and managed at last to drag him free. Then I struggled toward the edge of the pool, heaving him by his shoulders, lifting his head above water. His weight was dismaying. Eventually the girls waded out to help me.

But we were too late. When we dumped him on the concrete, his face stayed agape with horror; water lay stagnant in his mouth. I could see nothing wrong with his eyes. Carol grew hysterical, and it was Lorna who ran to the hospital, perhaps in order to get away from the sight of him. I only made Carol worse by demanding why they hadn't waited for us at the shelter; I wanted to feel they were to blame. But she denied they had written the message, and grew more hysterical when I asked why they hadn't waited at the island. The question, or the memory, seemed to frighten her.

I never saw her again. The few newspapers that bothered to report Mark's death gave the verdict "by misadventure." The police took a dislike to me after I insisted that there might be somebody else in the pool, for the draining revealed nobody. At least, I thought, whatever

was there had gone away. Perhaps I could take some credit
for that, at least.

But perhaps I was too eager for reassurance. The last
time I ventured near the shelter was years ago, one winter
night on the way home from school. I had caught sight of
a gleam in the depths of the shelter. As I went close,
nervously watching both the shelter and the pool, I saw
two discs glaring at me from the darkness beside the
bench. They were Coca-Cola caps, not eyes at all, and it
must have been a wind that set the pool slopping and sent
the caps scuttling toward me. What frightened me most as
I fled through the dark was that I wouldn't be able to see
where I was running if, as I desperately wanted to, I put
up my hands to protect my eyes.

# *Napier Court*

ALMA NAPIER sat up in bed. Five minutes ago she'd laid down *Victimes de Devoir* to cough, then stared round her bedroom heavy-eyed; the partly open door reflected panels of cold October sunlight, which glanced from the flowered wallpaper, glared from the glass-fronted bookcase, but left the metronome on top in shadow and failed to reach the corner where her music stand was standing. She'd thought she had heard footsteps on the stairs. Beyond the brilliant panel she could see the darker landing; she waited for someone to appear. Her clock, displayed within its glass tube, showed 11:03. It must be Maureen. Then she thought: could it be her parents? Had they decided to give up their holiday after all? She had looked forward to being left alone for a fortnight when her cold had confined her to the house; she wanted time to prove herself, to make her own way—she felt a stab of misery as she listened. Couldn't they leave her alone for two weeks? Didn't they trust her? The silence thickened; the darkness on the landing seemed to move. "Who's there? Is that you, Maureen?" she called and coughed. The darkness moved again. Of course it didn't, she said, willing her hands to unclench. She held up one; the little finger twitched. Don't be childish, she told herself, where's your strength? She slid out of the cocoon of warmth, slipped on her slippers and dressing gown, and went downstairs.

The house was empty. "You see?" she said aloud. What else had she expected? She entered the kitchen. On the windowsill sat the medicine her mother had bought. "I don't like to leave you alone," she'd said two hours ago. "Promise you'll take this and stay in bed until you're better. I've asked Maureen to buy anything you need while she's shopping." "Mother," Alma had protested, "I could have asked her. After all, she is *my* friend." "I know I'm being overprotective, I know I can't expect to be liked for it anymore," and oh, God, Alma thought, all the strain of calming her down, of parting friends; there was no longer any question of love. As her mother was leaving the bedroom while her father bumped the last case down to the car, she'd said: "Alma, I don't want to talk about Peter, as you well know, but you did promise—" "I've told you," Alma had replied somewhat sharply, "I shan't be seeing him again." That was all over. She wished everything was over, all this possessiveness which threatened to erase her completely; she wished she could be left alone with her music. But that was not to be, not for two years. There was the medicine bottle, incarnating her mother's continued influence in the house. Taking medicine for a cold was a sign of weakness, in Alma's opinion. But her chest hurt terribly when she coughed; after all, her mother wasn't imposing it on her, if she took it that was her own decision. She measured a spoonful and gulped it down. Then she padded determinedly through the hall, past the living room (her father's desk reflected in one mirror), the dining room (her mother's flower arrangements preserved under glass in another), and upstairs, past her mother's Victorian valentines framed above the ornate banister. Now, she ordered herself, to bed, and another chapter of *Victimes de Devoir* before Maureen arrived. She'd never make the Brichester French Circle if she carried on like this.

But as soon as she climbed into bed, trying to preserve its bag of warmth, she was troubled by something she remembered having seen. In the hall—what had been wrong? She caught it: as she'd mounted the stairs she'd seen a shape in the hall mirror. Maureen's coat hanging on the coat stand—but Maureen wasn't here. Certainly something pale had stood against the front door panes. About to investigate, she addressed herself: the house was empty, there could be nothing there. All right, she'd asked Maureen to check the story of the house in the library's files of the *Brichester Herald*—but that didn't mean she believed the hints she'd heard in the corner shop that day, before her mother had intervened with "Now, Alma, don't upset yourself" and to the shopkeeper: "Haunted, indeed! I'm afraid we grew out of that sort of thing in Severnford!" If she had seemed to glimpse a figure in the hall it merely meant she was delirious. She'd asked Maureen to check purely because she wanted to face up to the house, to come to terms with it. She was determined to stop thinking of her room as her refuge, where she was protected by her music. Before she left the house she wanted to make it a step toward maturity.

The darkness shifted on the landing. Tired eyes, she explained—yet again her room enfolded her. She reached out and removed her flute from its case; she admired its length, its shine, the perfection of its measurements as they fitted to her fingers. She couldn't play it now—each time she tried she coughed—but it seemed charged with beauty. Her appreciation over, she laid the instrument to rest in its long black box.

"You retreat into your room and your music." Peter had said that, but he'd been speaking of a retreat from Hiroshima, from the conditions in Lower Brichester, from all the horrid things he'd insisted she confront. That was over, she said quickly, and the house was empty. Yet her eyes strayed from *Victimes de Devoir*.

Footsteps on the stairs again. This time she recognized Maureen's. The others—which she hadn't heard, of course—had been indeterminate, even sexless. She thought she'd ask Maureen whether she'd left her coat in the hall; she might have entered while Alma had slept, with the key she'd borrowed. The door opened and the panel of sunlight fled, darkening the room. No, thought Alma; to inquire into possible delusions would be an admission of weakness.

Maureen dropped her carrier and sneezed. "I think I've got your cold," she said indistinctly.

"Oh, dear." Alma's mood had darkened with the room, with her decision not to speak. She searched for conversation in which to lose herself. "Have you heard yet when you're going to library school?" she asked.

"It's not settled yet. I don't know, the idea of a spinster career is beginning to depress me. I'm glad you're not faced with that."

"You shouldn't brood," Alma advised, restlessly stacking her books on the bedspread.

Maureen examined the titles. *"Victimes de Devoir, Therese Desqueyroux.* In the original French, good Lord. Why are you grappling with these?"

"So that I'll be an interesting young woman," Alma replied instantly. "I'm sure I've told you I feel guilty doing nothing. I can't practice, not with this cold. I only hope it's past before the Camside concert. Which reminds me, do you think I could borrow your transistor during the day? For the music program. To give me peace."

"All right. I can't today, I start work at one. Though I think—no, it doesn't matter."

"Go on."

"Well, I agree with Peter, you know that. You can't have peace and beauty without closing your eyes to the world. Didn't he say that to seek peace in music was to seek complete absence of sensation, of awareness?"

"He said that and you know my answer." Alma unwillingly remembered; he had been here in her room, taking in the music in the bookcase, the polished record player—

she'd sensed his disapproval and felt miserable; why couldn't he stay the strong forthright man she'd come to admire and love? "Really, darling, this is an immature attitude," he'd said. "I can't help feeling you want to abdicate from the human race and its suffering." Her eyes embraced the room. This was security, apart from the external chaos, the horrid part of life. "Even you appreciate the beauty of the museum exhibits," she told Maureen.

"I suppose that's why you work there. I admire them, yes, but in many cases by ignoring their history of cruelty."

"Why must you and Peter always look for the horrid things? What about this house? There are beautiful things here. That record player—you can look at it and imagine all the craftsmanship it took. Doesn't that seem to you fulfilling?"

"You know we leftists have a functional aesthetic. Anyway—" Maureen paused. "If that's your view of the house you'd best not know what I found out about it."

"Go on, I want to hear."

"If you insist. The *Brichester Herald* was useless—they reported the death of the owner and that was all—but I came across a chapter in Pamela Jones' book on local hauntings which gives the details. The last owner of the house lost a fortune in the stock market—I don't know how exactly, of course it's not my field—and he became a recluse in this house. There's worse to come, are you sure you want—? Well, he went mad. Things started disappearing, so he said, and he accused something he thought was living in the house, something that used to stand behind him or mock him from the empty rooms. I can imagine how he started having hallucinations, looking at this view—"

Alma joined her at the window. "Why?" she disagreed. "I think it's beautiful." She admired the court before the house, the stone pillars framing the iron flourish of the gates; then a stooped woman passed across the picture, heaving a pram from which overflowed a huge cloth bag of washing. Alma felt depressed again; the scene was spoiled.

"Sorry, Alma," Maureen said; her cold hand touched Alma's fingers. Alma frowned slightly and insinuated herself between the sheets. ". . . Sorry," Maureen said again. "Do you want to hear the rest? It's conventional, really. He gassed himself. The Jones book has something about a note he wrote—insane, of course: he said he wanted to 'fade into the house, the one possession left to me,' whatever that meant. Afterward the stories started; people used to see someone very tall and thin standing at the front door on moonlit nights, and one man saw a figure at an upstairs window with its head turning back and forth like clockwork. Yes, and one of the neighbors used to dream that the house was 'screaming for help'—the book explained that, but not to me I'm afraid. I shouldn't be telling you all this, you'll be alone until tonight."

"Don't worry, Maureen. It's just enjoyably creepy."

"A perceptive comment. It blinds you to what really happened. To think of him in this house, possessing the rooms, eating, sleeping—you forget he lived once, he was *real*. I wonder which room—?"

"You don't have to harp on it," Alma said. "You sound like Peter."

"Poor Peter, you *are* attacking him today. He'll be here to protect you tonight, after all."

"He won't, because we've parted."

"You could have stopped me talking about him, then. But how for God's sake did it happen?"

"Oh, on Friday. I don't want to talk about it." Walking hand in hand to the front door and as always kissing as Peter turned the key; her father waiting in the hall: "Now listen, Peter, this can't go on"—prompted by her mother, Alma knew, her father was too weak to act independently. She'd pulled Peter into the kitchen—"Go, darling, I'll try and calm them down," she'd said desperately—but her mother was waiting, immediately animated, like a fairground puppet by a penny: "You know you've broken my heart, Alma, marrying beneath you." Alma had slumped into a chair, but Peter leaned against the dresser, facing them all, her mother's prepared speech: "Peter, I will not have you marrying Alma—you're uneducated, you'll get nowhere at the library, you're obsessed with politics and you don't care how much they distress Alma—" and on and on. If only he'd come to her instead of standing pugnaciously apart! She'd looked up at him finally, tearful, and he'd said: "Well, darling, I'll answer any point of your mother's you feel is not already answered"—and suddenly everything had been too much; she'd run sobbing to her room. Below, the back door had closed. She'd wrenched open the window; Peter was crossing the garden beneath the rain. "Peter!" she'd cried out. "Whatever happens I still love you—" but her mother was before her, pushing her away from the window, shouting down: "Go back to your kennel!". . . "What?" she asked Maureen, distracted back.

"I said I don't believe it was your decision. It must have been your mother."

"That's irrelevant. I broke it off finally." Her letter: "It would be impossible to continue when my parents refuse to receive you but anyway I don't want to anymore, I want to study hard and become a musician"—she'd posted it on Saturday after a sleepless sobbing night, and immediately she'd felt released, at peace. Then the thought disturbed her: it must have reached Peter by now; surely he wouldn't try to see her? But he wouldn't be able to get in; she was safe.

"You can't tell me you love your mother more than Peter. You're simply taking refuge again."

"Surely you don't think I love her now. But I still feel I must be loyal. Is there a difference between love and loyalty?"

"Never having had either, I wouldn't know. Good God, Alma, stop barricading yourself with pseudophilosophy!"

"If you must know, Maureen, I shall be leaving them as soon as I've paid for my flute. They gave it to me for my twenty-first and now they're threatening to take it back. It'll take me two years, but I shall pay."

"And you'll be twenty-five. God Almighty, why? Bowing down to private ownership?"

"You wouldn't understand anymore than Peter would."

"You've returned the ring, of course."

"No." Alma shifted *Victimes de Devoir*. "Once I asked Peter if I could keep it if we broke up." Two weeks before their separation; she'd felt the pressures—her parents' crush, his horrors—misshaping her, callous as thumbs on plasticine. And he'd replied that there'd be no question of their breaking up, which she'd taken for assent.

"And Peter's feelings?" Maureen let the question resonate, but it was muffled by the music.

"Maureen, I just want to remember the happy times!"

"I don't understand that remark. At least, perhaps I do, but I don't like it."

"You don't approve."

"I do not." Maureen brandished her watch; from her motion she might have been about to slap Alma. "I can't discuss it with you. I'll be late." She buttoned herself into her coat on the landing. "I suppose I'll see Peter later," she said, and clumped downstairs.

With the slam Alma was alone. Her hot water bottle chilled her toes; she thrust it to the foot of the bed. The room was darker; rain patted the pane. The metronome stood stolid in the shadow as if stilled forever. Maureen might well see Peter later; they both worked at Brichester Central Library. What if Maureen should attempt to heal the breach, to lend Peter her key? It was the sort of thing Maureen might well do, particularly as she liked Peter. Alma recalled suggesting once that they take Maureen out—"she does seem lonely, Peter"—only to find the two of them ideologically united against her; the most difficult two hours she'd spent with either of them, listening to their agreement on Vietnam and the rest across the cocktail bar table: horrid. Later she'd go down and bolt the door. But now—she turned restlessly and *Victimes de Devoir* toppled to the floor. She felt guilty not to be reading on—but she yearned to fill herself with music.

The shadows weighed on her eyes; she pulled the cord for light. Spray laced the window like cobwebs on a misty morning; outside the world was slate. The needle on her record player was dulled, but she selected the first record, Britten's *Nocturne* ("Finnegan's Half-Awake" Peter had commented; she'd never understood what he meant). She placed the needle and let the music expand through her, flowing into troubled crevices. The beauty of Peter Pears' voice. Peter. Suddenly she was listening to the words: sickly light, huge seaworms— She picked off the needle; she didn't want it to wear away the beauty. Usually Britten could transmute all to beauty. Had Peter's pitiless vision thrown the horrid part into such relief? Once she'd taken him to a performance of the *War Requiem* and in the interval he'd commented: "I agree with you—Britten succeeds completely in beautifying war, which is precisely my objection." And later he'd admitted that for the last half hour he'd been pitying the poor cymbal player, bobbing up and down on cue as if in church. That was his trouble: he couldn't achieve peace.

Suppose he came to the house? she thought again. Her gaze flew to the bedroom door, the massed dark on the landing. For a moment she was sure that Peter was out there; wasn't someone watching from the stairs? She coughed jaggedly; it recalled her. Deliberately she lifted her flute from its case and rippled a scale before the next cough came. Later she'd practice, no matter how she coughed; her breathing exercises might cure her lungs. "I find all these exercises a little terrifying," said Peter: "a little robotic." She frowned miserably; he seemed to wait wherever she sought peace. But thoughts of him carried her to the dressing-table drawer, to her ring; she didn't have to remember, the diamond itself crystallized beauty. She turned the jewel but it refused to sparkle beneath the heavy sky. Had he been uneducated? Well, he'd known nothing about music, he'd never known what a cadenza was—"what's the point of your academic analysis, where does it touch life?" Enough. She snapped the lid on the ring and restored it to its drawer. From now on she'd allow herself no time for disturbing memories: downstairs for soup—she must eat—then her flute exercises followed by *Victimes de Devoir* until she needed sleep.

The staircase merged into the hall, vaguely defined beneath her drowsiness; the Victorian valentines seemed dusty in the dusk, neglected in the depths of an antique shop. As Alma passed the living room a stray light was caught in the mirror and a memory was trapped: herself and Peter on the couch, separating instantly, tongues retreating guiltily into mouths, each time the opening door flashed in the mirror: toward the end Peter would clutch her rebelliously, but she couldn't let her parents come on them embracing, not after their own marriage had been drained of love. "We'll be each other's peace," she'd once told Peter, secretly aware as she spoke that she was terrified of sex. Once they were engaged she'd felt a duty to give in—but she'd panted uncontrollably, her mouth gulping over his, shaming her. One dreadful night Peter had rested his head on her shoulder and she'd known that he was consulting his watch behind her back. And suddenly, weeks later, it had come right; she was at peace, soothed, her fears almost engulfed—which was precisely when her parents had shattered the calm, the door thrown open, jarring the mirror: "Peter, this is a respectable house, I won't have you keeping us all up like this until God knows what hour, even if you are used to that sort of thing—" and then that final confrontation— Quickly, Alma told herself, onward. She thrust the memories back into the darkness of the two dead rooms to be crushed by her father's desk, choked by her mother's flowers.

On the kitchen windowsill the medicine was black against the back garden, the gray grass plastered down by rain: it loomed like a poison bottle in a Hitchcock film. What was Peter doing at this moment? Where would he be tonight? She fumbled sleepily with the tin of tomato soup and watched it gush into the pan. Where would he be tonight? With someone else? If only he would try to contact her, to show her he still cared— Nonsense. She turned up the gas. No doubt he'd be at the cinema; he'd tried to force films on her, past her music. Such as the film they'd seen on the afternoon of their parting, the afternoon they'd taken off work together, *Hurry Sundown;* it hadn't been the theme of racism which had seemed so horrid, but those scenes with Michael Caine sublimating his sex drive through his saxophone—she'd brushed her hair against Peter's cheek, hopefully, desperately, but he was intent on the screen, and she could only guess his thoughts, too accurately. Perhaps he and Maureen would find each other; Alma hoped so—then she could forget about them both. The soup bubbled, and she poured it into a dish. Gas sweetened the air; she checked the control, but it seemed turned tight. The dresser—there he had stood, pugnaciously apart, watching her. She set the medicine before her on the table; she'd take it upstairs with her—she didn't want to come downstairs again. In her mind she overcame the suffocating shadow of the rooms, thick with years of tobacco smoke in one, with lavender water in another, by her shining flute, the sheets of music brightly turning.

A dim thin figure moved down the hall toward the kitchen; it hadn't entered by the front door—rather it had emerged from the twin vista in the hall mirror. Alma sipped her soup, not tasting it but warmed. The figure fingered the twined flowers, sat at her father's desk. Alma bent her head over the plate. The figure stood outside the kitchen door, one hand on the doorknob. Alma stood; her chair screeched; she saw herself pulled erect by panic in the familiar kitchen like a child in darkness, and willed herself to sit. The figure climbed the stairs, entered her room, padded through the shadows, examining her music, breathing on her flute. Alma's spoon tipped and the soup drained back into its disc. Then, determinedly, she dipped again.

She had to fasten her thoughts on something as she mounted the stairs, medicine in hand; she thought of the Camside orchestral concert next week—thank God she

wouldn't be faced with Peter chewing gum amid the ranks
of placid tufted eggs. She felt for her bedroom lightswitch.
Behind the bookcase shadows sprang back into hiding and
were defined. She smiled at the room and at herself; then
carefully she closed the door. After the soup she felt a
little hot, light-headed. She moved to the window and
admired the court set back from the bare street; above the
roofs the sky was diluted lime-and-lemon beneath clouds
like wads of stuffing. " 'Napier Court'—I see the point,
but don't you think that naming houses is a bit pretentious?"
Alma slid her feet through the cold sheets, recoiling from
the frigid bottle. She'd fill it later; now she needed rest.
She set aside *Victimes de Devoir* and lay back on the
pillow.

Alma awoke. Someone was outside on the landing. At
once she knew: Peter had borrowed Maureen's key. He
came into the room, and as he did so her mother appeared
from behind the door and drove the music stand into his
face. Alma awoke. She was swaddled in blankets, breathing through them. For a moment she lay inert; one hand
was limp between her legs, her ear pressed on the pillow;
these two parts of her felt miles distant, and something
vast throbbed silently against her eardrums. She catalogued
herself: slight delirium, a yearning for the toilet. She
drifted with the bed; she disliked to emerge, to be oriented
by the cold.

Nonsense, don't indulge your weakness, she told herself,
and poked her head out. Surely she'd left the light on?
Darkness blindfolded her, warm as the blankets. She reached
for the cord, and the blue window blackened as the room
appeared. The furniture felt padded by delirium. Alma
burned. She struggled into her dressing gown and saw the
clock: 12:05. Past midnight and Maureen hadn't come?
Then she realized: the clock had stopped—it must have
been around the time of Maureen's departure. Of course
Maureen wouldn't return; she'd been repelled by disapproval. Which meant that Alma would have no transistor,
no means of discovering the time. She felt as if she

floated, bodiless, disoriented, robbed of sensation, and went to the window for some indication; the street was deserted, as it might be at any hour soon after dark.

Turning from the pane she pivoted in the mirror; behind her the bed stood at her left. That wasn't right; right was where it stood. Or did it reverse in the reflection? She turned to look but froze; if she faced round she'd meet a figure waiting, hands outstretched, one side of its face incomplete, like those photographs from Vietnam Peter had insisted she confront— The thought released her; she turned to an empty room. So much for her delirium. Deliberately she switched out the light and padded down the landing.

On her way back she passed her mother's room; she felt compelled to enter. Between the twin beds, shelves displayed the Betjemans, the books on Greece, histories of the Severn Valley. On the beds the sheets were stretched taut as one finds them on first entering a hotel room. When Peter had stayed for weekends her father had moved back into this room. Her father—out every night to the pub with his friends; he hadn't been vindictive to her mother, just unfeeling and unable to adjust to her domestic rhythm. When her mother had accused Alma of "marrying beneath her" she'd spoken of herself. Deceptively freed by their absence, Alma began to understand her mother's hostility to Peter. "You're a handsome bugger," her mother had once told him; Alma had pinpointed that as the genesis of her hostility—it had preyed on her mother's mind, this lowering herself to say what she thought he'd like only to realize that the potential of this vulgarity lurked within herself. Now Alma saw the truth; once more sleeping in the same room as her husband, she'd had the failure of her marriage forced upon her; she'd projected it on Alma's love for Peter. Alma felt released; she had understood them, perhaps she could even come once more to love them, just as eventually she'd understood that buying Napier Court had fulfilled her father's ambition to own a house in Brichester—her father, trying to talk to Peter who never communicated to him (he might have been unable, but this was no longer important), finally walking away from Peter whistling "Release Me" which he'd reprised the day after the separation, somewhat unfeelingly she thought. Even this she could understand. To seal her understanding, she turned out the light and closed the door.

Immediately a figure rose before her mother's mirror, combing long fingers through its hair. Alma managed not to shudder; she strode to her own door, opened it on blackness, and crossed to her bed. She reached out to it and fell on her knees; it was not there.

As she knelt trembling, the house rearranged itself round her; the dark corridors and rooms, perhaps not empty as she prayed, watched pitilessly, came to bear upon her. She staggered to her feet and clutched the cord, almost touching a gaping face, which was not there when the light came on. Her bed was inches from her knees, where it had been when she left it, she insisted. Yet this failed to calm her. There was more than darkness in the house; she was no longer comfortingly alone in her warm and welcoming home. Had Peter borrowed Maureen's key? All at once she hoped he had; then she'd be in his arms, admitting that her promise to her mother had been desperate; she yearned for his protection—strengthened by it she believed she might confront horrors if he demanded them.

She watched for Peter from the window. One night while he was staying Peter had come to her room— She focused on the court; it seemed cut off from the world, imprisoning. Eclipsed by the gatepost, a pedestrian crossing's beacons exchanged signals without meaning; she thought of others flashing far into the night on cold lonely country roads, and shivered. He had come into her room; they'd caressed furtively and whispered so as not to wake her parents, though now she suspected that her mother had lain awake, listening through her father's snores. "Take me," she'd pleaded—but in the end she couldn't; the wall was too attentive. Now she squirmed at her remembered

endearments: "my nice Peter"—"my handsome Peter"—
"my lovely Peter"—and at last her halting praise of his
body, the painful search for new phrases. She no longer
cared to recall; she sloughed off the memories with an
epileptic shudder.

Suddenly a man appeared in the gateway of the court.
Alma stiffened. The figure passed; she relaxed, but only
for a moment; had there not been something strange about
its long loping strides, its trailing shadow? This was childish,
she rebuked herself; she'd no more need to become obsessed with someone hastening to a date than with Peter,
who was no longer in a position to protect her. She turned
from the window before the figure should form behind her,
and picked up her flute. Half an hour of exercises, then
sleep. She opened the case. It was empty.

It was as if her mother had returned and taken back the
flute; she felt the house again rise up round her. She
grasped an explanation; last time she'd fingered her flute—
when had that been? Time had slipped away—she hadn't
replaced it in its case. She threw the sheets back from the
bed; only the dead bottle was exposed. She knelt again and
peered beneath the bed. Something bent above her, waiting,
grinning. No, the flute hadn't rolled. She stood up and the
figure moved behind her. "Don't!" she whimpered. At
that moment she saw that the dressing-table drawer was
open. She took one step toward it, to her ring, but could
not look into it, knowing what was there—a face peering
up at her from the drawer, its eyes opening, infinitely
slowly, the lashes parting stickily— Delirium again? It
didn't matter. Alma's lips trembled. She could still escape.
She went to the wardrobe—but nothing could have made
her open it; instead she caught up her clothes from the
chair at the foot of the bed and dressed clumsily, dragging
her skirt round to reach the zip. The room was silent; her
music had fled, but any minute something else would take
its place.

Since she had to face the darkened house, she did so.
She trembled only once. The Victorian valentines hung

immobile; the mirrors extended the darkness, strengthened its power. The house waited. Alma fell into the court; from the cobblestones, the erect gateposts, the street beyond, she drew courage. Two years and she'd be far from here, a complete person. Freed from fear, she left the front door open. But she shivered; the night air knifed through the dangerous warmth of her cold. She must go—where? To Maureen's, she decided; that was not too far, and she knew Maureen to be kind. She'd forget her disapproval if she saw Alma like this. Alma strode toward the orange fan which flared from the beacon behind the gatepost, and stopped.

Resting against the beacon was a white bag, half as high as Alma. She'd seen such bags before, full of laundry. Yet she could not force herself to pull back the gates and pass. Suddenly the gates were her protection against the shapeless mass, for deep within herself she suppressed a horror that the bag might move toward her, flapping. It couldn't be what it appeared, who would have left it there at this time of night? A car hissed past on the glittering tarmac. Alma choked a scream for help. Screaming in the middle of the street—what would her mother have thought? Musicians didn't do that sort of thing. Besides, why shouldn't someone have left a bag of washing at the crossing while she went for help to heft it to the laundry? Alma touched the gates and withdrew, chilled; here she was, risking pneumonia in the night, and for what? The panic of delirium. As a child she'd screamed hoarsely through her cold that a man was bending over her; she was too old for that. Back to bed—no, to find her flute, and then to bed, to purge herself of these horrid visions. Ironically she thought: Peter would be proud of her if he knew. Her flute—must the two years any longer be meaningful? Still touched by understanding, she couldn't think that her parents would hold to their threat, made after all before she'd written to Peter. What must have been a night breeze moved the bag. Forcing her footsteps not to drag, Alma left the orange radiance and closed the door behind her; her last test.

In the hall the thing she had thought was Maureen's coat shifted wakefully. Alma ignored it, but her flesh crept hot and cold. At the far end of the hall mirror, a figure approached, arms extended as if blindly. Alma smiled; it was too like a childish fear to frighten her: "enjoyably creepy"—she tried to recapture her mood of the morning, but every organ of her body felt hot and pounding. She broke and ran to her room; the light, oddly, was still on.

In the rooms below, her father's desk creaked; the flower arrangements writhed. Did it matter? Alma argued desperately. There was no lock on her door, but she refused to barricade it; there was nothing solid abroad in the house, nothing to harm her but the lure of her own fears. Her flute—she wouldn't play it once she found it; she'd go to bed with its protection. She moved round the bed and saw the flute, overlaid by *Victimes de Devoir*. The flute was bent in half.

One tear pressed from Alma's eyes before she realized the full horror. As she whirled, completely disoriented, a mirror crashed below. Something shrieked toward her through the corridors. She sank onto the bed, defenseless, wishing all were over. Music blasted from the record player, the *Nocturne;* Alma leaped up and screamed. "In roaring he shall rise," the voice bawled, "and on the surface—" A music stand was hurled to the floor."—*die!*" The needle scraped across the record and clicked off. The walls seemed on the point of tearing, bulging inward. Alma no longer cared. She'd screamed once; she could do no more. Now she waited.

When the figure formed deep in the mirror she knew that all was over. She faced it, drained of feeling. It grew closer, arms stretched out, its face inflated gray by gas. Alma wept; it was horrid. She knew who it was; a shaft of truth had pierced the suffocating warmth of her delirium. The suicide had possessed the house, was the house; he had waited for someone like her. "Go on," she sobbed at him, "take me!" The bloated cheeks moved in a swollen grin; the arms stretched out for her and vanished.

The house was empty. Alma was surrounded by a vacuum into which something must rush. She stood up shaking and fell into the vacuum; her sight was torn away. She tried to move; there was no longer any muscle to respond. She felt nothing, but utter horror closed her in. Somewhere she sensed her body, moving happily on her bedroom carpet, picking up her ruined flute, breathing a hideous note into it. She tried to scream. Impossible.

Only in dreams can houses scream for help.

# Down There

"HURRY ALONG THERE," Steve called as the girls trooped down the office. "Last one tonight. Mind the doors."

The girls smiled at Elaine as they passed her desk, but their smiles meant different things: just like you to make things more difficult for the rest of us, looks like you've been kept in after school, suppose you've nothing better to do, fancy having to put up with him by yourself. She didn't give a damn what they thought of her. No doubt they earned enough without working overtime, since all they did with their money was squander it on makeup and new clothes.

She only wished Steve wouldn't make a joke of everything: even the lifts, one of which had broken down entirely after sinking uncontrollably to the bottom of the shaft all day. She was glad that hadn't happened to her, even though she gathered the sub-basement was no longer so disgusting. Still, the surviving lift had rid her of everyone now, including Mr. Williams, the union representative, who'd tried the longest to persuade her not to stay.

He still hadn't forgiven the union for accepting a temporary move to this building; perhaps he was taking it out on her. Well, he'd gone now, into the November night and rain.

It had been raining all day. The warehouses outside the windows looked like melting chocolate; the river and the canals were opaque with tangled ripples. Cottages and terraces, some of them derelict, crowded up the steep hills toward the disused mines. Through the skeins of water on the glass their infrequent lights looked shaky as candle flames.

She was safe from all that, in the long office above five untenanted floors and two basements. Ranks of filing cabinets stuffed with blue Inland Revenue files divided the office down the middle; smells of dust and old paper hung in the air. Beneath a fluttering fluorescent tube protruding files drowsed, jerked awake. Through the steamy window above an unquenchable radiator, she could just make out the frame where the top section of the fire escape should be.

"Are you feeling exploited?" Steve said.

He'd heard Mr. Williams' parting shot, calling her the employers' weapon against solidarity. "No, certainly not." She wished he would let her be quiet for a while. "I'm feeling hot," she said.

"Yes, it is a bit much." He stood up, mopping his forehead theatrically. "I'll go and sort out Mr. Tuttle."

She doubted that he would find the caretaker, who was no doubt hidden somewhere with a bottle of cheap rum. At least he tried to hide his drinking, which was more than one could say for the obese half-chewed sandwiches he left on windowsills, in the room where tea was brewed, even once on someone's desk.

She turned idly to the window behind her chair and watched the indicator in the lobby counting down. Steve had reached the basement now. The letter *B* flickered, then brightened: he'd gone down to the sub-basement, which had been meant to be kept secret from the indicator and from everyone except the holder of the key. Perhaps the finding of the cache down there had encouraged Mr. Tuttle to be careless with food.

She couldn't help growing angry. If the man who had built these offices had had so much money, why hadn't he put it to better use? The offices had been merely a disguise for the sub-basement, which was to have been his refuge. What had he feared? War, revolution, a nuclear disaster? All anyone knew was that he'd spent the months before he had been certified insane in smuggling food down there. He'd wasted all that food, left it there to rot, and he'd had no thought for the people who would have to work in the offices: no staircases, a fire escape that fell apart when someone tried to paint it—but she was beginning to sound like Mr. Williams, and there was no point in brooding.

The numbers were counting upward, slow as a child's first sum. Eventually Steve appeared, the solution. "No sign of him," he said. "He's somewhere communing with alcohol, I expect. Most of the lights are off, which doesn't help."

That sounded like one of Mr. Tuttle's ruses. "Did you go right down?" she said. "What's it like down there?"

"Huge. They say it's much bigger than any of the floors. You could play two football games at once in there." Was he exaggerating? His face was bland as a silent comedian's except for raised eyebrows. "They left the big doors open when they cleaned it up. If there were any lights I reckon you could see for miles. I'm only surprised it didn't cut into one of the sewers."

"I shouldn't think it could be any more smelly."

"It still reeks a bit, that's true. Do you want a look? Shall I take you down?" When he dodged toward her, as though to carry her away, she sat forward rigidly and held the arms of her chair against the desk. "No thank you," she said, though she'd felt a start of delicious apprehension.

"Did you ever hear what was supposed to have happened while they were cleaning up all the food? Tuttle told me, if you can believe him." She didn't want to hear; Mr.

Tuttle had annoyed her enough for one day. She leafed
determinedly through a file, until Steve went up the office
to his desk.

For a while she was able to concentrate. The sounds of
the office merged into a background discreet as muzak: the
rustle of papers, the rushes of the wind, the buzz of the
defective fluorescent like an insect trying to bumble its
way out of the tube. She maneuvered files across her desk.
This man was going to be happy, since they owed him
money. This fellow wasn't, since he owed them some.

But the thought of the food had settled on her like the
heat. Only this morning, in the room where the tea urn
stood, she'd found an ancient packet of Mr. Tuttle's sandwiches in the wastebin. No doubt the packet was still
there, since the cleaners were refusing to work until the
building was made safe. She seemed unable to rid herself
of the memory.

No, it wasn't a memory she was smelling. As she
glanced up, wrinkling her nostrils, she saw that Steve was
doing so too. ''Tuttle,'' he said, grimacing.

As though he'd given a cue, they heard movement on
the floor below. Someone was dragging a wet cloth across
linoleum. Was the caretaker doing the cleaners' job? More
likely he'd spilled a bottle and was trying to wipe away the
evidence. ''I'll get him this time,'' Steve said, and ran
toward the lobby.

Was he making too much noise? The soft moist dragging on the floor below had ceased. The air seemed thick
with heat and dust and the stench of food; when she lit a
cigarette, the smoke loomed reprovingly above her. She
opened the thin louvers at the top of the nearest window,
but that brought no relief. There was nothing else for it;
she opened the window that gave onto the space where the
fire escape should be.

It was almost too much for her. A gust of rain dashed
in, drenching her face while she clung to the handle. The
window felt capable of smashing wide, of snatching her
out into the storm. She managed to anchor the bar to the

sill, and leaned out into the night to let the rain wash away
the smell.

Nine feet below her she could see the fifth-floor platform of the fire escape, its iron mesh slippery and streaming.
The iron stairs that hung from it, poised to swing down to
the next platform, seemed to dangle into a deep pit of rain
whose sides were incessantly collapsing. The thought of
having to jump to the platform made her flinch back; she
could imagine herself losing her footing, slithering off into
space.

She was about to close the window, for the flock of
papers on her desk had begun to flap, when she glimpsed
movement in the unlit warehouse opposite and just below
her. She was reminded of a maggot, writhing in food. Of
course, that was because she was glimpsing it through the
warehouse windows, small dark holes. It was reflected
from her building, which was why it looked so large and
puffily vague. It must be Mr. Tuttle, for as it moved, she
heard a scuffling below her, retreating from the lifts.

She'd closed the window by the time Steve returned.
"You didn't find him, did you? Never mind," she said,
for he was frowning.

Did he feel she was spying on him? At once his face
grew blank. Perhaps he resented her knowing, first that
he'd gone down to the sub-basement, now that he'd been
outwitted. When he sat at his desk at the far end of the
office, the emptiness between them felt like a rebuff. "Do
you fancy some tea?" she said, to placate him.

"I'll make it. A special treat." He jumped up at once
and strode to the lobby.

Why was he so eager? Five minutes later, as she leafed
through someone's private life, she wondered if he meant
to creep up on her, if that was the joke he had been
planning behind his mask. Her father had used to pounce
on her to make her shriek when she was little—when he
had still been able to. She turned sharply, but Steve had
pulled open the doors of the out-of-work lift shaft and was

peering down, apparently listening. Perhaps it was Mr. Tuttle he meant to surprise, not her.

The tea was hot and fawn, but little else. Why did it seem to taste of the lingering stench? Of course, Steve hadn't closed the door of the room off the lobby, where Mr. Tuttle's sandwiches must still be festering. She hurried out and slammed the door with the hand that wasn't covering her mouth.

On impulse she went to the doors of the lift shaft where Steve had been listening. They opened easily as curtains; for a moment she was teetering on the edge. The shock blurred her vision, but she knew it wasn't Mr. Tuttle who was climbing the lift cord like a fat pale monkey on a stick. When she screwed up her eyes and peered into the dim well, of course there was nothing.

Steve was watching her when she returned to her desk. His face was absolutely noncommittal. Was he keeping something from her—a special joke, perhaps? Here it came; he was about to speak. "How's your father?" he said.

It sounded momentarily like a comedian's catchphrase. "Oh, he's happier now," she blurted. "They've got a new stock of large print books in the library."

"Is there someone who can sit with him?"

"Sometimes." The community spirit had faded once the mine owners had moved on, leaving the area honeycombed with mines, burdened with unemployment. People seemed locked into themselves, afraid of being robbed of the little they had left.

"I was wondering if he's all right on his own."

"He'll have to be, won't he." She was growing angry; he was as bad as Mr. Williams, reminding her of things it was no use remembering.

"I was just thinking that if you want to slope off home, I won't tell anyone. You've already done more work than some of the rest of them would do in an evening."

She clenched her fists beneath the desk to hold onto her temper. He must want to leave early himself and so was trying to persuade her. No doubt he had problems of his own—perhaps they were the secret behind his face—but he mustn't try to make her act dishonestly. Or was he testing her? She knew so little about him. "He'll be perfectly safe," she said. "He can always knock on the wall if he needs anyone."

Though his face stayed blank his eyes, frustrated now, gave him away. Five minutes later he was craning out of the window over the fire escape, while Elaine pinned flapping files down with both hands. Did he really expect his date, if that was his problem, to come out on a night like this? It would be just like a man to expect her to wait outside.

The worst of it was that Elaine felt disappointed, which was absurd and infuriating. She knew perfectly well that the only reason he was working tonight was that one of the seniors had to do so. Good God, what had she expected to come of an evening alone with him? They were both in their forties—they knew what they wanted by now, which in his case was bound to be someone younger than Elaine. She hoped he and his girl friend would be very happy. Her hands on the files were tight fists.

When he slammed the window she saw that his face was glistening. Of course it wasn't sweat, only rain. He hurried away without looking at her, and vanished into the lift. Perhaps the girl was waiting in the doorway, unable to rouse Mr. Tuttle to let her in. Elaine hoped Steve wouldn't bring her upstairs. She would be a distraction, that was why. Elaine was here to work.

And she wasn't about to be distracted by Steve and his attempts at jokes. She refused to turn when she heard the soft sounds by the lift. No doubt he was peering through the lobby window at her, waiting for her to turn and jump. Or was it his girl friend? As Elaine reached across her desk for a file she thought that the face was pale and very fat. Elaine was damned if she would give her the satisfaction of being noticed—but when she tried to work she couldn't concentrate. She turned angrily. The lobby was deserted.

In a minute she would lose her temper. She could see

where he was hiding, or they were: the door of the room off the lobby was ajar. She turned away, determined to work, but the deserted office wouldn't let her; each alley between the filing cabinets was a hiding place, the buzz of the defective light and the fusillade of rain could hide the sound of soft footsteps. It was no longer at all funny. He was going too far.

At last he came in from the lobby, with no attempt at stealth. Perhaps he had tired of the joke. He must have been to the street door, for his forehead was wet, though it didn't look like rain. Would he go back to work now, and pretend that the urn's room was empty? No, he must have thought of a new ruse, for he began pacing from cabinet to cabinet, glancing at files, stuffing them back into place. Was he trying to make her as impatient as he appeared to be? His quick sharp footsteps seemed to grow louder and more nerve-racking, like the ticking of the clock when she was lying awake, afraid to doze off in case her father needed her. "Steve, for heaven's sake what's wrong?"

He stopped in the act of pulling a file from its cabinet. He looked abashed, at a loss for words, like a schoolboy caught stealing. She couldn't help taking pity on him; her resentment had been presumptuous. "You didn't go down to find Mr. Tuttle just now, did you?" she said, to make it easier for him.

But he looked even less at ease. "No, I didn't. I don't think he's here at all. I think he left hours ago."

Why must he lie? They had both heard the caretaker on the floor below. Steve seemed determined to go on. "As a matter of fact," he said, "I'm beginning to suspect that he sneaks off home as soon as he can once the building's empty."

He was speaking low, which annoyed her: didn't he want his girl friend to hear? "But there's someone else in the building," he said.

"Oh, yes," she retorted, "I'm sure there is." Why did he have to dawdle instead of coming out with the truth? He was worse than her father when he groped among his memories.

He frowned, obviously not sure how much she knew. "Whoever it is, they're up to no good. I'll tell you the rest once we're out of the building. We mustn't waste any more time."

His struggles to avoid the truth amused and irritated her. The moisture on his forehead wasn't rain at all. "If they're up to no good," she said innocently, "we ought to wait until the police arrive."

"No, we'll call the police once we're out." He seemed to be saying anything that came into his head. How much longer could he keep his face blank? "Listen," he said, his fist crumpling the file, "I'll tell you why Tuttle doesn't stay here at night. The cleaners too, I think he told them. When the men were cleaning out the sub-basement, some of the food disappeared overnight. You understand what that means? Someone stole a hundredweight of rotten food. The men couldn't have cared less, they treated it as a joke, and there was no sign how anyone could have got in. But as he says, that could mean that whatever it was was clever enough to conceal the way in. Of course I thought he was drunk or joking, but now . . ."

His words hung like dust in the air. She didn't trust herself to speak. How dare he expect her to swallow such rubbish, as if she were too stupid to know what was going on? Her reaction must have shown on her face; she had never heard him speak coldly before. "We must go immediately," he said.

Her face was blazing. "Is that an order?"

"Yes, it is. I'll make sure you don't lose by it." His voice grew authoritative. "I'll call the lift while you fetch your coat."

Blind with anger, she marched to the cloakroom at the far end of the office from the lobby. As she grabbed her coat the hangers clashed together, a shrill violent sound which went some way toward expressing her feelings.

Since Steve had no coat, he would be soaked. Though that gave her no pleasure, she couldn't help smiling.

The windows were shaking with rain. In the deserted office her footsteps sounded high-pitched, nervous. No, she wasn't on edge, only furious. She didn't mind passing the alleys between the cabinets, she wouldn't deign to look, not even at the alley where a vague shadow was lurching forward; it was only the shadow of a cabinet, jerked by the defective light. She didn't falter until she came in sight of the lobby, where there was no sign of Steve.

Had he gone without her? Was he smuggling out his girl friend? They weren't in the room off the lobby, which was open and empty; the overturned wastebin seemed to demonstrate their haste. The doors of the disused lift shaft were open too. They must have opened when Steve had called the other lift. Everything could be explained; there was no reason for her to feel that something was wrong.

But something was. Between the two lift shafts, the call button was glowing. That could mean only one thing: the working lift hadn't yet answered the call. There was no other exit from the lobby—but there was no sign of Steve.

When she made herself go to the disused lift shaft, it was only in order to confirm that her thought was absurd. Clinging to the edges of the doorway, she leaned out. The lift was stranded in the sub-basement, where it was very dim. At first all she could distinguish was that the trapdoor in its roof was open, though the opening was largely covered by a sack. Could anything except a sack be draped so limply? Yes, for it was Steve, his eyes like glass that was forcing their lids wide, his mouth gagged with what appeared to be a torn-off wad of dough—except that the dough had fingers and a thumb.

She was reeling, perhaps over the edge of the shaft. No, she was stumbling back into the foyer, and already less sure what she'd glimpsed. Steve was dead, and she must get out of the building; she could think of nothing else. Thank God, she need not think, for the working lift had arrived. Was there soft movement in the disused shaft, a chorus of sucking like the mouthing of a crowd of babies? Nothing could have made her look. She staggered away, between the opening doors—into total darkness.

For a moment she thought she'd stepped out into an empty well. But there was a floor underfoot; the lift's bulb must have blown. As the doors clamped shut behind her, the utter darkness closed in.

She was scrabbling at the metal wall in a frantic bid to locate the buttons—to open the doors, to let in some light—before she controlled herself. Which was worse: a quick descent in the darkness, or to be trapped alone on the sixth floor? In any case, she needn't suffer the dark. Hurriedly she groped in her handbag for her lighter.

She flicked the lighter uselessly once, twice, as the lift reached the fifth floor. The sudden plunge in her guts wasn't only shock; the lift had juddered to a halt. She flicked the lighter desperately. It had just lit when the doors hobbled open.

The fifth floor was unlit. Beyond the lobby she could see the windows of the untenanted office, swarming with rain and specks of light. The bare floor looked like a carpet of dim fog, interrupted by angular patches of greater dimness, blurred rugs of shadow. There was no sign of Mr. Tuttle or whoever she'd heard from above. The doors were closing, but she wasn't reassured: if the lift had begun to misbehave, the least it could do would be to stop at every floor.

The doors closed her in with her tiny light. Vague reflections of the flame hung on the walls and tinged the grayish metal yellow; the roof was a hovering blotch. All the lighter had achieved was to remind her how cramped the lift was. She stared at the doors, which were trembling. Was there a movement beyond them other than the out-bursts of rain?

When the doors parted, she retreated a step. The fourth floor was a replica of the fifth—bare floors colorless with dimness, windows that looked shattered by rain—but the shuffling was closer. Was the floor of the lobby glistening in patches, as though from moist footsteps? The doors were hesitating, she was brandishing her tiny flame as though it might defend her—then the doors closed reluctantly, the lift faltered downward.

She'd had no time to sigh with relief, if indeed she had meant to, when she heard the lobby doors open above her. A moment later the lift shook. Something had plumped down on its roof.

At once, with a shock that felt as though it would tear out her guts, she knew what perhaps she had known, deep down, for a while: Steve hadn't been trying to frighten her—he had been trying not to. She hadn't heard Mr. Tuttle on the fifth floor, nor any imaginary girl friend of Steve's. Whatever she had heard was above her now, fumbling softly at the trapdoor.

It couldn't get in. She could hear that it couldn't, not before the lift reached the third—O God, make the lift be quick! Then she could run for the fire escape, which wasn't damaged except on the sixth. She was thinking quickly now, almost in a trance that carried her above her fear, aware of nothing except the clarity of her plan—and it was no use.

The doors were only beginning to open as they reached the third when the lift continued downward without stopping. Either the weight on its roof, or the tampering, was sending it down. As the doors gaped to display the brick wall of the shaft, then closed again, the trapdoor clanged back and something like a hand came reaching down toward her.

It was very large. If it found her, it would engulf her face. It was the color of ancient dough, and looked puffed up as if by decay; patches of the flesh were torn and ragged, but there seemed to be no blood, only grayness. She clamped her left hand over her mouth, which was twitching uncontrollably, and thrust the lighter at the swollen groping fingers.

They hissed in the flame and recoiled, squirming. Whitish beads had broken out on them. In a way the worst thing was the absence of a cry. The hand retreated through the opening, scraping the edge, and a huge vague face peered down with eyes like blobs of dough. She felt a surge of hysterical mirth at the way the hand had fled—but she choked it back, for she had no reason to feel triumphant. Her skirmish had distracted her from the progress of the lift, which had reached the bottom of the shaft.

Ought she to struggle with the doors, try to prevent them from opening? It was too late. They were creeping back, they were open now, and she could see the sub-basement.

At least she could see darkness which her light couldn't even reach. She had an impression of an enormous doorway, beyond which the darkness, if it was in proportion, might extend for hundreds of yards; she thought of the mouth of a sewer or a mine. The stench of putrid food was overwhelming, parts of the dark looked restless and puffy. But when she heard scuttling, and a dim shape came darting toward her, it proved to be a large rat.

Though that was bad enough, it mustn't distract her from the thing above her, on the lift. It had no chance to do so. The rat was yards away from her, and darting aside from her light, when she heard a spongy rush and the rat was overwhelmed by a whitish flood like a gushing of effluent. She backed away until the wall of the lift arrested her. She could still see too much—but how could she make herself put out the flame, trap herself in the dark?

For the flood was composed of obese bodies which clambered over one another, clutching for the trapped rat. The rat was tearing at the pudgy hands, ripping pieces from the doughy flesh, but that seemed not to affect them at all. Huge toothless mouths gaped in the puffy faces, collapsed inward like senile lips, sucking loudly, hungrily. Three of the bloated heads fell on the rat, and she heard its squeals above their sucking.

Then the others that were clambering over them, out of the dark, turned toward her. Great moist nostrils were

dilating and vanishing in their noseless faces. Could they
see her light with their blobs of eyes, or were they smelling
her terror? Perhaps they'd had only soft rotten things to eat
down here, but they were learning fast. Hunger was their
only motive, ruthless, all-consuming.

They came jostling toward the lift. Once, delirious,
she'd heard all the sounds around her grow stealthily
padded, but this softness was far worse. She was trying
both to stand back and to jab the lift button, quite uselessly;
the doors refused to budge. The doughy shapes would pile
in like tripe, suffocating her, putting out the flame, gorg-
ing themselves on her in the dark. The one that had ridden
the lift was slithering down the outside to join them.

Perhaps its movement unburdened the lift, or jarred a
connection into place, for all at once the doors were
closing. Swollen hands were thumping them, soft fingers
like grubs were trying to squeeze between them, but already the lift was sailing upward. Oh, God, suppose it
went straight up to the sixth floor! But she'd found the
ground floor button, though it twitched away from her,
shaken by the flame, and the lift was slowing. Through the
slit between the doors, beyond the glass doors to the street,
a streetlamp blazed like the sun.

The lift's doors opened, and the doughy face lurched in,
its fat white blind eyes bulging, its avid mouth huge as a
fist. It took her a moment prolonged as a nightmare to
realize that it had been crushed between lift and shaft—
for as the doors struggled open, the face began to tear.
Screaming, she dragged the doors open, tearing the body
in half. As she ran through it she heard it plump at the foot
of the shaft, to be met by a soft eager rush—but she was
fleeing blindly into the torrent of rain, toward the steep
maze of unlit streets, her father at the fireside, his quiet
vulnerable demand to know all that she'd done today.

# Heading
# Home

SOMEWHERE ABOVE you can hear your wife and the young man talking. You strain yourself upward, your muscles trembling like water, and manage to shift your unsteady balance onto the next stair.

They must think he finished you. They haven't even bothered to close the cellar door, and it's the trickle of flickering light through the crack that you're striving toward. Anyone else but you would be dead. He must have dragged you from the laboratory and thrown you down the stairs into the cellar, where you regained consciousness on the dusty stone. Your left cheek still feels like a rigid plate, slipped into your flesh where it struck the floor. You rest on the stair you've reached and listen.

They're silent now. It must be night, since they've lit the hall lamp whose flame is peeking into the cellar. They can't intend to leave the house until tomorrow, if at all. You can only guess what they're doing now, alone in the house. Your numb lips crack again as you grin. Let them enjoy themselves while they can.

He didn't leave you many muscles you can use; it was a thorough job. No wonder they feel safe. Now you have to concentrate yourself in those muscles that still function. Swaying, you manage to raise yourself momentarily to a position where you can grip the next higher stair. You clench on your advantage. Then, pushing with muscles you'd almost forgotten you had, you manage to lever yourself one step higher.

You maneuver yourself until you're sitting upright. There's less risk that way of your losing your balance for a moment and rolling all the way down to the cellar floor, where you began climbing hours ago. Then you rest. Only six more stairs.

You wonder again how they met. Of course you should have known that it was going on, but your work was your wife and you couldn't spare the time to watch over the woman you'd married. You should have realized that when she went to the village she would meet people and mightn't be as silent as at home. But her room might have been as far from yours as the village is from the house: you gave little thought to the people in either.

Not that you blame yourself. When you met her—in the town where you attended the University—you'd thought she understood how important your work was. It wasn't as if you'd intended to trick her. It was only when she tried to seduce you from your work, both for her own gratification and because she was afraid of it, that you barred her from your companionship by silence.

You can hear their voices again. They're on the upper floor. You don't know whether they're celebrating or comforting each other as guilt settles on them. It doesn't matter. So long as he didn't close the laboratory door when he returned from the cellar. If it's closed you'll never be able to open it. And if you can't get into the laboratory he's killed you after all. You raise yourself, your muscles shuddering with the effort, your cheeks chafing against the wooden stair. You won't relax until you can see the laboratory door.

You're reaching for the top stair when you slip. Your chin comes down on it and slides back. You grip the stair with your jaws, feeling splinters lodge between your teeth. Your neck scrapes the lower stair, but it has lost all feeling save an ache fading slowly into dullness. Only your jaws are preventing you from falling back where you started, and they're throbbing as if nails are being driven into the hinges with measured strokes. You close them tighter, pounding with pain, then you overbalance yourself onto the top stair. You teeter for a moment, then you're secure.

But you don't rest yet. You edge yourself forward and sit up so that you can peer out of the cellar. The outline of the laboratory door billows slightly as the lamp flickers. It occurs to you that they've lit the lamp because she's terrified of you, lying dead beyond the main staircase as she thinks. You laugh silently. You can afford to. When the flame steadies you can see darkness gaping for inches around the laboratory door.

You listen to their voices upstairs, and rest. You know he's a butcher, because he once helped one of the servants to carry the meat from the village. In any case, you could have told his profession from what he has done to you. You're still astonished that she should have taken up with him. From the little you knew of the village people you were delighted that they avoided your house.

You remember the day the new priest came to see you. You could tell he'd heard all the wildest village tales about your experiments. You were surprised he didn't try to ward you off with a cross. When he found you could argue his theology into a corner, he left, a twitch pulling his smile awry. He'd tried to persuade both of you to attend church, but your wife sat silent throughout. It had been then that you decided to trust her to go to the village. As you paid off the servants you told yourself she would be less likely to talk. You grin fiercely. If you'd been as inaccurate in your experiments you would be dead.

Upstairs they're still talking. You rock forward and try to wedge yourself between the cellar door and its frame.

With your limited control it's difficult, and you find yourself leaning in the crack without any purchase on the wood. Your weight hasn't moved the door, which is heavier than you have ever before had cause to realize. Eventually you manage to wedge yourself in the crack, gripping the frame with all your strength. The door rests on you, and you nudge your weight clumsily against it.

It creaks away from you a little, then swings back, crushing you. It has always hung unevenly and persisted in standing ajar; it never troubled you before. Now the strength he left you, even focused like light through a burning-glass, seems unequal to shifting the door. Trapped in the crack, you relax for a moment. Then, as if to take it unawares, you close your grip on the frame and shove against the door, pushing yourself forward as it swings away.

It comes back, answering the force of your shove, and you aren't clear. But you're still falling into the hall, and as the door chops into the frame you fall on your back, beyond the sweep of the door. You're free of the cellar, but on your back you're helpless. The slowing door can move more than you can. All the muscles you've been using can only work aimlessly and loll in the air. You're laid out on the hall floor like a laboratory subject, beneath the steadying flame.

Then you hear the butcher call to your wife, "I'll see," and start downstairs.

You begin to twitch all the muscles on your right side frantically. You roll a little toward that side, then your wild twitching rocks you back. The flame shakes above you, making your shadow play the cruel trick of achieving the movement you're struggling for. He's at the halfway landing now. You work your right side again and hold your muscles still as you begin to turn that way. Suddenly you've swung over your point of equilibrium and are lying on your right side. You strain your aching muscles to inch you forward, but the laboratory is several feet away, and you're by no means moving in a straight line. His footsteps resound. Then you hear your wife's terrified voice, entreating him back. There's a long pondering silence. Then he hurries back upstairs.

You don't let yourself rest until you're inside the laboratory, although by then your ache feels like a cold stiff surface within your flesh and your mouth tastes like a dusty hole in stone. Once beyond the door you sit still, gazing about. Moonlight is spread from the window to the door. Your gaze seeks the bench where you were working when he found you. He hasn't cleared up any of the material which your convulsions threw to the floor. Glinting on the floor you can see a needle, and nearby the surgical thread which you never had occasion to use. You relax to prepare for your last concerted effort, and remember.

You recall the day you perfected the solution. As soon as you'd quaffed it you felt your brain achieve a piercing alertness, become precisely and continually aware of the messages of each nerve and preside over them, making minute adjustments at the first hint of danger. You knew this was what you'd worked for, but you couldn't prove it to yourself until the day you felt the stirrings of cancer. Then your brain seemed to condense into a keen strand of energy that stretched down and seared the cancer out. That was proof. You were immortal.

Not that some of the research you'd had to carry out wasn't unpleasant. It had taken you a great deal of furtive expenditure at the mortuaries to discover that some of the extracts you needed for the solution had to be taken from the living brain. The villagers thought the children had drowned, for their clothes were found on the riverbank. Medical progress, you told yourself, has always involved suffering.

Perhaps your wife suspected something of this stage of your work, or perhaps she and the butcher had simply decided to rid themselves of you. In any case, you were working at your bench, trying to synthesize your discovery, when you heard him enter. He must have rushed at you, for before you could turn you felt a blazing slash gape in the back of your neck. Then you awoke on the cellar floor.

You edge yourself forward across the laboratory. Your greatest exertion is past, but this is the most exacting part. When you're nearly touching your prone body you have to turn round. You move yourself with your jaws and steer with your tongue. It's difficult, but less so than tonguing yourself upright on your neck to rest on the stairs. Then you fit yourself to your shoulders, groping with your mind to feel the nerves linking again.

Now you'll have to hold yourself unflinching or you'll roll apart. With your mind you can do it. Gingerly, so as not to part yourself, you stretch out your arm for the surgical needle and thread.

# *The Proxy*

WHEN her spade struck the obstacle she thought it was another stone. Among the sunlit lumps of earth that bristled with uprooted grass, soil trickled down her balked spade. She tried to dig around the object, to dislodge it. It and her spade ground as if they were subterranean teeth. It was longer than she'd thought: inches—no, feet. She scraped away its covering of earth. It was composed not of stone but of bricks.

The remains of a wall? She glanced at the neighboring houses. Within their small front gardens they stood close to the pavement, in pairs. Only hers hung back within its larger garden, as though the others had stepped forward to meet the rank of trees along the avenue. Hers was newer; it didn't know the drill.

The disinterred bricks looked charred, as had some of the earth she'd turned. She was still pondering when she saw Paul's car. He had to halt abruptly as another driver, impatient with the lethargic traffic lights, swung across his path, into the side road. As Paul drove by to lock up their car he waved to her. His wave looked feeble, preoccupied.

When he returned she said, "How was your day?"

"Oh," he groaned. "Not bad," he added quickly, smiling—but the groan had been the truth. He wouldn't be able to tell her more: she didn't even know the exact nature of his job—something to do with the Ministry of Defense.

He mixed drinks and brought them outside. They sat sipping on the bench he'd made, and gazed at the upheaved earth. The shadow of an adjacent house boxed in the garden. Eclipsed by roofs, the sunlight still flooded the sky with lemon.

When they had been silent for a while she said, "Did you see what I unearthed?"

"A bit of wall."

"Don't you think it could be an old foundation? See—if there were a house just there, it would be in line with all the others."

"It would if it were, but what makes you think it was?"

"I think it burnt down. Come and see."

He was rubbing his forehead, trying to smooth it. "I'll look later." His words tripped loosely over one another.

Perhaps it was only a wall. It wasn't important now; what mattered was that Paul was on edge. She wiped specks of earth from her glasses, then she turned on the pressure cooker and uncorked the wine. When she went to call him, he was gazing at his empty glass. The rectangular shadow had engulfed the garden. As the afterglow faded from her dazzled eyes, it looked as though an entire foundation had sprouted, dark and vague, from the earth.

He chattered and joked throughout dinner. Whenever he had problems at work he always laughed more, to pretend he had none. She'd grown used to the fact that part of him was marked Government Property—a part she would never know. She was used to telling people that she didn't know her husband's job. But when he was worried, as now, she couldn't help feeling cut off from him.

Boxy shadows stretched into the house. She drew the curtains, to make the rooms cosier. The radiators twanged as hot water expanded their veins. Beyond the curtains in the front bedroom a blurred light shone: a car, turning.

They played backgammon. The circular men tapped around the board, knocking one another onto the central bar, leaping back into the fray. When Paul had drunk enough to be able to sleep, she preceded him upstairs.

Was that the same light beyond the curtains? It seemed to be flickering slowly—perhaps a child was playing with a flashlight in the house opposite. It held her attention, so that she failed to hear Paul entering the room.

He was staring expectantly at her. "Sorry, what was that?" she said.

"I said, what were you looking at?"

"That light."

"Light?" He sounded confused, a little irritable.

"That one." She parted the curtains, but there was only the tree before the streetlamp, an intricate cutout flattened by the sodium light. Had the child hidden on glimpsing her shadow? She lay beside Paul, and felt him twitch repeatedly back from the edge of sleep. His restlessness made her want to raise her head and peer toward the window. She lay, eyes closed, trying to share her sleepiness with him.

The bricks refused to shift. Very well, she'd build a rockery over them. In the afternoon she walked down to the beach. The sea leaped up the rocks and shouted in her ears. The high wind nuzzled her face violently, deafening her. As she tramped home with an armful of rocks, sand stung her eyes and swarmed on her glasses.

Though her eyes were watering, she piled her collection on top of the bricks. The arrangement looked sparse; she would need at least one more forage before it looked impressive. Still, it hid the bricks.

She had to keep dabbing her eyes while she prepared dinner. The gas sounded jerky—but that was only her hearing, trying to return to her. After dinner, when she drew the curtains, she could hardly see out of the bedroom window or hear the murmur of the town. Was the child playing tricks again? Certainly a light was flickering. She groped her way to the bathroom, to mop her eyes.

All evening Paul told jokes, some of which she hadn't heard before. "Have another drink," he kept insisting, as though that would make her a more appreciative audience. Oh, what was worrying him? Could it be the very nature of his job? No, he'd come to terms with that long ago. Though she had never seen him so much as threaten violence, he felt no such reticence over national defense.

She followed him upstairs. He was swaying a little beneath the burden of alcohol; she hoped it would drag him down into sleep. When he went into the bathroom she could still feel his tension, entangled with her nerves. She'd neglected to draw the bedroom curtains when her eyes had been smarting. She strode to the window and halted, coughing with shock.

Perhaps the streetlamp had failed, robbing her of the silhouetted tree. For a moment, alcohol hindered her thoughts sufficiently for her to think so. But how could that explain the dark vague bulk, so close that it must be in her garden? What was this silence that clung to her as though she were in the grip of a trance?

As she stared, unable to look away, a pale patch grew clearer within the bulk. It was a window, at about the same level as hers. Within it dim light moved slowly as the glow of embers. By its size, the window must belong to a back bedroom. She was gazing at the back of a house, where no house could be.

She forced herself to turn away, to recapture some sense of her bedroom, her house, light, familiarity. A figure was lying in the bed. She hadn't heard him enter. "Oh, God," she cried inadvertently, starting.

He jerked nervously. "What? What's wrong?"

"That is. That! Can't you see?"

Now she was frightened in a new way, for she realized

he could not. "What?" he demanded, staring straight at the dim unsteady rectangle. "What are you talking about?"

The threat of a night's insomnia edged his voice. Was she going to add to his worries? She swallowed; her fear sank into her guts. "Nothing. It's gone now," she lied.

"Come to bed then, for heaven's sake."

She closed her eyes before dragging the curtains shut. "I think I'll just have a nightcap first."

In fact she downed two more drinks before she felt able to peer out of the living room. The tree stood beyond the hedge; the branches sprinkled with buds, and the privet leaves were lurid with sodium light. The longer she stared, trying to fix the view in her mind, the less familiar and more unreal it seemed.

Paul lay on his back, his lips trembling with snores. She slipped in beside him. At last, when she'd stared at the sodium glow through the curtains for minutes, she took off her glasses. Her stomach felt calmer. Alcohol was melting the icy lump of fear.

She lay teeming with thoughts. Had Paul's tension infected her? Was it making her imagine things? She preferred the alternative: that she'd seen a house which was no longer there. Why should she feel menaced? Good Lord, what could a house which no longer existed *do?* Her eyes grew heavy, but still she reopened them, to check that the light wasn't flickering. Around her, unsharpened by her glasses, the room was very vague.

She stared at the place where the bricks were hidden. Rocks gleamed, polished by the sea. It seemed impossible that there was no trace of what she'd seen—but she was stubbornly convinced that she'd seen it: there could be nothing wrong with her mind. Perhaps more rocks would help bury what was there, if there was anything. Besides, a walk to the beach would take her away from the house. Her gladness dismayed her.

Today the sea was calm. The sun made a shoal of glittering fish that swam in all the rock pools. Over the

beach crept the incessant mouthless whispering of waves.
She selected rocks, and wished she felt closer to the
stillness.

She set down the rocks. The growth of the cairn was
satisfying, but would it be enough? Would the pile act as a
gravestone, or something of the kind? Though she knew
she had dug it herself, the earth looked as it would have if
it had been upheaved from beneath.

She was being stupid. All right, she had seen the house
which had used to stand here. Was that so terrible? The
length of the garden separated the previous house from
hers. Surely that was reassuring. After all, houses couldn't
move.

If only she could tell Paul! Well, in time she would be
able to. At least that hope was heartening. Perhaps, she
thought as he opened the gate, she could tell him soon, for
he looked somehow relieved.

"I've got to go away," he said at once.

She felt her hope being squeezed to death in her stomach.
"When?" Her voice sounded dwindled, as she felt.

"Tomorrow." He was staring at her. "Oh, come on,
Elaine," he said, all at once nervously irritable. "I've got
enough problems."

"I'm sorry." She let her anxiety sound.

"I'll be back tomorrow night."

Presumably he'd meant to stay away overnight, but now
was trying to reassure her. "Take care," she said, suddenly anxious in another way.

After dinner he helped clear up and dried the dishes.
She washed slowly, too meticulously. When they'd finished she said, "Make me another drink." She was afraid
to go upstairs.

The longer she dawdled, the more afraid she would be.
Why, it wasn't even dark; the lower reaches of the sky
glowed rustily. Drawn curtains ought to make her feel safe
in her house—not that there was anything to fear. When
she forced herself to hurry upstairs her footsteps sounded
like an eager child's clambering. She strode into the bed-

room and grabbed the curtains—but her hands clenched spasmodically.

The dark house loomed over her. She could see no streetlamp, nor the glowing sky. It was as though the house had choked all light with smoke. Only the dim window was lit. Although it was very grubby or veiled with smoke, she could see into its room.

The room looked cramped, though it was difficult to be sure; the unquiet glow brought the walls billowing sluggishly forward. Apart from a long prone shape, the room looked bare.

What was the shape? It emerged lethargically from the dimness, as from mud. As she stared, unaware that her nails were piercing her palms through the curtains, the silence held her fast, like amber. The shape was only a bed. But was there a form lying beneath its gray blankets?

All at once she clashed the curtains together, restoring sounds to herself. She was ready to clatter downstairs in panic—but she made herself wait with her back to the window until she could walk down. The very fact that she could turn her back proved she was still in control.

Nevertheless she tried to stay downstairs as long as possible. She mixed drinks and proposed new games. But Paul refused to stay up late; he wanted to leave early next morning. "The sooner I go the sooner I'll be back."

She retreated into bed without going to the window. A dim vague light crept back and forth on the curtains, as though seeking entry. There was nothing to fear except the strangeness. The glimpses had developed slowly as a primitive photograph; the process was too sluggish for anything to happen before Paul returned home. Should she tell him then? She clung to him, but he was busy snoring.

When she woke Paul had gone. He mustn't have wanted to disturb her. She lay hanging onto sleep, unwilling to open her eyes. Abruptly she struggled out of bed and fumbled back the curtains to gaze at the tree.

Later, while she was shopping, she met an old lady who

lived nearby. Beneath the severe purple-rinsed coiffure the eyes blinked once; the pale lips doled out "Good day." It was almost a reproof. But Elaine was determined not to miss her opportunity. "Could I ask you something?" she said, her friendly tone disguising her tension.

After a pause the other admitted, "You may."

"Where I live now—was there ever a fire?"

"In your *house*, do you mean?"

Beneath the deftness there seemed to be resentment, perhaps contempt. "No," Elaine said, restraining her impatience. "Before my house was built."

"I believe there was something of the kind."

The old lady's shopping trolley turned, ready to move on. "Who started the fire?" Elaine said, too eagerly. "How was it started?"

"Oh, I really couldn't tell you. There was quite a family living there. One of the children was retarded. Now I must be about my tasks." She was almost at the end of the aisle of tins when she called back, "Of course it was during the war. I should think it would have been a bomb."

Her words confused Elaine. They refused to fit together logically. Perhaps they couldn't; perhaps that had been the woman's intention. As Elaine unpacked the shopping they faded, leaving her mind open to more immediate and disturbing speculations.

She wished she could go out visiting—but she wouldn't know when Paul had returned. She didn't like to leave him alone in the house until she had told him what she had seen. Should she continue to build the rockery? Suppose the rockery was aggravating what was happening?

Eventually she walked down to the beach. Often the sea helped her grow calm. But today the sky was walled off by slate; the beach was trapped in its own brooding glow. At least the prospect slowed down her thoughts. When sunset began smouldering beneath the enormous gray wall, she made herself walk home.

Each street she traversed was darker. Sudden light threaded the lines of streetlamps. If the dark house was standing inside her gate, what would she do? Absurdly, she found herself wondering obsessively what it might look like from the front. But the garden was bare except for the lumpy heap of rocks above the churned earth. The sight was frailly reassuring.

She prepared dinner, then she made herself a snack. She'd eat dinner with Paul, if he wasn't home too late. Surely he wouldn't be. The sound of her chewing filled her ears and seemed to occupy the house, which was hollow with silence.

It was dark now. She should have drawn the curtains earlier—but then she wouldn't know what was beyond them. Nothing was outside the living room but the rockery, the tree, the lamp. She reached into the hall and into rooms, switching on all the lights. At last she ventured into the bedroom. Apprehension stirred deep in her. She averted her face as she stepped forward to the curtains.

But the silence seized her, and she had to look.

The house was there, of course. She couldn't pretend that it was easier to live with now that it had grown familiar; her fists crumpled the curtains. Within the smoky window, muffled light crawled somnolently. Something lay on the vague bed.

Very gradually—so gradually that she lost all sense of time—she began to distinguish its shape. It was a figure, supine and still, though the uneasy light made the blankets seem to squirm like a cocoon. It was wholly covered. Was it a corpse?

Her mind was struggling to regain control of her limbs, to drag her away. Her fascination held her; the figure seemed too shapeless for a corpse, it reminded her of— When she managed to think, fear clutched her stomach. The shape beneath the blankets was exactly like a dummy made of pillows, the sort of dummy children left to represent them while they sneaked away.

Momentarily her terror, not yet quite defined, weakened her fascination, and she became aware of a nagging sense that she ought to be hearing a sound. What sound? Her

nervous frustration made her hands shake. All of a sudden
they banged together, nearly wrenching the curtains from
their rail.

It was the call of the telephone. She ran downstairs,
almost falling headlong. Oh, please don't let the caller ring
off! Her footsteps resounded in the deserted living room as
she snatched the receiver from the hall table. "Yes?" she
gasped. "Hello? Yes?"

"I've just stopped off to tell you I'm on my way," Paul
said. "Are you all right? You sound—I don't know."

"Yes, I'm all right." She sounded unconvincing, but
the truth would take too long. "You'll be quick, won't
you? Please be quick."

As she set down the buzzing receiver she noticed the
crack between the living room curtains. It ought to be
orange with sodium light, but instead it was blocked by a
dark bulk. High in the bulk, light flickered lethargically.

She was retreating, unable to think, toward the back
door when her earlier terror came clear and froze her. If
the thing in the bed was pretending to be someone, where
was that someone now? Who was abroad in the night, and
to what purpose?

Her panic sent her stumbling upstairs. She left the bedroom door open, so as to hear any sound in the house. She
sat trembling on the bed and stared at the tight curtains.
Only the restless light troubled the darkness beyond them.

Where had Paul called from? Oh, please let him have
been nearly home! He wouldn't be long now—not long,
please not long. She wished she had a drink to quiet her,
but that would have meant going downstairs, closer to
whatever was roaming the night.

If anything was. Mightn't her imagination, made hectic
by all the strangeness, have got the better of her? Surely
the figure in the bed could be a corpse. In the circumstances that would be reassuring. However disturbing, a
corpse was hardly a threat.

Minutes later she reached the window. Her reluctance
made the carpet feel hindering as a marsh. At the curtains,

her will seemed unequal to the struggle with her hands. But her hands sneaked past her fear, to the curtains, and opened a crack for her to peer through.

Silence closed around her. It drew her head forward, and parted her hands to widen the gap between the curtains. Dim light wavered over the gray window, which appeared to hover in a block of night. With a painful slowness that released her breath in infrequent gasps, she made out what was beyond.

The blankets were rolled back from the bed; they slumped against the footboard. On the exposed mattress lay an old stained bolster. The whitish patches that protruded from it here and there must be lumps of stuffing. Over it the stifled light crawled.

She was staring dully, aching with fear, when something in the room moved. A shadow faltered on the blurred wall. Was someone unseen making for the window? Dry fear clutched her throat. Perhaps it was only the unsteady light, perhaps there was no shadow—for the light was making the bolster appear to shift.

Then, as her lungs agonized for breath, she saw that the object on the bed was indeed moving. It was struggling to raise itself. The lumps of stuffing might be, or might be trying to be, limbs. The swellings and discolorations at the top of the bolster could have been the beginnings of a travesty of a face.

Her mind fought to open her claws of hands, to thrust her away from the window. Was her fascination causing the nightmare to be played out before her? She was still striving to turn when the shadow fled across the wall, and its source appeared beyond the gray window. His face was wrenched out of shape by terror, so that it took her moments to be sure it was Paul. He had gone into the wrong house.

Her sobbing cry released her. She fell on the stairs, but dragged herself erect with her bruised hands. A notion was trying to declare itself—that there had been a sound she ought to have heard. She hurled open the front door. The rockery glowed sodium, tangled in shadows of branches.

As she stood trying to control her mind, to fit together what might have happened, she glimpsed the flashing at the intersection. How could traffic lights be blue? When she realized that it was an ambulance, she began to trudge toward it like a sleepwalker. Already she could see that one of the cars was Paul's. She hardly needed the sight of the draped body the men in white were bearing away from his car to suggest how he'd been able to enter a house that no longer existed.

She stood on the pavement, and began to shake. Could she enter that house too? But when she glanced back, her garden was bare beneath the orange glow. Only the rockery stood there like a cairn over a grave.

# The Depths

As Miles emerged, a woman and a pink-eyed dog stumped by. She glanced at the house; then, humming tunelessly, she aimed the same contemptuous look at Miles. As if the lead was a remote control, the dog began to growl. They thought Miles was the same as the house.

He almost wished that were true; at least it would have been a kind of contact. He strolled through West Derby village and groped in his mind for ideas. Pastels drained from the evening sky. Wood pigeons paraded in a treelined close. A mother was crying, "Don't you dare go out of this garden again." A woman was brushing her driveway and singing that she was glad she was Bugs Bunny. Beyond a brace of cars, in a living room that displayed a bar complete with beer pumps, a couple listened to Beethoven's Greatest Hits.

Miles sat drinking beer at a table behind the Crown, at the edge of the bowling green. Apart from the click of bowls the summer evening seemed as blank as his mind. Yet the idea had promised to be exactly what he and his publisher needed: no more days of drinking tea until his head swam, of glaring at the sheet of paper in the typewriter while it glared an unanswerable challenge back at him. He hadn't realized until now how untrustworthy inspirations were.

Perhaps he ought to have foreseen the problem. The owners had told him that there was nothing wrong with the house—nothing except the aloofness and silent disgust of their neighbors. If they had known what had happened there they would never have bought the house; why should they be treated as though by living there they had taken on the guilt?

Still, that was no more unreasonable than the crime itself. The previous owner had been a bank manager, as relaxed as a man could be in his job; his wife had owned a small boutique. They'd seemed entirely at peace with each other. Nobody who had known them could believe what he had done to her. Everyone Miles approached had refused to discuss it, as though by keeping quiet about it they might prevent it from having taken place at all.

The deserted green was smudged with darkness. "We're closing now," the barmaid said, surprised that anyone was still outside. Miles lifted the faint sketch of a tankard and gulped a throatful of beer, grimacing. The more he researched the book, the weaker it seemed to be.

To make things worse, he'd told the television interviewer that it was near completion. At least the program wouldn't be broadcast for months, by which time he might be well into a book about the locations of murder—but it wasn't the book he had promised his publisher, and he wasn't sure that it would have the same appeal.

Long dark houses slumbered beyond an archway between cottages, lit windows hovered in the arch. A signboard reserved a weedy patch of ground for a library. A gray figure was caged by the pillars of the village cross. On the roof of a pub extension, gargoyles began barking, for they were dogs. A cottage claimed to be a sawmill, but the smell seemed to be of manure. Though his brain was taking notes, it wouldn't stop nagging.

He gazed across Lord Sefton's estate toward the tower blocks of Cantril Farm. Their windows were broken ranks of small bright perforations in the night. For a moment, as his mind wobbled on the edge of exhaustion, the unstable patterns of light seemed a code which he needed to break to solve his problems. But how could they have anything to do with it? Such a murder in Cantril Farm, in the concrete barracks among which Liverpool communities had been scattered, he might have understood; here in West Derby it didn't make sense.

As he entered the deserted close, he heard movements beneath eaves. It must be nesting birds, but it was as though the sedate house had secret thoughts. He was grinning as he pushed open his gate, until his hand recoiled. The white gate was stickily red.

It was paint. Someone had written SADIST in an ungainly dripping scrawl. The neighbors could erase that—he wouldn't be here much longer. He let himself into the house.

For a moment he hesitated, listening to the dark. Nothing fled as he switched on the lights. The hall was just a hall, surmounted by a concertina of stairs; the metal and vinyl of the kitchen gleamed like an Ideal Home display; the corduroy suite sat plump and smug on the dark green pelt of the living room. He felt as though he were lodging in a show house, without even the company of a shelf of his books.

Yet it was here, from the kitchen to the living room, that everything had happened—here that the bank manager had systematically rendered his wife unrecognizable as a human being. Miles stood in the empty room and tried to imagine the scene. Had her mind collapsed, or had she been unable to withdraw from what was being done to her? Had her husband known what he was doing, right up to the moment when he'd dug the carving knife into his throat and run headlong at the wall?

It was no good: here at the scene of the crime, Miles found the whole thing literally unimaginable. For an uneasy moment he suspected that that might have been true of the killer and his victim also. As Miles went upstairs, he was planning the compromise to offer his publisher: *Murderers' Houses? Dark Places of the World?* Perhaps it mightn't be such a bad book, after all.

When he switched off the lights, darkness came upstairs from the hall. He lay in bed and watched the shadows of the curtains furling and unfurling above him. He was touching the gate, which felt like flesh; it split open, and his hand plunged in. Though the image was unpleasant it seemed remote, drawing him down into sleep.

The room appeared to have grown much darker when he woke in the grip of utter panic.

He didn't dare move, not until he knew what was wrong. The shadows were frozen above him, the curtains hung like sheets of lead. His mouth tasted metallic, and made him think of blood. He was sure that he wasn't alone in the dark. The worst of it was that there was something he mustn't do—but he had no idea what it was.

He'd begun to search his mind desperately when he realized that was exactly what he ought not to have done. The threat had been waiting in his mind. The thought which welled up was so atrocious that his head began to shudder. He was trying to shake out the thought, to deny that it was his. He grabbed the light cord, to scare it back into the dark.

Was the light failing? The room looked steeped in dimness, a grimy fluid whose sediment clung to his eyes. If anything the light had made him worse, for another thought came welling up like bile, and another. They were worse than the atrocities which the house had seen. He had to get out of the house.

He slammed his suitcase—thank God he'd lived out of it, rather than use the wardrobe—and dragged it onto the landing. He was halfway down, and the thuds of the case on the stairs were making his scalp crawl, when he realized that he'd left a notebook in the living room.

He faltered in the hallway. He mustn't be fully awake: the carpet felt moist underfoot. His skull felt soft and porous, no protection at all for his mind. He had to have the notebook. Shouldering the door aside, he strode blindly into the room.

The light which dangled spiderlike from the central plaster flower showed him the notebook on a fat armchair. Had the chairs soaked up all that had been done here? If he touched them, what might well up? But there was worse in his head, which was seething. He grabbed the notebook and ran into the hall, gasping for air.

His car sounded harsh as a saw among the sleeping houses. He felt as though the neat hygenic facades had cast him out. At least he had to concentrate on his driving, and was deaf to the rest of his mind. The road through Liverpool was as unnaturally bright as a playing field. When the Mersey Tunnel closed overhead he felt that an insubstantial but suffocating burden had settled on his scalp. At last he emerged, only to plunge into darkness.

Though his sleep was free of nightmares, they were waiting whenever he jerked awake. It was as if he kept struggling out of a dark pit, having repeatedly forgotten what was at the top. Sunlight blazed through the curtains as though they were tissue paper, but couldn't reach inside his head. Eventually, when he couldn't bear another such awakening, he stumbled to the bathroom.

When he'd washed and shaved he still felt grimy. It must be the lack of sleep. He sat gazing over his desk. The pebbledashed houses of Neston blazed like the cloudless sky; their outlines were knife-edged. Next door's drain sounded like someone bubbling the last of a drink through a straw. All this was less vivid than his thoughts—but wasn't that as it should be?

An hour later he still hadn't written a word. The nightmares were crowding everything else out of his mind.

Even to think required an effort that made his skin feel infested, swarming.

A random insight saved him. Mightn't it solve both his problems if he wrote the nightmares down? Since he'd had them in the house in West Derby—since he felt they had somehow been produced by the house—couldn't he discuss them in his book?

He scribbled them out until his tired eyes closed. When he reread what he'd written he grew feverishly ashamed. How could he imagine such things? If anything was obscene, they were. Nothing could have made him write down the idea which he'd left until last. Though he was tempted to tear up the notebook, he stuffed it out of sight at the back of a drawer and hurried out to forget.

He sat on the edge of the promenade and gazed across the Dee marshes. Heat-haze made the Welsh hills look like piles of smoke. Families strolled as though this were still a watering place; children played carefully, inhibited by parents. The children seemed wary of Miles; perhaps they sensed his tension, saw how his fingers were digging into his thighs. He must write the book soon, to prove that he could.

Ranks of pebbledashed houses, street after street of identical Siamese twins, marched him home. They reminded him of cells in a single organism. He wouldn't starve if he didn't write—not for a while, at any rate—but he felt uneasy whenever he had to dip into his savings; their unobtrusive growth was reassuring, a talisman of success. He missed his street and had to walk back. Even then he had to peer twice at the street name before he was sure it was his.

He sat in the living room, too exhausted to make himself dinner. Van Gogh landscapes, frozen in the instant before they became unbearably intense, throbbed on the walls. Shelves of Miles' novels reminded him of how he'd lost momentum. The last nightmare was still demanding to be written, until he forced it into the depths of his mind. He would rather have no ideas than that.

When he woke, the nightmare had left him. He felt enervated but clean. He lit up his watch and found he'd slept for hours. It was time for the Book Programme. He'd switched on the television and was turning on the light when he heard his voice at the far end of the room, in the dark.

He was on television, but that was hardly reassuring; his one television interview wasn't due to be broadcast for months. It was as though he'd slept that time away. His face floated up from the gray of the screen as he sat down, cursing. By the time his book was published, nobody would remember this interview.

The linkman and the editing had invoked another writer now. Good God, was that all they were using of Miles? He remembered the cameras following him into the West Derby house, the neighbors glaring, shaking their heads. It was as though they'd managed to censor him, after all.

No, here he was again. "Jonathan Miles is a crime novelist who feels he can no longer rely on his imagination. Desperate for new ideas, he lived for several weeks in a house where, last year, a murder was committed." Miles was already losing his temper, but there was worse to come: they'd used none of his observations about the creative process, only the sequence in which he ushered the camera about the house like Hitchcock in the *Psycho* trailer. "Viewers who find this distasteful," the linkman said unctuously, "may be reassured to hear that the murder in question is not so topical or popular as Mr. Miles seems to think."

Miles glared at the screen while the program came to an end, while an announcer explained that "Where Do You Get Your Ideas?" had been broadcast ahead of schedule because of an industrial dispute. And now here was the news, all of it as bad as Miles felt. A child had been murdered, said a headline; a Chief Constable had described it as the worst case of his career. Miles felt guiltily resentful; no doubt it would help distract people from his book.

Then he sat forward, gaping. Surely he must have misheard; perhaps his insomnia was talking. The newsreader looked unreal as a talking bust, but his voice went on, measured, concerned, inexorable. "The baby was found in a microwave oven. Neighbors broke into the house on hearing the cries, but were unable to locate it in time." Even worse than the scene he was describing was the fact that it was the last of Miles' nightmares, the one he had refused to write down.

Couldn't it have been coincidence? Coincidence, coincidence, the train chattered, and seemed likely to do so all the way to London. If he had somehow been able to predict what was going to happen, he didn't want to know—especially not now, when he could sense new nightmares forming.

He suppressed them before they grew clear. He needed to keep his mind uncluttered for the meeting with his publisher; he gazed out of the window, to relax. Trees turned as they passed, unraveling beneath foliage. On a platform a chorus line of commuters bent to their luggage, one by one. The train drew the sun after it through clouds, like a balloon.

Once out of Euston Station and its random patterns of swarming, he strolled to the publishers. Buildings glared like blocks of salt, which seemed to have drained all moisture from the air. He felt hot and grimy, anxious both to face the worst and to delay. Hugo Burgess had been ominously casual: "If you happen to be in London soon we might have a chat about things. . . ."

A receptionist on a dais that overlooked the foyer kept Miles waiting until he began to sweat. Eventually a lift produced Hugo, smiling apologetically. Was he apologizing in advance for what he had to say? "I suppose you saw yourself on television," he said when they reached his office.

"Yes, I'm afraid so."

"I shouldn't give it another thought. The telly people are envious buggers. They begrudge every second they give to discussing books. Sometimes I think they resent the competition and get their own back by being patronizing." He was pawing through the heaps of books and papers on his desk, apparently in search of the phone. "It did occur to me that it would be nice to publish fairly soon," he murmured.

Miles hadn't realized that sweat could break out in so many places at once. "I've run into some problems."

Burgess was peering at items he had rediscovered in the heaps. "Yes?" he said without looking up.

Miles summarized his new idea clumsily. Should he have written to Burgess in advance? "I found there simply wasn't enough material in the West Derby case," he pleaded.

"Well, we certainly don't want padding." When Burgess eventually glanced up he looked encouraging. "The more facts we can offer the better. I think the public is outgrowing fantasy, now that we're well and truly in the scientific age. People want to feel informed. Writing needs to be as accurate as any other science, don't you think?" He hauled a glossy pamphlet out of one of the piles. "Yes, here it is. I'd call this the last gasp of fantasy."

It was a painting, lovingly detailed and photographically realistic, of a girl who was being simultaneously mutilated and raped. It proved to be the cover of a new magazine, *Ghastly*. Within the pamphlet the editor promised "a quarterly that will wipe out the old horror pulps—everything they didn't dare to be."

"It won't last," Burgess said. "Most people are embarrassed to admit to reading fantasy now, and that will only make them more so. The book you're planning is more what they want—something they know is true. That way they don't feel they're indulging themselves." He disinterred the phone at last. "Just let me call a car and we'll go into the West End for lunch."

Afterward they continued drinking in Hugo's club. Miles thought Hugo was trying to midwife the book. Later he dined alone, then lingered for a while in the hotel bar; his spotlessly impersonal room had made him feel isolated.

Over the incessant trickle of muzak he kept hearing Burgess:
"I wonder how soon you'll be able to let me have sample
chapters. . . ."

Next morning he was surprised how refreshed he felt,
especially once he'd taken a shower. Over lunch he unburdened himself to his agent. "I just don't know when I'll be
able to deliver the book. I don't know how much research
may be involved."

"Now look, you mustn't worry about Hugo. I'll speak
to him. I know he won't mind waiting if he knows it's for
the good of the book." Susie Barker patted his hand; her
bangles sounded like silver castanets. "Now here's an idea
for you. Why don't you do up a sample chapter or two on
the West Derby case? That way we'll keep Hugo happy,
and I'll do my best to sell it as an article."

When they'd kissed good-bye Miles strolled along Char-
ing Cross Road, composing the chapter in his head and
looking for himself in bookshop displays. Miles, Miles,
books said in a window stacked with crime novels. NIGHT
OF ATROCITIES, headlines cried on an adjacent newspaper
stand.

He dodged into Foyles. That was better: he occupied
half a shelf, though his earliest titles looked faded and
dusty. When he emerged he was content to drift with the
rush-hour crowds—until a newsvendor's placard stopped
him. BRITAIN'S NIGHT OF HORROR, it said.

It didn't matter, it had nothing to do with him. In that
case, why couldn't he find out what had happened? He
didn't need to buy a paper, he could read the report as the
newsvendor snatched the top copy to reveal the same
beneath. "Last night was Britain's worst night of murders
in living memory. . . ."

Before he'd read halfway down the column the noise of
the crowd seemed to close in, to grow incomprehensible
and menacing. The newsprint was snatched away again
and again as if he were the victim of a macabre card trick.
He sidled away from the newsstand as though from the
scene of a crime, but already he'd recognized every detail.

If he hadn't repressed them on the way to London he could have written the reports himself. He even knew what the newspaper had omitted to report: that one of the victims had been forced to eat parts of herself.

Weeks later the newspapers were still in an uproar. Though the moderates pointed out that the murders had been unrelated and unmotivated, committed by people with no previous history of violence or of any kind of crime, for most of the papers that only made it worse. They used the most unpleasant photographs of the criminals that they could find, and presented the crimes as evidence of the impotence of the law, of a total collapse of standards. Opinion polls declared that the majority was in favor of an immediate return of the death penalty. "MEN LIKE THESE MUST NOT GO UNPUNISHED," a headline said, pretending it was quoting. Miles grew hot with frustration and guilt— for he felt he could have prevented the crimes.

All too soon after he'd come back from London, the nightmares had returned. His mind had already felt raw from brooding, and he had been unable to resist; he'd known only that he must get rid of them somehow. They were worse than the others: more urgent, more appalling.

He'd scribbled them out as though he was inspired, then he'd glared blindly at the blackened page. It hadn't been enough. The seething in his head, the crawling of his scalp, had not been relieved even slightly. This time he had to develop the ideas, imagine them fully, or they would cling and fester in his mind.

He'd spent the day and half the night writing, drinking tea until he hardly knew what he was doing. He'd invented character after character, building them like Frankenstein out of fragments of people, only to subject them to gloatingly prolonged atrocities, both the victims and the perpetrators.

When he'd finished, his head felt like an empty rusty can. He might have vomited if he had been able to stand. His gaze had fallen on a paragraph he'd written, and he'd swept the pages onto the floor, snarling with disgust.

"Next morning he couldn't remember what he'd done—but when he reached in his pocket and touched the soft object his hand came out covered with blood. . . . "

He'd stumbled across the landing to his bedroom, desperate to forget his ravings. When he'd awakened next morning he had been astonished to find that he'd fallen asleep as soon as he had gone to bed. As he'd lain there, feeling purged, an insight so powerful it was impossible to doubt had seized him. If he hadn't written out these things they would have happened in reality.

But he had written them out: they were no longer part of him. In fact they had never been so, however they had felt. That made him feel cleaner, absolved him of responsibility. He stuffed the sloganeering newspapers into the wastebasket and arranged his desk for work.

By God, there was nothing so enjoyable as feeling ready to write. While a pot of tea brewed he strolled about the house and reveled in the sunlight, his release from the nightmares, his surge of energy. Next door a man with a beard of shaving foam dodged out of sight, like a timid Santa Claus.

Miles had composed the first paragraph before he sat down to write, a trick that always helped him write more fluently—but a week later he was still struggling to get the chapter into publishable shape. All that he found crucial about his research—the idea that by staying in the West Derby house he had tapped a source of utter madness, which had probably caused the original murder—he'd had to suppress. Why, if he said any of that in print they would think he was mad himself. Indeed, once he'd thought of writing it, it no longer seemed convincing.

When he could no longer bear the sight of the article, he typed a fresh copy and sent it to Susie. She called the following day, which seemed encouragingly quick. Had he been so aware of what he was failing to write that he hadn't noticed what he'd achieved?

"Well, Jonathan, I have to say this," she said as soon

as she'd greeted him. "It isn't up to your standard. Frankly, I think you ought to scrap it and start again."

"Oh." After a considerable pause he could think of nothing to say except "All right."

"You sound exhausted. Perhaps that's the trouble." When he didn't answer she said, "You listen to your Auntie Susie. Forget the whole thing for a fortnight and go away on holiday. You've been driving yourself too hard— you looked tired the last time I saw you. I'll explain to Hugo, and I'll see if I can't talk up the article you're going to write when you come back."

She chatted reassuringly for a while, then left him staring at the phone. He was realizing how much he'd counted on selling the article. Apart from royalties, which never amounted to as much as he expected, when had he last had the reassurance of a check? He couldn't go on holiday, for he would feel he hadn't earned it; if he spent the time worrying about the extravagance, that would be no holiday at all.

But wasn't he being unfair to himself? Weren't there stories he could sell?

He turned the idea over gingerly in his mind, as though something might crawl out from beneath—but really, he could see no arguments against it. Writing out the nightmares had drained them of power; they were just stories now. As he dialled Hugo's number, to ask him for the address of the magazine, he was already thinking up a pseudonym for himself.

For a fortnight he walked around Anglesey. Everything was hallucinatorily intense: beyond cracks in the island's grassy coastline, the sea glittered as though crystallizing and shattering; across the sea, Welsh hills and mist appeared to be creating each other. Beaches were composed of rocks like brown crusty loaves decorated with shells. Anemones unfurled deep in glassy pools. When night fell he lay on a slab of rock and watched the stars begin to swarm.

As he strolled he was improving the chapters in his mind, now that the first version had clarified his themes. He wrote the article in three days, and was sure it was publishable. Not only was it the fullest description yet of the murder, but he'd managed to explain the way the neighbors had behaved: they'd needed to dramatize their repudiation of all that had been done in the house, they'd used him as a scapegoat to cast out, to proclaim that it had nothing to do with them.

When he'd sent the manuscript to Susie he felt pleasantly tired. The houses of Neston grew silver in the evening, the horizon was turning to ash. Once the room was so dark that he couldn't read, he went to bed. As he drifted toward sleep he heard next door's drain bubbling to itself.

But what was causing bubbles to form in the grayish substance that resembled fluid less than flesh? They were slower and thicker than tar, and took longer to form. Their source was rushing upward to confront him face to face. The surface was quivering, ready to erupt, when he awoke.

He felt hot and grimy, and somehow ashamed. The dream had been a distortion of the last thing he'd heard, that was all; surely it wouldn't prevent him from sleeping. A moment later he was clinging to it desperately; its dreaminess was comforting, and it was preferable by far to the ideas that were crowding into his mind. He knew now why he felt grimy.

He couldn't lose himself in sleep; the nightmares were embedded there, minute, precise, and appalling. When he switched on the light it seemed to isolate him. Night had bricked up all the windows. He couldn't bear to be alone with the nightmares—but there was only one way to be rid of them.

The following night he woke, having fallen asleep at his desk. His last line met his eyes: "Hours later he sat back on his haunches, still chewing doggedly . . ." When he gulped the lukewarm tea it tasted rusty as blood. His surroundings seemed remote, and he could regain them only by purging his mind. His task wasn't even half finished.

His eyes felt like dusty pebbles. The pen jerked in his hand, spattering the page.

Next morning Susie rang, wrenching him awake at his desk. "Your article is tremendous. I'm sure we'll do well with it. Now I wonder if you can let me have a chapter breakdown of the rest of the book to show Hugo?"

Miles was fully awake now, and appalled by what had happened in his mind while he had been sleeping. "No," he muttered.

"Are there any problems you'd like to tell me about?"

If only he could! But he couldn't tell her that while he had been asleep, having nearly discharged his task, a new crowd of nightmares had gathered in his mind and were clamoring to be written. Perhaps now they would never end.

"Come and see me if it would help," Susie said.

How could he, when his mind was screaming to be purged? But if he didn't force himself to leave his desk, perhaps he never would. "All right," he said dully. "I'll come down tomorrow."

When tomorrow came it meant only that he could switch off his desk lamp; he was nowhere near finishing. He barely managed to find a seat on the train, which was crowded with football fans. Opened beer cans spat; the air grew rusty with the smell of beer. The train emerged roaring from a tunnel, but Miles was still in his own, which was far darker and more oppressive. Around him they were chanting football songs, which sounded distant as a waveband buried in static. He wrote under cover of his briefcase, so that nobody would glimpse what he was writing.

Though he still hadn't finished when he reached London, he no longer cared. The chatter of the wheels, the incessant chanting, the pounding of blood and nightmares in his skull had numbed him. He sat for a while in Euston. The white tiles glared like ice, a huge voice loomed above him.

As soon as she saw him Susie demanded, "Have you seen a doctor?"

Even a psychiatrist couldn't help him. "I'll be all right," he said, hiding behind a bright false smile.

"I've thought of some possibilities for your book," she said over lunch. "What about that house in Edinburgh where almost the same murder was committed twice, fifty years apart? The man who did the second always said he hadn't known about the first. . . ."

She obviously hoped to revive him with ideas—but the nightmare which was replaying itself, endless as a loop of film, would let nothing else into his skull. The victim had managed to tear one hand free and was trying to protect herself.

"And isn't there the lady in Sutton who collects bricks from the scenes of crimes? She was meaning to use them to build a miniature Black Museum. She ought to be worth tracing," Susie said as the man seized the flailing hand by its wrist. "And then if you want to extend the scope of the book there's the mother of the Meathook Murder victims, who still gets letters pretending to be from her children."

The man had captured the wrist now. Slowly and deliberately, with a grin that looked pale as a crack in clay, he— Miles was barely able to swallow; his head, and every sound in the restaurant, was pounding. "They sound like good ideas," he mumbled, to shut Susie up.

Back at her office, a royalty fee had arrived. She wrote him a check at once, as though that might cure him. As he slipped it into his briefcase, she caught sight of the notebooks in which he'd written on the train. "Are they something I can look at?" she said.

His surge of guilt was so intense that it was panic. "No, it's nothing, it's just something, no," he stammered.

Hours later he was walking. Men loitered behind boys playing pinball; the machines flashed like fireworks, splashing the men's masks. Addicts were gathering outside the all-night chemist's on Piccadilly; in the subterranean Gents', a starved youth washed blood from a syringe. Off Regent Street, Soho glared like an amusement arcade. On Oxford

Street figures in expensive dresses, their bald heads gleaming, gestured broken-wristed in windows.

He had no idea why he was walking. Was he hoping the crowds would distract him? Was that why he peered at their faces, more and more desperately? Nobody looked at all reassuring. Women were perfect as corpses, men seemed to glow with concealed aggression; some were dragons, their mouths full of smoke.

He'd walked past the girl before he reacted. Gasping, he struggled through a knot of people on the corner of Dean Street and dashed across, against the lights. In the moments before she realized that he'd dodged ahead of her and was staring, he saw her bright quick eyes, the delicate web of veins beneath them, the freckles that peppered the bridge of her nose, the pulsing of blood in her neck. She was so intensely present to him that it was appalling.

Then she stepped aside, annoyed by him, whatever he was. He reached out, but couldn't quite seize her arm. He had to stop her somehow. "Don't," he cried.

At that, she fled. He'd started after her when two policemen blocked his path. Perhaps they hadn't noticed him, perhaps they wouldn't grab him—but it was too late; she was lost in the Oxford Street crowd. He turned and ran, fleeing the police, fleeing back to his hotel.

As soon as he reached his room he began writing. His head felt stuffed with hot ash. He was scribbling so fast that he hardly knew what he was saying. How much time did he have? His hand was cramped and shaking, his writing was surrounded by a spittle of ink.

He was halfway through a sentence when, quite without warning, his mind went blank. His pen was clawing spasmodically at the page, but the urgency had gone; the nightmare had left him. He lay in the anonymous bed in the dark, hoping he was wrong.

In the morning he went down to the lobby as late as he could bear. The face of the girl he'd seen in Oxford Street stared up at him from a newspaper. In the photograph her eyes looked dull and reproachful, though perhaps they

seemed so only to him. He fled upstairs without reading
the report. He already knew more than the newspaper
would have been able to tell.

Eventually he went home to Neston. It didn't matter
where he went; the nightmares would find him. He was an
outcast from surrounding reality. He was focused inward
on his raw wound of a mind, waiting for the next outbreak
of horrors to infest him.

Next day he sat at his desk. The sunlit houses opposite
glared back like empty pages. Even to think of writing
made his skin prickle. He went walking, but it was no
good: beyond the marshes, factories coughed into the sky;
grass blades whipped the air like razors; birds swooped,
shrieking knives with wings. The sunlight seemed violent
and pitiless, vampirizing the landscape.

There seemed no reason why the nightmares should ever
stop. Either he would be forced to write them out, to
involve himself more and more deeply in them, or they
would be acted out in reality. In any case he was at their
mercy; there was nothing he could do.

But wasn't he avoiding the truth? It hadn't been coincidence that had given him the chance he'd missed in Oxford Street. Perhaps he had been capable of intervention all
along, if he had only known. However dismaying the
responsibility was, surely it was preferable to helplessness.
His glimpse in Oxford Street had made all the victims
unbearably human.

He sat waiting. Pale waves snaked across the surface of
the grass; in the heat-haze they looked as though water was
welling up from the marshes. His scalp felt shrunken, but
that was only nervousness and the storm that was clotting
overhead. When eventually the clouds moved on, unbroken,
they left a sediment of twilight that clung to him as he
trudged home.

No, it was more than that. His skin felt grimy, unclean.
The nightmares were close. He hurried to let his car out of
the garage, then he sat like a private detective in the

driver's seat outside his house. His hands clenched on the steering wheel. His head began to crawl, to swarm.

He mustn't be trapped into self-disgust. He reminded himself that the nightmares weren't coming from him, and forced his mind to grasp them, to be guided by them. Shame made him feel coated in hot grease. When at last the car coasted forward, was it acting out his urge to flee? Should he follow that street sign, or that one?

Just as the signs grew meaningless because he'd stared too long, he knew which way to go. His instincts had been waiting to take hold, and they were urgent now. He drove through the lampless streets, where lit curtains cut rectangles from the night, and out into the larger dark.

He found he was heading for Chester. Trees beside the road were giant scarecrows, brandishing tattered foliage. Gray clouds crawled grublike across the sky; he could hardly distinguish them from the crawling in his skull. He was desperate to purge his mind.

Roman walls loomed between the timber buildings of Chester, which were black and white as the moon. A few couples were window-shopping along the enclosed rows above the streets. On the bridge that crossed the main street, a clock perched like a moonfaced bird. Miles remembered a day when he'd walked by the river, boats passing slowly as clouds, a brass band on a small bandstand playing "Blow the Wind Southerly." How could the nightmare take place here?

It could, for it was urging him deeper into the city. He was driving so fast through the spotless streets that he almost missed the police station. Its blue sign drew him aside. That was where he must go. Somehow he had to persuade them that he knew where a crime was taking place.

He was still yards away from the police station when his foot faltered on the accelerator. The car shuddered and tried to jerk forward, but that was no use. The nearer he came to the police station, the weaker his instinct became.

Was it being suppressed by his nervousness? Whatever the reason, he could guide nobody except himself.

As soon as he turned the car the urgency seized him. It was agonizing now. It rushed him out of the center of Chester, into streets of small houses and shops that looked dusty as furniture shoved out of sight in an attic. They were deserted except for a man in an ankle-length overcoat, who limped by like a sack with a head.

Miles stamped on the brake as the car passed the mouth of an alley. Snatching the keys, he slammed the door and ran into the alley, between two shops whose posters looked ancient and faded as Victorian photographs. The walls of the alley were chunks of spiky darkness above which cramped windows peered, but he didn't need to see to know where he was going.

He was shocked to find how slowly he had to run, how out of condition he was. His lungs seemed to be filling with lumps of rust, his throat was scraped raw. He was less running than staggering forward. Amid the uproar of his senses, it took him a while to feel that he was too late.

He halted as best he could. His feet slithered on the uneven flagstones, his hands clawed at the walls. As soon as he began to listen he wished he had not. Ahead in the dark, there was a faint incessant shriek that seemed to be trying to emerge from more than one mouth. He knew there was only one victim.

Before long he made out a dark object farther down the alley. In fact it was two objects, one of which lay on the flagstones while the other rose to its feet, a dull gleam in its hand. A moment later the figure with the gleam was fleeing, its footsteps flapping like wings between the close walls.

The shrieking had stopped. The dark object lay still. Miles forced himself forward, to see what he'd failed to prevent. As soon as he'd glimpsed it he staggered away, choking back a scream.

\*       \*       \*

He'd achieved nothing except to delay writing out the rest of the horrors. They were breeding faster in his skull, which felt as though it were cracking. He drove home blindly. The hedgerows and the night had merged into a dark mass that spilled toward the road, smudging its edges. Perhaps he might crash—but he wasn't allowed that relief, for the nightmares were herding him back to his desk.

The scratching of his pen, and a low half-articulate moaning which he recognized sometimes as his voice, kept him company. Next day the snap of the letter box made him drop his pen; otherwise he might not have been able to force himself away from the desk.

The package contained the first issue of *Ghastly*. "Hope you like it," the editor gushed. "It's already been banned in some areas, which has helped sales no end. You'll see we announce your stories as coming attractions, and we look forward to publishing them." On the cover the girl was still writhing, but the contents were far worse. Miles had read only a paragraph when he tore the glossy pages into shreds.

How could anyone enjoy reading that? The pebbledashed houses of Neston gleamed innocently back at him. Who knew what his neighbors read behind their locked doors? Perhaps in time some of them would gloat over his pornographic horrors, reassuring themselves that this was only horror fiction, not pornography at all: just as he'd reassured himself that they were only stories now, nothing to do with reality—certainly nothing to do with him, the pseudonym said so—

The Neston houses gazed back at him, self-confident and bland: they looked as convinced of their innocence as he was trying to feel—and all at once he knew where the nightmares were coming from.

He couldn't see how that would help him. Before he'd begun to suffer from his writer's block, there had been occasions when a story had surged up from his unconscious and demanded to be written. Those stories had been products of his own mind, yet he couldn't shake them off except by writing—but now he was suffering nightmares on behalf of the world.

No wonder they were so terrible, nor that they were growing worse. If material repressed into the unconscious was bound to erupt in some less manageable form, how much more powerful that must be when the unconscious was collective! Precisely because people were unable to come to terms with the crimes, repudiated them as utterly inhuman or simply unimaginable, the horrors would reappear in a worse form and possess whoever they pleased. He remembered thinking that the patterns of life in the tower blocks had something to do with the West Derby murder. They had, of course. Everything had.

And now the repressions were focused in him. There was no reason why they should ever leave him; on the contrary, they seemed likely to grow more numerous and more peremptory. Was he releasing them by writing them out, or was the writing another form of repudiation?

One was still left in his brain. It felt like a boil in his skull. Suddenly he knew that he wasn't equal to writing it out, whatever else might happen. Had his imagination burned out at last? He would be content never to write another word. It occurred to him that the book he'd discussed with Hugo was just another form of rejection: knowing you were reading about real people reassured you they were other than yourself.

He slumped at his desk. He was a burden of flesh that felt encrusted with grit. Nothing moved except the festering nightmare in his head. Unless he got rid of it somehow, it felt as though it would never go away. He'd failed twice to intervene in reality, but need he fail again? If he succeeded, was it possible that might change things for good?

He was at the front door when the phone rang. Was it Susie? If she knew what was filling his head, she would never want to speak to him again. He left the phone ringing in the dark house and fled to his car.

The pain in his skull urged him through the dimming

fields and villages to Birkenhead, where it seemed to abandon him. Not that it had faded—his mind felt like an abscessed tooth—but it was no longer able to guide him. Was something anxious to prevent him from reaching his goal?

The bare streets of warehouses and factories and terraces went on for miles, brick-red slabs pierced far too seldom by windows. At the peak hour the town center grew black with swarms of people, the Mersey Tunnel drew in endless sluggish segments of cars. He drove jerkily, staring at faces.

Eventually he left the car in Hamilton Square, over-looked by insurance offices caged by railings, and trudged toward the docks. Except for his footsteps, the streets were deserted. Perhaps the agony would be cured before he arrived wherever he was going. He was beyond caring what that implied.

It was dark now. At the ends of rows of houses whose doors opened onto cracked pavement he saw docked ships, glaring metal mansions. Beneath the iron mesh of swing bridges, a scum of neon light floated on the oily water. Sunken rails snagged his feet. In pubs on street corners he heard tribes of dockers, a sullen wordless roar that sounded like a warning. Out here the moan of a ship on the Irish Sea was the only voice he heard.

When at last he halted, he had no idea where he was. The pavement on which he was walking was eaten away by rubbly ground; he could smell collapsed buildings. A roofless house stood like a rotten tooth, lit by a single streetlamp harsh as lightning. Streets still led from the opposite pavement, and despite the ache—which had aborted nearly all his thoughts—he knew that the street directly opposite was where he must go.

There was silence. Everything was yet to happen. The lull seemed to give him a brief chance to think. Suppose he managed to prevent it? Repressing the ideas of the crimes only made them erupt in a worse form—how much worse might it be to repress the crimes themselves?

Nevertheless he stepped forward. Something had to cure him of his agony. He stayed on the treacherous pavement of the side street, for the roadway was skinless, a mass of bricks and mud. Houses pressed close to him, almost forcing him into the road. Where their doors and windows ought to be were patches of new brick. The far end of the street was impenetrably dark.

When he reached it, he saw why. A wall at least ten feet high was built flush against the last houses. Peering upward, he made out the glint of broken glass. He was closed in by the wall and the plugged houses, in the midst of desolation.

Without warning—quite irrelevantly, it seemed—he remembered something he'd read about years ago while researching a novel: the Mosaic ritual of the Day of Atonement. They'd driven out the scapegoat, burdened with all the sins of the people, into the wilderness. Another goat had been sacrificed. The images chafed together in his head; he couldn't grasp their meaning—and then he realized why there was so much room for them in his mind. The aching nightmare was fading.

At once he was unable to turn away from the wall, for he was atrociously afraid. He knew why this nightmare could not have been acted out without him. Along the bricked-up street he heard footsteps approaching.

When he risked a glance over his shoulder, he saw that there were two figures. Their faces were blacked out by the darkness, but the glints in their hands were sharp. He was trying to claw his way up the wall, though already his lungs were laboring. Everything was over—the sleepless nights, the poison in his brain, the nightmare of responsibility—but he knew that while he would soon not be able to scream, it would take him much longer to die.

# *Out of*

# *Copyright*

THE WIDOW gazed wistfully at the pile of books. "I thought they might be worth something."

"Oh, some are," Tharne said. "That one, for instance, will fetch a few pence. But I'm afraid your husband collected books indiscriminately. Much of this stuff isn't worth the paper it's printed on. Look, I'll tell you what I'll do—I'll take the whole lot off your hands and give you the best price I can."

When he'd counted out the notes, the wad over his heart was scarcely reduced. He carried the bulging cartons of books to his van, down three gloomy flights of stairs, along the stone path which hid beneath lolling grass, between gateposts whose stone globes grew continents of moss. By the third descent he was panting. Nevertheless he grinned as he kicked grass aside; the visit had been worthwhile, certainly.

He drove out of the cracked and overgrown streets, past rusty cars laid open for surgery, old men propped on front steps to wither in the sun, prams left outside houses as though in the hope that a thief might adopt the baby. Sunlight leaping from windows and broken glass lanced his eyes. Heat made the streets and his perceptions waver. Glimpsed in the mirror or sensed looming at his back, the cartons resembled someone crouching behind him. They smelled more dusty than the streets.

Soon he reached the crescent. The tall Georgian houses shone white. Beneath them the van looked cheap, a tin toy littering the street. Still, it wasn't advisable to seem too wealthy when buying books.

He dumped the cartons in his hall, beside the elegant curve of the staircase. His secretary came to the door of her office. "Any luck?"

"Yes indeed. Some first editions and a lot of rare material. The man knew what he was collecting."

"Your mail came," she said in a tone which might have announced the police. This annoyed him: he prided himself on his legal knowledge, he observed the law scrupulously. "Well, well," he demanded, "who's saying what?"

"It's that American agent again. He says you have a moral obligation to pay Lewis' widow for those three stories. Otherwise, he says—let's see—'I shall have to seriously consider recommending to my clients that they boycott your anthologies.' "

"He says that, does he? The bastard. They'd be better off boycotting him." Tharne's face grew hot and swollen; he could hardly control his grin. "He's better at splitting infinitives than he is at looking after his people's affairs. He never renewed the copyright on those stories. We don't owe anyone a penny. And by God, you show me an author who needs the money. Rolling in it, all of them. Living off their royalties." A final injustice struck him; he smote his forehead. "Anyway, what the devil's it got to do with the widow? She didn't write the stories."

To burn up some of his rage, he struggled down to the cellar with the cartons. His blood drummed wildly. As he unpacked the cartons, dust smoked up to the light bulbs.

The cellar, already dim with its crowd of bookshelves, grew dimmer.

He piled the books neatly, sometimes shifting a book from one pile to another, as though playing Patience. When he reached the ace, he stopped. *Tales Beyond Life*, by Damien Damon. It was practically a legend; the book had never been reprinted in its entirety. The find could hardly have been more opportune. The book contained "The Dunning of Diavolo"—exactly what he needed to complete the new Tharne anthology, *Justice from Beyond the Grave*. He knocked lumps of dust from the top of the book, and turned to the story.

Even in death he would be recompensed. Might the resurrectionists have his corpse for a toy? Of a certainty—but only once those organs had been removed which his spirit would need, and the Rituals performed. This stipulation he had willed on his death-bed to his son. Unless his corpse was pacified, his curse would rise.

Undeed, had the father's estate been more readily available to clear the son's debts, this might have been an edifying tale of filial piety. Still, on a night when the moon gleamed like a sepulture, the father was plucked tuber-pallid from the earth.

Rather than sow superstitious scruples in the resurrectionists, the son had told them naught. Even so, the burrowers felt that they had mined an uncommon seam. Voiceless it might be, but the corpse had its forms of protest. Only by seizing its wrists could the corpse-miners elude the cold touch of its hands. Could they have closed its stiff lids, they might have borne its grin. On the contrary, neither would touch the gelatinous pebbles which bulged from its face . . .

Tharne knew how the tale continued: Diavolo, the father, was dissected, but his limbs went snaking round the town in search of those who had betrayed him, and crawled down the throats of the victims to drag out the twins of those organs of which the corpse had been robbed. All good Gothic stuff—gory and satisfying, but not to be taken too seriously. They couldn't write like that nowadays; they'd lost the knack of proper Gothic writing. And yet they whined that they weren't paid enough!

Only one thing about the tale annoyed him: the misprint "undeed" for "indeed." Amusingly, it resembled "undead"—but that was no excuse for perpetrating it. The one reprint of the tale, in the twenties, had swarmed with literals. Well, this time the text would be perfect. Nothing appeared in a Tharne anthology until it satisfied him.

He checked the remaining text, then gave it to his secretary to retype. His timing was exact: a minute later the doorbell announced a book collector, who was as punctual as Tharne. They spent a mutually beneficial half hour. "These I bought only this morning," Tharne said proudly. "They're yours for twenty pounds apiece."

The day seemed satisfactory until the phone rang. He heard the girl's startled squeak. She rang through to his office, sounding flustered. "Ronald Main wants to speak to you."

"Oh, God. Tell him to write, if he still knows how. I've no time to waste in chatting, even if he has." But her cry had disturbed him; it sounded like a threat of inefficiency. Let Main see that someone round here wasn't to be shaken! "No, wait—put him on."

Main's orotund voice came rolling down the wire. "It has come to my notice that you have anthologized a story of mine without informing me."

Trust a writer to use as many words as he could! "There was no need to get in touch with you," Tharne said. "The story's out of copyright."

"That is hardly the issue. Aside from the matter of payment, which we shall certainly discuss, I want to take up with you the question of the text itself. Are you aware that whole sentences have been rewritten?"

"Yes, of course. That's part of my job. I am the editor, you know." Irritably Tharne restrained a sneeze; the smell of dust was very strong. "After all, it's an early story of yours. Objectively, don't you think I've improved it?" He oughtn't to sound as if he was weakening. "Anyway, I'm afraid that legally you've no rights."

Did that render Main speechless, or was he preparing a stronger attack? It scarcely mattered, for Tharne put down the phone. Then he strode down the hall to check his secretary's work. Was her typing as flustered as her voice had been?

Her office was hazy with floating dust. No wonder she was peering closely at the book—though she looked engrossed, almost entranced. As his shadow fell on the page she started; the typewriter carriage sprang to its limit, ringing. She demanded, "Was that you before?"

"What do you mean?"

"Oh, nothing. Don't let it bother you." She seemed nervously annoyed—whether with him or with herself he couldn't tell.

At least her typing was accurate, though he could see where letters had had to be retyped. He might as well write the introduction to the story. He went down to fetch *Who's Who in Horror and Fantasy Fiction*. Dust teemed around the cellar lights and chafed his throat.

Here was Damien Damon, real name Sidney Drew: b. Chelsea, 30 April 1876; d.? 1911? "His life was even more bizarre and outrageous than his fiction. Some critics say that that is the only reason for his fame . . ."

A small dry sound made Tharne glance up. Somewhere among the shelved books, a face peered at him through a gap. Of course it could be nothing of the sort, but it took him a while to locate a cover which had fallen open in a gap, and which must have resembled a face.

Upstairs he wrote the introduction. ". . . Without the help of an agent, and with no desire to make money from his writing, Damon became one of the most discussed in whispers writers of his day. Critics claim that it was scandals that he practiced magic which gained him fame. But his posthumously published *Tales Beyond Life* shows that he was probably the last really first-class writer in the tradition of Poe . . .'' Glancing up, Tharne caught sight of himself, pen in hand, at the desk in the mirror. So much for any nonsense that he didn't understand writers' problems. Why, he was a writer himself!

Only when he'd finished writing did he notice how quiet the house had become. It had the strained unnatural silence of a library. As he padded down the hall to deliver the text to his secretary his sounds felt muffled, detached from him.

His secretary was poring over the typescript of Damon's tale. She looked less efficient than anxious—searching for something she would rather not find? Dust hung about her in the amber light, and made her resemble a waxwork or a faded painting. Her arms dangled, forgotten. Her gaze was fixed on the page.

Before he could speak, the phone rang. That startled her so badly that he thought his presence might dismay her more. He retreated into the hall, and a dark shape stepped back behind him—his shadow, of course. He entered her office once more, making sure he was audible.

"It's Mr. Main again," she said, almost wailing.

"Tell him to put it in writing."

"Mr. Tharne says would you please send him a letter." Her training allowed her to regain control, yet she seemed unable to put down the phone until instructed. Tharne enjoyed the abrupt cessation of the outraged squeaking. "Now I think you'd better go home and get some rest," he said.

When she'd left he sat at her desk and read the typescript. Yes, she had corrected the original; "undeed" was righted. The text seemed perfect, ready for the printer. Why then did he feel that something was wrong? Had she omitted a passage or otherwise changed the wording?

He'd compare the texts in his office, where he was more comfortable. As he rose, he noticed a few faint dusty marks on the carpet. They approached behind his secretary's chair, then veered away. He must have tracked dust from the cellar, which clearly needed sweeping. What did his housekeeper think she was paid for?

Again his footsteps sounded muted. Perhaps his ears were clogged with dust; there was certainly enough of it about. He had never noticed how strongly the house smelled of old books, nor how unpleasant the smell could be. His skin felt dry, itchy.

In his office he poured himself a large Scotch. It was late enough, he needn't feel guilty—indeed, twilight seemed unusually swift tonight, unless it was an effect of the swarms of dust. He didn't spend all day drinking, unlike some writers he could name.

He knocked clumps of dust from the book; it seemed almost to grow there, like gray fungus. Airborne dust whirled away from him and drifted back. He compared the texts, line by line. Surely they were identical, except for her single correction. Yet he felt there was some aspect of the typescript which he needed urgently to decipher. This frustration, and its irrationality, unnerved him.

He was still frowning at the pages, having refilled his glass to loosen up his thoughts, when the phone rang once. He grabbed it irritably, but the earpiece was as hushed as the house. Or was there, amid the electric hissing vague as a cascade of dust, a whisper? It was beyond the grasp of his hearing, except for a syllable or two which sounded like Latin—if it was there at all.

He jerked to his feet and hurried down the hall. Now that he thought about it, perhaps he'd heard his secretary's extension lifted as his phone had rung. Yes, her receiver was off the hook. It must have fallen off. As he replaced it, dust sifted out of the mouthpiece.

Was a piece of paper rustling in the hall? No, the hall was bare. Perhaps it was the typescript, stirred on his desk by a draft. He closed the door behind him, to exclude any draft—as well as the odor of something very old and dusty.

But the smell was stronger in his room. He sniffed gingerly at *Tales Beyond Life*. Why, there it was: the book reeked of dust. He shoved open the French windows, then he sat and stared at the typescript. He was beginning to regard it with positive dislike. He felt as though he had been given a code to crack; it was nerve-racking as an examination. Why was it only the typescript that bothered him, and not the original?

He flapped the typed pages, for they looked thinly coated with gray. Perhaps it was only the twilight, which seemed composed of dust. Even his Scotch tasted clogged. Just let him see what was wrong with this damned story, then he'd leave the room to its dust—and have a few well-chosen words for his housekeeper tomorrow.

There was only one difference between the texts: the capital *I*. Or had he missed another letter? Compulsively and irritably, refusing to glance at the gray lump which hovered at the edge of his vision, he checked the first few capitals. *E, M, O, R, T* . . . Suddenly he stopped, parched mouth open. Seizing his pen, he began to transcribe the capitals alone.

*E mortuis revoco.*

*From the dead I summon thee.*

Oh, it must be a joke, a mistake, a coincidence. But the next few capitals dashed his doubts. *From the dead I summon thee, from the dust I recreate thee* . . . The entire story concealed a Latin invocation. It had been Damien Damon's last story and also, apparently, his last attempt at magic.

And it was Tharne's discovery. He must rewrite his introduction. Publicized correctly, the secret of the tale could help the book's sales a great deal. Why then was he unwilling to look up? Why was he tense as a trapped animal, ears straining painfully? Because of the thick smell of dust, the stealthy dry noises that his choked ears were unable to locate, the gray mass that hovered in front of him?

When at last he managed to look up, the jerk of his head twinged his neck. But his gasp was of relief. The gray blotch was only a chunk of dust, clinging to the mirror.

Admittedly it was unpleasant; it resembled a face masked with dust, which also spilled from the face's dismayingly numerous openings. Really, he could live without it, much as he resented having to do his housekeeper's job for her.

When he rose, it took him a moment to realize that his reflection had partly blotted out the gray mass. In the further moment before he understood, two more reflected gray lumps rose beside it, behind him. Were they hands, or wads of dust? Perhaps they were composed of both. It was impossible to tell, even when they closed over his face.

# The
# Invocation

HE OPENED the gate stealthily; perhaps she wouldn't see him. But he had hardly touched the path when she unbent from the garden. "There you are, Ted," she said, waving a fistful of weeds at him in vague reproof. "A young man was asking for you."

That would have been Ken, about their holiday. "Thank you, Mrs. Dame," he said, and made to hurry up the path.

"Call me Cecily." She'd taken to saying that every time she saw him. "I've asked Mr. Mellor if I can plant some flowers. I like to see a bit of color. If you want something done there's no use waiting for someone else to do it," she said, kicking the calf-high grass.

"Oh, right." He had no chance now of hurrying away; the cats from the ground-floor flat were drawing themselves about his legs, like eager fur stoles.

She added the weeds to a heap and mopped her forehead. "Isn't it hot. You'd think they could give us a breeze. Still, it won't be long before we're complaining about the cold. We're never satisfied, are we?"

I would be, Ted thought, if you'd shut up for just a few minutes. I must be going, he opened his mouth to say as cats surged around his feet.

"Well, I'd better let you go. You'll be wanting to get on with your studies." But her gaze halted him. "I've said it before and I'll say it again," she said, "you remind me of my son."

Oh, no, he thought. God, not this anecdote again. Her wiry body had straightened, her hands were clasped behind her back as if she were a child reciting to an audience. "He was always in his books, never ready for his dinner," she said. "Him and his father, sitting all over the place with their feet up, in their books. It was always: just let me finish this chapter. And after his father died he got worse."

Cats streamed softly over Ted's feet, birds rose clapping from trees along the dual carriageway as she went on. "He was sitting there reading that *Finian's Wake*, and I happened to know it hadn't any chapters. I don't know how anyone can waste their time with such stuff. Just let me finish this chapter, he said, while his dinner went cold. I was so furious I picked up a cream puff and threw it at him. I didn't mean it to go on his book, but he said I did and used that as an excuse to leave me."

Last time the cream puff had been a plate of baked beans on toast. "Yeah, well," Ted muttered, shaking a kitten from his ankle. "I'm keeping you from your work."

As he stamped upstairs, the wood amplified his peevishness. Right, sure, she was lonely, she wanted someone to talk to. But he had work to do. And really, there was no wonder she was lonely. Few people would be prepared to suffer her for long.

In his flat his essay was waiting, but he didn't feel like writing now. He cursed: on the way home he had made himself ready to sit down and write. He tried to phone Ken, but the party line was occupied by two women, busy surpassing each other's ailments.

He opened the window. The flowers in the decanter on the sill had withered, and he threw them toward the pile of weeds two stories below. Mrs. Dame was nowhere in sight. After a while he heard her climbing the stairs, wheezing a little. For a moment he feared she might knock, for a chat. But the wheezing faded upward, and soon he heard her footsteps overhead.

His essay lay on the table, surrounded by texts. *Butcher's Films; a Structuralist History. Les Films "Z+" de BUTCH-ERS et ses amis. The Conventions of the British B-Feature and the Signature of Montgomery Tully: a Problem in Decipherment.* When he'd chosen cinema as a subject he had expected to enjoy himself. Well, at least there was Hitchcock to look forward to next term.

The last line he'd written waited patiently. "The local-rep conventions of the British B-feature—" How on earth had he meant to continue? He liked the phrase too much to delete it. He stared emptily at the page. At last he stood up. Perhaps when he'd found out what Ken wanted he would be able to write.

As soon as he picked up the phone he heard Mrs. Dame's voice. "He said I distracted him from his reading. He sat there with his feet up and said that."

God, no! He would never get through now. She saved up her phone calls for the evenings, when they were cheaper; then she would chatter for hours. Before he could utter the sound he was tempted to make, he slammed the receiver into its cradle. Her voice—muttering through the ceiling, drifting down into the open window—faltered for a moment, then went on. The occasional word or phrase came clear, plucking at his attention, tempting his ears to strain.

He couldn't write unless he carried everything to the library, and that was a mile away. Surely he could read. He gazed at *Les Films "Z+"*, translating mentally from the point at which he'd stopped reading. "Within the most severe restrictions of the budget, these gleams of imagination are like triumphant buds. One feels the delight of the naturalist who discovers a lone flower among apparently barren rocks." But the room was growing darker as the sky filled with cloud. As he peered more closely at the text, Mrs. Dame's voice insinuated words into his translation. "Consider too the moment (one of the most beautiful in the entire British cinema) in *Master Spy* where June Thorburn discovers that her suspicions of Stephen Murray are, after all, unfounded. The direction and acting are simply the invisible frame of the script. Such simplicity and direct-ness are a cream puff."

"God!" He shoved his chair back violently; it clawed the floorboards. Her muttering seeped into the room, her words formed and dissolved. The heat made him feel limp and cumbersome, the heavy dimness strained his eyes. He went to the window to breathe, to find calm.

As he reached the window her voice ceased. Perhaps her listener had interrupted. Silence touched him softly through the window, like a breeze. The thickening sky changed slowly, almost indiscernibly. The traffic had gone home to dinner. The trees along the carriageway held their poses, hardly trembling. The hole which had been advancing along the roadway was empty and silent now, surrounded by dormant warning lights. Ted leaned his elbows on the sill.

But the silence wasn't soothing. It was unnatural, the product of too many coincidences; it couldn't last for long. His nerves were edgily alert for its breaking. Overhead a ragged black mass was descending, blotting out half the sky. It seemed to compress the silence. No doubt because he was unwillingly alert, Ted felt as though he was being watched too. Surely the silence, in its brittleness and tension, must be like the silence of a forest when a pred-ator was near.

He started. Mrs. Dame's voice had recommenced, an insistent bumbling. It nagged violently at him. Even if he shut the window, trapping himself with the heat, there was nowhere in his flat he could escape her voice. He began to curse loudly: "Jesus God almighty . . ." He combined everything sexual, religious, or scatological he could think of, and found that he knew a good many words.

When at last he was silent he heard Mrs. Dame's voice, wandering unchecked. His chest felt tight, perhaps holding back a scream of rage. His surroundings seemed to have altered subtly, for the worse. Beyond the trees that divided the carriageway, the houses brooded, gloomily luminous, beneath the slumped dark sky. Dull red blobs hung around the hole in the road; the sullenly glowing foliage looked paralyzed. The ominous mumbling of the city, faint yet huge, surrounded him. He felt more strongly as though he was being watched. He blamed everything he felt on her voice. "I wish something would shut you up for a while," he said as loudly as he could, and began to turn away.

Something halted him. The silence was closer, more oppressive; it seemed actually to have muffled Mrs. Dame's voice. Everything shone luridly. A dark hugeness stooped toward him. The mass of black cloud had altered; it was an enormous slowly smouldering head. Its eyes, sooty unequal blotches, shifted lethargically; jagged teeth lengthened and dissolved in the tattered smile. As the mass spread almost imperceptibly across the gray, its smile widening, it seemed to lean toward him. It pressed darkness into the room.

He flinched back, and saw that the decanter was toppling from the sill. He must have knocked it over. It was odd he hadn't felt the impact. He caught the decanter and replaced it on the sill. No wonder he hadn't felt it, no wonder his imagination was getting in his way: Mrs. Dame's muttering had won.

When he switched on the light it looked dim, cloaked by smoke. Darkness still made its presence felt in the room; so did the sense of watching. He'd had enough. There was no point in trying to work. Another evening wasted. He clumped downstairs angrily, tensely determined to relax. Overhead the clouds were moving on, still keeping their rain to themselves.

Ken wasn't in any of the pubs: not the Philharmonic, nor O'Connor's, nor the Grapes, nor the Augustus John. Ted became increasingly frustrated and depressed. He must

make sure of this holiday. He was going away with Ken
for a long weekend in three days, if they were going at all.
Just a few days' break from Mrs. Dame would let him
work, he was sure. He managed to chat, and to play bar
billiards. More and more students crowded in, the ceiling
of smoke thickened and sank. His tankards huddled together on the table.

When at last he rambled home from an impromptu
party, Mrs. Dame's light was out. The sight heartened
him. Perhaps now he could write. And perhaps not, he
thought, laughing at his beery clumsiness as he fumbled
with his sandals.

The decanter caught his attention. A small dark object
was visible inside it, at the bottom. He raised the sash in
the hope of a breeze, then he examined the decanter. The
facets of cut glass distorted the object; so did the beer. He
couldn't make it out. A lump of soot, a shifting pool of
muddy fluid, a dead insect? No doubt it would be clearer
in the morning. His sandals flopped underfoot on the
floorboards, like loose tongues. He extricated his feet at
last, and slid into bed.

Pounding woke him. He rose carefully and took two
aspirins. After a while some of the pounding went away;
the rest stayed outside, in the road. He gazed from the
window, palms over his ears. A pneumatic drill was inching the hole along the roadway toward him.

He squinted painfully at the decanter. Something had
lodged in it, but what? The cut glass confused his view.
As he turned the decanter in his hands the object seemed to
swell, to move of its own accord; there was a suggestion
of long feelers or legs. Yet when he peered down the glass
throat the decanter looked empty, and when he shook it
upside down nothing rattled or fell out. Perhaps when he'd
knocked over the decanter it had cracked, perhaps he was
seeing a flaw. He hoped not; he'd found the decanter black
with grime in a junk shop nearby, he had been proud of his
find once he'd cleaned it. Maybe one day, he thought, I'll

have something to decant. That woman upstairs will make
me into a wino.

He hurried to class and blinked at the film. Mono-
chrome figures posed, reading their lines. He might just as
well have his eyes closed. He listened to the heroine's
description of the plot so far. She'd missed out a scene—no,
his mind had; he'd blacked out for a moment. He blinked
at a talking tableau, then his eyes sank closed again; just
let him rest them a moment longer. Music woke him: THE
END. Afterward, fellow students applauded his honest
response.

At least he managed to contact Ken, who had retrieved
his tent and sleeping bags from a borrower. He would call
for Ted in his van. Ted relaxed. Now nothing could disturb him in his flat, not even Mrs. Dame.

When he heard her as he neared the house he smiled
wryly. She didn't bother him so much now. She had a
friend to tea; he heard spoons rattling demurely in china.
The evening grew cold, and he closed the window. Voices
penetrated the ceiling; occasionally he heard Mrs. Dame's
friend, chattering shrilly in an attempt to outdistance Mrs.
Dame, who headed her off easily and began another
anecdote. Rather her than me, Ted thought, laughing. He
turned to his essay and quickly wrote several pages.

Later he became less tolerant. He couldn't be expected
to endure her waking him up. When he went to bed the
night seemed oppressively tense, as though clouds were
hanging low and electric, although the sky was clear. He
felt restless and irritable, but eventually slept—only to be
awakened by Mrs. Dame. He could tell by the cadence of
her voice that she was talking, almost shouting, in her
sleep. Perhaps the tension of the night was affecting her.
Can't she even shut up when she's asleep? he thought,
glaring at the dark.

As he lay on his side he could see a faint distorted ghost
of the decanter, projected by the streetlamps onto the fitted
wardrobe. It was moving. No, a darker shadow was squeezing out of the watery outline of the neck. He turned his

head sharply. Some kind of insect, or a spider, was emerging; he saw long legs twitching on the glass lip. He hoped it would go out through the gap he'd left beneath the sash. If only it were a genie emerging from the bottle it could go and silence Mrs. Dame. He closed his eyes, reaching for slumber before he woke entirely, and tried to lull the crick in his neck to sleep.

A cry woke him. Was it one of the ground-floor cats? He lay in his own warmth and tried not to care, but his heart kept him awake. A bell tolled two o'clock. The next cry was louder. His heart leaped, racing, though he realized now that it was Mrs. Dame, crying out in her sleep. Couldn't she even have a nightmare quietly? He might just as well be in bed with her, God forbid. She was moaning now; muffled as it was, it sounded rather like a singer's doodling. After a while it soothed him to sleep.

Good God, what now? He kept his eyes determinedly shut. It must be dawn, for light was filtering through his eyelids. Soon he heard the sound again: a faint squeaking of claws on glass. It would be one of the cats—they often appeared on the sill, furry ghosts mopping at the window. He sighed. All we need now is a brass band, to play me a lullaby. He dragged more of the blanket over his ear.

The decanter was rocking. Something was struggling to squeeze back into the glass mouth. The legs scrabbled, squeaking on the glass, trying to force the swollen body down. But the body was larger than the mouth of the decanter. The decanter tipped over, fell, smashed. Ted woke gasping and leaped out of bed.

The decanter lay in fragments. His head felt as if it had been cracked open too. He sat on the bed and made himself calm down. The glimpse of the insect, the sound of the cat's claws, the fall of the decanter: these were the sources of his dream, which must have lasted only the second before he woke. Yesterday he must have replaced the decanter unstably. His head throbbed jaggedly, his heart jerked. Glaring upward made him feel a little better. It was all that woman's fault.

\*   \*   \*

The day's lectures examined the theme of misunderstanding in Butcher's films. Ted's eyes burned. The lecturer swam forward, hot and bright, droning. Misunderstanding. Here again we see the theme. Once more the theme of misunderstanding. When Ted walked home at last his mind was dull, featureless. Tonight he'd have an early night.

If that woman let him sleep. Well, tonight he'd wake her if he had to. She had no right to keep other people awake with her restlessness. He couldn't hear her as he approached the house; that was encouraging. An old woman was hobbling up the front path, stopping to rest her shopping bag. "I'll carry that for you," he said, and she turned. It was Mrs. Dame.

He managed to disguise his gasp as a cough. Once before he'd seen her ill, white faced, when she had tripped on the stairs. But now, for the first time, she looked old. She was stooped, her skin hung slumped on her; she massaged her ankles, which were clearly painful. "Thank you," she said when he picked up the shopping bag. She seemed hardly to recognize him.

"Can I get you anything?" he said, dismayed.

She smiled weakly at him. Her face looked like wax, a little melted. "No, thank you. I'm all right now."

He could hardly believe that he wished she were more talkative. "Have you been to the doctor?"

"I don't need him," she said with a hint of her old vitality. "He's got enough old crocks to see to without me wasting his time. I'll be all right when my legs have had a bit of a rest."

He left the bag outside her door. He felt vaguely guilty: now he'd have some peace—but good God, it wasn't he who'd made her ill, was it? Nevertheless he felt embarrassed when, going down, he met her on his landing. "Thank you," she said as she began to clamber up the last flight of stairs. He smiled nervously, blushing for no reason he understood, and fled into his flat.

Later he brought home his dinner. As he ate the curry from its plastic container, he felt uneasy. The city wound down quietly into evening; a few boys shouted around a football, occasional cars swished past, but they weren't what he was straining to hear. He was waiting irritably, anxiously, for Mrs. Dame's voice.

She would be all right. She had been when she'd fallen on the stairs. Or perhaps she wouldn't be; after all, she was getting old. In any case, there was nothing he could do. He washed up his fork, and turned to his essay. His eyes felt as though they were smouldering.

The interchangeable personalities of many British B-feature performers, he wrote. The white page glared; his eyes twitched. Around him the room wavered in sympathy, and something scuttled across the wardrobe. When he glanced round, there was only the noise of a car emerging from the side street opposite. It must have been that: the car's headlights hurrying the shadow of branches over the wardrobe, like a bunch of long rapid legs.

He finished his sentence somehow. Some performances actually imitate the performances of stars, he went on, which sometimes has the effect  The silence distracted him, as if someone was watching, mutely reproving; his eyes felt hot and huge. What effect? Reproving him for what? He sighed, and capped his pen. At least he was going away tomorrow. There was no point in forcing himself to write now, when he was so aware of waiting to hear Mrs. Dame's voice.

Later he heard her, when he went upstairs to the toilet; there was none on his floor. Beneath the unshaded bulb the bare dusty stairs looked old and cheerless. As he climbed them he heard a sound like the song of a wind in a cranny. Not until he reached the top landing did he realize that the sound was composed of words—that it was her voice.

"Leave my legs," she was pleading feebly. "Leave them now." Her voice sounded slurred, as if she was drunk. She was only talking in her sleep, that was why she sounded so odd. He heard a violent snore, then silence.

After a while her voice recommenced. What was she saying now? He tiptoed across the landing and stooped carefully toward her door.

As his ear touched the panel he heard a sound beyond. Had she fallen out of bed? Certainly something large and soft had fallen, and it seemed to be surrounded by a pattering on the carpet. The time switch clicked out, blinding him with darkness.

In a moment he heard her voice. "Leave them now," she moaned, "leave them." She was all right, she must have pushed something off the bed: probably the bedspread. If he knocked he would only wake her. He fumbled in the dark for the time switch. Behind him her voice slurred, moaning.

When he returned to his flat he found that now he'd heard her voice, he could still hear it: an almost inaudible blurred sound, rising and falling. It reminded him unpleasantly of the sound a fly's wings make, struggling as a spider feasts. The night seemed very cold. He closed the window and filled a hot water bottle. Her voice buzzed, trapped.

It must have been that unpleasant resemblance that led, when sleep overtook him at last, to the dream. Something was tapping on the window, softly, insistently. He turned his head reluctantly. Dawn coated everything like smoke, but he could see a large dark shape dangling beyond the pane, spinning slowly, swaying lightly toward the glass, bumping against it. It was a package with a withered face: Mrs. Dame's face, which had grown a thick gray beard. No, the beard was web, filling her slack mouth as though it were a yawning crevice. Her face bobbed up in the window frame; she was being reeled in from above. He tried to wake, but sleep dragged him down, gray and vague as the dawn.

Eventually the pneumatic drill woke him. He lay sweating, tangled in the blankets. Sunlight filled the room, which was very hot. Gradually, too gradually, the dream faded. He lay welcoming the light. At last he fished out the hot water bottle, which flopped under the bed. He was enormously glad to get up—and about time; he had overslept. Ken would be here soon.

He opened the windows and ate breakfast hastily. The flat overhead was silent, so far as he could hear over the chattering of the drill. Should he go up and knock? But then he mightn't be able to escape her conversation, when he ought to be getting ready for the weekend. Her friends would look after her if she needed help. He might go up, if he had time before Ken arrived.

He hurried about, checking that plugs were unplugged, sockets switched off. The space between the fitted wardrobe and the ceiling distracted him. The gap was dim, but at the back, against the wall, he could see a large dark mass. He must clean up the flat. A horn was shouting a tune below, in the road. It was Ken's van.

He closed the window and grabbed his bulging rucksack. The road repairers were directly outside now; as he slammed the door of the flat and shoved it to make sure, it sounded as though the drill was in his room. The sound like scuttling on the floorboards must be a vibration from the drill.

Ken drove through the Saturday morning traffic. The van plunged into the Mersey Tunnel, and out to North Wales. Neither Ken nor Ted had any lectures until Tuesday. They walked and climbed in the sharp air; they drank, and drove singing back to their tent. Above them mountains and stars glittered, distant and cold.

When they returned to Liverpool on Monday night they were famished. They ate at the Kebab House. O'Connor's was just down the block; friends cheered as they entered. Several hours later the barman got rid of them at last. "If you're driving I'm walking," Ted told Ken, trying to hold a shop front still.

He walked home, from side to side of the back streets. Moonlight glinted on the smooth red sandstone of the Anglican cathedral, at the top of its tremendous steps; nearby he heard a smash of glass, shouts, screams. Fragments of streets led down toward the river. Along Princes

Road, trees and lamp standards stood unmoving; Ted tried to compete with them, but couldn't manage it. His leaning pushed him forward, almost at a run, to the house. He couldn't remember when he'd been so drunk; he ought to have had more than one meal today. Mrs. Dame's window was dark and silent. She must be asleep.

His flat was full of a block of silence. The silence seemed lifeless, his flat unwelcoming—bare floorboards, the previous tenant's paint on the walls. Surely he wasn't yearning to hear that woman's voice. Something rustled as he entered the main room: a page among the books on the table. Some performances actually imitate the performances of stars, it said, which sometimes has the effect   What effect? Never mind. He'd finish that tomorrow.

He gazed at the tousled bed. What a mess to come home to. But the way he felt at the moment, he could sleep on anything. The tangled tunnel of blankets looked warmer than the chill flat. Some performances actually imitate   The sentence nagged him like a tune whose conclusion he couldn't remember. Forget it. Brush teeth, wash face, fall into bed.

He pushed the kitchen door farther open, and heard something move away from it, rustling faintly. They were still rustling when he found the light switch: a couple of moths, several large flies, all withered. Well, it was the spider season, but he wished the spiders would clear up after themselves.

He stooped to pick up the dustpan, and frowned. Beneath the window lay a scattering of small bones, of a mouse or a bird. Of course, he'd forgotten to close the kitchen window before leaving. One of the cats from downstairs must have slipped in; it was probably responsible for the insects too.

Water clanked and squeaked in the pipes. The tap choked on knots as he splashed icy water on his face, gasping. As he dabbed water from his eyes, a shadow scuttled over the fitted wardrobe. The wardrobe door rattled, and then the floorboards in the main room. Only headlights through branches, only vibrations from the road. Some performances actually

He padded across the cold boards and switched off the lights, then he slid into the tangle of blankets. God, they weren't so warm; his toes squirmed. And he'd forgotten to take out last week's hot water bottle, damn it. He could feel it dragging at the bedclothes; it was hanging down beyond the mattress, in a sack of loose blanket. He tried to hook it with his toes, but couldn't reach it. At least it wouldn't chill his feet.

The bed drifted gently on a sea of beer. Some performances have the  Oh, come on, he thought angrily. He glared at the room, to tire his eyes. It glowed faintly with moonlight, as though steeped in luminous paint. He glared at the glimmering wardrobe, at the dark gap above. What was that, at the back? It must be the accumulation of dust which he had to clean out, but it was pale as the moonlight, of which its appearance must be an effect. It looked like a tiny body, its head in the shadows, its limbs drawn up into a withered tangle. God, it looked like a colorless baby; he could even see one of its hands, could count the shrivelled fingers. What on earth was it? But the wardrobe was sailing sideways on his beer. He closed his eyes and drifted down, down into sleep.

A figure lay on a bed. Its face was dim, as was the dark shape crouched at the foot of the bed. Limbs—many of them, it seemed—reached for the sleeper, inching it down the bed. The figure writhed helplessly, its hands fluttered feebly as the wings of an ensnared fly. It moaned.

Ted woke. His eyes opened, fleeing the dream; the room sprang up around him, glowing dimly. He lay on his back, while his heart thudded like a huge soft drum. The luminous room looked hardly more reassuring than the dream. God, he would almost have preferred Mrs. Dame's muttering to this.

And now he wouldn't be able to sleep, because he was painfully cold. He couldn't feel his legs, they were so numb. He reached down to massage them. His hands seemed retarded and clumsy; they touched his legs and found them stiff, but his legs couldn't feel his fingers at all. Had he been lying awry, or was it the cold? He rubbed his thighs and cursed his awkwardness.

He couldn't move his feet. Though he strained, the dim hump in the blankets at the far end of the bed stood absolutely still. Panic was gathering. He lifted the blankets and pushed them back. His blood felt slow and thick; so did he.

Before he had uncovered his legs, the hump in the blankets collapsed, although he hadn't felt his feet move. Something dragged at the bedclothes, and he heard it thump the floor softly, in the sack of blankets beyond the mattress. Only the hot water bottle. At once he remembered that he had fished the bottle out of bed last week.

He managed to sit up, and threw the blankets away violently. Panic filled him, overwhelming but vague. He was swaying; he had to punch the mattress in order to prop himself up. His shadow dimmed the bed, he could hardly see his legs. They looked short, perhaps because of the dimness, and oddly featureless, like smooth glistening sticks. He couldn't move them at all.

As he stared down, struggling feebly and frantically to clear his mind, the dim hump came groping hungrily out on the tangle of blankets

# The Little
# Voice

WHEN Edith Locketty went downstairs the old man was already staring. She couldn't draw the curtains; during the night her curtain rail had collapsed again. On the wall that divided the yards, weeds nodded helplessly beneath rain. Beyond them, through his window that was the twin of hers, the old man stared at her.

He was smiling. She pursed her lips, frowning at his baggy face and veined dome, patched with gray hair and discolored skin as if abandoned to dust and spiders. His eyes were wide, but were they innocent? His smile looked sleepy, sated, reminiscent; reminiscent of . . .

She remembered her dream. Her face became a cold disgusted mask. Filthy old creature, it was written on his face what he was. But he couldn't know what she had dreamed. No doubt his smile referred to something equally disgusting. She cracked her egg viciously, as though it were a tiny cranium.

He turned away. Good of him to let her eat in peace! Bars of rain struggled down the window; beyond them, at the edge of her vision, he was a dim feeble shifting that felt like an irritation in her eye. The downpour hissed in the backyard and the alley beyond, prattled in the gutters. Gradually, through the liquid clamor, she made out another sound. In the old man's house the child was chattering.

She glanced reluctantly across. She knew neither its sex nor its age. Again she wondered whether he kept the child out of sight deliberately because he knew she was a teacher. Did it ever go to school? If it wasn't old enough, what possessed him to keep it awake at all hours?

Perhaps the child was beyond his control, and kept him awake. His smile might have been weary rather than sleepy, and meant for the child rather than for her. He sat at the dim bare table, gazing into the underwater room, at the muffled childish piping.

She dropped the crushed shell into the pedal bin, glad to be ready to leave. There was something nasty about him, she'd seen it skulking in his eyes. And he couldn't be helping the child to develop. She'd never heard the thin incessant voice pronounce a recognizable word.

The pavements glittered, bejeweled with rain and snatches of sun. The clouds had almost drained, the last shafts of rain hurried away on the wind; puddles puckered vanishing mouths. To think of leaving a child alone with him! If she had ever had a child— She halted her thoughts firmly. That was long past.

Nearing the school, she became her role: Miss Locketty the teacher. The children knew where they were with her, as they needed to. But the old man was troubling her: his stare, his sly pleasure, her recurring dream of his dry piebald flesh groping over her in bed.

She shook off the memory, squirming. How could anyone allow him near? His housekeeper might have, if that was what she was; perhaps the child was theirs. To think of his flesh jerking spasmodically like an old machine! One man had been enough to disgust her for life. She strode furiously into the schoolyard.

Mr. Prince was on yard duty. His hair was longer than

most of the girls'. It was his last day at this school, and he seemed not to care what the children did—although, in her opinion, he never had cared. Children sat on their wet raincoats. "Hang those up, please," she said, and they did so at once. Others were kicking puddles at each other, but ceased when she said, "You're too old for that." Already she felt calmer, more sure.

After assembly she led her class to their room. "You may play games quietly." They fought pen-and-paper battles, but noise came blundering through the wall from Mr. Prince's class. On the other side, the murmur of Sue Thackeray's children was hardly audible. At least it was Prince's last day.

Drat it, she'd forgotten to bring the Enid Blyton book to read to her class, their end-of-term treat. At lunchtime she made for the gates. A woman was reaching through the railings, as though the street were a cage. Her hand was bones gloved in skin, groping for the children, beckoning. In her pocket a bottle dribbled wine around its rakish stopper. "Come away from there, please," the teacher told the children. Poor woman; probably beyond help. As she turned away, the woman's eyes puckered wistfully.

The teacher strode home. More rain loomed overhead; the glum sky doled out light. The book lay on the kitchen table, where she'd left it to remind her. The old man sat at his table, reaching for, and talking to, the obscure gloom. His hands were playing some complicated game.

When he turned to stare at her, his smile looked gloating. Somewhere near him the voice clamored thinly for attention. "Yes, I can see you, you dirty old swine," she said loudly without thinking. "Just you watch yourself." She hurried away, for she thought he'd begun to tremble—though surely he couldn't have heard her words. His staring face looked frail as shadow.

She read her book to her class, and watched their faces dull. Ranks of uniformed waxworks stared at her, drooping a little. Did they think they were too old for the story, or that she was out of date? She saw the old man trembling.

Noise from next door floundered about her room, like a
clumsy intruder. If she didn't act she would lose control of
herself. "Talk quietly until I come back," she said.

When Mr. Prince deigned to answer his door, she said,
"Will you control your class, please? You're making it
impossible for me to read."

Sandwiched in her book, her finger pointed at him. He
glanced at the cover with a motion like spitting. His mouth
quirked, meaning: Jesus, that's just what you'd expect of
her. "Never mind what you think of it," she blurted.
"Just do as you're told. I could teach you a few of the
basics of teaching."

He stared incredulously at her. "Oh piss off and leave
us alone."

The head listened to her tale, sucking his pipe loudly;
she could tell he'd been looking forward to a quiet smoke.
"I'd have smacked a child for saying it," she said.

"I hope you'd do nothing of the kind." As she stared,
feeling betrayed, he added more gently, "Besides, it's his
last day. No point in unpleasantness. We all need a rest,"
he said, as though to excuse her. "It's time we all went
home."

From her window she watched her class crossing the
schoolyard, eager for freedom. "Have a good Easter,"
one had said, but had that been sarcasm? She could feel
only the burning knot of anger in her guts. And she was
faced with two weeks of the old man's stare.

But the house next to hers was silent. Only the dark,
uncurtained window gaped at her, vaguely framed by twilit
brick. She immersed herself in peace. Her anger dulled
and went out, or at least became a vague shadow in her
mind.

She served herself dinner on the Wedgwood service,
which her parents had kept for best. The window opposite
reminded her of an empty aquarium, grimy with neglect; it
made her kitchen feel more comfortable. Tomorrow she'd
put up the curtain rail. She read Georgette Heyer until
exhaustion began to disintegrate the phrases.

She was sitting at a table, gazing across it at darkness. Very gradually a shape began to accumulate twilight, scarcely more distinct than the dark: a developing fetus? It must be too dark for her eyes to function properly, for surely no fetus ever took that shape, or moved so swiftly around a table. When she woke, the silence seemed chill and very large, alive with memories. She had to urge herself to climb the stairs to bed.

Someone was knocking, but not at her door; she turned comfortably within her own warmth, and slept again. It was the sounds of the crowd, of footsteps booming muffled through the house, that woke her.

They were next door, she realized, as she blinked herself aware of the midday sunshine. She peered between the curtains, annoyed that she felt guiltily furtive. A policeman was emerging from the old man's house; a police car squatted outside.

At last she let go of the curtains. She rushed herself to the bathroom and slapped her face with water, scrubbed her armpits. What she'd said had served the old man right. Surely he hadn't— In the mirror her face deplored her faltering. She must find out what had happened.

Her body fumbled as though to hinder her dressing. As she strode down the path, trailing grasses clung to her ankles. Her stomach clenched—but she couldn't retreat, for the housekeeper had seen her. "What's wrong?" the teacher called, and felt forced to hold her breath.

The woman dragged her coat tighter, shivering in the April wind that fought for the parcel in her hands. "Mr. Wajda has died," she said.

He'd been a foreigner? Questions struggled half formed behind the teacher's lips: How did he? Why did he? It seemed safest to ask, "Who found him?"

"The postman. He was trying to deliver this." The woman held out the parcel; her small eyes looked careful, limited, determined not to speculate. "He saw Mr. Wajda at the bottom of the stairs."

"He fell downstairs?" The teacher tried not to sound as hopeful as she felt.

"They think there was a loose stair rod. Of course, he couldn't see it."

She managed to keep her relief from her face. But "Of course?" she repeated, puzzled.

"Yes, of course. He was blind."

"I see," she lied, and retreated mumbling, "If there's anything I can do." The housekeeper looked as bewildered as the teacher felt, and was staring at the opened parcel, which contained a skipping rope.

So the old man had been staring only at her sounds. His wide eyes hadn't meant to pretend innocence. No doubt his hearing had been acute; he must have heard her words. Still, blindness didn't make him innocent; indeed, it explained the way he had fumbled over her in her dreams. Enough of that. His death had been nothing to do with her, he would have fallen anyway, of course he would. She could forget him.

But she could not. He must be lying still in the dark house. His gloomy window looked ominous, as though threatening to stage an unpleasant surprise. It unnerved her from climbing up to replace her curtain rail. Instead she cleaned her house before it annoyed her further. Somewhere a child was either sobbing or laughing.

Next day the hearse arrived. Quick work: perhaps he'd had friends in the business. Now the house next door felt simply empty. She smiled at the flat blank window. No hurry now to put up the rail.

A child sang tunelessly: *la, la, la*. The teacher went shopping beneath a thick gray sky, and told children to leave the old man's garden. The news must have spread that his house was no-man's-land. Returning, she had to chase the children again. "Do you want the police?" she demanded, and watched while they fled.

*La, la, la*. She unpacked her purchases. *La, la, la*. The sound was above her. In the adjoining house. The childless black couple must have a visitor, and she wished they'd keep it quiet. Just a fortnight without children, that was all she wanted.

In her bedroom it was closer. *La, la, la.* She pressed her ear to the wall; a faint blurred thudding of reggae filtered through. Jungle drums, she thought automatically, and then her thoughts froze. The child's voice was beyond the far wall, in the old man's house.

It sounded alone and preoccupied. Perhaps it had been with the children she'd chased. If it had heard her threat of the police it mightn't dare to venture out. Suppose the stair rod were still loose?

The sky was sinking beneath its burden of unshed rain. Thick fringes of grass flopped over the old man's path. Her own garden was untidy as the blind man's; she must take it in hand. His windows were curtained with grime. The actual curtains, drooping within, looked like fat ropes of dust.

About to knock, she halted. A stair rod wedged the front door, too timidly ajar to be noticeable from the pavement. Perhaps this was the lethal stair rod—but it meant the child was a meddler, dangerous to itself. She pushed the door wide.

A dim staircase rose from the hall, which might have been a mirror's version of her own—except that she hoped that hers was infinitely cleaner. The woman could have done nothing but his shopping. Above the stairs, festoons of dust transformed a lampshade into a chandelier.

"Come here, please. Before you hurt yourself." Muffled as dust, the house dulled her voice, as though she were shouting into blankets. No answer came. Perhaps the child was downstairs now. She strode toward the kitchen, unwilling to climb toward the box of secret darkness.

The house smelled of dank wallpaper. The sky's lid allowed scant light into the kitchen. When she switched on the bulb, as gray as an old pear, the light felt thick as oil. The room was empty—perhaps too empty: there was no chair opposite the old man's at the table. Nothing else in the long cluttered room seemed worth noting, except a spillage of cans of baby food surrounding a bin beneath the sink. Beyond the window, her own kitchen looked darkly unfamiliar, hardly hers at all.

Enough dawdling. She hurried back toward the stairs; her echoes seemed indefinably wrong. She halted. Had there been a high sound, perhaps an inadvertent snatch of song, among her last echoes? "Come down here, please. I'm not going to hurt you."

The dark above her swallowed her call, and kept its secret. It stood blocking the top of the stairs. Good God, was she going to let her nervousness in an empty house prevent her from saving a child? She tramped upstairs. "Come here to me," she called.

At once there was movement in the dark. Someone came running toward her, down what sounded like an impossibly long hall. Above her the dark seemed crowded with sound, and about to hurl the source of that sound at her. The child was going to play a trick, to leap at her as she stood vulnerable on the stairs.

Her loss of dignity angered her, but she ran. Once she reached the hall she'd give the child a piece of her mind. The noise raced toward her, sounding thin, hollow, dry, and far too large—deformed by dust and echoes, of course. It was close behind her. Her clutching hand scraped a wad of dust from the banister.

The noise had halted. She gripped the banister tight as a weapon as she turned, for fear of an unbalancing prank. But the stairs were deserted.

Outside, the muddy sky gave her less light than she'd hoped. Of course, all the sounds must have come from the house beyond the old man's. The threat of rain filled her mind, like fog. She had almost reached her front door when it slammed in her face. She fumbled irritably for her key. Enough tricks for today.

*La, la, la.* Determined to ignore the sound, which seemed to have moved above her, she dined at the nearby Chinese restaurant. Mellowed by Riesling, she ambled home through streets polished by rain. Shops displayed beds, bright and

deserted. Her house displayed darkness. As she climbed
the stairs her echoes sounded more numerous than she
thought they should, as though someone were imitating
her. Of course, that was what had sounded wrong in the
old man's house. She smiled vaguely and went to bed.

Pale quick movement woke her. For a moment it hovered;
it had opened the ceiling to peer down at her. She was still
trying to prop her eyes open when it slid away, gliding
down the wall to the floor. It must have been the stray
light of a car.

Her eyelids settled shut. Then her brow tautened. She
must be half engulfed in a dream, for she thought she
remembered the pale oval crossing the floor and hiding
beneath her bed. No car's beam could have reached so far.
Determinedly, she relaxed. Her brow was beginning to
squeeze forth a headache.

She dozed amid distractions. The tick of her clock was
shouting, like an ignored child; a drip in the kitchen
seemed eager to remind her how largely empty the house
was. Something—a fly, it must have been—kept touching
her face lightly, silently. Grumbling, she withdrew beneath the blankets. Somewhere in a dream she could still
feel the timid touch.

She must have dreamed that it managed to pluck the
blankets away and crawl in beside her face. Daylight
showed her a deserted room. Perhaps the fly had fallen
under the bed to die; she wasn't looking. She ate breakfast
and stared at the weeds on the yard wall; lingering raindrops made their leaves crystalline. The weeds wept on her
fingers as she uprooted them triumphantly. She'd left them
growing to avoid arguments with the old man—and of
course he wouldn't have noticed.

She read the Heyer. The street sounded like a schoolyard;
footballs beat like irregular hearts. Later, the library was
quiet, until children came in for a chase. She couldn't
escape them at all, it seemed. She smiled wryly at the
harassed librarian.

*La, la, la.* Couldn't they teach the child a few more notes, or at least to stay firmly on the one? She added her coat to the load on the hall stand, straining her ears to determine the location of the sound. It was above her, on the old man's side. It moved slowly to the other side. But it couldn't do that unless it was in her house.

She ran upstairs. Her footsteps filled the house, but there was no need for stealth; the child was in her bedroom, trapped. It sang on, indifferent to her. She'd smack its bottom for that as well. She flung open the bedroom door.

The bed was spread with sunlight, the room blazed. The singing persisted ahead of her, tantalizingly, as she forced her eyes not to blink; then it moved through the wall into the spare bedroom. Just an acoustic trick. She was disconcertingly unsure what she felt now she'd been robbed of the naughty child. The house walls were too thin, that was for sure. She sat downstairs, riffling through her new books. When the singing recommenced she pursed her lips. She'd been tricked once.

She woke. She was sitting in the chair, an open book roofed her knee. For a moment she forgot that it was the next day, that she'd been to bed meanwhile. Some perversity of her metabolism always exhausted her after the end of term.

No doubt the tapping of rain had wakened her; the panes looked cracked by water, the room was crowded with dim giant amoebae. But the movement, or the version of it that her sleep had admitted, had sounded heavier. Though she quashed the memory at once, she thought of the departed footsteps of her parents. The sound came again, rumbling in the cupboard in the corner of the room.

Reluctantly she tiptoed closer. Dry waves of rain flooded down the cupboard door. With one hand she switched on the standard lamp, with the other she snatched open the door. The gas meter peered up at her, twitching its indicator. There was nothing else, not even a mouse hole. It must have been the black couple, being far too noisy.

In the kitchen all the cupboards were open. Their interiors looked very dark, and more full than they should have, especially where they were darkest. Wake up! She slapped her face, none too gently. What was her mind playing, hide and seek? She slammed the doors, refusing to peer within.

Her mind tried slyly to persuade her to dine out. Nonsense, she couldn't afford that every night. After dinner she wrote to Sue, suggesting a restaurant, then tried to read. Didn't they ever put that child to bed? It was such a dismal sound, it made her house seem so empty.

Next day she lost patience. Never mind sitting about, moping. Who was going to put up the curtain rail, her father? This time she'd do it properly. She replenished the sockets in the plaster with filler. Replacing the screws was more tiring than she'd thought; halfway through she was prickly with sweat. "Shut up with your la, la, la," she snarled. She'd complain, if she only knew where. Gasping triumphantly, she tightened the last screw and stood gazing at her handiwork, ignoring the blisters on her palms.

The singing insinuated itself among the words of her books, it began to pick apart her thoughts. What annoyed her most was its stupidity. It sounded mindless as a dripping tap.

On Good Friday she rode a bus into unexpected sunshine, but there seemed to be an indefinable thin barrier between her and her enjoyment. Among the children who crowded the fields and the woods a tuneless song kept appearing. She returned home before she'd planned to, toward slabs of cloud.

She lay listening furiously. *La, la, la.* It was hours past midnight, hours since she'd tried to sleep. Tomorrow she would track down the child's parents—except that deep in her mind she dreaded that nobody would know what she was talking about. She knew none of her neighbors well enough for a calculated chat.

On Easter Sunday she went to church, in search of

peace, though she hadn't been for years. Above the altar
Christ rose up, pure, perfected. She gazed in admiration,
surprised how much she'd forgotten. There was a real
man, probably the only one. She'd never met one like
him.

The choir sang. Boyish trebles pierced the hymn: *la, la,
la,* one sang tunelessly. Her shoulders writhed and
shuddered, but she managed to stay kneeling. She'd had
hallucinations with insomnia before: bushes that smiled,
trees that raised their heads from grazing. The choir was in
tune now. She sat back gratefully. But when the sermon
mentioned spirits—ghosts—she found she was trying not
to hear.

She strode into her home. Now, no more nonsense. She
hooked her coat onto the stand, and at once heard it fall
behind her. The fall sounded far too heavy for a coat. On
the floor, whose shadows seemed thickened rather than
diluted by the light that leaked beneath the door, all the
coats lay in a mound—her parents' too, which she kept
meaning to give away. The mound looked as if a lumpy
shape were hiding underneath.

They were coats. Nothing but coats. Good God, it
wasn't as if they were moving. But if the lurker were
holding itself still, waiting to be uncovered . . . She stumbled forward and snatched away the coats. She stood
glaring defiantly at the bare floor. The coats didn't seem
bulky enough to have composed so large a mound.

She felt strange, handling her parents' clothes so roughly.
Had she left them on the stand because she hadn't known
how to touch them? That afternoon she took them to the
presbytery for the rummage sale.

Her house seemed very empty; the restless prattling
made it more so. All she needed was sleep. After midnight
she slept fitfully, when the voice allowed her. Surely she
wouldn't need a doctor. Sometimes, when her self-control
was barely equal to her job, she'd dreaded that. *La, la, la.*

On Monday Sue Thackeray came visiting. They returned from the Chinese restaurant companioned by a bot-

tle of gin. Edith was glad of Sue, whose throaty laugh gave the echoes no chance to sound hollow.

Sue's armchair wheezed as she sat back bulging, tenderly cradling her refilled glass. Her arms were almost as thick as the stuffed chair's. Memories of her parents, whom she had recently lost, floated up on the gin. "At least you lived here with yours," she said. "I didn't see mine for months."

"But the house seems so empty now."

"Well, it will. I thought you looked a bit peaky, love." She stared hard and blearily at Edith. "You want to get away."

"I'm going to Minorca this summer. I can't afford to go anywhere else as well."

They fell silent. The silence rustled with the approach of rain. "Anyway," Sue said, slapping her knee, beginning to grin. Edith hushed her. "Can you hear that?" she blurted.

*La, la, la.* "Rain," Sue said.

"No, I don't mean that." It was so difficult to force the words past her confusion that surely the effort must be worthwhile. "Can't you hear the child?" she demanded, almost pleading.

Sue gazed at her rather sadly before saying "No." She thought it was Edith's imagination, did she? She thought Edith had wished a child into her mind, did she?

"Did you ever want to adopt a child?"

"No," Edith declared angrily, "I never did, and I don't want one now. I have enough of them at school. I like my freedom, thank you." Why was she shouting, with only Sue to hear?

"All right, all right," Sue said grumpily. "I didn't mean—"

The crash turned her next word into a gape. Edith was already running to the door. But it had warped somehow, and refused to budge. She mustn't lose her temper, things were like children sometimes. But she must get out to see

what had happened! At the third wrench the door set her
free.

The fallen rail lay tangled in its curtains, scattered with
plaster. Above it, her filled sockets had been gouged.
"Look at that," she said incredulously. "It's been torn
down."

"Don't be silly," Sue rebuked her. "It's just fallen."

When Sue left, hurrying bowed beneath rain, Edith stood
staring at the dull street. The air was latticed with transparent slashes. Just fallen, indeed! How could the woman be
so smug about her blindness? At least her smugness had
convinced Edith that the child must exist objectively outside her own mind, however unnaturally. The gin allowed
her thoughts to be comfortably vague. Whatever it was, it
wouldn't drive her out of her own house. "You'll go
first," she shouted to her echoes.

A child was laughing. The sound seemed peaceful.
Perhaps she might enjoy having a child in the house. She
woke to the touch of cold rubber on her feet; the hot water
bottle felt dead. No, she didn't want a child. The hard hot
poking that preceded it had been bad enough: that, and the
doctor's groping to get rid of it, and the sight of it—it
hadn't looked at all human, it had never had the chance.
She had had it murdered. She could never have had a child
after that, even if she had wanted to.

"I want no child," she snarled at the dark. Then she
froze, remembering what she'd felt as she had awakened.

Of course it had been a dream: the face nuzzling hers
eagerly, the hand reaching playfully to touch her feet and
the bottle. Only in dreams was such a reach possible. But
she lay stiffly, trying to hush her breath, willing the bed to
be empty, willing the dark not to nuzzle her face. Perhaps
she lay thus for hours before, inadvertently, she fell asleep.

In the kitchen, a dim face was staring at her from the
empty house. Has it gone back? she thought, immediately
anxious not to understand what she meant. But it was the
housekeeper, who hadn't kept house. Impulsively Edith

ran to the yard wall. "Excuse me," she called. "Excuse me."

Eventually the door opened to let out the reluctant face. Edith felt drained of words, tricked by her own impulse. "When Mr. Er died," she said, still unwilling to think what she meant. "Was the child there?"

The woman's eyes narrowed, though they hadn't much scope to do so. "What child?"

"The one who lived with him." Perhaps she could shock the woman into truth. "It was your child, wasn't it?"

"It certainly was not," the woman said, turning away.

"But he had a child," Edith pleaded.

"I don't know who's been talking. He never had one that lived," the woman muttered resentfully. "It killed my aunt before she could bear it."

Perhaps her aunt had been married to him. Or perhaps not. Dirty old man. Irrelevant, Edith thought impatiently. She pointed behind the woman. "Surely there must have been a child. What about all that baby food?"

"He had no teeth," the woman said smugly. Her eyes reminded Edith of a pig's: small, dull, penned in. She was closing the door. "But the skipping rope," Edith protested.

"Listen," the woman said, "whatever he may have done, he's dead now. I won't discuss it. And you better hadn't, either."

The door snapped shut, like disapproving lips. Perhaps he'd lured children to his house for sexual purposes; no doubt most men would, given the chance; but that wasn't the point. That wasn't what the woman, too stupid to realize she had done so, had confirmed. Her very stupidity, her refusal to think, had confirmed it. There *had* been a child in that house, but nobody had seen it—because it couldn't be seen.

Now it had come into Edith's house. Today she found the thought of its objective existence less comforting. But at least it meant there was nothing wrong with her. "Yes, la, la, la,'' she said loudly; it was distant and muffled. "Go on, keep it up as long as you like.''

Sometimes she managed to switch off her awareness, as she often did with her class. Whenever she heard the sound again she laughed pityingly. It was no worse than the cries of children outside, though they had become aggressively distracting. She tried to doze. The library might be more restful, but she wouldn't be driven out of her own house. When the song became more insistent, frustrated by being ignored, she laughed louder.

A bath might relax her. She turned on the taps, and the steam expurgated her reflection, diluted her colors, softened her swollen curves; she no longer looked heavily fleshy—almost attractive, she thought. Steam surrounded her reflected face with a vignette's oval that shrank like an iris in an old film.

She sank into the water, wallowing, yet she couldn't relax. As her muscles loosened they seemed to liquefy, and her mind felt helplessly afloat and vulnerable. The walls looked insubstantial, as though infiltrated by fog that muffled the room, deafening her to anything that might be approaching the door.

She felt she was being watched. She washed quickly and rose sloshing. She rubbed herself roughly with the towel. Was something playfully touching her? She whirled, and glimpsed a face.

It had been spying on her from the mirror, through the peeling steam. Her own face, of course, and she wiped the mirror clear. But as the steam re-formed she seemed to glimpse beyond it a dim movement, with eyes. Instinctively, infuriatingly, she covered herself with the towel. She wrenched at the door, which had warped shut. She closed her eyes, trapping her cry behind her lips, and tugged until the door pulled free.

As she dressed she grew coldly furious. It wouldn't get the better of her again. She read, determined not to hear the tuneless babbling. She slept a little, despite the almost insubstantial groping at her face in the dark.

A pile of cans was waiting to fall on her when she opened a cupboard door. How stupid and infantile. She pushed them back and checked the other cupboards, which were innocent. She smiled grimly—oh no, it wouldn't play that trick on her—and climbed the stairs slowly, examining the stair rods.

All of its tricks were moronic, and some were disgusting, but none was worth her notice. Amid the clamor in the street a voice prattled, distant or muffled. She refused to hear its words. It might be only her lack of sleep that made it rush toward her.

She dreamed that she had died and that the house was full of laughter. The dream shifted: something was kissing or licking her cheek. When she struggled awake it was there on her pillow—a fat encrusted earthworm. Stupid, disgusting. She hurried downstairs to throw it out, but not too fast to check the stair rods.

Hadn't she read this page before, more than once? The window cleaner gazed at her, making her feel caged, on show. His sluggish progress round the house, his dull dabbing at the panes, unnerved her. Nor did he seem to have lightened the rooms. She had never realized how many dark corners the house contained. Many of them had begun to acquire objects, some of which moved, none of which was there when she strode close.

Once, when the cries of children outside seemed especially violent and threatening, she heard an object being dragged upstairs. She ran into the hall, and seemed to glimpse a dim movement as it climbed onto the landing. It seemed dreadfully large, or shaped like a nightmare, or both.

Whatever it was, she wasn't having it in her house. She climbed, scrutinizing the stair rods. She heard her bedroom door open, and the fall of something moist and fat within. Had it been dragging a burden that it had now dropped? Was that why it had looked so grotesque? Her hand clenched on the doorknob when she heard the giggling within; it took her minutes to open the door. But the room was mockingly bare. She went downstairs white-faced . . . checking the rods.

She had to sit down, to calm her heart. Her tormentor had almost reached her. To have let such stupidity touch her! She wouldn't again. She found herself looking forward to next term: school would make her sure of herself again. Only three more days. In the corners, objects kept her company. She slept, when she managed to sleep, with the light on. Only two days. *La, la, la.* Only one.

The sight of the fallen rail depressed her. If she replaced the rail it would only be torn down again. No point in moping. Less than one more day. To cheer herself up, she ate dinner using the Wedgwood service.

She must go to bed early and try to sleep, but not just yet. She could read, except that her books didn't interest her. But what in God's name stopped her going to the library to change them? She wouldn't be trapped anymore than she would be driven out. She washed up swiftly and left the plates on the table.

A few children ran among the tables, for a last chase. "We'll be glad to give them back to you," the librarian said wryly. There were no books that appealed to Edith, except ones she'd read. Impulsively she chose some new children's books, to find out what they read these days. Maybe she'd read them to her children.

It had begun to rain. Buds of water grew on the hedges, gleaming orange with sodium light. The lampposts were rooted in shallow glaring pools. Rain pecked at her; houses streamed, their windows tight and snug.

Her own house looked bedraggled; its windows drooled. The unkempt lawn struggled to stand beneath the rain. Water snatched at her as she slammed the door behind her. The slam resounded through the house, as though all the doors were mocking her.

The darkness became still, preparing its next trick. She wouldn't give it the chance. Clutching her books, she switched on the hall light. The hall stand appeared beside her, its head swollen with coats. With the adjacent switch she drove back the dark on the landing, then she hurried into the front room. The house hemmed her in with echoes. Only echoes.

The window was frosted with rain; watery shapes crawled about the room. Would her groping hand meet the light switch, or something soft and tongued? Of course it was the switch, and the light destroyed the shapes. She drew the curtains, trying to make the room cozier.

As she did so, what had been hiding behind a chair rose up, to scare her. She refused to look, although the grinning object seemed too large, and grotesquely lacking. She couldn't have glimpsed so much from the corner of her eye, but hadn't the object been held up by a hand rather than a neck, even though it had rolled its eyes? Rubbish. She clashed the curtains together as if cutting off a play, and turned to confront the empty room.

She stalked to the kitchen, ignoring the crowd of her sounds. The Wedgwood was arrayed on the table. The sight of the empty window deformed by rain troubled her; as she moved, the window twitched like a nervous blind eye. She gazed out at the hectic night. Tomorrow she'd put up the rail. This time she'd make sure it stayed up.

Something in her room was very wrong.

She stood trapped, trying to recall what she'd seen, afraid to turn until she knew. The night was vicious with glittering. Suddenly she turned: of course, she'd used only part of the Wedgwood, yet the entire service was laid out. How stupid—hardly even a trick.

She reached for a plate. But her hand faltered and hung slackly as she moaned, unable to accept what she was seeing. She had to pick miserably at a plate before she was convinced. Although they had been reassembled with terrible minuteness, every item of the service was shattered into fragments.

Her panic threw her stumbling toward the hall. The hollow desertion of the house overwhelmed her. But she was not entirely alone, for although the switch stayed on, something was clapped over the light, trapping her in darkness.

The room whirled as she did. The blind window gazed across, streaming grimily. She wrenched at the door, which had warped shut more stubbornly than the others. She stumbled across the flowing room toward the door to the yard, groping feverishly for her keys.

She halted, squeezing her eyes tight in terror and rage. Whatever it did, she was determined not to see it. She could hear it running toward her, large and unbalanced, as though crippled. It was about to leap on her. Let it do its worst.

The light blazed again, through her eyelids. Her tormentor was standing before her, waiting to be seen. Her forehead felt as though her skull were shrinking, squeezing out needles of sweat. She clenched her eyelids desperately.

It touched her. Its large loose face crawled moistly over hers. Its hands plucked at her. They felt unformed, and terribly far apart. Its face returned and clung to hers, snuffling. Nothing could have forced her to open her eyes.

Her whole body squirmed with a convulsion beyond nausea. She was terrified to move: what might she touch blindly? Suddenly, in utter desperation, her mouth opened. Words came uncontrollably as retching, but slowly, deliberately: "Get away from me, you filthy thing."

She felt it leave her, and stood frozen. Was the stillness a trick? At last she had to open her eyes, for the aching void made her giddy. The room felt as empty as it looked, and she sat down before she could fall. Eventually she swept the Wedgwood into the bin. She switched on all the lights, then opened the front-room curtains and sat with her back to the window. Before her, her faint outline trembled incessantly with rain.

Dawn seeped into the room. Her eyes felt hot and bloated. When she switched off the lights the room turned ashen. She sipped boiling tea, trying to taste it; her stomach writhed. The colors of the house struggled with the gray.

She trudged through the soaked streets. She'd forgotten to bring the library books. No time now. She wouldn't have been reading them today, she must make herself sure of her children again. They needed to be sure of one another, she and the children. She felt uneasy, unwilling to face them. As she trudged she grew tense. Her legs were aching, and her mind.

Through the bars she could see some of her class. Thank God, they weren't looking at her; she hadn't decided how to approach them. Their cries sounded alarmingly jagged, menacing. She was still trying to decide as her automatic trudging took her into the schoolyard.

At once the crying began.

How could the other children ignore it, that inconsolable, atrociously miserable cry? But she knew what it was. She strode glaring toward the school. Once she was inside and away from the sound she'd be all right.

But the cry wrenched at her. It was so thin and feeble, yet so penetrating; so helpless and desolate, beyond any hope of being comforted. She couldn't bear it. As she strode toward the children she could hear it coming closer. They gaped at her as she hurried among them, pulling them aside to peer for the abandoned wailing.

She faltered, and gazed at them. The plight of the crying victim could be no worse than theirs, with their home lives, their stupidity, their inability to find themselves. Wasn't there a plea deep in their dull eyes? She couldn't reach the crying; but at least she could touch these children; that must be worth something.

Her eyes spilled her grief. "I'm sorry," she said to the gaping children. "It's all right," she said, reaching out, trying to embrace them as they began to back away. "Come here, I won't hurt you. I'm sorry. I'm sorry." Surely her cries must drain some of the enormous guilt that bowed her down.

At last, when the schoolyard was empty of children, and Sue and her colleagues had ceased trying to coax her into the school, she stumbled away. The crying accompanied her home, and everywhere she went. Sometimes, as they emerged from school, her children saw her. They fled, leaving her pleading with the air, trying to embrace it. Surely the crying must stop eventually, surely the voice must grow happy again. "La, la, la," she pleaded. "La, la, la."

# Drawing In

No WONDER the rent was so low. There were cracks everywhere; new ones had broken out during the night— one passed above the foot of his bed, through the elaborate molding, then trailed toward the parquet floor. Still, the house didn't matter; Thorpe hadn't come here for the house.

He parted the curtains. Act one, scene three. Mist lingered; the lake was overlapped by a ghost of itself. Growing sunlight renewed colors from the mist: the green fur of the hills, the green spikes of pines. All this was free. He'd little reason to complain.

As always when he emerged from his room, the height of the ceiling made him glance up. Above the stairs, another new crack had etched the plaster. Suppose the house fell on him while he was asleep? Hardly likely—the place looked far too solid.

He hesitated, staring at the door which stood ajar. Should he give in to curiosity? It wasn't as simple as that: he'd come here to recuperate; he could scarcely do so if curios-

ity kept him awake. Last night he'd lain awake for hours
wondering. Feeling rather like a small boy who'd crept
into this deserted house for a dare, he pushed open the
door.

The room was smaller than his, and darker—though
perhaps all that was because of the cabinets, high as the
ceiling and black as drowned timber, that occupied all the
walls. The cabinets were padlocked shut, save one whose
broken padlock dangled from the half-open door. Beyond
the door was darkness, dimly crowded. Speculations on
the nature of that crowding had troubled his sleep.

He ventured forward. Again, as the cabinet loured over
him, he felt like a small boy. Ignoring doubts, he tugged
the door wide. The padlock fell, loud in the echoing
room—and from high in the cabinet, dislodged objects
toppled. Some opened as they fell, and their contents
scuttled over him.

The containers rattled on the parquet as he flinched
back. They resembled pillboxes of transparent plastic. They
were inscribed in a spidery handwriting, which seemed
entirely appropriate, for each had contained a spider. A
couple of dark furry blotches clung with long legs to his
sleeve. He picked them off, shuddering. He couldn't rid
himself of an insidious suspicion that some of the creatures
were not quite dead.

He peered reluctantly at them. Bright pinheads of eyes
peered back, dead as metal; beside them, palpi bristled.
The lifeless fur felt unpleasantly cold on his palm. Eventually he'd filled all the containers, God only knew how
correctly. If he were an audience watching himself, this
would be an enjoyable farce. As he replaced the boxes on
the high shelf, he noticed a padlocked container, large as a
hatbox, lurking at the back of the cabinet. Let it stay there.
He'd had enough surprises for one day.

Besides, he must report the cracks. Eventually the bus
arrived, laden with climbers. Some of their rucksacks
occupied almost as much space as they did. Camps smoked
below the hills.

Outside the estate agent's office, cows plodded to market. The agent listened to the tale of the cracks. "You surprise me. I'll look in tomorrow." His fingertips brushed his gray hair gently, abstractedly. He glanced up as Thorpe hesitated. "Something else?"

"The owner of the house—what line is he in?"

"Anarach—narach—" The agent shook his head irritably to clear it of the blockage. "*An* arachnologist," he pronounced at last.

"I thought it must be something of the kind. I looked in one of the cabinets—the one with the broken lock."

"Ah, yes, his bloodsuckers. That's what he likes to call them. All these writers are eccentric in some way, I suppose. I should have asked you not to touch anything," he said reprovingly.

Thorpe had been glad to confess, but felt embarrassed now. "Well, perhaps no harm's done," the agent said. "He went to Eastern Europe six months ago, in search of some rarity—having fixed the amount of the rent."

Was that comment a kind of reproof? It sounded wistful. But the agent stood up smiling. "Anyway, you look better for the country," he said. "You've much more color now."

And indeed Thorpe felt better. He was at his ease in the narrow streets; he was able to make his way between cars without flinching—without feeling jagged metal bite into him, the windscreen shatter into his face. The scars of his stitches no longer plucked at his cheeks. He walked part of the way back to the house, until weakness overtook him.

He sat gazing into the lake. Fragmented reflections of pines wavered delicately. When mist began to descend the hills he headed back, in time to glimpse of group of hikers admiring the house. Pleased, he scanned it himself. Mist had settled on the chimney stacks. The five squat horned blurs looked as though they were playing a secret game, trying to hide behind one another. One, the odd man out, lacked horns.

After dinner Thorpe strolled through the house, sipping

malt whisky. Rooms resounded around him. They sounded like an empty stage, where he was playing owner of the house. He strode up the wide stairs, beneath the long straight crack, and halted outside the door next to his.

He wouldn't be able to sleep unless he looked. Besides, he had found the agent's disapproval faintly annoying. If Thorpe wasn't meant to look in the cabinets, why hadn't he been told? Why had one been left ajar?

He strode in, among the crowd of dark high doors. This time, as he opened the cabinet he made sure the padlock didn't slip from its hold. Piled shelves loomed above him as he stooped into the dimness, to peer at the hatbox or whatever it was.

It wasn't locked. It had been, but its fastening was split: a broken padlock lay on top. On the lid, wisps of handwriting spelled *Carps: Trans: C. D.* The obscure inscription was dated three months ago.

Thorpe frowned. Then, standing back, he poked gingerly at the lid with his foot. As he did so, he heard a shifting. It was the padlock, which landed with a thud on the bottom of the cabinet. Unburdened, the lid sprang up at once. Within was nothing but a crack in the metal of the container. He closed the cabinet and then the room, wondering why the metal box appeared to have been forced open.

And why was the date on the lid so recent? Was the man so eccentric that he could make such a mistake? Thorpe lay pondering that and the inscription. Half-dozing, he heard movement in one of the rooms: a trapped bird scrabbling in a chimney? It troubled him almost enough to make him search. But the whisky crept up on him, and he drifted with his thoughts.

How did the arachnologist bring his prizes home—in his pocket, or stowed away with the rest of the livestock on the voyage? Thorpe stood on a dockside, awaiting a package which was being lowered on a rope. Or was it a rope? No, for as it swung close the package unclenched and grabbed him. As its jaws closed on his face he awoke gasping.

In the morning he searched the house, but the bird seemed to have managed to fly. The cracks had multiplied; there was at least one in every room, and two now above the stairs. The scattering of plaster on the staircase looked oddly like earth.

When he heard the agent's car he buttoned his jacket and gave his hair a rapid severe brushing. Damn it, the bird was still trapped; he heard it stir behind him, though there was no hint of it in the mirror. It must be in the chimney, for it sounded far too large to be otherwise invisible.

The agent scrutinized the rooms. Was he looking only for cracks, or for evidence that Thorpe had been peeking? "This is most unexpected," he said as though Thorpe might be responsible. "I don't see how it can be subsidence. I'll have it looked at, though I don't think it's anything serious."

He was dawdling in Thorpe's room, perhaps to reassure himself that Thorpe had done it no injury. "Ah, here he is," he said without warning, and stooped to grope beneath the bed. Who had been skulking there while Thorpe was asleep? The owner of the house, it seemed—or at least a photograph of him, which the agent propped curtly on the bedside table, to supervise the room.

When the agent had left, Thorpe peered up the chimneys. Their furred throats looked empty, but were very dark. The flickering beam of the flashlight he'd found groped upward. A soft dark mass plummeted toward him. It missed him, and proved to be a fall of soot, but was discouraging enough. In any case, if the bird was still up there, it was silent now.

He confronted the photograph. So that was what an arachnologist looked like: a clump of hair, a glazed expression, an attempt at a beard—the man seemed hypnotized, but no doubt was preoccupied. Thorpe found his dusty presence disconcerting.

Why stand here challenging the photograph? He felt healthy enough to make a circuit of the lake. As he strolled, the inverted landscape drifted with him. He could feel his strength returning, as though he was absorbing it from the hills. For the first time since he'd left the hospital, his hands looked enlivened by blood.

From the far end of the lake he admired the house. Its inverted chimneys swayed, rooted deep in the water. Suddenly he frowned, and squinted. It must be an effect of the distance, that was all—but he kept glancing at the house as he returned along the lakeside. Once he was past the lake he had no chance to doubt. There were only four chimney stacks.

It must have been yesterday's mist that had produced the appearance of a fifth stack, lurking. Nevertheless it was odd. Doubts clung to his mind as he climbed the stairs, until his start of surprise demolished his thoughts. The glass of the photograph was cracked from top to bottom.

He refused to be blamed for that. The agent ought to have left it alone. He laid it carefully on its back on the bedside table. Its crack had made him obsessively aware of the others; some, he was sure, were new—including one in a downstairs window, a crack which, curiously, failed to pass right through the thickness of the pane. The staircase was sprinkled again; the scattering not only looked like, but seemed to smell like, earth. That night, as he lay in bed, he thought he heard dust whispering down from the cracks.

Though he ridiculed thoughts that the house was unsafe, he felt vulnerable. The shifting shadow of a branch looked like a new crack, digging into the wall. In turn, that made the entire room appear to shift. Whenever he woke from fitful dozing, he seemed to glimpse a stealthy movement of the substance of the room. It must be an optical effect, but it reminded him of the way a quivering of ornaments might betray the presence of an intruder.

Once he awoke, shocked by an image of a tufted face

that peered upside down through the window. It infuriated
him to have to sit up to make sure the window was blank.
Its shutter of night was not reassuring. His subconscious
must have borrowed the image of inversion from the lake,
that was all. But the room seemed to be trembling, as he
was.

Next day he waited impatiently for the surveyor, or
whoever the agent was sending. He rapidly grew irritable.
Though it could be nothing but a hangover from his insomnia, to stay in the house made him nervous. Whenever he
glanced in a mirror, he felt he was being invisibly watched.
The dark fireplaces looked ominous, prosceniums awaiting
a cue. At intervals he heard a pattering in other rooms: not
of tiny feet, but of the fall of debris from new cracks.

Why was he waiting? He hadn't felt so nervously aim-
less since the infancy of his career, when he'd loitered,
clinging to a single line, in the wings of a provincial
theatre. The agent should have given his man a key to let
himself in; if he hadn't, that was his problem. Thorpe
strode over the slopes that surrounded the lake. He enjoyed
the intricately true reflections in the still water, and felt a
great deal healthier.

Had the man let himself in? Thorpe seemed to glimpse a
face, groping into view at a twilit upper window. But the
only sound in the house was a feeble scraping, which he
was unable to locate. The face must have been a fragment
of his dream, tangled in his lingering insomnia. His
imagination, robbed of sleep, was everywhere now. As he
climbed the stairs, he thought a face was spying on him
from a dark corner of the ceiling.

When he descended, fallen debris crunched underfoot.
During his meal he drank a bottle of wine, as much for
distraction as for pleasure. Afterward he surveyed the
house. Yes, the cracks were more numerous; there was
one in every surface now, except the floors. Had the older
cracks deepened? Somehow he was most disturbed by the
dust beneath the cracked windows. It looked like earth, not
like pulverized glass at all.

He wished he'd gone into town to stay the night. It was too late now—indeed, the last bus had gone by the time he'd returned to the house. He was too tired to walk. He certainly couldn't sit outside all night with the mists. It was absurd to think of any other course than going to bed, to try and sleep. But he drained the bottle of whisky before doing so.

He lay listening. Yes, the trapped bird was still there. It sounded even feebler now; it must be dying. If he searched for it he would lose his chance of sleep. Besides, he knew already that he couldn't locate it. Its sounds were so weak that they seemed to shift impossibly, to be fumbling within the fabric of the walls.

He was determined to keep his eyes closed, for the dim room appeared to be jerking. Perhaps this was a delayed effect of his accident. He let his mind drift him out of the room, into memories: the wavering of trees and of their reflections, the comedy sketch of his encounter with the piled cabinet, Carps, Trans.

Darkness gathered like soot on his eyes. A dark mass sank toward him, or he was sinking into dark. He was underground. Around him, unlit corridors dripped sharply. The beam of his flashlight explored the figure that lay before him on dank stone. The figure was pale as a spider's cocoon. As the light fastened on it, it scuttled apart.

When he awoke, he was crying out not at the dream but at his stealthy realization. He'd solved the inscription in his sleep, at least in part. Eastern Europe was the key. Carps meant Carpathians, Trans was Transylvania. But C. D.—no, what he was thinking was just a bad joke. He refused to take it seriously.

Nevertheless it had settled heavily on his mind. Good God, he'd once had to keep a straight face throughout a version of the play, squashed into a provincial stage: the walls of Castle Dracula had quaked whenever anyone had opened a door, the rubber bat had plummeted into the stalls. C. D. could mean anything—anything except that. Wouldn't it be hilarious if that *was* what the bemused old spider-man had meant? But in the dark it seemed less than hilarious, for near him in the room, something was stirring.

He groped for the cord of the bedside lamp. It was long and furry, and seemed unexpectedly fat. When he pulled it the light went on, and he saw at once that the cracks were deeper; he had been hearing the fall of debris. Whether the walls had begun to jerk rhythmically, or whether that was a delayed symptom of his accident, he had no time to judge. He must get out while he had the chance. He swung his feet to the floor, and knocked the photograph from the table.

Too bad, never mind, come on! But the shock of its fall delayed him. He glanced at the photograph, which had fallen upside down. The inverted tufted face stared up at him.

All right, it was the face he had dreamed in the window; why shouldn't it be? Just let him drag clothes over his pyjamas—he'd spend the night outside if need be. Quickly, quickly—he thought he could hear the room twitching. The twitches reminded him not of the stirring of ornaments, but of something else: something of which he was terrified to think.

As he stamped his way into his trousers, refusing to think, he saw that now there were cracks in the floor. Perhaps worse, all the cracks in the room had joined together. He froze, appalled, and heard the scuttling.

What frightened him most was not how large it sounded, but the fact that it seemed not to be approaching over floors. Somehow he had the impression that it hardly inhabited the space of the house. Around him the cracks stood out from their surfaces. They looked too solid for cracks.

The room shook repetitively. The smell of earth was growing. He could hardly keep his balance in the unsteady room; the lines that weren't cracks at all were jerking him toward the door. If he could grab the bed, drag himself along it to the window— His mind was struggling to withdraw into itself, to deny what was happening. He was fighting not only to reach the window but to forget the image which had seized his mind: a spider perched at the center of its web, tugging in its prey.

# The Pattern

Di seemed glad when he went outside. She was sitting on the settee, legs shoved beneath her, eyes squeezed tight, looking for the end of her novel. She acknowledged the sound of the door with a short nod, pinching her mouth as if he'd been distracting her. He controlled his resentment; he'd often felt the same way about her, while painting.

He stood outside the cottage, gazing at the spread of green. Scattered buttercups crystallized the yellow tinge of the grass. At the center of the field a darker green rushed up a thick tree, branching, multiplying; toward the edges of the field, bushes were foaming explosions, blue-green, red-edged green. Distant trees displayed an almost transparent papery spray of green. Beyond them lay curves of hills, toothed with tiny pines and a couple of random towers, all silver as mist. As Tony gazed, sunlight spilled from behind clouds to the sound of a huge soft wind in the trees. The light filled the greens, intensifying them; they blazed.

Yes, he'd be able to paint here. For a while he had

feared he wouldn't. He'd imagined Di struggling to find her final chapter, himself straining to paint, the two of them chafing against each other in the little cottage. But good Lord, this was only their second day here. They weren't giving themselves time. He began to pace, looking for the vantage point of his painting.

There were patterns and harmonies everywhere. You only had to find them, find the angle from which they were clear to you. He had seen that one day, while painting the microcosm of patterns in a patch of verdure. Now he painted nothing but glimpses of harmony, those moments when distant echoes of color or movement made sense of a whole landscape; he painted only the harmonies, abstracted. Often he felt they were glimpses of a total pattern that included him, Di, his painting, her writing, life, the world: his being there and seeing was part of the pattern. Though it was impossible to perceive the total pattern, the sense was there. Perhaps that sense was the purpose of all real art.

Suddenly he halted. A May wind was passing through the landscape. It unfurled through the tree in the field; in a few moments the trees beyond the field responded. It rippled through the grass, and the lazy grounded swaying echoed the leisurely unfolding of the clouds. All at once he saw how the clouds elaborated the shapes of the trees and bushes, subtracting color, lazily changing their shapes as they drifted across the sky.

He had it now. The wind passed, but it didn't matter. He could paint what he'd seen; he would see it again when the breeze returned. He was already mixing colors in his mind, feeling enjoyment begin: nobody could ever mass-produce the colors he saw. He turned toward the cottage, to tiptoe upstairs for his canvas and the rest without disturbing Di.

Behind him someone screamed.

In the distance, across the field. One scream: the hills echoed curtly. Tony had to grab an upright of the cottage porch to steady himself. Everything snapped sharp, the cottage garden, the uneven stone wall, the overgrown path beyond the wall, the fence, and the wide empty flower-sprinkled field. There was nobody in sight. The echoes of the cry had stopped at once, except in Tony's head. The violence of the cry reverberated there. Of what emotion? Terror, outrage, disbelief, agony? All of them?

The door slammed open behind him. Di emerged, blinking red-eyed, like an angrily roused sleeper. "What's wrong?" she demanded nervously. "Was that you?"

"I don't know what it was. Over there somewhere."

He was determined to be calm. The cry had unnerved him; he didn't want her nervousness to reach him too—he ignored it. "It might have been someone with their foot in a trap," he said. "I'll see if I can see."

He backed the car off the end of the path, onto the road. Di watched him over the stone wall, rather anxiously. He didn't really expect to find the source of the cry; probably its cause was past now. He was driving away from Di's edginess, to give her a chance to calm down. He couldn't paint while he was aware of her nervousness.

He drove. Beside the road the field stretched placidly, easing the scream from his mind. Perhaps someone had just stumbled, had cried out with the shock. The landscape looked too peaceful for anything worse. But for a while he tried to remember the sound, some odd quality about it that nagged at him. It hadn't sounded quite like a cry; it had sounded as if— It was gone.

He drove past the far side of the field beyond the cottage. A path ran through the trees along the border; Ploughman's Path, a sign said. He parked and ventured up the path a few hundred yards. Patches of light flowed over the undergrowth, blurring and floating together, parting and dimming. The trees were full of the intricate trills and chirrups of birds. Tony called out a few times: "Anyone there? Anybody hurt?" But the leaves hushed him.

He drove farther uphill, toward the main road. He would return widely around the cottage, so that Di could be alone for a while. Sunlight and shadow glided softly over the

Cotswold hills. Trees spread above the road, their trunks lagged with ivy. Distant foliage was a bank of green folds, elaborate as coral.

On the main road he found a pub, the Farmer's Rest. That would be good in the evenings. The London agent hadn't mentioned that; he'd said only that the cottage was isolated, peaceful. He'd shown them photographs, and though Tony had thought the man had never been near the cottage, Di had loved it at once. Perhaps it was what her book needed.

He glimpsed the cottage through a gap in the hills. Its mellow Cotswold stone seemed concentrated, a small warm amber block beyond the tiny tree-pinned field, a mile below. The green of the field looked simple now, among the fields where sheep and cattle strolled sporadically. He was sorry he'd come so far from it. He drove toward the turnoff that would take him behind the cottage and eventually back to its road.

Di ran to the garden wall as he drove onto the path. "Where were you?" she said. "I was worried."

Oh, Christ, he thought, defeated. "Just looking. I didn't find anything. Well, I found a pub on the main road."

She tutted at him, smiling wryly: just like him, she meant. "Are you going to paint?"

She couldn't have made any progress on her book; she would find it even more difficult now. "I don't think so," he said.

"Can't you work either? Oh, let's forget it for today. Let's walk to the pub and get absolutely pissed."

At least the return journey would be downhill, he thought, walking. A soft wind tugged at them whenever they passed gaps; green light and shadow swarmed among branches. The local beer was good, he found. Even Di liked it, though she wasn't fond of beer. Among the Toby jugs and bracketed rifles, farmers discussed dwindling profits, the delivery of calves, the trapping of foxes, the swollen inflamed eyes of myxomatosis. Tony considered asking one of them about the scream, but now they were all intent on the dartboard; they were a team, practicing somberly for a match. "I know there's an ending that's right for the book," Di said. "It's just finding it."

When they returned to the cottage, amber clouds floated above the sunset. The horizon was the color of the stone. The field lay quiet and chill. Di gazed at the cottage, her hands light on the wall. After a while he thought of asking why, but her feelings might be too delicate, too elusive. She would tell him if she could.

They made love beneath the low dark beams. Afterward he lay in her on their quilt, gazing out at the dimming field. The tree was heavy with gathering darkness; a sheep bleated sleepily. Tony felt peaceful, in harmony. But Di was moving beneath him. "Don't squash," she said. As she lay beside him he felt her going into herself, looking for her story. At the moment she didn't dare risk the lure of peace.

When he awoke, the room was gloomy. Di lay face upturned, mouth slackly open. Outside the ground hissed with rain beneath a low gray sky; the walls of the room streamed with the shadows of water.

He felt dismally oppressed. He had hoped to paint today. Now he imagined himself and Di hemmed in by the rain, struggling with their balks beneath the low beams, wandering irritably about the small rooms, among the fat mock-leather furniture and stray electric fires. He knew Di hoped this book would make her more than just another children's novelist, but it couldn't while he was in the way.

Suddenly he glimpsed the landscape. All the field glowed sultry green. He saw how the dark sky and even the dark framing room were necessary to call forth the sullen glow. Perhaps he could paint that glimpse. After a while he kissed Di awake. She'd wanted to be awakened early.

After breakfast she reread *The Song of the Trees*. She turned over the last page of the penultimate chapter and stared at the blank table beneath. At last she pushed herself away from the table and began to pace shortly. Tony tried to keep out of her way. When his own work was frustrated she seemed merely an irritation; he was sure she must feel the same of him. "I'm going out for a walk," she called, opening the front door. He didn't offer to walk with her. He knew she was searching for her conclusion.

When the rain ceased he carried his painting materials outside. For a moment he wished he had music. But they couldn't have transported the stereo system, and their radio was decrepit. As he left the cottage he glanced back at Di's flowers, massed minutely in vases.

The gray sky hung down, trapping light in ragged flourishes of white cloud. Distant trees were smudges of mist; the greens of the field merged into a dark glow. On the near side of the fence the path unfurled innumerable leaves, oppressive in their dark intricacy, heavy with raindrops. Even the raindrops were relentlessly green. Metallic chimes and chirrs of birds surrounded him, as did a thick rich smell of earth.

Only the wall of the garden held back the green. The heavy jagged stones were a response to the landscape. He could paint that, the rough texture of stone, the amber stone spattered with darker ruggedness, opposing the overpoweringly lush green. But it wasn't what he'd hoped to paint, and it didn't seem likely to make him much money.

Di liked his paintings. At his first exhibition she'd sought him out to tell him so; that was how they'd met. Her first book was just beginning to earn royalties; she had been working on her second. Before they were married he'd begun to illustrate her work.

If exhibiting wasn't too lucrative, illustrating books was less so. He knew Di felt uneasy as the breadwinner; sometimes he felt frustrated that he couldn't earn them more— the inevitable castration anxiety. That was another reason why she wanted *The Song of the Trees* to sell well: to promote his work. She wanted his illustrations to be as important as the writing.

He liked what there was of the book. He felt his paintings could complement the prose; they'd discussed ways of setting out the pages. The story was about the last dryads of a forest, trapped among the remaining trees by a fire that had sprung from someone's cigarette. As they watched picnickers sitting on blackened stumps amid the ash, breaking branches from the surviving trees, leaving litter and matches among them, the dryads realized they must escape before the next fire. Though it was unheard of, they managed to relinquish the cool green peace of the trees and pass through the clinging dead ash to the greenery beyond. They coursed through the greenery, seeking welcoming trees. But the book was full of their tribulations: a huge grim oak-dryad who drove them away from the saplings he protected; willow-dryads who let them go deep into their forest, but only because they would distract the dark thick-voiced spirit of a swamp; glittering birch-dryads, too cold and aloof to bear; morose hawthorns, whose flowers farted at the dryads, in case they were animals come to chew the leaves.

He could tell Di loved writing the book—perhaps too much so, for she'd thought it would produce its own ending. But she had been balked for weeks. She wanted to write an ending that satisfied her totally; she was determined not to fake anything. He knew she hoped the book might appeal to adults too. "Maybe it needs peace," she'd said at last, and that had brought them to the cottage. Maybe she was right. This was only their third day, she had plenty of time.

As he mused, the sluggish sky parted. Sunlight spilled over an edge of cloud. At once the greens that had merged into green emerged again, separating: a dozen greens, two dozen. Dots of flowers brightened over the field, colors filled the raindrops piercingly. He saw the patterns at once: almost a mandala. The clouds were whiter now, fragmented by blue; the sky was rolling open from the horizon. He began to mix colors. Surely the dryads must have passed through such a landscape.

The patterns were emerging on his canvas when, beyond the field, someone screamed.

It wasn't Di. He was sure it wasn't a woman's voice. It was the voice he'd heard yesterday, but more outraged still; it sounded as if it were trying to utter something too dreadful for language. The hills swallowed its echoes at once, long before his heart stopped pounding loudly.

As he tried to breathe in calm, he realized what was odd about the scream. It had sounded almost as much like an echo as its reiteration in the hills: louder, but somehow lacking a source. It reminded him—yes, of the echo that sometimes precedes a loud sound-source on a record.

Just an acoustic effect. But that hardly explained the scream itself. Someone playing a joke? Someone trying to frighten the intruders at the cottage? The local simpleton? An animal in a trap, perhaps, for his memory of the scream contained little that sounded human. Someone was watching him.

He turned sharply. Beyond the nearby path, at the far side of the road, stood a clump of trees. The watcher was hiding among them; Tony could sense him there—he'd almost glimpsed him skulking hurriedly behind the trunks. He felt instinctively that the lurker was a man.

Was it the man who'd screamed? No, he hadn't had time to make his way round the edge of the field. Perhaps he had been drawn by the scream. Or perhaps he'd come to spy on the strangers. Tony stared at the trees, waiting for the man to betray his presence, but couldn't stare long; the trunks were vibrating restlessly, incessantly—heat-haze, of course, though it looked somehow odder. Oh, let the man spy if he wanted to. Maybe he'd venture closer to look at Tony's work, as people did. But when Tony rested from his next burst of painting, he could tell the man had gone.

Soon he saw Di hurrying anxiously down the road. Of course, she must have heard the scream. "I'm all right, love," he called.

"It was the same, wasn't it? Did you see what it was?"

"No. Maybe it's children. Playing a joke."

She wasn't reassured so easily. "It sounded like a man,"

she said. She gazed at his painting. "That *is* good," she said, and wandered into the cottage without mentioning her book. He knew she wasn't going in to write.

The scream had worried her more than she'd let him see. Her anxiety lingered even now she knew he was unharmed. Something else to hinder her book, he thought irritably. He couldn't paint now, but at least he knew what remained to be painted.

He sat at the kitchen table while she cooked a shepherd's pie in the range. Inertia hung oppressively about them. "Do you want to go to the pub later?" he said.

"Maybe. I'll see."

He gazed ahead at the field in the window, the cooling tree; branches swayed a little behind the glass. In the kitchen something trembled—heat over the electric stove. Di was reaching for the teapot with one hand, lifting the kettle with the other; the steaming spout tilted above her bare leg. Tony stood up, mouth opening—but she'd put the kettle down. "It's all right," he answered her frown, as he scooped up spilled sugar from the table.

She stood at the range. "Maybe the pub might help us to relax," he said.

"I don't want to relax! That's no use!" She turned too quickly, and overbalanced toward the range. Her bare arm was going to rest on the metal that quivered with heat. She pushed herself back from the wall, barely in time. "You see what I mean?" she demanded.

"What's the matter? Clumsiness isn't like you."

"Stop watching me, then. You make me nervous."

"Hey, you can't just blame me." How would she have felt if she had been spied on earlier? There was more wrong with her than her book and her irrationally lingering worry about him, he was sure. Sometimes she had what seemed to be psychic glimpses. "Is it the cottage that's wrong?" he said.

"No, I like the cottage."

"The area, then? The field?"

She came to the table, to saw bread with a carving

knife; the cottage lacked a bread knife. "I like it here. It's probably just me," she said, musing about something.

The kettle sizzled, parched. "Bloody clean simplicity," she said. She disliked electric stoves. She moved the kettle to a cold ring and turned back. The point of the carving knife thrust over the edge of the table. Her turn would impale her thigh on the blade.

Tony snatched the knife back. The blade and the wood of the table seemed to vibrate for a moment. He must have jarred the table. Di was staring rather abstractedly at the knife. "That's three," he said. "You'll be all right now."

During dinner she was abstracted. Once she said, "I really like this cottage, you know. I really do." He didn't try to reach her. After dinner he said, "Look, I'm sorry if I've been distracting you," but she shook her head, hardly listening. They didn't seem to be perceiving each other very well.

He was washing up when she said, "My God." He glanced anxiously at her. She was staring up at the beams. "Of course. Of course," she said, reaching for her notebook. She pushed it away at once and hurried upstairs. Almost immediately he heard her begin typing.

He tried to paint, until darkness began to mix with his colors. He stood gazing as twilight collected in the field. The typewriter chattered. He felt rather unnecessary, out of place. He must buy some books in Camside tomorrow. He felt restless, a little resentful. "I'm going down to the pub for a while," he called. The typewriter's bell rang, rang again.

The pub was surrounded by jeeps, sports cars, floridly painted vans. Crowds of young people pressed close to the tables, on stools, on the floor; they shouted over each other, laughed, rolled cigarettes. One was passing around a sketchbook, but Tony didn't feel confident enough to introduce himself. A few of the older people doggedly practiced darts, the rest surrounded Tony at the bar. He chatted about the weather and the countryside, listened to prices of grain. He hoped he'd have a chance to ask about the scream.

He was slowing in the middle of his second pint when the barman said, "One of the new ones, aren't you?"

"Yes, that's right." On an impulse he said loudly enough for the people around him to hear: "We're in the cottage across the field from Ploughman's Path."

The man didn't move hurriedly to serve someone else. Nobody gasped, nobody backed away from Tony. Well, that was encouraging. "Are you liking it?" the barman said.

"Very much. There's just one odd thing." Now was his chance. "We keep hearing someone screaming across the field."

Even then the room didn't fall silent. But it was as if he'd broken a taboo; people withdrew slightly from him, some of them seemed resentful. Three women suddenly excused themselves from different groups at the bar, as if he were threatening to become offensive. "It'll be an animal caught in a trap," the barman said.

"I suppose so." He could see the man didn't believe it either.

The barman was staring at him. "Weren't you with a girl yesterday?"

"She's back at the cottage."

Everyone nearby looked at Tony. When he glanced at them, they looked away. "You want to be sure she's safe," the barman muttered, and hurried to fill flourished glasses. Tony gulped down his beer, cursing his imagination, and almost ran to the car.

Above the skimming patch of lit tarmac, moths ignited; a rabbit froze, then leaped. Discovered trees rushed out of the dark, to be snatched back at once by the night. The light bleached the leaves, the rushing tunnels of boles seemed subterraneously pale. The wide night was still. He could hear nothing but the hum of the car. Above the hills hung enormous dim clouds, gray as rocks.

He could see Di as he hurried up the path. Her head was

silhouetted on the curtain; it leaned at an angle against the back of the settee. He fumbled high in the porch for the hidden key. Her eyes were closed, her mouth was loosely open. Her typescript lay at her feet.

She was blinking, smiling at him. He could see both needed effort; her eyes were red, she looked depressed—she always did when she'd finished a book. "See what you think of it," she said, handing him the pages. Beneath her attempt at a professional's impersonality he thought she was offering the chapter to him shyly as a young girl.

Emerging defeated from a patch of woodland, the dryads saw a cottage across a field. It stood in the still light, peaceful as the evening. They could feel the peace filling its timbers: not a green peace but a warmth, stillness, stability. As they drew nearer they saw an old couple within. The couple had worked hard for their peace; now they'd achieved it here. Tony knew they were himself and Di. One by one the dryads passed gratefully into the dark wood of the beams, the doors.

He felt oddly embarrassed. When he managed to look at her he could only say, "Yes, it's good. You've done it."

"Good," she said. "I'm glad." She was smiling peacefully now.

As they climbed the stairs she said, "If we have children they'll be able to help me too. They can criticize."

She hoped the book would let them afford children. "Yes, they will," he said.

The scream woke him. For a moment he thought he'd dreamed it, or had cried out in his sleep. But the last echo was caught in the hills. Faint as it was, he could feel its intolerable horror, its despair.

He lay blinking at the sunlight. The white-painted walls shone. Di hadn't awakened; he was glad. The scream throbbed in his brain. Today he must find out what it was.

After breakfast he told Di he was going into Camside. She was still depressed after completing the book; she looked drained. She didn't offer to accompany him. She stood at the garden wall, watching him blindly, dazzled by the sun. "Be careful driving," she called.

The clump of trees opposite the end of the path was quivering. Was somebody hiding behind the trunks? Tony frowned at her. "Do you feel—" but he didn't want to alarm her unnecessarily "—anything? Anything odd?"

"What sort of thing?" But he was wondering whether to tell her when she said, "I like this place. Don't spoil it."

He went back to her. "What will you do while I'm out?"

"Just stay in the cottage. I want to read through the book. Why are you whispering?" He smiled at her, shaking his head. The sense of someone watching had faded, though the tree trunks still quivered.

Plushy white-and-silver layers of cloud sailed across the blue sky. He drove the fifteen miles to Camside, a slow roller-coaster ride between green quilts spread easily over the hills. Turned earth displayed each shoot on the nearer fields; trees met over the roads and parted again.

Camside was wholly the colors of rusty sand; similar stone framed the wide glass of the library. Mullioned windows multiplied reflections. Gardens and walls were thick with flowers. A small river coursed beneath a bridge; in the water, sunlight darted incessantly among pebbles. He parked outside a pub, The Wheatsheaf, and walked back. Next to the library stood an odd squat building of the amber stone, a square block full of small windows whose open casements were like griddles filled with panes; over its door a new plastic sign said *Camside Observer*. The newspaper's files might be useful. He went in.

A girl sat behind a low white Swedish desk; the crimson bell of her desk lamp clanged silently against the white walls, the amber windowsills. "Can I help you?"

"I hope so. I'm, I'm doing some research into an area near here, Ploughman's Path. Have you heard of it?"

"Oh, I don't know." She was glancing away, looking

for help to a middle-aged man who had halted in a door-way behind her desk. "Mr. Poole?" she called.

"We've run a few stories about that place," the man told Tony. "You'll find them in our files, on microfilm. Next door, in the library."

"Oh, good. Thanks." But that might mean hours of searching. "Is there anyone here who knows the background?"

The man frowned, and saw Tony realize that meant yes. "The man who handled the last story is still on our staff," he said. "But he isn't here now."

"Will he be here later?"

"Yes, probably. No, I've no idea when." As Tony left he felt the man was simply trying to prevent his colleague from being pestered.

The library was a long room, spread with sunlight. Sunlight lay dazzling on the glossy tables, cleaved shade among the bookcases; a trolley overflowed with thrillers and romances. Ploughman's Path? Oh, yes—and the librarian showed him a card file that indexed local personalities, events, areas. She snapped up a card for him, as if it were a tarot's answer. Ploughman's Path: see Victor Hill, *Legendry and Customs of the Severn Valley.* "And there's something on microfilm," she said, but he was anxious to make sure the book was on the shelf.

It was. It was bound in op-art blues. He carried it to a table; its blues vibrated in the sunlight. The index told him the passage about Ploughman's Path covered six pages. He riffled hastily past photographs of standing stones, a trough in the binding full of breadcrumbs, a crushed jagged-legged fly. Ploughman's Path—

Why the area bounding Ploughman's Path should be dogged by ill luck and tragedy is not known. Folk living in the cottage nearby have sometimes reported hearing screams produced by no visible agency. Despite the similarity of this to banshee legends, no such legend appears to have grown up locally. But Ploughman's Path, and the area bounding it farthest from the cottage (see map), has been so often visited by tragedy and misfortune that local folk dislike to even mention the name, which they fear will bring bad luck.

Farthest from the cottage. Tony relaxed. So long as the book said so, that was all right. And the last line told him why they'd behaved uneasily at the Farmer's Rest. He read on, his curiosity unmixed now with apprehension.

But good Lord, the area was unlucky. Rumors of Roman sacrifices were only its earliest horrors. As the history of the place became more accurately documented, the tragedies grew worse. A gallows set up within sight of the cottage, so that the couple living there must watch their seven-year-old daughter hanged for theft; it had taken her hours to die. An old woman accused of witchcraft by gossip, set on fire and left to burn alive on the path. A mute child who'd fallen down an old well: coping stones had fallen on him, breaking his limbs and hiding him from searchers—years later his skeleton had been found. A baby caught in an animal trap. God, Tony thought. No wonder he'd heard screams.

A student was using the microfilm reader. Tony went back to the *Observer* building. A pear-shaped red-faced man leaned against the wall, chatting to the receptionist; he wore a tweedy pork-pie hat, a blue shirt and waistcoat, tweed trousers. "Watch out, here's trouble," he said as Tony entered.

"Has he come in yet?" Tony asked the girl. "The man who knows about Ploughman's Path?"

"What's your interest?" the red-faced man demanded.

"I'm staying in the cottage near there. I've been hearing odd things. Cries."

"Have you now." The man pondered, frowning. "Well, you're looking at the man who knows," he decided to say, thumping his chest. "Roy Burley. Burly Roy, that's me. Don't you know me? Don't you read our paper? Time you did, then." He snatched an *Observer* from a rack and stuffed it into Tony's hand.

"You want to know about the path, eh? It's all up here." He tapped his hat. "I'll tell you what, though, it's a hot day for talking. Do you fancy a drink? Tell old Puddle I'll be back soon," he told the girl.

He thumped on the door of The Wheatsheaf. "They'll open up. They know me here." At last a man reluctantly opened the door, glancing discouragingly at Tony. "It's all right, Bill, don't look so bloody glum," Roy Burley said. "He's a friend of mine."

A girl set out beer mats; her radio sang that everything was beautiful, in its own way. Roy Burley bought two pints and vainly tried to persuade Bill to join them. "Get that down you," he told Tony. "The only way to start work. You'd think they could do without me over the road, the way some of the buggers act. But they soon start screaming if they think my copy's going to be late. They'd like to see me out, some of them. Unfortunately for them, I've got frends. There I am," he said, poking a thick finger into the newspaper: "The Countryside This Week," by Countryman. "And there, and there." "Social Notes," by A. Guest. "Entertainments," by D. Plainman. "What's your line of business?" he demanded.

"I'm an artist, a painter."

"Ah, the painters always come down here. And the advertising people. I'll tell you, the other week we had a photographer—"

By the time it was his round Tony began to suspect he was just an excuse for beers. "You were going to tell me about the screams," he said when he returned to the table.

The man's eyes narrowed warily. "You've heard them. What do you think they are?"

"I was reading about the place earlier," Tony said, anxious to win his confidence. "I'm sure all those tragedies must have left an imprint somehow. A kind of recording. If there are ghosts, I think that's what they are."

"That's right." Roy Burley's eyes relaxed. "I've always thought that. There's a bit of science in that, it makes sense. Not like some of the things these spiritualists try to sell."

Tony opened his mouth to head him off from the next anecdote: too late. "We had one of them down here, trying to tell us about Ploughman's Path. A spiritualist or a medium, same thing. Came expecting us all to be yokels, I shouldn't wonder. The police weren't having any, so he tried it on us. Murder brings these mediums swarming like flies, so I've heard tell."

"What murder?" Tony said, confused.

"I thought you read about it." His eyes had narrowed again. "Oh, you read the book. No, it wouldn't be in there, too recent." He gulped beer; everything is beautiful, the radio sang. "Why, it was about the worst thing that ever happened at Ploughman's Path. I've seen pictures of what Jack the Ripper did, but this was worse. They talk about people being flayed alive, but—Christ. Put another in here, Bill."

He half emptied the refilled glass. "They never caught him. I'd have stopped him, I can tell you," he said in vague impotent fury. "The police didn't think he was a local man, because there wasn't any repetition. He left no clues, nobody saw him. At least, not what he looked like. There was a family picnicking in the field the day before the murder, they said they kept feeling there was someone watching. He must have been waiting to catch someone alone.

"I'll tell you the one clever suggestion this medium had. These picnickers heard the scream, what you called the recording. He thought maybe the screams were what attracted the maniac there."

Attracted him there. That reminded Tony of something, but the beer was heavy on his mind. "What else did the medium have to say?"

"Oh, all sorts of rubbish. You know, this mystical

stuff. Seeing patterns everywhere, saying everything is a pattern.''

"Yes?"

"Oh, yes," Roy Burley said irritably. "He didn't get that one past me, though. If everything's a pattern it has to include all the horror in the world, doesn't it? Things like this murder? That shut him up for a bit. Then he tried to say things like that may be necessary too, to make up the pattern. These people," he said with a gesture of disgust, "you can't talk to them."

Tony bought him another pint, restraining himself to a half. "Did he have any ideas about the screams?"

"God, I can't remember. Do you really want to hear that rubbish? You wouldn't have liked what he said, let me tell you. He didn't believe in your recording idea." He wiped his frothy lips sloppily. "He came here a couple of years after the murder," he reluctantly answered Tony's encouraging gaze. "He'd read about the tragedies. He held a three-day vigil at Ploughman's Path, or something. Wouldn't it be nice to have that much time to waste? He heard the screams, but—this is what I said you wouldn't like—he said he couldn't feel any trace of the tragedies at all.''

"I don't understand."

"Well, you know these people are shupposed to be senshitive to sush things." When he'd finished laughing at himself he said, "Oh, he had an explanation, he was full of them. He tried to tell the police and me that the real tragedy hadn't happened yet. He wanted us to believe he could see it in the future. Of course he couldn't say what or when. Do you know what he tried to make out? That there was something so awful in the future it was echoing back somehow, a sort of ghost in reverse. All the tragedies were just echoes, you see. He even made out the place was trying to make this final thing happen, so it could get rid of it at last. It had to make the worst thing possible happen, to purge itself. That was where the traces of the tragedies had gone—the psychic energy, he called it. The place had converted all that energy, to help it make the thing happen. Oh, he was a real comedian.''

"But what about the screams?"

"Same kind of echo. Haven't you ever heard an echo on a record before you hear the sound? He tried to say the screams were like that, coming back from the future. He was entertaining, I'll give him that. He had all sorts of charts, he'd worked out some kind of numerical pattern, the frequency of the tragedies or something. Didn't impress me. They're like statistics, those things, you can make them mean anything.'' His eyes had narrowed, gazing inward. "I ended up laughing at him. He went off very upset. Well, I had to get rid of him, I'd better things to do than listen to him. It wasn't my fault he was killed," he said angrily, "whatever some people may say.''

"Why, how was he killed?"

"Oh, he went back to Ploughman's Path. If he was so upset he shouldn't have been driving. There were some children playing near the path. He must have meant to chase them away, but he lost control of the car, crashed at the end of the path. His legs were trapped and he caught fire. Of course he could have fitted that into his pattern,'' he mused. "I suppose he'd have said that was what the third scream meant.''

Tony started. He fought back the shadows of beer, of the pub. "How do you mean, the third scream?"

"That was to do with his charts. He'd heard three screams in his vigil. He'd worked out that three screams meant it was time for a tragedy. He tried to show me, but I wasn't looking. What's the matter? Don't be going yet, it's my round. What's up, how many screams have you heard?"

"I don't know," Tony blurted. "Maybe I dreamt one.'' As he hurried out he saw Roy Burley picking up his abandoned beer, saying, "Aren't you going to finish this?"

It was all right. There was nothing to worry about, he'd just better be getting back to the cottage. The key groped clumsily for the ignition. The rusty yellow of Camside rolled back, rushed by green. Tony felt as if he were floating in a stationary car, as the road wheeled by beneath him—as if he were sitting in the front stalls before a cinema screen, as the road poured through the screen, as the bank of a curve hurtled at him: look out! Nearly. He slowed. No need to take risks. But his mind was full of the memory of someone watching from the trees, perhaps drawn there by the screams.

Puffy clouds lazed above the hills. As the Farmer's Rest whipped by, Tony glimpsed the cottage and the field, laid out minutely below; the trees at Ploughman's Path were a tight band of green. He skidded into the side road, fighting the wheel; the road seemed absurdly narrow. Scents of blossoms billowed thickly at him. A few birds sang elaborately, otherwise the passing countryside was silent, deserted, weighed down by heat.

The trunks of the trees at the end of Ploughman's Path were twitching nervously, incessantly. He squeezed his eyes shut. Only heat-haze. Slow down. Nearly home now.

He slammed the car door, which sprang open. Never mind. He ran up the path and thrust the gate back, breaking its latch. The door of the cottage was ajar. He halted in the front room. The cottage seemed full of his harsh panting.

Di's typescript was scattered over the carpet. The dark chairs sat fatly; one lay on its side, its fake leather ripped. Beside it a small object glistened red. He picked it up, staining his fingers. Though it was thick with blood he recognized Di's wedding ring.

When he rushed out after searching the cottage he saw the trail at once. As he forced his way through the fence, sobbing dryly, barbed wire clawed at him. He ran across the field, stumbling and falling, toward Ploughman's Path. The discolored grass of the trail painted his trouser cuffs and hands red. The trees of Ploughman's Path shook violently, with terror or with eagerness. The trail touched their trunks, leading him beneath the foliage to what lay on the path.

It was huge. More than anything else it looked like a tattered cutout silhouette of a woman's body. It gleamed red beneath the trees; its torso was perhaps three feet wide. On the width of the silhouette's head two eyes were arranged neatly.

The scream ripped the silence of the path, an outraged cry of horror beyond words. It startled him into stumbling forward. He felt numb and dull. His mind refused to grasp what he was seeing; it was like nothing he'd ever seen. There was most of the head, in the crotch of a tree. Other things dangled from branches.

His lips seemed glued together. Since reaching the path he had made no sound. He hadn't screamed, but he'd heard himself scream. At last he recognized that all the screams had been his voice.

He began to turn about rapidly, staring dull-eyed, seeking a direction in which he could look without being confronted with horror. There was none. He stood aimlessly, staring down near his feet, at a reddened gag.

As all the trees quivered like columns of water he heard movement behind him.

Though he had no will to live, it took him a long time to turn. He knew the pattern had reached its completion, and he was afraid. He had to close his eyes before he could turn, for he could still hear the scream he was about to utter.

# The Show
# Goes On

THE NAILS were worse than rusty; they had snapped. Under cover of several coats of paint, both the door and its frame had rotted. As Lee tugged at the door it collapsed toward him with a sound like that of an old cork leaving a bottle.

He hadn't used the storeroom since his father had nailed the door shut to keep the rats out of the shop. Both the shelves and the few items which had been left in the room—an open tin of paint, a broken-necked brush—looked merged into a single mass composed of grime and dust.

He was turning away, having vaguely noticed a dark patch that covered much of the dim wall at the back of the room, when he saw that it wasn't dampness. Beyond it he could just make out rows of regular outlines like teeth in a gaping mouth: seats in the old cinema.

He hadn't thought of the cinema for years. Old resurrected films on television, shrunken and packaged and robbed of flavor, never reminded him. It wasn't only that Cagney and Bogart and the rest had been larger than life, huge hovering faces like ancient idols; the cinema itself had had a personality—the screen framed by twin theater boxes from the days of the music hall, the faint smell and muttering of gaslights on the walls, the manager's wife and daughter serving in the auditorium and singing along with the musicals. In the years after the war you could get in for an armful of lemonade bottles, or a bag of vegetables if you owned one of the nearby allotments; there had been a greengrocer's old weighing machine inside the paybox. These days you had to watch films in concrete warrens, if you could afford to go at all.

Still, there was no point in reminiscing, for the old cinema was now a back entry for thieves. He was sure that was how they had robbed other shops on the block. At times he'd thought he heard them in the cinema; they sounded too large for rats. And now, by the look of the wall, they'd made themselves a secret entrance to his shop.

Mrs. Entwistle was waiting at the counter. These days she shopped here less from need than from loyalty, remembering when his mother used to bake bread at home to sell in the shop. "Just a sliced loaf," she said apologetically.

"Will you be going past Frank's yard?" Within its slippery wrapping the loaf felt ready to deflate, not like his mother's bread at all. "Could you tell him that my wall needs repairing urgently? I can't leave the shop."

Buses were carrying stragglers to work or to school. Ninety minutes later—he could tell the time by the passengers, which meant he needn't have his watch repaired—the buses were ferrying shoppers down to Liverpool city center, and Frank still hadn't come. Grumbling to himself, Lee closed the shop for ten minutes.

The February wind came slashing up the hill from the Mersey, trailing smoke like ghosts of the factory chimneys. Down the slope a yellow machine clawed at the remains of houses. The Liver Buildings looked like a monument in a graveyard of concrete and stone.

Beyond Kiddiegear and The Wholefood Shop, Frank's

yard was a maze of new timber. Frank was feeding the
edge of a door to a shrieking circular blade. He gazed at
Lee as though nobody had told him anything. When Lee
kept his temper and explained, Frank said, "No problem.
Just give a moan when you're ready."

"I'm ready now."

"Ah, well. As soon as I've finished this job I'll whiz
round." Lee had reached the exit when Frank said, "I'll
tell you something that'll amuse you . . ."

Fifteen minutes later Lee arrived back, panting, at his
shop. It was intact. He hurried around the outside of the
cinema, but all the doors seemed immovable, and he
couldn't find a secret entrance. Nevertheless he was sure
that the thieves—children, probably—were sneaking in
somehow.

The buses were full of old people now, sitting stiffly as
china. The lunchtime trade trickled into the shop: men who
couldn't buy their brand of cigarettes in the pub across the
road, children sent on errands while their lunches went
cold on tables or dried in ovens. An empty bus raced along
the deserted street, and a scrawny youth in a leather jacket
came into the shop, while his companion loitered in the
doorway. Would Lee have a chance to defend himself, or
at least to shout for help? But they weren't planning theft,
only making sure they didn't miss a bus. Lee's heart felt
both violent and fragile. Since the robberies had begun
he'd felt that way too often.

The shop was still worth it. "Don't keep it up if you
don't want to," his father had said, but it would have been
admitting defeat to do anything else. Besides, he and his
parents had been even closer here than at home. Since
their death, he'd had to base his stock on items people
wanted in a hurry or after the other shops had closed:
flashlights, canned food, light bulbs, cigarettes. Lee's Home-
Baked Bread was a thing of the past, but it was still Lee's
shop.

Packs of buses climbed the hill, carrying home the

rush-hour crowds. When the newspaper van dumped a stack of the evening's *Liverpool Echo* on the doorstep, he knew Frank wasn't coming. He stormed round to the yard, but it was locked and deserted.

Well then, he would stay in the shop overnight; he'd nobody to go home for. Why, he had even made the thieves' job easier by helping the door to collapse. The sight of him in the lighted shop ought to deter thieves—it better had, for their sakes.

He bought two pork pies and some bottles of beer from the pub. Empty buses moved off from the stop like a series of cars on a fairground ride. He drank from his mother's Coronation mug, which always stood by the electric kettle.

He might as well have closed the shop at eight o'clock; apart from an old lady who didn't like his stock of cat food, nobody came. Eventually he locked the door and sat reading the paper, which seemed almost to be written in a new language: *Head Raps Shock Axe,* said a headline about the sudden closing of a school.

Should he prop the storeroom door in place, lest he fall asleep? No, he ought to stay visible from the cinema, in the hope of scaring off the thieves. In his childhood they would hardly have dared sneak into the cinema, let alone steal—not in the last days of the cinema, when the old man had been roaming the aisles.

Everyone, perhaps even the manager, had been scared of him. Nobody Lee knew had ever seen his face. You would see him fumbling at the dim gaslights to turn them lower, then he'd begin to make sounds in the dark as though he was both muttering to himself and chewing something soft. He would creep up on talkative children and shine his flashlight into their eyes. As he hissed at them, a pale substance would spill from his mouth.

But they were scared of nothing these days, short of Lee's sitting in the shop all night, like a dummy. Already he felt irritable, frustrated. How much worse would he feel after a night of doing nothing except waste electricity on the lights and the fire?

He wasn't thinking straight. He might be able to do a great deal. He emptied the mug of beer, then he switched off the light and arranged himself on the chair as comfortably as possible. He might have to sit still for hours.

He only hoped they would venture close enough for him to see their faces. A flashlight lay ready beside him. Surely they were cowards who would run when they saw he wasn't scared of them. Perhaps he could chase them and find their secret entrance.

For a long time he heard nothing. Buses passed downhill, growing emptier and fewer. Through their growling he heard faint voices, but they were fading away from the pub, which was closing. Now the streets were deserted, except for the run-down grumble of the city. Wind shivered the window. The edge of the glow of the last few buses trailed vaguely over the storeroom entrance, making the outlines of cinema seats appear to stir. Between their sounds he strained his ears. Soon the last bus had gone.

He could just make out the outlines of the seats. If he gazed at them for long they seemed to waver, as did the storeroom doorway. Whenever he closed his eyes to rest them he heard faint tentative sounds: creaking, rattling. Perhaps the shop always sounded like that when there was nothing else to hear.

His head jerked up. No, he was sure he hadn't dozed: there had been a sound like a whisper, quickly suppressed. He hunched himself forward, ears ringing with strain. The backs of the cinema seats, vague forms like charcoal sketches on a charcoal background, appeared to nod toward him.

Was he visible by the glow of the electric fire? He switched it off stealthily, and sat listening, eyes squeezed shut. The sudden chill held him back from dozing.

Yes, there were stealthy movements in a large enclosed place. Were they creeping closer? His eyes sprang open to take them unawares, and he thought he glimpsed movement, dodging out of sight beyond the gap in the wall.

He sat absolutely still, though the cold was beginning to

insinuate cramp into his right leg. He had no way of measuring the time that passed before he glimpsed movement again. Though it was so vague that he couldn't judge its speed, he had a nagging impression that someone had peered at him from the dark auditorium. He thought he heard floorboards creaking.

Were the thieves mocking him? They must think it was fun to play games with him, to watch him gazing stupidly through the wall they'd wrecked. Rage sprang him to his feet. Grabbing the flashlight, he strode through the doorway. He had to slow down in the storeroom, for he didn't want to touch the shelves fattened by grime. As soon as he reached the wall he flashed the light into the cinema.

The light just managed to reach the walls, however dimly. There was nobody in sight. On either side of the screen, which looked like a rectangle of fog, the theater boxes were cups of darkness. It was hard to distinguish shadows from dim objects, which perhaps was why the rows of seats looked swollen.

The thieves must have retreated into one of the corridors, toward their secret entrance; he could hear distant muffled sounds. No doubt they were waiting for him to give up— but he would surprise them.

He stepped over a pile of rubble just beyond the wall. They mustn't have had time to clear it away when they had made the gap. The flashlight was heavy, reassuring; they'd better not come too near. As soon as he reached the near end of a row of seats and saw that they were folded back out of his way, he switched off the light.

Halfway down the row he touched a folding seat, which felt moist and puffy—fatter than it had looked. He didn't switch on the light, for he oughtn't to betray his presence more than was absolutely necessary. Besides, there was a faint sketchy glow from the road, through the shop. At least he would be able to find his way back easily—and he'd be damned if anyone else got there first.

When he reached the central aisle he risked another

blink of light, to make sure the way was clear. Shadows
sat up in all the nearest seats. A few springs had broken;
seats lolled, spilling their innards. He paced forward in the
dark, stopping frequently to listen. Underfoot, the carpet
felt like perished rubber; occasionally it squelched.

At the end of the aisle he halted, breathing inaudibly.
After a while he heard movement resounding down a
corridor to his left. All at once—good Lord, he'd forgotten
that—he was glad the sounds weren't coming from his
right, where the Gents' had been and still was, presumably.
Surely even thieves would prefer to avoid the yard beyond
that window, especially at night.

Blinking the light at the floor, he moved to his left. The
darkness hovering overhead seemed enormous, dwarfing
his furtive sounds. He had an odd impression that the
screen was almost visible, as an imperceptible lightening
of the dark above him. He was reminded of the last days
of the cinema, in particular one night when the projection-
ist must have been drunk or asleep: the film had slowed
and dimmed very gradually, flickering; the huge almost
invisible figures had twitched and mouthed silently, unable
to stop—it had seemed that the cinema was senile but
refusing to die, or incapable of dying.

Another blink of light showed him the exit, a dark arch
a head taller than he. A few scraps of linoleum clung to
the stone floor of a low corridor. He remembered the way:
a few yards ahead the corridor branched; one short branch
led to a pair of exit doors, while the other turned behind
the screen, toward a warren of old dressing rooms.

When he reached the pair of doors he tested them, this
time from within the building. Dim light drew a blurred
sketch of their edges. The bars which ought to snap apart
and release the doors felt like a single pole encrusted with
harsh flakes. His rusty fingers scraped as he rubbed them
together. Wind flung itself at the doors, as unable to move
them as he was.

He paced back to the junction of the corridors, feeling

his way with the toes of his shoes. There was a faint sound far down the other branch. Perhaps the thieves were skulking near their secret entrance, ready to flee. One blink of the light showed him that the floor was clear.

The corridor smelled dank and musty. He could tell when he strayed near the walls, for the chill intensified. The dark seemed to soak up those of his sounds that couldn't help being audible—the scrape of fallen plaster underfoot, the flap of a loose patch of linoleum which almost tripped him and which set his heart palpitating. It seemed a very long time before he reached the bend, which he coped with by feeling his way along the damp crumbling plaster of the wall. Then there was nothing but musty darkness for an even longer stretch, until something taller than he was loomed up in front of him.

It was another pair of double doors. Though they were ajar, and their bars looked rusted in the open position, he was reluctant to step through. The nervous flare of his light had shown him a shovel leaning against the wall; perhaps it had once been used to clear away fallen plaster. Thrusting the shovel between the doors, he squeezed through the gap, trying to make no noise.

He couldn't quite make himself switch off the flashlight. There seemed to be no need. In the right-hand wall were several doorways; he was sure one led to the secret entrance. If the thieves fled, he'd be able to hear which doorway they were using.

He crept along the passage. Shadows of dangling plaster moved with him. The first room was bare, and the color of dust. It would have been built as a dressing room, and perhaps the shapeless object, huddled in a corner and further blurred by wads of dust, had once been a costume. In the second deserted room another slumped, arms folded bonelessly. He had a hallucinatory impression that they were sleeping vagrants, stirring wakefully as his light touched them.

There was only one movement worth his attention: the

stealthy restless movement he could hear somewhere ahead. Yes, it was beyond the last of the doorways, from which—he switched off the flashlight to be sure—a faint glow was emerging. That must come from the secret entrance.

He paused just ahead of the doorway. Might they be lying in wait for him? When the sound came again—a leathery sound, like the shifting of nervous feet in shoes—he could tell that it was at least as distant as the far side of the room. Creeping forward, he risked a glance within.

Though the room was dimmer than fog, he could see that it was empty: not even a dusty remnant of clothing or anything else on the floor. The meager glow came from a window barred by a grille, beyond which he heard movement, fainter now. Were they waiting outside to open the grille as soon as he went away? Flashlight at the ready, he approached.

When he peered through the window, he thought at first there was nothing to see except a cramped empty yard: gray walls which looked furred by the dimness, gray flagstones, and—a little less dim—the sky. Another grille covered a window in an adjoining wall.

Then a memory clenched on his guts. He had recognized the yard.

Once, as a child, he had been meant to sneak into the Gents' and open the window so that his friends could get in without paying. He'd had to stand on the toilet seat in order to reach the window. Beyond a grille whose gaps were thin as matchsticks, he had just been able to make out a small dismal space enclosed by walls which looked coated with darkness or dirt. Even if he had been able to shift the grille he wouldn't have dared to do so, for something had been staring at him from a corner of the yard.

Of course it couldn't really have been staring. Perhaps it had been a half-deflated football; it looked leathery. It must have been there for a long time, for the two socketlike dents near its top were full of cobwebs. He'd fled, not

caring what his friends might do to him—but in fact they
hadn't been able to find their way to the yard. For years he
hadn't wanted to look out of that window, especially when
he'd dreamed—or had seemed to remember—that something had moved, gleaming, behind the cobwebs. When
he'd been old enough to look out of the window without
climbing up, the object was still there, growing dustier.
Now there had been a gap low down in it, widening as
years passed. It had resembled a grin stuffed with dirt.

Again he heard movement beyond the grille. He couldn't
quite make out that corner of the yard, and retreated,
trying to make no noise, before he could. Nearly at the
corridor, he saw that a door lay open against the wall. He
dragged the door shut as he emerged—to trap the thieves,
that was all; if they were in the yard that might teach them
a lesson. He would certainly have been uneasy if he had
still been a child.

Then he halted, wondering what else he'd heard.

The scrape of the door on bare stone had almost covered
up another sound from the direction of the cinema. Had
the thieves outwitted him? Had they closed the double
doors? When he switched on the flashlight, having fumbled
and almost dropped it lens first, he couldn't tell: perhaps
the doors were ajar, but perhaps his nervousness was
making the shadow between them appear wider than it
was.

As he ran, careless now of whether he was heard,
shadows of dead gaslights splashed along the walls, swelling.
Their pipes reminded him obscurely of breathing tubes,
clogged with dust. In the bare rooms, slumped dusty forms
shifted with his passing.

The doors were still ajar, and looked untouched. When
he stepped between them, the ceiling rocked with shadows;
until he glanced up he felt that it was closing down. He'd
done what he could in here, he ought to get back to the
shop—but if he went forward, he would have to think. If
the doors hadn't moved, then the sound he had almost

heard must have come from somewhere else: perhaps the unlit cinema.

Before he could help it, he was remembering. The last weeks of the cinema had been best forgotten: half the audience had seemed to be there because there was nowhere else to go, old men trying to warm themselves against the grudging radiators; sometimes there would be the thud of an empty bottle or a fallen walking stick. The tattered films had jerked from scene to scene like dreams. On the last night Lee had been there, the gaslights had gone out halfway through the film, and hadn't been lit at the end. He'd heard an old man falling and crying out as though he thought the darkness had come for him, a little girl screaming as if unable to wake from a nightmare, convinced perhaps that only the light had held the cinema in shape, prevented it from growing deformed. Then Lee had heard something else: a muttering mixed with soft chewing. It had sounded entirely at home in the dark.

But if someone was in the cinema now, it must be the thieves. He ought to hurry, before they reached his shop. He was hurrying, toward the other branch of the corridor, which led to the exit doors. Might he head off the thieves that way? He would be out of the building more quickly, that was the main thing—it didn't matter why.

The doors wouldn't budge. Though he wrenched at them until his palms smarted with rust, the bars didn't even quiver. Wind whined outside like a dog, and emphasized the stuffy mustiness of the corridor.

Suddenly he realized how much noise he was making. He desisted at once, for it would only make it more difficult for him to venture back into the cinema. Nor could he any longer avoid realizing why.

Once before he'd sneaked out to this exit, to let in his friends who hadn't been able to find their way into the yard. Someone had told the usherette, who had come prowling down the central aisle, poking at people with her flashlight beam. As the light crept closer, he had been unable to move; the seat had seemed to box him in, his mouth and throat had felt choked with dust. Yet the panic he'd experienced then had been feeble compared to what he felt now—for if the cinema was still guarded against intruders, it was not by the manager's daughter.

He found he was trembling, and clawed at the wall. A large piece of plaster came away, crunching in his hand. The act of violence, mild though it was, went some way toward calming him. He wasn't a child, he was a shop-keeper who had managed to survive against the odds; he had no right to panic as the little girl had, in the dark. Was the knot that was twisting harder, harder in his guts re-newed panic, or disgust with himself? Hoping that it was the latter, he made himself hurry toward the auditorium.

When he saw what he had already noticed but managed to ignore, he faltered. A faint glow had crept into the corridor from the auditorium. Couldn't that mean that his eyes were adjusting? No, the glow was more than that. Gripping the edge of the archway so hard that his fingers twitched painfully, he peered into the cinema.

The gaslights were burning.

At least blurred ovals hovered on the walls above their jets. Their light had always fallen short of the central aisle; now the glow left a swath of dimness, half as wide as the auditorium which it divided. If the screen was faintly lit—if huge vague flattened forms were jerking there, rather than merely stains on the canvas—it failed to illumi-nate the cinema. He had no time to glance at the screen, for he could see that not all the seats were empty.

Perhaps they were only a few heaps of rubbish which were propped there—heaps which he hadn't been able to distinguish on first entering. He had begun to convince himself that this was true, and that in any case it didn't matter, when he noticed that the dimness was not al-together still. Part of it was moving.

No, it was not dimness. It was a glow, which was crawling jerkily over the rows of seats, toward the first of the objects propped up in them. Was the glow being carried along the central aisle? Thank God, he couldn't quite distinguish its source. Perhaps that source was making a faint sound, a moist somewhat rhythmic muttering that sounded worse than senile, or perhaps that was only the wind.

Lee began to creep along the front of the cinema, just beneath the screen. Surely his legs wouldn't let him down, though they felt flimsy, almost boneless. Once he reached the side aisle he would be safe and able to hurry, the gaslights would show him the way to the gap in his wall. Wouldn't they also make him more visible? That ought not to matter, for—his mind tried to flinch away from thinking—if anything was prowling in the central aisle, surely it couldn't outrun him.

He had just reached the wall when he thought he heard movement in the theater box above him. It sounded dry as an insect, but much larger. Was it peering over the edge at him? He couldn't look up, only clatter along the bare floorboards beneath the gaslights, on which he could see no flames at all.

He still had yards to go before he reached the gap when the roving glow touched one of the heaps in the seats.

If he could have turned and run blindly, nothing would have stopped him; but a sickness that was panic weighed down his guts, and he couldn't move until he saw. Perhaps there wasn't much to see except an old coat, full of lumps of dust or rubble, that was lolling in the seat; nothing to make the flashlight shudder in his hand and rap against the wall. But sunken in the gap between the lapels of the coat was what might have been an old Halloween mask overgrown with dust. Surely it was dust that moved in the empty eyes—yet as the flashlight rapped more loudly against the wall, the mask turned slowly and unsteadily toward him.

Panic blinded him. He didn't know who he was nor where he was going. He knew only that he was very small and at bay in the vast dimness, through which a shape was directing a glow toward him. Behind the glow he could almost see a face from which something pale dangled. It wasn't a beard, for it was rooted in the gaping mouth.

He was thumping the wall with the flashlight as though to remind himself that one or the other was there. Yes, there was a wall, and he was backing along it: backing where? Toward the shop, his shop now, where he wouldn't need to use the flashlight, mustn't use the flashlight to illuminate whatever was pursuing him, mustn't see, for then he would never be able to move. Not far to go now, he wouldn't have to bear the dark much longer, must be nearly at the gap in the wall, for a glow was streaming from behind him. He was there now, all he had to do was turn his back on the cinema, turn quickly, just turn—

He had managed to turn halfway, trying to be blind without closing his eyes, when his free hand touched the object which was lolling in the nearest seat. Both the overcoat and its contents felt lumpy, patched with damp and dust. Nevertheless the arm stirred; the object at the end of it, which felt like a bundle of sticks wrapped in torn leather, tried to close on his hand.

Choking, he pulled himself free. Some of the sticks came loose and plumped on the rotten carpet. The flashlight fell beside them, and he heard glass breaking. It didn't matter, he was at the gap, he could hear movement in the shop, cars and buses beyond. He had no time to wonder who was in there before he turned.

The first thing he saw was that the light wasn't that of streetlamps; it was daylight. At once he saw why he had made the mistake: the gap was no longer there. Except for a single brick, the wall had been repaired.

He was yelling desperately at the man beyond the wall, and thumping the new bricks with his fists—he had begun to wonder why his voice was so faint and his blows so feeble—when the man's face appeared beyond the brick-sized gap. Lee staggered back as though he was fainting.

Except that he had to stare up at the man's face, he might have been looking in a mirror.

He hadn't time to think. Crying out, he stumbled forward and tried to wrench the new bricks loose. Perhaps his adult self beyond the wall was aware of him in some way, for his face peered through the gap, looking triumphantly contemptuous of whoever was in the dark. Then the brick fitted snugly into place, cutting off the light.

Almost worse was the fact that it wasn't quite dark. As he began to claw at the bricks and mortar, he could see them far too clearly. Soon he might see what was holding the light, and that would be worst of all.

## The Puppets

THAT was the summer when I thought I could see everything. Because I knew I'd passed to go to University, my focus wasn't narrowed down to textbooks. More than that, I had what I thought I wanted—which shows that I wasn't seeing very clearly, after all.

Yet I was seeing so much for the first time: how the shadow of the church spire made the village square into a sundial (ten o'clock at Millie's Woollens, eleven at the Acorn, just as the bar was opening); how the campers' tents beside Delamere Forest resembled orange wedges of processed cheese; the workmen's sentry box guarding the pit outside the post office, where they were supposed to be improving the telephone exchange, and the way passersby both frowned at the intrusion and muttered "about time." Even Mr. Ince's Punch and Judy show seemed new to me, a childhood delight it would do me no harm to recapture. Again I was wrong: in the end, horribly so.

In its season, Mr. Ince's little theater always stood beneath a clump of trees at the edge of the village green.

There seemed hardly to be room in the striped box for Mr. Ince and his sharp elbows, which protruded when he walked. The puppets nodded and pecked and squabbled like birds on a window ledge; sometimes their ledge was so crowded with movement that you might have thought he had more than two hands.

It was his skill that kept me watching. Sometimes on my way home past his cottage, I'd seen him carving his figures with infinite care; now I saw that care in the gestures of their tiny hands, the birdlike cocking of their heads, the timing of their actions. Perhaps at midsummer, when he went traveling, his audiences appreciated his skill.

Of course I liked to think of myself as the only intelligent sensitive person in a village of dullards—or almost the only one. Was she my real reason for loitering near the theater? Beyond the clump of trees, through the gap in the buildings of the village square, I might, if I was lucky, watch her: Rebecca.

Sometimes she appeared at the window of her parents' antique shop. Sometimes I only thought I glimpsed her, among the elaborate furniture, the delicate clocks, the plates like circular miniatures. When she came out of the shop—the frills of her unfashionably long skirts and petticoats billowing, her blonde hair streaming—it was as though a porcelain figure had come to life.

I'd wanted her for years. Perhaps when I was younger I might have approached her, but brooding over the possibility had made me worse and worse. Years at a boys' school had driven me further into myself. There were girls to be had in the village, despite their giggling pretence of aloofness, but they weren't worth even the meager effort they required. I could only lie in bed with an illusion of Rebecca, and feel feverish with guilt afterward. No doubt those nights left me even less prepared for the day she came to the house.

My father was a dentist; my mother, his anesthetist. They had brought me up to take care of my teeth, and though he fished inside my mouth with a mirror twice a year, I never needed treatment. Often I imagined what he did with his hooks and drills and pliers, especially when his victim was someone I didn't like. I felt smug when I saw the victims in the waitingroom, chatting bravely or louring over spineless magazines.

One morning quite early in my long holiday I finished a book by Camus. When I'd stared at the forested horizon for a while, depressing myself with thoughts of suffering, I went downstairs. I glanced into the waitingroom, past the stand whose curlicues were bare of coats, and there was Rebecca.

At once I saw how little reassurance there was in the framed Edwardian comic postcards on the walls, the simian chatter of a radio announcer and his records. Only I could comfort her, for she was alone—and all I could do was dodge out of sight, afraid that she would catch me watching.

I patrolled the hallway several times before I managed to enter. "Hello," I mumbled, but she seemed not to hear me; I had scarcely heard myself. My momentum carried me to the magazine table, where at least I needn't face her while I pretended to look for something to read.

Impulsively I grabbed the least dog-eared of the magazines and swung round. I wasn't fast enough, for my face was already a mask that must be blazing visibly, my stiff tongue thrust painfully against my bottom teeth. I could only poke the magazine toward her while slowly, very slowly, she looked up.

Her smile almost overbalanced me. "Oh, no thank you," she said, and let her hand stray toward a magazine which lay abandoned at her feet.

Though my face was puffing up with embarrassment, I managed to read the title: *Musical Times*. "Do you like music?" I stammered, and wished my gaping mouth were even larger, for then I might swallow myself.

"Very much. I play a little. I play the violin."

"Oh, was that you?" Perhaps she had glimpsed me

dawdling past her house and gawping at the melodies beyond the trees, thinking that someone besides myself appreciated good music. I had never dreamed that Rebecca herself had been playing.

"Can I be heard all over the village?" She seemed dismayed. "Oh, you heard me as you were passing. I'm afraid I don't play very well—I wish I had the courage to perform for an audience, then I might make myself play better."

"Why, you play—" "Marvelously, beautifully, magnificently" might expose my feelings about her too soon. "You play quite well," I said.

"Thank you very much." I thought she must be thanking me for distracting her. "Are you very knowledgeable about music?"

"Oh, yes." At once I wished I hadn't said that, but if I had denied it my compliment would have been rendered meaningless. "I particularly like Strauss—Richard Strauss, obviously. And Mozart, of course. And Beethoven, especially Beethoven," I babbled. "Beethoven is—" God knows what I might have said if my father hadn't taken Rebecca away.

He'd saved me from one kind of agony only to afflict me with worse. When the drill began, my hands became spastic claws which struggled to cover my ears. Good God, what was he doing to her? I stumbled about the house like a parody of an expectant father outside a delivery room.

When she emerged she looked as bad as I'd feared. Her face was white as china, and I had the impression that she was barely able to walk. "Come and sit down," I blurted, not minding my father's surprised but relieved grin behind her: I was developing—not before time, he seemed to say. "Would you like some tea or something?" I said.

"No, thank you. I must get home," she said, nervous as Cinderella.

Just in time I realized that I had another chance. I was

tempted not to take it, but my father was watching. "I'd better see you home," I said.

Halfway down the hedged path which led, after several diversions, to the green, she stumbled and I dared to take her arm. The leaves of the hedges were plated with light and pricked with rainbows from last night's rain; everything smelled moist and growing. I was too entranced by walking with Rebecca to speak.

The path bent sharply around Mr. Ince's garden. Beyond the clipped lawn and the birdbath on its pedestal, the trees from which he carved his puppets crowded about the cottage. I hadn't realized how thick they had grown; I couldn't even see the shed in which he kept the barrow on which he wheeled his theater, the ramshackle van he used for longer tours. Mr. Ince stood still as a tree before the cottage; birds were pecking crumbs from his hands, the sleeves of his old jacket looked stained with droppings. Rebecca glanced aside, wrinkling her nose.

We'd reached the square, and I had let go of her arm as soon as we'd come in sight of people, before I realized that if we were to meet again except by chance, I would have to speak. Perhaps I would summon up the courage on the way to her house—but she halted in front of the antique shop. "Thank you so much," she said.

"I thought you said you were going home."

"I meant here." As I turned away, detesting my bashfulness, she said, "Do you go to many concerts?"

"Yes, in Manchester. Sometimes in Liverpool." I was edging away from her, not caring how rude I seemed, when suddenly I wondered if she was as glad to find someone like herself as I had been. Staring anywhere but at her, I mumbled, "Would you like to go to one sometime?"

"Well, I haven't much spare time. I'm making costumes for the pageant." A good excuse, I thought bitterly, walking away. "But I'd love to go," she said. "Will you find out what's on and tell me tomorrow?"

I would have dashed home at once and back to the shop

with the information, except that it might have been fatal to show how I felt. For hours I wandered around the outskirts of the village, blinded by my good luck. When I reached home I didn't mind my parents' knowing grins. It was only when I woke next morning that I wondered how all this could possibly be happening to me.

But we went to a concert in Manchester, and that was only the beginning. Soon we were strolling hand in hand through the village, and I hoped everyone noticed. Everything—the church rummage sales where I bought Rabelais and Boccaccio, afternoon teas in Mrs. Winder's Olde English Tea Shoppe, the Sunday cricket match in which our team beat the next village—was our backdrop. One evening we sat beside the green, which was spread with a sheet of moonlight, and told each other our dreams. Both of us dreamed of touring the world, she to play for audiences, I because I was famished for newness. After that, even when I wasn't with her, I felt drugged by our closeness.

Our first disagreement—quite minor, it seemed at the time—was about Mr. Ince.

That evening I'd played her a record of Mahler's Third. As we strolled toward her house, we were content to be quiet together for a while. The hedges that walled the path were quivering in breezes; overhead, clouds flooded by. The dimness merged our surroundings like a spoiled painting, and I had almost passed Mr. Ince's cottage before I saw the theater.

Though she resisted, I turned back. The striped booth faced the cottage; I had to crane over the hedge to distinguish the stage. My first hallucinatory glimpse had been accurate. On the dark stage, beneath miniature curtains that fluttered in the wind, Punch and Judy were performing.

They weren't squabbling now. Indeed, they made no sound at all. They seemed to be dancing: bowing to each other, twirling gracefully though their flapping costumes tugged at them, retreating a few precise steps then gliding together again. Perhaps the dimness helped smooth their movements, made them appear more lifelike, as it did their faces. Their only audience was the trees that loomed above the cottage, shifting restlessly and hissing, dissatisfied giants.

"Come on, Jim," Rebecca was murmuring urgently. "I should be home by now."

"Wait just a minute." There was some aspect of the pirouetting figures I wanted to define. Once I'd seen Mr. Ince gazing wistfully at birds that splashed in the birdbath, then sailed away on the wind. Did he wish he could create movements as tiny and perfect as theirs? But tonight's rehearsal didn't look much like that; in an obscure way I was reminded of a dance of trees.

"I'm going, Jim. We've been staying out too late. My parents will be angry again."

Again? It was the first I'd heard of it, and it seemed far less important than the puppets that were dancing just for us. "You want to watch this, don't you?"

"No, I don't." She pulled away violently. She must be frightened of her parents, surely—not of the puppets. But good God, we were adults: I was eighteen, she was twenty.

I caught up with her in the middle of the green. She was very tense; for a moment I thought she would flinch away. Instead she said in a tone which offered both consolation and, vulnerably, trust: "I want you to come home tomorrow night and hear me play."

By the next evening I was nervous. Until recently I'd hardly noticed her parents. Now I sometimes encountered them when I met Rebecca at their shop, where they were guardedly polite to me; I was sure they didn't like me very much. I cut myself while shaving, and had to waste five minutes dabbing at myself. If I had visited the antique shop in that state, heaven knows what I would have broken.

Mr. Ince was sitting in a homemade chair as I hurried past his garden. He was staring into the entangled dimness beneath the trees. A large figure which he had begun to carve lay abandoned at his feet. Stumps of branches protruded from the faceless head, like boils.

I was shocked by how much he had aged. Had this been

a gradual process which I'd been too preoccupied to notice? He looked drained, exhausted, past caring about the large figure which he had agreed to carve for the pageant. My passing must have roused him, for he swayed to his feet and dragged chair and figure into the cottage, beneath the dark wings of the trees.

When I reached Rebecca's my carefully combed hair was snatching at my face, my armpits were prickly from hurrying. Her father gazed at me as though I were a salesman whose unwelcomeness he was too polite to show. He said nothing as he ushered me down the oak-paneled hall, which was barnacled with horse brasses.

If he and his wife tried to make me feel at home, in the large stony room where the panels of the walls were as heavy and dark as the piano, it was only for the sake of Rebecca, whose strain was painfully apparent. She seemed afraid to venture near me—because of her parents or because, like an examiner, I'd come to hear her play? She wore a severe black dress, a musician's uniform. Together with everything else, it robbed me of all sense of the times we'd shared.

Eventually her father sat down at the piano. As soon as she tucked the violin beneath her chin she seemed to forget everything except the technical problems of the music. It was as though she and her father were helping each other with tasks set by Mozart and Beethoven; I felt she would never be enough at her ease to let the music flow. Of course, at the end of each piece I applauded wildly.

I drank a lot of sherry in an attempt to calm my nerves; her mother's lips grew more pursed each time she refilled my glass. Mostly to show that I was quite at home, I sang fragments of Verdi in the bathroom, and perhaps that prompted Rebecca's mother to ask me, "What are you doing in the pageant?"

Though Rebecca had tried to coax me into participating, I'd managed to avoid the whole thing, in which her parents were heavily involved. "I hadn't really thought," I mumbled.

"We have a song for you." She sat waiting for me to stand up and take the music from her. "Rebecca will accompany you."

"I thought you didn't like to play for audiences," I said to Rebecca.

There was an appalled and wounded silence, which I tried to ignore by glaring at the music, which proved to be an Elizabethan ballad. "Shall I play it for you?" Rebecca said.

"Can't he sight-read?" Her father made me sound no longer worth noticing. She played the melody for me, and I managed to follow it through the staves. "Now you sing it, James," her mother said.

Could she tell I disliked my full name, because it made me sound like a butler? When at last I finished, and the throbbing of my red-hot face began to lessen, she said, "You'll need a lot of practice." She sounded almost accusing, though I had never claimed to be a musician.

After an awkward half hour, during which Rebecca's parents and I confirmed we had nothing in common, I said that I thought I'd better go. "Oh, Rebecca is going to be very busy. She may not see you before the pageant. She'll need to make you a costume." To Rebecca, with an emphasis I thought vindictive, she said, "I've invited Alan for his fitting tomorrow. I expect you'll want him to stay for dinner."

Though Rebecca tried to say good-bye at the door, I made her walk along the tree-lined drive. As soon as we were out of earshot of the house I demanded, "Who's Alan?"

"Just the son of some friends of theirs." She halted me and squeezed my hand. "They're trying to match us, but you mustn't worry. He and I are friends, that's all. It's you I want." Gripping my shoulders hard and gazing into my eyes, she said, "I've always done what they want, but not over this."

Her lingering kiss convinced me more than her words, yet before I reached home I was wondering how, if she

had always obeyed her parents, she could be sure of
changing now. Was love enough? I felt like Mr. Ince's
cottage, brooding darkly in its cage of trees.

I saw little of her during the next week, though her
mother spent five minutes brusquely measuring me in the
shop. If her parents answered the phone, she was in the
bath, or too busy to be called, or not at home. Once she
suggested that I could sit with her while she worked, but
that would have entailed suffering her parents. I preferred
to go to Liverpool or Manchester; somehow the violence I
felt toward her parents seemed appropriate to city streets.

The night before the pageant, her mother summoned me
to try on my costume. Since Rebecca was watching eagerly,
I had to conceal my dismay. In the doublet and hose I felt
less like an actor than a transvestite. The following day I
felt even worse.

Almost the whole of the village was there, either trudging in procession toward the green or lining the square and
the main street to watch. Perhaps all this was meant to
celebrate the village anniversary, yet I suspected the pageant of trying to show that the village was an enclave of
craftsmanship and culture, not just the site of the fair that
would be opening next week.

Rebecca clearly enjoyed wearing her crinoline. I thought
of how seldom I'd touched her, how she seemed happiest
concealing her body. Alan, a burly fellow several years
older than I, was wearing doublet and hose. Worse still,
her mother had made us walk together behind Rebecca,
like rival suitors. His round face resembled a football I
would have loved to kick.

When we took our places on the green, and he began to
declaim an Elizabethan description of the village, I realized that he belonged to the village repertory company. No
wonder he was so good at posing, I thought bitterly: no
wonder he looked so convincing in drag. He was rewarded
with an outburst of applause—and then it was my turn.

Though at least I had Rebecca, whereas he had been
alone, I didn't do as well. I'd been practicing last night

and the whole of this morning, but her father had refused to let me rehearse with her; he said it would be less genuine. Did he want me to embarrass her? When I sang, my voice in the middle of the green sounded thinner than a bird's. Children tittered, at me or at Rebecca, who was strumming her violin like a lute.

At the end, which was received by a drizzle of applause, Rebecca told me, "You were super. So were you," she said to Alan, and doled out a kiss to each of us.

I was furious. I hardly spoke to her for the rest of the day, except to complain that the pageant was pretentious, trivial, a waste of time. When the festivities began, I drank pint after pint of beer from the table which Mr. Blundell of the Acorn kept replenishing; then I loitered near Alan, in the hope that he would say something to which I could take exception, so that I could knock him down. When at last I grew tired of loitering, I found that Rebecca had gone.

I wandered until it grew dark. Trudging home, I thought for a moment that Mr. Ince had come back; as usual, he'd gone touring in his van once the fair was due on the green. No, he must still be away, for the cottage was dark and grass sprawled over the garden path—but then what had I heard in the cottage? It had sounded rather like brooms falling over in a cupboard, then falling again. No doubt it was branches tapping the cottage; I really didn't care.

Next morning, when my head had stopped drumming savagely, I went to the shop to apologize to Rebecca, while her parents looked forbidding in the background. That night at the fair she refused to go on most of the rides, and when I persuaded her into a Dodgem car she felt withdrawn, stony within the clasp of my arm. As I walked her home I nagged her until she agreed to go to a concert in Manchester the following week.

At least she was grateful for the concert. It was Beethoven's Ninth; I'd learned she was happiest with familiar things, though I refused to believe that summed her up.

The applause was so rapturous that it provoked an encore, and we missed the train.

I couldn't see that it mattered; there would be another in less than an hour. I tried to keep her occupied, on a bare bench as far as possible from the sullen yellowish lights, but she kept starting up to peer along the line, a couple of sketched gleams embedded in sooty darkness. Overhead a large metallic voice announced trains to places I'd never heard of. Could she hear other voices, demanding what she meant by coming home so late? "They'll have to get used to it eventually," I said.

"Why will they *have* to?"

"Because you're an adult," I said incredulously. "You can't let them tell you what to do."

"Is it adult to behave irresponsibly?"

I thought she was growing pompous. Besides, we were wasting time when we could be necking. "If you always did what they wanted," I pointed out, "you'd never see me again."

"I know that." She seemed close to tears. All at once I saw how to cheer her up and clear the way for myself. "Look," I said, "if they bother you so much, why don't you move away and get a job?"

"A job?" She made it sound insulting. "I don't want a job. I'm only helping in the shop to keep my parents happy." She added more gently, "When I'm married I'll want to devote my time to my music."

That stopped me. Were we planning marriage all of a sudden? She'd said she would resist her parents' choice; who else could she mean except me? I wasn't ready to discuss marriage—and besides, I'd realized at last that her dream of seeing the world was nothing but a dream; Manchester was about as far as she cared to venture.

The romantic mood seemed worth preserving. "You know, I'd wanted to meet you for years," I said. "I could never work out how to, until that day you had to come for treatment. And then I'll bet I suffered more than you did. I never told you," I laughed, feeling that a secret ought to bring us closer together, "but when someone I didn't like was in there, I used to stand outside and listen to the drill."

When she pulled away from me and hurried to the edge of the platform, I thought she was going to vomit, but she was only hoping for the train. Nevertheless she looked sickened when I tried to coax her back to the bench. On the train she tolerated my embrace, but shook her head dismally when I demanded what was wrong. Her parents were waiting on the lit stage of the porch, and I left her at the gate; I'd had enough.

I didn't see her for days. I yearned to, yet I was afraid she might insist on talking marriage; that would force me to ponder our relationship, which I didn't want to do. Why couldn't we just enjoy it, forget our differences and enjoy each other as we had at first? If I'd thought beyond that, I would have had to wonder how, since she insisted on staying at home, we could stay together once I went to University.

As I wandered brooding around the village, I saw Mr. Ince. He was pushing his barrow, which was laden with the theater, toward the green, but it looked almost as though the barrow was dragging him. Not only his elbows but the rest of his bones appeared ready to tear his skin, which resembled tissue paper. Now that the workmen's booth had gone from outside the post office, there was nothing to take the children away from Mr. Ince's show, but they may have been as distressed by the performance as I was: Punch and Judy seemed to drag themselves limping along their ledge, their heads nodding as if they were senile, their limbs moving hardly at all.

The following day I received the card. Though the envelope bore Rebecca's return address, it was not in her handwriting. I knew instinctively that the sharp severe letters were her mother's. When I made myself tear open the flap, I found a printed invitation to Rebecca's twenty-first birthday.

I hadn't realized it was so close. What other secrets had

she kept from me? I replied that of course I would come, and rushed to Manchester to buy her a present which, I hoped, would let us share a happy memory: a recording of Beethoven's Ninth.

The birthday reception was at the country club, a converted mansion amid fields overlooked that night by flocks of stars. A uniformed girl took my coat, a liveried usher led me to the party, and Rebecca's mother tried to gain possession of my present. I wanted to hand it to Rebecca, who was surrounded by expensive-looking friends, but her mother said firmly, "Leave it on the table."

A long table laden with presents stood against one wall. I stared for a while in dismay; then, remembering the memory it was supposed to evoke, I dumped the record on the table and made in despair for the bar. The table already bore a complete set of Beethoven's symphonies.

I managed to kiss Rebecca before her mother steered her away. For a while I hung about on the edge of conversations, listening as Rebecca's friends agreed what was good (hanging, the birch, repatriation) and bad (unions, comprehensive education, the state of the world outside the village). What upset me most was that her young friends, Alan and the rest, sounded exactly like their elders. I don't know who or what provoked me to say, "Why don't you just build a wall around the village?"

"It strikes me you don't care much for our village," Rebecca's father said. "You seem happiest when you're away from it. Like that fellow Ince."

"Don't mention him," his wife said. "Letting us down like that over the pageant, not even bothering to stay."

"He wants locking up," Alan said. "God only knows what he thinks he's doing—I don't think he knows himself. I had a look at his show today. No wonder people are keeping their children away. It isn't entertainment, it's monstrous."

Before I could ask him what he was talking about, Rebecca said, "He's so restless. All that traveling. Like a gypsy." She wrinkled her nose, as though at a bad smell.

"What's wrong with gypsies?" I managed not to blurt, restraining myself not only because I could imagine the sort of reply she would make but because I'd suddenly realized the trap that had been set for me. Her parents had wanted her to see how out of place I was; perhaps they'd hoped I would make a scene to estrange her once and for all. Instead I drank, and smiled, and nodded, and cursed what I thought was my cowardice.

In the morning I had a mission: to save Rebecca from herself, from the attitudes of her parents and friends. She couldn't be as ingrown as they were, not yet; otherwise, how could she appreciate Beethoven's Ninth? But I couldn't reach her all day, and next morning a notice in the antique shop said that they had gone on holiday for two weeks.

Had her parents arranged this swiftly, or was it another secret she had kept from me? My anger couldn't feed on itself for more than a couple of days; before the week was over I felt almost guiltily free, able to do things I wanted to do without thinking of Rebecca. I walked all day through the spread countryside, toward a promise of hills which I never quite reached, and my mind grew attuned to the pace of the clouds. I stood beneath an oak in Delamere Forest and watched a storm fill, then burst, the sky.

The day after she returned, my nervousness infuriated me. I keyed myself up to braving the shop and her parents, only to find that they hadn't opened the shop. Whenever I called her house the phone was engaged, tooting monotonously. There was nothing for it but to go to the house.

I couldn't go in. I'd used up all my courage in braving the shop. I paced back and forth outside the gates, and grimaced furiously at myself in the dark. Wind rushed down the drive, trying to shoulder me away; along the drive, trees roared at me. Twice I strode halfway up the drive before I faltered.

I was still patrolling, almost suffocated by self-disgust, when the porch lit—like a refrigerator, I thought distractedly—and Rebecca emerged. I dodged out of sight, back toward the village. She was alone, and looked determined; perhaps she was going to my house.

I appeared from a lane. "Oh, hello," I said. "I didn't know you were back. I've been walking."

Was her start of pleasure or dismay? She didn't sound as glad to see me as I thought she should, but didn't resist when I took her hand. "Where are you going?" I said.

"Walking, like you."

Perhaps that was a riposte; I thought it best to gain an advantage. "Did you like your record?"

"Yes, very much." But I'd expected her at least to squeeze my hand. Surely she must be grateful not to be alone on the dark road; shouldn't I make the most of her gratitude? But when we reached the square I had to say, "You didn't tell me you were going on holiday."

"No." Her voice sounded as though it was trying to hide in the blustery wind.

"Why didn't you?"

"Because of the way I felt." Her hand jerked in mine. "Don't make me worse."

I hurried her past the antique shop, before I could grow too irritable to keep quiet, toward the green. The night we'd sat there, we had been closest. Perhaps the muted glow of the grass would calm us now.

Was it the tension between us that made the place seem too vivid? Large bruises blackened the green where the rides of the fair had stood. Around them the sparse grass looked oily with traces of rain. The glimmering blades were lurid as green wires which, when I gazed at them, seemed to flicker like dying neon. There was no peace here, for in the clump of trees at the edge of the green, someone was croaking.

Should I have guided Rebecca away, since she was growing more tense? Ultimately it would have made no difference between us. I crept toward the trees, but faltered before she did, my hand tightening inadvertently on hers. In the dark beneath the trees, Mr. Ince was standing upright in a coffin.

Of course it was the theater. The back of the stage, which concealed him from the audience, was gone. His head appeared above the ledge, dwarfing the performers. Though the puppets were croaking at each other as they nodded back and forth, in the dimness his mouth seemed not to be moving. Only his eyes rolled in their sockets like marbles in a fairground mask, watching the puppets.

Rebecca was trying to drag me away, but I wanted to hear what the voices were saying, all the more so since they sounded vicious almost to the point of incoherence. I could make out some of Judy's phrases now, though they seemed to ebb and flow like wind in trees: ". . . living like an animal . . . nobody to look after you . . . can't look after yourself . . ." The croaking rose almost to a shriek. ". . . might as well dig yourself a hole and live in it . . . that's where you're going anyway . . . deep in the dirt . . ."

I might have heard more if Rebecca hadn't held me back. Was he repeating accusations that had been leveled at him? I couldn't see how, since he had always lived alone. Was part of him accusing himself? "Come on," I said irritably to Rebecca, "don't be stupid. Nothing's going to hurt you."

"No, I won't." Her voice was so cold that it stopped me. "You watch by yourself if you want to. I don't enjoy watching people suffering."

"What do you mean by that?"

Her tone had already made it clear. "You told me how you enjoy listening to people in your father's surgery."

I thought this ridiculously unfair, so much so that I followed her away from the green. "Well, so would you," I said.

"No, I would not. Perhaps I was brought up differently."

"Yes, well," I said ominously, "maybe you'd better leave your parents out of this."

"Don't you dare say anything against my parents."

I felt possessed by an atrociously banal script. "Oh, don't they ever say anything against me?"

"Stop it. Let's talk about something else. I don't know what," she said miserably.

We were outside the antique shop; I was tempted to kick in the window. "I want to hear what they said," I persisted. "Go on. Go on, let's hear it."

"All right, you *shall* hear. The way I feel now, it doesn't matter." She was staring into the dim maze of antiques. "They say you're not like them or my friends. They say you've never tried to get to know them, and that you're a drunkard, and that you'd make me go out to work." As though to drive me away for good she added defiantly, "And they think you're probably a sadist."

I hadn't fully realized that she must have told them everything when I snarled, "If their opinion means so much to you, you'd better go to Alan."

"I was on my way to see him when I met you." When I froze, she added dully, "At least I feel peaceful with him."

"Well," I said, and wondered momentarily if I would be able to say anything so final, "you'd better piss off then, hadn't you?"

She gazed at me, then fled sobbing. I managed to leave the antique shop without committing any of the crimes that were seething in my head. As I stalked toward the green, I thought bitterly that the Punch and Judy show summed up our relationship. I was ready to enjoy it on that level, but the clump of trees was deserted. No doubt the creaking on the hedged path was Mr. Ince's barrow. As I passed his cottage he was stumbling in, and for a moment I thought two birds were riding on his shoulders—but no wonder my perceptions were disordered.

I spent the next day brooding over how much of the fault was mine. If I hadn't sworn at her, would she have run away? During my last few days in the village, I managed occasionally not to brood; there was packing to be done before I left for University, trees to be kicked in Delamere Forest, a whole string of curses it took me a quarter of an hour to shout one afternoon amid the fields, a kind of exorcism that didn't quite work. All week I avoided the village square. When I had to pass near it, I turned my face away.

Yet I was realizing that our relationship had been a bad mistake. That was why, on the night before I left, I strolled past Rebecca's house: to prove that I could. Beyond the ranks of trees her father was pounding the piano, a dark oppressive sound. I was turning away when Rebecca's violin began to sing. It sounded far more inspired than before.

I wasn't quite adjusted, after all. How dare she forget me so easily? Gusts of wind helped me storm toward the village; trees woke shouting, one after the other, beside the road. By the time I reached the square I was determined to speak to her.

Wind slammed the door of the telephone booth for me, and ruffled the directory. Had the wind also interfered with the line, or had the workmen left a fault? I couldn't rouse Rebecca's phone; beyond static vague as wind there was only a squabbling of faint squeaky voices. "Hello? Hello?" I demanded, and the voices seemed to parrot my words.

When I stepped out of the box I was free of Rebecca. Speaking to her could only have prolonged the unpleasantness. I gazed round the square, at the antique shop cramped by the other cramped buildings. I was free of the village too. Wind soared across the fields.

As I crossed the green, the wind made me feel I was sailing. Tomorrow I would be somewhere new. The clump of trees at the edge of the green lashed convulsively back and forth; I thought of a bird caught by the tail, unable to fly. Nothing stood among the trees.

The hedges were rocking, trying to erase the path with splashes of thicker dimness. The leaves sounded like rain, and seemed to scintillate like a million fragments of breaking glass. Large bluish patches raced through the clouds. Beyond the fields I thought I heard Delamere Forest, a deafening choir made faint by distance.

As I reached Mr. Ince's cottage, the sky was clearing.

Nevertheless I almost passed by, having observed casually that the trees were creaking, the grass of the unkempt garden was hissing. Had his tour exhausted him that he'd let the grass grow so long? Why, he had even left the theater standing beside the garden path—wedged there, as far as I could see, by a couple of large stones.

The theater wasn't deserted. Though there was no sign of Mr. Ince within the proscenium—I craned over the hedge, which pushed and clawed at me—Punch and Judy were on stage. Were they nailed to the ledge, and moving in the wind? Certainly their nodding and gesturing looked lifeless, all the more so when I made out that the paint of their faces and fixed eyes was peeling, yet I had a hallucinatory impression that they were actually fighting the wind. Apart from the rattle of wooden limbs on the ledge, they made no sound.

I was still peering, determined to make out exactly what I was seeing, when the wind dropped and the figures continued to move.

Perhaps there was still an imperceptible breeze; it wouldn't take much to make the figures totter and nod. But how could a breeze make Punch's cap writhe while failing to stir the miniature curtains? A moment later the edge of the cap gaped, and a snail crawled out down the face, leaving its trail across one flaking eye. The snail dangled from the set lips like a lolling tongue, then fell.

As I recoiled, a gust of wind rushed over the hedge and hurled the theater down so violently that the frame collapsed, leaving a canvas shape flattened on the grass. Above the wind I heard something, two things, fleeing through the long grass and scrabbling past the door of the cottage, which I now saw was open.

I should have fled, and then the village would have no hold on me, not even when I wake at four in the morning. But I was determined to find out what was happening—not least because Rebecca would never have let me.

I opened the gate, which had to be lifted on its crumbling hinges, and ventured up the path. Cold wet grass spilled over my ankles. A tree root bulged the path, a swollen muscle beneath cracked stone skin. The trees seemed to have closed even more oppressively about the cottage; I was unable to distinguish them from its walls.

I could see nothing through the small blackened windows. Though the entire cottage seemed to be creaking—no doubt that was the tossing of trees overhead—I made myself go to the door. It was stuck ajar, but when I pushed it, it swung wide.

It opened directly into a room. On the bare stone floor, beside a low table, Mr. Ince sat with his back to me, his legs splayed straight out before him, his hands gripping his thighs. He was facing a cold fireplace. Though the door had banged against the wall, he didn't stir.

Perhaps it was concern for him that made me enter, but still I was nervous enough to tiptoe quickly, ready to flee. Before I reached him I glimpsed the conditions under which he had been living—for how long? Both his clothes and the table were spattered with moldy food; the fireplace and the surrounding wall seemed to be trembling with soot; sagging wallpaper revealed cracks in the walls like the bulging crack in the path. Then I saw his face.

Was he alive? Barely, perhaps, but I hoped not when I realized why his face was more visible than the rest of the room; it was patchily whitish, like an old tree. How could he bear that if he were conscious? Still, that wasn't why I was backing away, too panicky to realize that I was retreating from the door. Two small things had crawled rattling from his pockets and were tugging, like terrified children, at his hands.

It was only wind that slammed the door, but I flinched back still farther. Perhaps the same wind moved Mr. Ince; perhaps I didn't really see his whitish mouth grimace in a parody of senile impatience—but he fell forward on his hands, splintering the objects within them.

My brain felt like a lump of metal. I couldn't grasp what was happening; I knew only that I had to get out of that room, from which the crowd of trees seemed to have drained all but a glimmer of light. Certainly the room was too dark for me to be sure that Mr. Ince had swayed upright again, that his arms were reaching out bundles that moved spasmodically. Nevertheless I grabbed a poker, which felt rotten with rust, from beside the fireplace before making for the door.

Did Mr. Ince stagger to his feet? Were his eyes gleaming, like those boils of sap that sometimes swell on trees? Amid the roar of foliage I thought something responded to his glare: something in a cupboard near the door. It sounded large and uncompleted, no longer much like falling brooms.

Perhaps the cottage door was wedged shut now. I fled to the farthest window and smashed the grimy pane. Panic helped me clamber through without wasting time in glancing back. As I tore myself free of a shard of glass, I thought I glimpsed a moist object swaying stiffly and laboriously out of the cupboard and across the room.

Next morning, after a sleepless night that seemed alive with creaking, I left home. A week later my mother's first letter gave me the news that Mr. Ince's cottage had burned down. The villagers thought he must have been careless with the fire; I suspected vandals might have seen the broken window. In any case I was glad, as glad as I could be while I was still so nervous. I hoped the trees had been destroyed too—for as I'd fled, past the eager tree root and the sprawled theater, I was sure that the branches had begun to twitch like the web of a spider robbed of its prey.

# Calling Card

DOROTHY HARRIS stepped off the pavement and into her hall. As she stooped groaning to pick up the envelopes the front door opened, opened, a yawn that wouldn't be suppressed. She wrestled it shut—she must ask Simon to see to it, though certainly not over Christmas—then she began to open the cards.

Here was Father Christmas, and here he was again, apparently after dieting. Here was a robin like a rosy apple with a beak, and here was an envelope whose handwriting staggered: Simon's and Margery's children, perhaps?

The card showed a church on a snowy hill. The hill was bare except for a smudge of ink. Though the card was unsigned, there was writing within. A Very Happy Christmas And A Prosperous New Year, the message should have said—but now it said A Very Harried Christmas And No New Year. She turned back to the picture, her hands shaking. It wasn't just a smudge of ink; someone had drawn a smeary cross on the hill: a grave.

Though the name on the envelope was a watery blur, the

address was certainly hers. Suddenly the house—the kitchen and living room, the two bedrooms with her memories stacked neatly against the walls—seemed far too large and dim. Without moving from the front door she phoned Margery.

"Is it Grandma?" Margery had to hush the children while she said, "You come as soon as you like, mummy."

Lark Lane was deserted. An unsold Christmas tree loitered in a shop doorway, a gargoyle craned out from the police station. Once Margery had moved away, the nearness of the police had been reassuring—not that Dorothy was nervous, like some of the old folk these days—but the police station was only a community center now.

The bus already sounded like a pub. She sat outside on the ferry, though the bench looked and felt like black ice. Lights fished in the Mersey, gulls drifted down like snowflakes from the muddy sky. A whitish object grabbed the rail, but of course it was only a gull. Nevertheless she was glad that Simon was waiting with the car at Woodside.

As soon as the children had been packed off to bed so that Father Christmas could get to work, she produced the card. It felt wet, almost slimy, though it hadn't before. Simon pointed out what she'd overlooked: the age of the stamp. "We weren't even living there then," Margery said. "You wouldn't think they would bother delivering it after sixty years."

"A touch of the Christmas spirit."

"I wish they hadn't bothered," Margery said. But her mother didn't mind now; the addressee must have died years ago. She turned the conversation to old times, to Margery's father. Later she gazed from her bedroom window, at the houses of Bebington sleeping in pairs. A man was creeping about the house, but it was only Simon, laden with presents.

In the morning the house was full of cries of delight, gleaming new toys, balls of wrapping paper big as cabbages. In the afternoon the adults, bulging with turkey and pudding, lolled in chairs. When Simon drove her home that night,

Dorothy noticed that the unsold Christmas tree was still there, a scrawny glistening shape at the back of the shop doorway. As soon as Simon left, she found herself thinking about the unpleasant card. She tore it up, then went determinedly to bed.

Boxing Day was her busiest time, what with cooking the second version of Christmas dinner, and making sure the house was impeccable, and hiding small presents for the children to find. She wished she could see them more often, but they and their parents had their own lives to lead.

An insect clung to a tinsel globe on the tree. When she reached out to squash the insect it wasn't there, neither on the globe nor on the floor. Could it have been the reflection of someone thin outside the window? Nobody was there now.

She liked the house best when it was full of laughter, and it would be again soon: "We'll get a sitter," Margery promised, "and first-foot you on New Year's Eve." She'd used to do that when she had lived at home—she'd waited outside at midnight of the Old Year so as to be the first to cross her mother's threshold. That reminded Dorothy to offer the children a holiday treat. Everything seemed fine, even when they went to the door to leave. "Grandma, someone's left you a present," little Denise cried.

Then she cried out, and dropped the package. Perhaps the wind had snatched it from her hands. As the package, which looked wet and moldy, struck the curb it broke open. Did its contents scuttle out and sidle away into the dark? Surely that was the play of the wind, which tumbled carton and wrapping away down the street.

Someone must have used her doorway for a wastebin, that was all. Dorothy lay in bed, listening to the wind which groped around the windowless side of the house, that faced onto the alley. She kept thinking she was on the ferry, backing away from the rail, forgetting that the rail was also behind her. Her nervousness annoyed her—she was acting like an old fogey—which was why, next afternoon, she walked to Otterspool promenade.

Gulls and planes sailed over the Mersey, which was deserted except for buoys. On the far bank, tiny towns and stalks of factory chimneys stood at the foot of an enormous frieze of clouds. Sunlight slipped through to Birkenhead and Wallasey, touching up the colors of microscopic streets; specks of windows glinted. She enjoyed none of this, for the slopping of water beneath the promenade seemed to be pacing her. Worse, she couldn't make herself go to the rail to prove that there was nothing.

Really, it was heartbreaking. One vicious card and she felt nervous in her own house. A blurred voice seemed to creep behind the carols on the radio, lowing out of tune. Next day she took her washing to Lark Lane, in search of distraction as much as anything.

The Westinghouse Laundromat was deserted. *O O O*, the washing machines said emptily. There was only herself, and her dervishes of clothes, and a black plastic bag almost as tall as she was. If someone had abandoned it, whatever its lumpy contents were, she could see why, for it was leaking; she smelled stagnant water. It must be a draft that made it twitch feebly. Nevertheless, if she had been able to turn off her machine she might have fled.

She mustn't grow neurotic. She still had friends to visit. The following day she went to a friend whose flat over-looked Wavertree Park. It was all very convivial—a rain-storm outside made the mince pies more warming, the chat flowed as easily as the whisky—but she kept glancing at the thin figure who stood in the park, unmoved by the downpour. The trails of rain on the window must be lending him their color, for his skin looked like a snail's.

Eventually the 68 bus, meandering like a drunkard's monologue, took her home to Aigburth. No, the man in the park hadn't really looked as though his clothes and his body had merged into a single grayish mass. Tomorrow she was taking the children for their treat, and that would clear her mind.

She took them to the aquarium. Piranhas sank stonily, their sides glittering like Christmas cards. Toads were bubbling lumps of tar. Finny humbugs swam, and darting fish wired with light. Had one of the tanks cracked? There seemed to be a stagnant smell.

In the museum everything was under glass: shrunken heads like sewn leathery handbags, a watchmaker's workshop, buses passing as though the windows were silent films. Here was a slum street, walled in by photographs of despair, real flagstones underfoot, overhung by streetlamps on brackets. She halted between a grid and a drinking fountain; she was trapped in the dimness between blind corners, and couldn't see either way. Why couldn't she get rid of the stagnant smell? Gray forlorn faces, pressed like specimens, peered out of the walls. "Come on, quickly," she said, pretending that only the children were nervous.

She was glad of the packed crowds in Church Street, even though the children kept letting go of her hands. But the stagnant smell was trailing her, and once, when she grabbed for little Denise's hand, she clutched someone else's, which felt soft and wet. It must have been nervousness which made her fingers seem to sink into the hand.

That night she returned to the aquarium and found she was locked in. Except for the glow of the tanks, the narrow room was oppressively dark. In the nearest tank a large dead fish floated toward her, out of weeds. Now she was in the tank, her nails scrabbling at the glass, and she saw that it wasn't a fish but a snail-colored hand, which closed spongily on hers. When she woke, her scream made the house sound very empty.

At least it was New Year's Eve. After tonight she could stop worrying. Why had she thought that? It only made her more nervous. Even when Margery phoned to confirm they would first-foot her, that reminded her how many hours she would be on her own. As the night seeped into the house, the emptiness grew.

A knock at the front door made her start, but it was only

the Harveys, inviting her next door for sherry and sand-wiches. While she dodged a sudden rainstorm, Mr. Harvey dragged at her front door, one hand through the letter box, until the latch clicked.

After several sherries Dorothy remembered something she'd once heard. "The lady who lived next door before me—didn't she have trouble with her son?"

"He wasn't right in the head. He got so he'd go for anyone, even if he'd never met them before. She got so scared of him she locked him out one New Year's Eve. They say he threw himself in the river, though they never found the body."

Dorothy wished she hadn't asked. She thought of the body, rotting in the depths. She must go home, in case Simon and Margery arrived. The Harveys were next door if she needed them.

The sherries had made her sleepy. Only the ticking of her clock, clipping away the seconds, kept her awake. Twenty past eleven. The splashing from the gutters sounded like wet footsteps pacing outside the window. She had never noticed she could smell the river in her house. She wished she had stayed longer with the Harveys; she would have been able to hear Simon's car.

Twenty to twelve. Surely they wouldn't wait until midnight. She switched on the radio for company. A master of ceremonies was making people laugh; a man was laughing thickly, sounding waterlogged. Was he a drunk in the street? He wasn't on the radio. She mustn't brood; why, she hadn't put out the sherry glasses; that was some-thing to do, to distract her from the intolerably measured counting of the clock, the silenced radio, the emptiness displaying her sounds—

Though the knock seemed enormously loud, she didn't start. They were here at last, though she hadn't heard the car. It was New Year's Day. She ran, and had reached the front door when the phone shrilled. That startled her so badly that she snatched the door open before lifting the receiver.

Nobody was outside—only a distant uproar of cheers and bells and horns—and Margery was on the phone. "We've been held up, mummy. There was an accident in the tunnel. We'll be over as soon as we can."

Then who had knocked? It must have been a drunk; she heard him stumbling beside the house, thumping on her window. He'd better take himself off, or she would call Mr. Harvey to deal with him. But she was still inside the doorway when she saw the object on her step.

Good God, was it a rat? No, just a shoe, so ancient that it looked stuffed with mold. It wasn't mold, only a rotten old sock. There was something in the sock, something that smelled of stagnant water and worse. She stooped to peer at it, and then she was struggling to close the door, fighting to make the latch click, no breath to spare for a scream. She'd had her first foot, and now—hobbling doggedly alongside the house, its hands slithering over the wall—here came the rest of the body.

## Above the
## World

NOBODY was at Reception when Knox came downstairs. The dinner gong hung mute in its frame; napkin pyramids guarded dining tables; in the lounge, chairs sat emptily. Nothing moved, except fish in the aquarium, fluorescent gleams amid water that bubbled like lemonade. The visitors' book lay open on the counter. He riffled the pages idly, seeking his previous visit. A Manchester address caught his attention: but the name wasn't his—not any longer. The names were those of his wife and the man.

It took him a moment to realize. They must have been married by then. So the man's name had been Tooley, had it? Knox hadn't cared to know. He was pleased to find that he felt nothing but curiosity. Why had she returned here— for a kind of second honeymoon, to exorcise her memories of him?

When he emerged, it was raining. That ought to wash the hills clean of all but the dedicated walkers; he might be alone up there—no perambulatory radios, no families marking their path with trailing children. Above the hotel, mist

228

wandered among the pines, which grew pale and blurred, a spiky frieze of gray, then solidified, regaining their green. High on the scree slope, the Bishop of Barf protruded like a single deformed tooth.

The sight seemed to halt time, to turn it back. He had never left the Swan Hotel. In a moment Wendy would run out, having had to go back for her camera or her rucksack or something. "I wasn't long, was I? The bus hasn't gone, has it? Oh dear, I'm sorry." Of course these impressions were nonsense: he'd moved on, developed since his marriage, defined himself more clearly—but it cheered him that his memories were cool, disinterested. Life advanced relentlessly, powered by change. The Bishop shone white only because climbers painted the pinnacle each year, climbing the steep scree with buckets of whitewash from the Swan.

Here came the bus. It would be stuffed with wet campers slow as turtles, their backs burdened with tubular scaffolding and enormous rucksacks. Only once had he suffered such a ride. Had nothing changed? Not the Swan, the local food, the unobtrusive service, the long white seventeenth-century building which had so charmed Wendy. He had a table to himself; if you wanted to be left alone, nobody would bother you. Tonight there would be venison, which he hadn't tasted since his honeymoon. He'd returned determined to enjoy the Swan and the walks, determined not to let memories deny him those pleasures— and he'd found that his qualms were groundless.

He strode down the Keswick road. Rain rushed over Bassenthwaite Lake and tapped on the hood of his windbreaker. Why did the stone wall ahead seem significant? Had Wendy halted there once, because the wall was singing? "Oh, look, aren't they beautiful." As he stooped toward the crevice, a cluster of hungry beaks had sprung out of the darkness, gaping. The glimpse had unnerved him: the inexorable growth of life, sprouting everywhere, even in stone. Moss choked the silent crevice now.

Somehow that image set him wondering where Wendy

and the man had died. Mist had caught them, high on one or other of the hills; they'd died of exposure. That much he had heard from a friend of Wendy's, who had grown aloof from him and who had seemed to blame him for entrusting Wendy to an inexperienced climber—as if Knox should have taken care of her even after the marriage! He hadn't asked for details. He'd felt relieved when Wendy had announced that she'd found someone else. Habit, familiarity, and introversion had screened them from each other well before they'd separated.

He was passing a camp in a field. He hadn't slept in a tent since early in his marriage, and then only under protest. Rain slithered down bright canvas. The muffled voices of a man and a woman paced him from tent to tent. Irrationally, he peered between the tents to glimpse them— but it must be a radio program. Though the voices sounded intensely engrossed in discussion, he could distinguish not a word. The camp looked deserted. Everyone must be under canvas, or walking.

By the time he reached Braithwaite village, the rain had stopped. Clouds paraded the sky; infrequent gaps let out June sunlight, which touched the heights of the surrounding hills. He made for the cafe at the foot of the Whinlatter Pass—not because Wendy had loved the little house, its homemade cakes and its shelves of books, but for something to read: he would let chance choose his reading. But the shop was closed. Beside it Coledale Beck pursued its wordless watery monologue.

Should he climb Grisedale Pike? He remembered the view from the summit, of Braithwaite and Keswick the colors of pigeons, white and gray amid the palette of fields. But climbers were toiling upward, toward the intermittent sun. Sometimes the spectacle of plodding walkers, hill boots creaking, sticks shoving at the ground, red faces puffing like trains in distress, made his climb seem a mechanical compulsion, absurd and mindless. Suppose the height was occupied by a class of children, heading like lemmings for the edge?

He'd go back to Barf: that would be lonely—unless one had Mr. Wainwright's guidebook, Barf appeared unclimbable. Returning through the village, he passed Braithwaite post office. That had delighted Wendy—a house just like the other small white houses in the row, except for the counter and grille in the front hall, beside the stairs. A postcard came fluttering down the garden path. Was that a stamp on its corner, or a patch of moss? Momentarily he thought he recognized the handwriting—but whose did it resemble? A breeze turned the card like a page. Where a picture might have been there was a covering of moss, which looked vaguely like a blurred view of two figures huddled together. The card slid by him, into the gutter, and lodged trembling in a grid, brandishing its message. Impulsively he made a grab for it—but before he could read the writing, the card fell between the bars.

He returned to the road to Thornthwaite. A sheen of sunlight clung to the macadam brows; hedges dripped dazzling silver. The voices still wandered about the deserted campsite, though now they sounded distant and echoing. Though their words remained inaudible, they seemed to be calling a name through the tents.

At Thornthwaite, only the hotel outshone the Bishop. As Knox glanced toward the coaching inn, Wendy appeared in his bedroom window. Of course it was a chambermaid—but the shock reverberated through him, for all at once he realized that he was staying in the room which he had shared with Wendy. Surely the proprietress of the Swan couldn't have intended this; it must be coincidence. Memories surged, disconcertingly vivid—collapsing happily on the bed after a day's walking, making love, not having to wake alone in the early hours. Just now, trudging along the road, he'd thought of going upstairs to rest. Abruptly he decided to spend the afternoon in walking.

Neither the hard road nor the soggy margin of Bassenthwaite Lake tempted him. He'd climb Barf, as he had intended. He didn't need Mr. Wainwright's book; he knew the way. Wendy had loved those handwritten guidebooks;

she'd loved searching through them for the self-portrait of
Mr. Wainwright which was always hidden among the
hand-drawn views—there he was, in Harris tweed, over-
looking Lanthwaite Wood. No, Knox didn't need those
books today.

The beginning of the path through Beckstones larch
plantation was easy. Soon he was climbing beside Beckstones Gill, his ears full of its intricate liquid clamor as the
stream tumbled helplessly downhill, confined in its rocky
groove. But the path grew steep. Surely it must have been
elsewhere that Wendy had run ahead, mocking his slowness,
while he puffed and cursed. By now most of his memories
resembled anecdotes he'd overheard or had been told—
blurred, lacking important details, sometimes contradictory.

He rested. Around him larches swayed numerous limbs,
engrossed in their tethered dance. His breath eased; he
ceased to be uncomfortably aware of his pulse. He stumped
upward, over the path of scattered slate. On both sides of
him, ferns protruded from decay. Their highest leaves
were wound into a ball, like green caterpillars on stalks.

A small rockface blocked the path. He had to scramble
across to the continuation. Lichen made the roots of trees
indistinguishable from the rock. His foot slipped; he
slithered, banging his elbow, clutching for handholds. Good
Lord, the slope was short, at worst he would turn his
ankle, he could still grab hold of rock, in any case someone was coming, he could hear voices vague as the stream's
rush that obscured them. At last he was sure he was safe,
though at the cost of a bruised hip. He sat and cursed his
pounding heart. He didn't care who heard him—but perhaps nobody did, for the owners of the voices never
appeared.

He struggled upward. The larches gave way to spruce
firs. Fallen trunks, splintered like bone, hindered his
progress. How far had he still to climb? He must have
labored half a mile by now; it felt like more. The forest
had grown oppressive. Elaborate lichens swelled brittle
branches; everywhere he looked, life burgeoned parasitically,

consuming the earth and the forest, a constant and ruthless renewal. He was sweating, and the clammy chill of the place failed to cool him.

Silence seized him. He could hear only the restless creaking of trees. For a long time he had been unable to glimpse the Swan; the sky was invisible, too, except in fragments caged by branches. All at once, as he climbed between close banks of mossy earth and rock, he yearned to reach the open. He felt suffocated, as though the omnipresent lichen were thick fog. He forced himself onward, panting harshly.

Pain halted him—pain that transfixed his heart and paralyzed his limbs with shock. His head felt swollen, burning, deafened by blood. Beyond that uproar, were there voices? Could he cry for help? But he felt that he might never draw another breath.

As suddenly as it had attacked him, the pain was gone, though he felt as if it had burned a hollow where his heart had been. He slumped against rock. His ears rang as though metal had been clapped over them. Oh, God, the doctor had been right; he must take things easy. But if he had to forgo rambling, he would have nothing left that was worthwhile. At last he groped upward out of the dank trough of earth, though he was still light-headed and unsure of his footing. The path felt distant and vague.

He reached the edge of the forest without further mishap. Beyond it, Beckstones Gill rushed over broken stones. The sky was layered with gray clouds. Across the stream, on the rise to the summit, bracken shone amid heather.

He crossed the stream and climbed the path. Below him the heathery slope plunged toward the small valley. A few crumbs of boats floated on Bassenthwaite. A constant quivering ran downhill through the heather; the wind dragged at his windbreaker, whose fluttering deafened him. He felt unnervingly vulnerable, at the mercy of the gusts. His face had turned cold as bone. Sheep dodged away from him. Their swiftness made his battle with the air seem ridiculous, frustrating. He had lost all sense of time before he reached the summit—where he halted, entranced. At last his toil had meaning.

The world seemed laid out for him. Light and shadow drifted stately over the hills, which reached toward clouds no vaster than they. Across Bassenthwaite, hills higher than his own were only steps on the ascent to Skiddaw, on whose deceptively gentle outline gleamed patches of snow. A few dots, too distant to have limbs, crept along that ridge. The hills glowed with all the colors of foliage, grass, heather, bracken, except where vast tracts of rock broke through. Drifts of shadow half-absorbed the colors; occasional sunlight renewed them.

The landscape was melting; he had to blink. Was he weeping, or had the wind stung his eyes? He couldn't tell; the vastness had charmed away his sense of himself. He felt calm, absolutely unselfconscious. He watched light advancing through Beckstones plantation, possessing each successive rank of foliage. When he gazed across the lake again, that sight had transfigured the landscape.

Which lake was that on the horizon? He had never before noticed it. It lay like a fragment of slate, framed by two hills dark as storms—but above it, clouds were opening. Blue sky shone through the tangle of gray; veils of light descended from the ragged gap. The lake began to glow from within, intensely calm. Beyond it fields and trees grew clear, minute and luminous. Yes, he was weeping.

After a while he sat on a rock. Its coldness was indistinguishable from his own stony chill. He must go down shortly. He gazed out for a last view. The hills looked smooth, alluringly gentle; valleys were trickles of rock. He held up his finger for a red bug to crawl along. Closer to him, red dots were scurrying; ladybirds, condemned to explore the maze of grass blades, to change course at each intersection. Their mindless urgency dismayed him.

They drew his gaze to the heather. He gazed deep into a tangled clump, at the breathtaking variety of colors, the intricacies of growth. As many must be hidden in each

patch of heather: depths empty of meaning, and intended
for no eye. All around him plants reproduced shapes
endlessly: striving for perfection, or compelled to repeat
themselves without end? If his gaze had been microscopic,
he would have seen the repetitions of atomic particles,
mindlessly clinging and building, possessed by the compulsion of matter to form patterns.

Suddenly it frightened him—he couldn't tell why. He
felt unsafe. Perhaps it was the mass of cloud which had
closed overhead like a stone lid. The colors of the summit
had turned lurid, threatening. He headed back toward the
wood. The faces of sheep gleamed like bone—he had
never noticed before how they resembled munching skulls.
A group of heads, chewing mechanically, glared white
against the sky and kept their gaze on him.

He was glad to cross the stream, though he couldn't feel
the water. He must hurry down before he grew colder.
The hush of the woods embraced him. Had a sheep followed him? No, it was only the cry of a decaying trunk.
He slipped quickly down the path, which his feet seemed
hardly to touch.

The movement of silver-green lattices caged him.
Branches and shadows swayed everywhere, entangled. The
tips of some of the firs were luminously new. Winds
stalked the depths of the forest, great vague forms on
creaking stilts. Scents of growth and decay accompanied
him. When he grabbed a branch to make sure of his
footing, it broke, scattering flakes of lichen.

Again the forest grew too vivid; the trees seemed victims of the processes of growth, sucked dry by the lichen
which at the same time lent them an elaborate patina of
life. Wherever he looked, the forest seemed unbearably
intricate. How, among all that, could he glimpse initials?
Somehow they had seized his attention before he knew
what they were. They were carved on a cracked and
wrinkled tree: Wendy's initials, and the man's.

Or were they? Perhaps they were only cracks in the
bark. Of course she and the man might well have climbed

up here—but the more Knox squinted, the less clear the letters seemed. He couldn't recapture the angle of vision at which they had looked unmistakable.

He was still pacing back and forth before the trunk, as though trapped in a ritual, when stealthy movement made him turn. Was it the shifting of gray trees beneath the lowering largely unseen sky? No—it was a cloud or mist, descending swiftly from the summit, through the woods.

He glanced ahead for the path—and, with a shock that seemed to leave him hollow, realized that it was not there. Nor was it visible behind him as far back as the wall of mist. His reluctant fascination with the forest had lured him astray.

He strode back toward the mist, hushing his doubts. Surely the path couldn't be far. But the mist felt thick as icy water, and blinded him. He found himself slithering on decay toward a fall which, though invisible, threatened to be steep. A grab at a crumbling trunk saved him; but when he'd struggled onto safer ground, he could only retreat toward the tree which he had thought was inscribed.

He must press on, outdistancing the mist, and try to head downward. Wasn't there a forest road below, quite close? But whenever he found an easy slope, it would become abruptly dangerous, often blocked by treacherous splintered logs. He was approaching panic. As much as anything, the hollow at the center of himself dismayed him. He had tended to welcome it when it had grown there, in his marriage and afterward; it had seemed safe, invulnerable. Now he found he had few inner resources with which to sustain himself.

The mist was only yards away. It had swallowed all the faint sounds of the wood. If he could only hear the stream, or better still a human voice, a vehicle on the forest road—if only he had gone back to the hotel for his whistle and compass— But there was a sound. Something was blundering toward him. Why was he indefinably distressed, rather than heartened?

Perhaps because the mist obscured it as it scuttled down

the slope toward him; perhaps because it sounded too small for an adult human being, too swift, too lopsided. He thought of a child stumbling blindly down the decayed slope. But what child would be so voiceless? As it tumbled limping through the mist, Knox suppressed an urge to flee. He saw the object stagger against a misty root, and collapse there. Before he had ventured forward he saw that it was only a rucksack.

Yet he couldn't quite feel relieved. The rucksack was old, discolored and patched with decay; mist drained it of color. Where had it come from? Who had abandoned it, and why? It still moved feebly, as though inhabited. Of course there was a wind: the mist was billowing. Nevertheless he preferred not to go closer. The blurred tentative movements of the overgrown sack were unpleasant, somehow.

Still, perhaps the incident was opportune. It had made him glance upward for an explanation. He found none—but he caught sight of a summit against the clouds. It wasn't Barf, for between the confusion of trees he could just distinguish two cairns, set close together. If he could reach them, he ought to be able to see his way more clearly. Was he hearing muffled voices up there? He hoped so, but hadn't time to listen.

He wasn't safe yet. The mist had slowed, but was still pursuing him. The slope above him was too steep to climb. He retreated between the trees, avoiding slippery roots which glistened dull silver, glancing upward constantly for signs of a path. For a while he lost sight of the unknown summit. Only a glimpse of the cairns against the darkening sky mitigated his panic. Were they cairns, or figures sitting together? No, they were the wrong color for people.

Above him the slope grew steeper. Worse, twilight was settling like mist into the woods. He glared downhill, but the fall was dim and precipitous; there was no sign of a road, only the gray web of innumerable branches. He groped onward, careless of his footing, desperate to glimpse

a way. Surely a path must lead to the cairns. But would he
reach it before dark? Could he heave himself up the slope
now, using trees for handholds? Wait: wasn't that a path
ahead, trailing down between the firs? He stumbled forward,
afraid to run in case he slipped. He reached out to grab a
tree, to lever himself past its trap of roots. But his fingers
recoiled—the encrusted glimmering bark looked unnervingly like a face.

He refused to be reminded of anyone. He clung to the
hollow within himself and fought off memories. Yet as he
passed close to the next tree, he seemed to glimpse the hint
of a face composed of cracks in the bark, and of twilight.
His imagination was conspiring with the dimness, that was
all—but why, as he grasped a trunk to thrust himself
onward, did each patch of lichen seem to suggest a face?
The more closely he peered, enraged by his fears, the
smaller and more numerous the swarming faces seemed.
Were there many different faces, or many versions of a
couple? Their expressions, though vague, seemed numerous and disturbing.

For a moment he was sure that he couldn't back away—
that he must watch until the light was entirely gone, must
glimpse faces yet smaller and clearer and more numerous.
Panic hurled him away from the lichen, and sent him
scrabbling upward. His fingers dug into decay; ferns writhed
and snapped when he grabbed them; the surrounding dimness teemed with faces. He kicked himself footholds, gouged
the earth with his heels. He clutched at roots, which
flaked, moist and chill. More than once he slithered back
into the massing darkness. But his panic refused to be
defeated. At last, as twilight merged the forest into an
indistinguishable crowd of dimness, he scrambled up a
slope that had commenced to be gentle, to the edge of the
trees.

As soon as he had done so, his triumph collapsed beneath dismay. Even if he glimpsed a path from the summit,
night would engulf it before he could make his way down.
The sky was blackening. Against it loomed two hunched

forms, heads turned to him. Suddenly joy seized him. He could hear voices—surely the sound was more than the muttering of wind. The two forms were human. They must know their way down, and he could join them.

He scrambled upward. Beyond the trees, the slope grew steep again; but the heather provided easy holds, though his clambering felt almost vertical. The voices had ceased; perhaps they had heard him. But when he glanced up, the figures hadn't moved. A foot higher, and he saw that the faces turned to him were patches of moss; the figures were gray, composed roughly of fragments of slate. They were cairns, after all. It didn't matter: companionship waited at the summit; he'd heard voices, he was sure that he'd heard them, please let him have done so. And indeed, as he struggled up the last yards of the slope, the two gray figures rose with a squeaking and rattling of slate, and advanced heavily toward him.

# *Baby*

WHEN the old woman reached the shops Dutton began to lag farther behind. Though his hands were as deep in his pockets as they could go, they were shaking. It's all right, he told himself, stay behind. The last thing you want is for her to notice you now. But he knew he'd fallen behind because he was losing his nerve.

The November wind blundered out of the side streets and shook him. As he hurried across each intersection, head trembling deep in his collar, he couldn't help searching the doorways for Tommy, Maud, even old Frank, anyone with a bottle. But nobody sat against the dull paint of the doors, beneath the bricked-up windows; nothing moved except tangles of sodden paper and leaves. No, he thought, trying to seize his mind before it began to shake like his body. He hadn't stayed sober for so long to lapse now, when he was so close to what he'd stayed sober for.

She'd drawn ahead; he was four blocks behind now. Not far enough behind. He'd better dodge into the next side street before she looked back and saw him. But then one of the shopkeepers might see him hiding and call the police. Or she might turn somewhere while he was hiding, and he would lose her. The stubble on his cheeks crawled with sweat, which clung to the whole of his body; he couldn't tell if it was boiling or frozen. For a couple of steps he limped rapidly to catch up with the old woman, then he held himself back. She was about to look at him.

Fear flashed through him as if his sweat were charged. He made himself gaze at the shops, at the stalls outside: water chestnuts, capsicums, aubergines, dhal—the little notices on sticks said so, but they were alien to him; they didn't help him hold onto his mind. Their price flags fluttered, tiny and nerve-racking as the prickling of his cheeks.

Then he heard the pram. Its sound was deep in the blustering of the wind, but it was unmistakable. He'd heard it too often, coming toward the house, fading into the room below his. It sounded like the start of a rusty metal yawn, abruptly interrupted by a brief squeal, over and over. It was the sound of his goal, of the reason why he'd stayed sober all night. He brought the pockets of his coat together, propping the iron bar more securely against his chest inside the coat.

She had reached the maze of marshy ground and broken houses beyond the shops. At last, Dutton thought, and began to run. The bar thumped his chest until it bruised. His trousers chafed his thighs like sandpaper, his calves throbbed, but he ran stumbling past the morose shoppers, the defiantly cheerful shopkeepers, the continuing almost ghostly trade of the street. As soon as she was out of sight of the shops, near one of the dilapidated houses, he would have her. At once he halted, drenched in sweat. He couldn't do it.

He stood laughing mirthlessly at himself as newspapers swooped at him. He was going to kill the old woman, was he? Him, who hadn't been able to keep a job for more than a week for years? Him, who had known he wasn't going to keep a job before he started working at it, until the social security had reluctantly agreed with him? Him, who could boast of nothing but the book he cashed weekly at the post office? He was going to kill her?

His mind sounded like his mother. Too much so to dishearten him entirely: it wasn't him, he could answer back. He remembered when he'd started drinking seriously. He'd felt then that if the social security took an interest in him he would be able to hold down a job; but they hadn't bothered to conceal their indifference, and soon after that they'd given him his book. But now it was different. He didn't need anyone's encouragement. He'd proved that by not touching a drink since yesterday afternoon. If he could do that, he could do anything.

He shoved past a woman wheeling a pramful of groceries, and ran faster to outdistance the trembling that spread through his body. His shoes crackled faintly with the plastic bags in which his feet were wrapped. He was going to kill her, because of the contemptuous way she'd looked at him in the hall, exactly as his mother had used to; because while he was suffering poverty, she had chosen worse and flaunted her happiness; because, although her coat had acquired a thick hem of mud from trailing, though the coat gaped like frayed lips between her shoulders, she was always smiling secretly, unassailably. He let the thoughts seep through his mind, gathering darkly and heavily in the depths. He *was* going to kill her—because she looked too old for life, too ugly and wizened to live; because she walked as if to do so were a punishment; because her smile must be a paralyzed grimace of pain, after all; because her tuneless crooning often kept him awake half the night, though he stamped on her ceiling; because he needed her secret wealth. She had turned and was coming back toward him, past the shops.

His face huddled into his collar as he stumbled away, across the road. That was enough. He'd tried, he couldn't do more. If circumstances hadn't saved him he would have failed. He would have been arrested, and for nothing. He shifted the bar uneasily within his coat, anxious to be rid of it. He gazed at the burst husk of a premature firework, lying trampled on the pavement. It reminded him of himself. He turned hastily as the old woman came opposite him, and stared in a toy-shop window.

An orange baby with fat wrinkled dusty joints stared back at him. Beside it, reflected in a dark gap among the early Christmas toys and fireworks for tomorrow night, he saw the old woman. She had pushed her pram alongside the greengrocer's stall; now she let it go. Dutton peered closer, frowning.

He was sure she hadn't pushed the pram before letting go. Yet it had sped away, past the greengrocer's stall, then halted suddenly. He was still peering when she wheeled it out of the reflection, into the depths full of toys. He began to follow her at once, hardly shaking. Even if he hadn't needed her wealth to give him a chance in life, he had to know what was in that pram.

What wealth? How did he know about it? He struggled to remember. Betty, no, Maud had told him, the day she hadn't drunk too much to recall. She'd read about the old woman in the paper, years ago: about how she'd been swindled by a man whom nobody could trace. She'd given the man her money, her jewels, her house, and her relatives had set the police on him. But then she had been in the paper herself, saying she hadn't been swindled at all, that it was none of their business what she'd gained from the trade; and Maud supposed they'd believed her, because that was the last she had seen of the woman in the paper.

But soon after that Maud had seen her in town, wheeling her pram and smiling to herself. She'd often seen her in the crowds, and then the old woman had moved into the room beneath Dutton, older and wearier now but still smiling. "That shows she got something out of it," Maud said. "What else has she got to smile about? But where she keeps it, that's the thing." She'd shown Dutton a bit she had kept of the paper, and it did look like the old woman, smiling up from a blot of fluff and sweat.

The old woman had nearly reached home now. Dutton

stumbled over a paving stone that had cracked and collapsed like ice on a pool. The iron bar nudged his chest impatiently, tearing his skin. Nearly there now. He had to remember why he was doing this. If he could hold all that in his mind he would be able to kill her. He muttered; his furred tongue crawled in his mouth like a dying caterpillar. He must remember.

He'd gone into her room one day. A month ago, two? Never mind! he thought viciously. He'd been drunk enough to take the risk, not too drunk to make sense of what he'd found. He'd staggered into the house and straight into her room. Since he knew she didn't lock the door, he'd expected to find nothing; yet he was astonished to find so little. In the strained light through the encrusted window, stained patches of wallpaper slumped and bulged. The bed knelt at one corner, for a leg had given way; the dirty sheets had slipped down to conceal the damage. Otherwise the room was bare, no sign even of the pram. The pram. Of course.

He had tried to glimpse what was in the pram. He'd pressed his cheek against his window whenever he heard her approaching, but each time the pram's hood was in the way. Once he'd run downstairs and peered into the pram as she opened her door, but she had pulled the pram away like a chair in a practical joke, and gazed at him with amazement, amusement, profound contempt.

And last week, in the street, he'd been so drunk he had reeled at her and wrenched the pram's handle from her grasp. He'd staggered around to look beneath the hood— but she had already kicked the pram, sending it sailing down a canted side road, and had flown screaming at him, her nails aimed straight for his eyes. When he'd fallen in the gutter she had turned away, laughing with the crowd. As he had pushed himself unsteadily to his feet, his hand deep in sodden litter, he was sure he'd glimpsed the pram halting inches short of crashing into a wall, apparently by itself.

He had decided then, as his hand slithered in the pulp.

In his mind she'd joined the people who were laughing inwardly at him: the social security, the clerks in the post office. Only she was laughing aloud, encouraging the crowd to laugh. He would kill her for that. He'd persuaded himself for days that he would. She'd soon have no reason to laugh at his poverty, at the book he hid crumpled in his hand as he waited in the post office. And last night, writhing on his bed amid the darkly crawling walls, listening to her incessant contented wailing, he'd known that he would kill her.

He would kill her. Now.

He was running, his hands gloved in his pockets and swinging together before him at the end of the metal bar, running past a shop whose windows were boarded up with dislocated doors, past the faintly whistling waste ground and, beneath his window in the side of the house, a dormant restlessly creaking bonfire taller than himself. She must have reached her room by now.

The street was deserted. Bricks lay in the roadway, unmoved by the tugging of the wind. He wavered on the front steps, listening for sounds in the house. The baby wasn't crying in the cellar, which meant those people must be out; nobody was in the kitchen; even if the old man in the room opposite Dutton's were home, he was deaf. Dutton floundered into the hall, then halted as if at the end of a chain.

He couldn't do it here. He stared at the smudged and faded whorls of the wallpaper, the patterns of numbers scribbled above the patch where the telephone had used to be, the way the stairs turned sharply in the gloom just below the landing. The bar hung half out of his coat. He could have killed her beyond the shops, but this was too familiar. He couldn't imagine a killing here, where everything suffocated even the thought of change—everything, even the creaking of the floorboards.

The floorboards were creaking. She would hear them. All at once he felt he was drowning in sweat. She would come out and see the iron bar, and know what he'd meant to do.

She would call the police. He pulled out the bar, tearing a buttonhole, and blundered into her room.

The old woman was at the far end of the room, her back to him. She was turning away from the pram, stooped over as if holding an object against her belly. From her mouth came the sound that had kept him awake so often, a contented lulling sound. For the first time he could hear what she was saying. "Baby," she was crooning, "baby." She might have been speaking to a lover or a child.

In a moment she would see him. He limped swiftly forward, his padding footsteps puffing up dust to discolor the dim light more, and swung the iron bar at her head.

He'd forgotten how heavy the bar was. It pulled him down toward her, by his weakened arms. He felt her head give, and heard a muffled crackling beneath her hair. Momentarily, as he clung to the bar as it rested in her head against the wall, he was face to face with her, with her eyes and mouth as they worked spasmodically and went slack.

He recoiled, most of all because there was the beginning of a wry smile in her eyes until they faded. Then she fell with a great flat thud, shockingly heavy and loud. Dust rolled out from beneath her, rising about Dutton's face as he fought a sneeze, settling on the dark patch that was spreading over the old woman's colorless hair.

Dutton closed his eyes and gripped the bar, propping it against the wall, resting his forehead on the lukewarm metal. His stomach writhed, worse than in the mornings, sending convulsions through his whole body. At last he managed to open his eyes and look down again. She lay with one cheek in the dust, her hair darkening, her arms sprawled on either side of her. They had been holding nothing to her belly. In the dim light she looked like a sleeping drunk, a sack, almost nothing at all. Dutton remembered the crackling of her head and found himself giggling hysterically, uncontrollably.

He had to be quick. Someone might hear him. Stepping

over her, he unbuttoned the pram's apron and pulled it back.

At first he couldn't make out what the pram contained. He had to crane himself over, holding his body back from obscuring the light. The pram was full of groceries—cabbage, sprouts, potatoes. Dutton shook his head, bewildered, suspecting his eyes of practical joking. He pulled the pram over to the window, remembering only just in time to disguise his hand in the rag he kept as a handkerchief.

The windowpanes looked like the back of a fireplace. Dutton rubbed them with his handkerchief but succeeded only in smudging the grime. He peered into the pram again. It was still almost packed with groceries; only, near the head of the pram, there was a clear space about a foot in diameter. It was empty.

He began to throw out the vegetables. Potatoes trundled thundering over the floorboards, a rolling cabbage scooped up dust in its leaves. The vegetables were fresh, yet she had entered none of the shops, and he was sure he hadn't seen her filching. He was trying to recall what in fact he had seen when his wrapped hand touched something at the bottom of the pram: something hard, round, several round objects, a corner beneath one, a surface that struck cold through his handkerchief—glass. He lifted the corner and the framed photograph came up out of the darkness, its round transparent cargo rolling. They almost rolled off before he laid the photograph on the corner of the pram, for his grip had slackened as the globes rolled apart to let the old woman stare up at him.

She was decades younger, and there was no doubt she was the woman Maud had shown him. And here were her treasures, delivered to him on her photograph as if on a tray. He grinned wildly and stooped to admire them. He froze in that position, hunched over in disbelief.

There were four of the globes. They were transparent, full of floating specks of light that gradually settled. He stared numbly at them. Close to his eyes threads of sunlight through the window selected sparkling motes of dust,

then let them go. Surely he must be wrong. Surely this
wasn't what he'd suffered all night for. But he could see
no other explanation. The old woman had been wholly
mad. The treasures that had kept her smiling, the treasures
she had fought him for, were nothing but four fake snow-
storm globes of the kind he'd seen in dozens of toy shops.

He convulsed as if seized by nausea. With his wrapped
hand he swept all four globes off the photograph, snarling.

They took a long time to fall. They took long enough
for him to notice, and to stare at them. They seemed to be
sinking through the air as slowly as dust, turning enormously like worlds, filling the whole of his attention. In
each of them a faint image was appearing: in one a
landscape, in another a calm and luminous face.

It must be the angle at which you held them to the light.
They were falling so slowly he could catch them yet, could
catch the face and the landscape which he could almost
see, the other images which trembled at the very edge of
recognition, images like a sweet and piercing song, approaching from inaudibility. They were falling slowly—
yet he was only making to move toward them when the
globes smashed on the floor, their fragments parting like
petals. He heard no sound at all.

He stood shaking in the dimness. He had had enough.
He felt his trembling hands wrap the stained bar in his
handkerchief. The rag was large enough; it had always
made a companionable bulge in his pocket. He sniffed,
and wondered if the old woman's pockets were empty. It
was only when he stooped to search that he saw the
enormous bulge in her coat, over her belly.

Part of his mind was warning him, but his fingers
wrenched eagerly at her buttons. He threw her coat open,
in the dust. Then he recoiled, gasping. Beneath the faded
flowers of her dress she was heavily pregnant.

She couldn't be. Who would have touched her? Her coat
hadn't bulged like that in the street, he was sure. But there
was no mistaking the swelling of her belly. He pushed

himself away from her, his hands against the damp wall. The light was so dim and thick he felt he was struggling in mud. He gazed at the swollen lifeless body, then he turned and ran.

Still there was nobody in the street. He stumbled to the waste ground and thrust the wrapped bar deep in the bonfire. Tomorrow night the blood would be burned away. As he limped through the broken streets, the old woman's room hung about him. At last, in a doorway two streets distant, he found Tommy.

He collapsed on the doorstep and seized the bottle Tommy offered him. The cloying wine poured down his throat; bile rose to meet it, but he choked them down. As the wind blustered at his chest it seemed to kindle the wine in him. There was no pregnant corpse in the settling dust, no room thick with dim light, no crackling head. He tilted his head back, gulping.

Tommy was trying to wrest the bottle from him. The neck tapped viciously against Dutton's teeth, but he held it between his lips and thrust his tongue up to hurry the last drops; then he hurled the bottle into the gutter, where it smashed, echoing between the blank houses. As he threw it, a police car entered the road.

Dutton sat inert while the policemen strolled toward him. Tommy was levering himself away rapidly, crutch humping. Dutton knew one of the policemen: Constable Wayne. "We can't pretend we didn't see that, Billy," Wayne told him. "Be a good boy and you'll be out in the morning."

The wine smudged the world around Dutton for a while. The cell wall was a screen on which he could put pictures to the sounds of the police station: footsteps, shouts, telephones, spoons rattling in mugs. His eyes were coaxing the graffiti from beneath the new paint when, distant but clear, he heard a voice say, "What about Billy Dutton?"

"Him knock an old woman's head in?" Wayne's voice said. "I don't reckon he could do that, even sober. Besides,

I brought him in around the time of death. He wasn't capable of handling a bottle, let alone a murder.''

Later a young policeman brought Dutton a mug of tea and some aging cheese sandwiches wrapped in greaseproof paper, then stood frowning with mingled disapproval and embarrassment while Dutton was sick. Yet though Dutton lay rocking with nausea for most of the night, though frequently he stood up and roamed unsteadily about the cell and felt as if his nausea was sinking deep within him like dregs, always he could hear Wayne's words. The words freed him of guilt. He had risked, and lost, and that was all. When he left the cell he could return to his old life. He would buy a bottle and celebrate with Tommy, Maud, even old Frank.

He could hear an odd sound far out in the night, separate from the musings of the city, the barking dogs, the foghorns on the Mersey. He propped himself on one elbow to listen. Now that it was coming closer he could make it out: a sound like an interrupted metal yawn. It was groaning toward him; it was beside him. He awoke shouting and saw Wayne opening his cell. It must have been the hinges of the door.

''It's about time you saw someone who can help you,'' Wayne said.

Perhaps he was threatening to give Dutton's address to a social worker or someone like that. Let him, Dutton thought. They couldn't force their way into his room so long as he didn't do wrong. He was sure that was true; it must be.

Three doors away from the police station was a pub, a Wine Lodge. They must have let him sleep while he could; the Wine Lodge was already open. Dutton bought a bottle and crossed to the opposite pavement, which was an edge of the derelict area toward which he'd pursued the old woman.

The dull sunlight seemed to seep out of the ruined walls. Dutton trudged over the orange mud, past stagnant puddles in the shape of footprints; water welled up around his shoes, the mud sucked them loudly. As soon as there were walls between him and the police station he unstoppered the bottle and drank. He felt like a flower opening to the sun. Still walking, he hadn't lowered the bottle when he caught sight of old Frank sitting on the step of a derelict house.

"Here's Billy," Frank shouted, and the others appeared in the empty window. At the edge of the waste land a police car was roving; that must be why they had taken refuge.

They came forward as best they could to welcome him. "You won't be wanting to go home tonight," Maud said.

"Why not?" In fact there was no reason why he shouldn't know—he could have told them what he'd overheard Wayne discussing—but he wouldn't take that risk. They were ready to suspect anyone, these people; you couldn't trust them.

"Someone did for that old woman," Frank said. "The one in the room below you. Bashed her head in and took her pram."

Dutton's throat closed involuntarily; wine welled up from his lips, around the neck of the bottle. "Took her pram?" he coughed, weeping. "Are you sure?"

"Sure as I was standing outside when they carried her out. The police knew her, you know, her and her pram. They used to look in to make sure she was all right. She wouldn't have left her pram anywhere, they said. Someone took it."

"So you won't be wanting to go home tonight. You can warm my bed if you like," Maud said toothlessly, lips wrinkling.

"What would anyone want to kill her for?" Betty said, dragging her gray hair over the scarred side of her face. "She hadn't got anything."

"She had once. She was rich. She bought something with all that," Maud said.

"Don't care. She didn't have anything worth killing her for. Did she, Billy?"

"No," Dutton said, and stumbled hurriedly on: "There wasn't anything in that pram. I know. I looked in it once when she was going in her room. She was poorer than us."

"Unless she was a witch," Maud said.

Dutton shook the bottle to quicken the liquor. In a moment it would take hold of him completely, he'd be floating on it, Maud's words would drift by like flotsam on a warm sea. "What?" he said.

"Unless she was a witch. Then she could have given everything she owned, and her soul as well, to that man they never found, and still have had something for it that nobody could see, or wouldn't understand if they did see." She panted, having managed her speech, and drank.

"That woman was a witch right enough," Tommy said, challenging the splintered floor with his crutch. "I used to go by there at night and hear her singing to herself. There was something not right there."

"I sing," Frank said, standing up menacingly, and did so: "Rock of Ages." "Am I a witch, eh? Am I a witch?"

"They weren't hymns she was singing, I'll be bound. If I hadn't seen her in the street I'd have said she was a darky. Jungle music, it was. Mumbo-jumbo."

"She was singing to her baby," Dutton said loosely.

"She didn't have a baby, Billy," Maud said. "Only a pram."

"She was going to have one."

"You're the man who should know, are you?" Frank demanded. "She could have fooled me. She was flat as a pancake when they carried her out. Flat as a pancake."

Dutton stared at Frank for as long as he could, before he had to look away from the deformed strawberry of the man's nose. He seemed to be telling the truth. Two memories were circling Dutton, trying to perch on his thoughts: a little girl who'd been peering in the old woman's window one day, suddenly running away and calling back— inappropriately, it had seemed at the time—"Fat cow";

the corpse on the dusty floor, indisputably pregnant even in the dim light. "Flat as a pancake," Frank repeated.

Dutton was still struggling to understand when Maud said, "What's that?"

Dutton could hear nothing but the rushing of his blood. "Sounds like a car," Betty said.

"Too small for a car. Needs oiling, whatever it is."

What were they talking about? Why were they talking about things he couldn't understand, that he couldn't even hear, that disturbed him? "What?" Dutton yelled.

They all stared at him, focusing elaborately, and Tommy thumped his crutch angrily. "It's gone now," Maud said at last.

There was a silence until Betty said sleepily, "If she was a witch where was her familiar?"

"Her what?" Dutton said, as the bottle blurred and dissolved above his eyes. She didn't know what she was talking about. Nor did he, he shouted at himself. Nor did he.

"Her familiar. A kind of, you know, creature that would do things for her. Bring her food, that kind of thing. A cat, or something. She hadn't anything like that. She wouldn't have been able to hide it."

Nowhere to hide it, Dutton thought. In her pram—but her pram had been empty. The top of his head was rising, floating away; it didn't matter. Betty's hand wobbled at the edge of his vision, spilling wine toward him. He grabbed the bottle as her eyes closed. He tried to drink but couldn't find his mouth. Somehow he managed to stopper the bottle with his finger, and a moment later was asleep.

When he awoke he was alone in the dark.

Among the bricks that were bruising his chest was the bottle, still glued to his finger. He clambered to his feet, deafened by the clattering of bricks, and dug the bottle into his pocket for safety, finger and all. He groped his way out of the house, sniffing, searching vainly for his handkerchief. A wall reeled back from him and he fell, scraping his shoulder. Eventually he reached the doorway.

Night had fallen. Amid the mutter of the city, fireworks were already sputtering; distant chimneys sprang up momentarily against a spray of white fire. Far ahead, between the tipsily shifting walls, the lights of the shops blinked faintly at Dutton. He took a draft to fend off the icy plucking of the wind, then he stuffed the bottle in his pocket and made for the lights.

The mud was lying in wait for him. It swallowed his feet with an approving sound. It poured into his shoes, seeping into the plastic bags. It squeezed out from beneath unsteady paving stones, where there were any. He snarled at it and stamped, sending it over his trouser cuffs. It stretched glistening faintly before him as far as he could see.

Cars were taking a short cut from the main road, past the shops. Dutton stood and waited for their lights to sweep over the mud, lighting up his way. He emptied the bottle into himself. Headlights swung toward him, blazing abruptly in puddles, pinching up silver edges of ruts from the darkness, touching a small still dark object between the walls to Dutton's left.

He glared toward that, through the pale fading firework display on his eyeballs. It had been low and squat, he was sure; part of it had been raised, like a hood. Suddenly he recoiled from the restless darkness and began to run wildly. He fell with a flat splash and heaved himself up, his hands gloved in grit and mud. He stumbled toward the swaying lights and glared about whenever headlights flashed between the walls. Around him the walls seemed as unstable as the ground.

He was close enough to the shops for the individual sounds of the street to have separated themselves from the muted anonymous roar of the city, when he fell again. He fell into darkness behind walls, and scrabbled in the mud, slithering grittily. When he regained his feet he peered desperately about, trying to hold things still. The lights of the street, sinking, leaping back into place and sinking,

sinking; the walls around him, wavering and drooping; a dwarfish fragment of wall close to him, on his left. Headlights slipped past him and corrected him. It wasn't a fragment of wall. It was a pram.

In that moment of frozen clarity he could see the twin claw-marks its wheels had scored in the mud, reaching back into darkness. Then the darkness rushed at him as his ankles tangled and he lost his footing. He was reeling helplessly toward the pram.

A second before he reached it he lashed out blindly with one foot. He tottered in a socket of mud, but he felt his foot strike metal, and heard the pram fall. He whirled about, running toward the whirling lights, changing his direction when they steadied. The next time headlights passed him he twisted about to look. The force of his movement spun him back again and on, toward the lights. But he was sure he'd seen the pram upturned in the mud, and shaking like a turtle trying to right itself.

Once among the shops he felt safe. This was his territory. People were hurrying home from work, children were running errands; cars laden with packages butted their way toward the suburbs, honking. He'd stay here, where there were people; he wouldn't go home to his room.

He began to stroll, rolling unsteadily. He gazed in the shop windows, whose contents sank like a loose television image. When he reached a launderette he halted, frowning, and couldn't understand why. Was it something he'd heard? Yes, there was a sound somewhere amid the impatient clamor of the traffic: a yawn of metal cut short by a high squeal. It was something like that, not entirely, not the sound he remembered, only the sound of a car. Within the launderette things whirled, whirled; so did the launderette; so did the pavement. Dutton forced himself onward, cursing as he almost fell over a child. He shoved the child aside and collided with a pram.

Bulging out from beneath its hood was a swollen faceless head of blue plastic. Folds of its wrinkled wormlike body squeezed over the side of the pram; within the blue transparent body he could see white coils and rolls of washing, like tripe. Dutton thrust it away, choking. The woman wheeling it aimed a blow at him and pushed the pram into the launderette.

He ran helplessly forward, trying to retrieve his balance. Mud trickled through the burst plastic in his shoes and grated between his toes. He fell, slapping the pavement with himself. When someone tried to help him up he snarled and rolled out of their reach.

He was cold and wet. His coat had soaked up all the water his falls had squeezed out of the mud. He couldn't go home, couldn't warm himself in bed; he had to stay here, out on the street. His mouth tasted like an abandoned bottle. He glared about, roaring at anyone who came near. Then, over the jerking segments of the line of car roofs, he saw Maud hurrying down a side street, carrying a bottle wrapped in newspaper.

That was what he needed. A ball of fire sprang up spinning and whooping above the roofs. Dutton surged toward the pedestrian crossing, whose two green stick figures were squeaking at each other across the path through the cars. He was almost there when a pram rushed at him from an alley.

He grappled with it, hurling it from him. It was only a pram, never mind, he must catch up with Maud. But a white featureless head nodded toward him on a scrawny neck, craning out from beneath the hood; a head that slipped awry, rolling loose on its neck, as the strings that tied it came unknotted. It was only a guy begging pennies for cut-price fireworks. Before he realized that, Dutton had overbalanced away from it into the road, in front of a released car.

There was a howl of brakes, another, a tinkle of glass. Dutton found himself staring up from beneath a front bumper. Wheels blocked his vision on either side, like huge oppressive earmuffs. People were shouting at each other, someone was shouting at him, the crowd was chattering, laughing. When someone tried to help him to his feet he kicked out and clung to the bumper. Nothing could touch him now, he was safe, they wouldn't dare to. Eventually someone took hold of his arm and wouldn't let go until he stood up. It was Constable Wayne.

"Come on, Billy," Wayne said. "That's enough for today. Go home."

"I won't go home!" Dutton cried in panic.

"Do you mean to tell me you're sending him home and that's all?" a woman shouted above the yapping of her jacketed Pekinese. "What about my headlight?"

"I'll deal with him," Wayne said. "My colleague will take your statements. Don't give me any trouble, Billy," he said, taking a firmer hold on Dutton's arm.

Dutton found himself being marched along the street, toward his room. "I'm not going home," he shouted.

"You are, and I'll see that you do." A fire engine was elbowing its way through the traffic, braying. In the middle of a side street, between walls that quaked with the light of a huge bonfire, children were stoning firemen.

"I won't," Dutton said, pleading. "If you make me I'll get out again. I've drunk too much. I'll do something bad, I'll hurt someone."

"You aren't one of those. Go home now and sleep it off. You know we've no room for you on Saturday nights. And tonight of all nights we don't want to be bothered with you."

They had almost reached the house. Wayne gazed up at the dormant bonfire on the waste ground. "We'll have to see about that," he said. But Dutton hardly heard him. As the house swayed toward him, a rocket exploded low and snatched the house forward for a moment from the darkness. In the old woman's room, at the bottom of the windowpane, he saw a metal bar: the handle of a pram.

Dutton began to struggle again. "I'm not going in there!" he shouted, searching his mind wildly for anything. "I killed that old woman! I knocked her head in, it was me!"

"That's enough of that, now," Wayne said, dragging him up the steps. "You're lucky I can see you're drunk."

Dutton clutched the front door frame with both hands. "There's something in there!" he screamed. "In her room!"

"There's nothing at all," Wayne said. "Come here and I'll show you." He propelled Dutton into the hall and switching on his flashlight, pushed open the old woman's door with his foot. "Now, what's in here?" he demanded. "Nothing."

Dutton looked in, ready to flinch. The flashlight beam swept impatiently about the room, revealing nothing but dust. The bed had been pushed beneath the window during the police search. Its headrail was visible through the pane: a metal bar.

Dutton sagged with relief. Only Wayne's grip kept him from falling. He turned as Wayne hurried him toward the stairs, and saw the mouth of darkness just below the landing. It was waiting for him, its lips working. He tried to pull back, but Wayne was becoming more impatient. "See me upstairs," Dutton pleaded.

"Oh, it's the horrors, is it? Come on now, quickly." Wayne stayed where he was, but shone his flashlight into the mouth, which paled. Dutton stumbled upstairs as far as the lips, which flickered tentatively toward him. He heard the constable clatter up behind him, and the darkness fell back farther. Before him, sharp and bright amid the darkness, was his door.

"Switch on your light, be quick," Wayne said.

The room was exactly as Dutton had left it. And why not? he thought, confident all at once. He never locked it, there was nothing to steal, but now the familiarity of everything seemed welcoming: the rumpled bed; the wardrobe, rusted open and plainly empty; the washbasin; the grimy coin-meter. "All right," he called down to Wayne, and bolted the door.

He stood for a long time against the door while his head swam slowly back to him. The wind reached for him through the wide-open window. He couldn't remember having opened it so wide, but it didn't matter. Once he was steady he would close it, then he'd go to bed. The blankets were raised like a cowl at the pillow, waiting for him. He heard Constable Wayne walk away. Eventually he heard the children light the bonfire.

When blackening tatters of fire began to flutter toward the house he limped to close the window. The bonfire was roaring; the heat collided with him. He remembered with a shock of pleasure that the iron bar was deep in the blaze. He sniffed and groped vainly for his handkerchief as the smoke stung his nostrils. Never mind. He squinted at the black object at the peak of the bonfire, which the flames had just reached. Then he fell back involuntarily. It was the pram.

He slammed the window. Bright orange faces glanced up at him, then turned away. There was no mistaking the pram, for he saw the photograph within the hood strain with the heat, and shatter. He tested his feelings gingerly and realized he could release the thoughts he'd held back, at last. The pursuit was over. It had given up. And suddenly he knew why.

It had been the old woman's familiar. He'd known that as soon as Betty had mentioned the idea, but he hadn't dared think in case it heard him thinking; devils could do that. The old woman had taken it out in her pram, and it had stolen food for her. But it hadn't lived in the pram. It had lived inside the old woman. That was what he'd seen in her room, only it had got out before the police had found the body.

He switched off the light. The room stayed almost as bright, from the blaze. He fumbled with his buttons and removed his outer clothes. The walls shook; his mouth was beginning to taste like dregs again. It didn't matter. If he couldn't sleep he could go out and buy a bottle. Tomorrow he could cash his book. He needn't be afraid to go out now.

It must have thrown itself on the bonfire because devils lived in fire. It must have realized at last that he wasn't like the old woman, that it couldn't live inside him. He stumbled toward the bed. A shadow was moving on the pillow. He balked, then he saw it was the shadow of the blanket's cowl. He pulled the blanket back.

He had just realized how like the hood of a pram the shape of the blanket had been when the long spidery arms unfolded from the bed, and the powerful claws reached eagerly to part him.

# In the Bag

THE BOY'S FACE struggled within the plastic bag. The bag labored like a dying heart as the boy panted frantically, as if suffocated by the thickening mist of his own breath. His eyes were gray blank holes, full of fog beneath the plastic. As his mouth gaped desperately the bag closed on his face, tight and moist, giving him the appearance of a wrapped fish, not quite dead.

It wasn't his son's face. Clarke shook his head violently to clear it of the notion as he hurried toward the assembly hall. It might have been, but Peter had had enough sense and strength to rip the bag with a stone before trying to pull it off. He'd had more strength than . . . Clarke shook his head hurriedly and strode into the hall. He didn't propose to let himself be distracted. Peter had survived, but that was no thanks to the culprit.

The assembled school clattered to its feet and hushed. Clarke strode down the side aisle to the sound of belated clatters from the folding seats, like the last drops of rain after a downpour. Somewhere amid the muted chorus of nervous coughs, someone was rustling plastic. They wouldn't dare breathe when he'd finished with them. Five strides took him onto the stage. He nodded curtly to the teaching staff and faced the school.

"Someone put a plastic bag over a boy's head today," he said. "I had thought all of you understood that you come here to learn to be men. I had thought that even those of you who do not shine academically had learned to distinguish right from wrong. Apparently I was mistaken. Very well. If you behave like children, you must expect to be treated like children."

The school stirred; the sound included the crackling of plastic. Behind him Clarke heard some of the teachers sit forward, growing tense. Let them protest if they liked. So long as this was his school its discipline would be his.

"You will all stand in silence until the culprit owns up."

Tiers of heads stretched before him, growing taller as they receded, on the ground of their green uniform. Toward the middle he could see Peter's head. He'd forgotten to excuse the boy from assembly, but it was too late now. In any case, the boy looked less annoyed by the oversight than embarrassed by his father's behavior. Did he think Clarke was treating the school thus simply because Peter was his son? Not at all; three years ago Clarke had used the same method when someone had dropped a firework in a boy's duffel hood. Though the culprit had not come forward, Clarke had had the satisfaction of knowing he had been punished among the rest.

The heads were billiard balls, arranged on baize. Here and there one swayed uneasily then hurriedly steadied as Clarke's gaze seized it. A whole row shifted restlessly, one after another. Plastic crackled softly, jarring Clarke from his thoughts.

"It seems that the culprit is not a man but a coward," he said. "Very well. Someone must have seen what he did and who he is. No man will protect a coward from his just desserts. Don't worry that your fellows may look down on

you for betraying him. If they do not admire you for
behaving like a man, they are not men.''

The ranks of heads swayed gently, hypnotically. One of
them must have seen what had happened to Peter: someone
running softly behind him as he crossed the playing field,
dragging the bag over his head, twisting it tight about his
neck and stretching it into a knot at the back . . . Plastic
rustled secretly, deep in the hall, somewhere near Peter.
Was the culprit taunting Clarke? He grew cold with fury.
He scrutinized the faces, searching for the unease which
those closest to the sound must feel; but all the faces were
defiantly bland, including Peter's. So they refused to help
him even so meagerly. Very well.

"No doubt some of you think this is an easy way to
avoid your lessons," he said. "I think so, too. Instead,
from tomorrow you will all assemble here when school is
over and stand in silence for an hour. This will continue
until the culprit is found. Please be sure to tell your parents
tonight. You are dismissed.''

He strode to his office without a backward glance; his
demeanor commanded his staff to carry on his discipline.
But he had not reached his office when he began to feel
dissatisfied. He was grasping the door handle when he
realized what was wrong. Peter must still feel himself
doubly a victim.

A class came trooping along the corridor, protesting
loudly, hastily silent. "Henry Clegg," he said. "Go to
IIIA and tell Peter Clarke to come to my office immediately.''

He searched the faces of the passing boys for furtiveness.
Then he noticed that although he'd turned the handle and
was pushing, the door refused to move. Within, he heard a
flurried crackling rustle. He threw his weight against the
door, and it fell open. Paper rose from his desk and sank
back limply. He closed the window, which he'd left ajar;
mist was inching toward it, across the playing field. He
must have heard a draft fumbling with his papers.

A few minutes later Peter knocked and entered. He

stood before Clarke's desk, clearly unsure how to address his father. Really, Clarke thought, the boy should call him sir at school; there was no reason why Peter should show him less respect than any other pupil.

"You understand I didn't mean that you should stay after school, Peter," he said. "I hope that won't cause embarrassment between you and your friends. But you must realize that I cannot make an exception of them, too."

For an unguarded moment he felt as though he were justifying himself to his son. "Very well," Peter said. "Father."

Clarke nodded for him to return to his lesson, but the boy stood struggling to speak. "What is it?" Clarke said. "You can speak freely to me."

"One of the other boys . . . asked Mr. Elland if you were . . . right to give the detention and Mr. Elland said he didn't think you were."

"Thank you, Peter. I shall speak to Mr. Elland later. But for now, you had better return to his class."

He gazed at the boy, and then at the closed door. He would have liked to see Peter proud of his action, but the boy looked self-conscious and rather disturbed. Perhaps he would discuss the matter with him at home, though that broke his own rule that school affairs should be raised with Peter only in school. He had enough self-discipline not to break his own rules without excellent reason.

Self-discipline must be discussed with Elland later. Clarke sat at his desk to draft a letter to the parents. Laxity in the wearing of school uniform. A fitting sense of pride. The school as a community. Loyalty, a virtue we must foster at all costs. The present decline in standards.

But the rustle of the paper distracted him. He'd righted the wrong he had done Peter, he would deal with Elland later; yet he was dissatisfied. With what? The paper prompted him, rustling. There was no use pretending. He must remember what the sound reminded him of.

It reminded him of the sound the plastic bag had made once he'd put it over Derek's head.

His mind writhed aside, distracting him with memories that were more worthy of his attention. They were difficult enough to remember—painful indeed. Sometimes it had seemed that his whole life had been contrived to force him to remember.

Whenever he had sat an examination someone had constantly rustled paper behind him. Nobody else had heard it; after one examination, when he'd tackled the boy who had been sitting behind him, the others had defended the accused. Realizing that the sound was in himself, in the effect of stress on his senses, Clarke had gone to examinations prepared to hear it; he'd battled to ignore it, and had passed. He'd known he must; that was only justice.

Then there had been the school play: that had been the worst incident, the most embarrassing. He had produced the play from his own pared-down script, determined to make an impression in his first teaching post. But Macbeth had stalked onto the heath to a sound from the wings as of someone straining to blow up a balloon, wheezing and panting faintly. Clarke had pursued the sound through the wings, finding only a timidly bewildered boy with a thunder sheet. Nevertheless, the headmaster had applauded rapidly and lengthily at the curtain. Eventually, since he himself hadn't been blamed, Clarke ceased cross-examining his pupils.

Since then his career had done him more than justice. Sitting at his desk now, he relaxed; he couldn't remember when he'd felt so much at ease with his memories. Of course there had been later disturbing incidents. One spring evening he had been sitting on a park bench with Edna, courting her, and had glanced away from the calm green sunset to see an inflated plastic bag caught among branches. The bag had seemed to pant violently in its struggles with the breeze; then it had begun to nod sluggishly. He'd run across the lawn in panic, but before he reached the bag it had been snatched away, to retreat nodding into the darkness between the trees. For a moment, vaguely amid his panic, it had made him think of the unidentified boy who had appeared beside him in a class photograph, face blurred into a gray blob. Edna had asked him no questions, and he'd been grateful to forget the incident. But the panic still lay in his memory, now he looked.

It was like the panic he'd felt while awaiting Peter's birth. That had been late in the marriage; there might have been complications. Clarke had waited, trying to slow his breath, holding himself back; panic had been waiting just ahead. If there were any justice, Edna at least would survive. He'd heard someone approaching swiftly beyond the bend in the hospital corridor: a purposeful crackling rustle—a nurse. He had felt pinned down by panic; he'd known that the sound was bearing death toward him. But the nurse must have turned aside beyond the bend. Instead, a doctor had appeared to call him in to see his wife and son. For the only time in his life, Clarke had rushed away to be sick with relief.

As if he had vomited out what haunted him, the panic had never seized him again. But Derek remained deep in his mind, waiting. Each time his thoughts brushed the memory they shrank away; each time it seemed more shameful and horrible. He had never been able to look at it directly.

But why not? He had looked at all these memories without flinching. He had dealt with Peter, later he would deal with Elland. He felt unassailably right, incapable of wrong. He would not be doing himself justice if he did not take this chance.

He sat forward, as if to interview his memory. He coaxed his mind toward it, trying to relax, reassuring himself. There was nothing to fear, he was wholly secure. He must trust his sense of innate rightness; not to remember would be to betray it. He braced himself, closing his eyes. At the age of ten, he had killed another boy.

He and Derek had been playing at the end of the street, near the disused railway line. They weren't supposed to be there, but their parents rarely checked. The summer sun had been trying to shake off trails of soot that rose from the factory chimneys. The boys had been playing at spacemen, inspired by the cover of a magazine crumpled among the rubble. They'd found a plastic bag.

Clarke had worn it first. It had hung against his ears like blankets when he breathed; his ears had been full of his breathing, the bag had grown stuffily hot and misty at once, clinging to his face. Then Derek had snatched it for himself.

Clarke hadn't liked him really, hadn't counted him as much of a friend. Derek was sly, he grabbed other people's toys, he played vindictive tricks on others, then whined if they turned on him. When he did wrong he tried to pass the blame to someone else—but that day Clarke had had nobody else to play with. They'd wanted to play spacemen chasing Martians over the waste ground of the moon, but Derek's helmet had kept flying off. Clarke had pulled it tight at the back of Derek's neck, to tie a careful knot.

They ran until Derek fell down. He'd lain kicking on the rubble, pulling at the bag, at his neck. The bag had ballooned, then had fastened on his face like gray skin, again and again. His fingernails had squeaked faintly on the plastic; he'd sounded as though he were trying to cough. When Clarke had stooped to help him he'd kicked out blindly and viciously. Dismayed by the sight, infuriated by the rebuff, Clarke had run away. Realizing that he didn't know where he was running to, he'd panicked and had hidden in the outside toilet for hours, long after the woman's screams had gone by, and the ambulance.

Though nobody had known he and Derek had been together—since Derek's sister and her boyfriend were supposed to have kept the boy with them in the park—Clarke had waited, on the edge of panic, for Derek's father to knock at the front door. But the next day his mother had told him Derek had had an accident; he'd been warned never to play with plastic bags, and that was all. It wasn't enough, he'd decided years later, while watching a fight;

too many of his classmates' parents weren't enough for
their children; he'd known then what his career was to be.
By then he had been able to relax, except for the depths of
his mind.

He'd allowed himself to forget; yet today he was hound-
ing a boy for a lesser crime.

No. It wasn't the same. Whoever had played that trick
on Peter must have known what he was doing. But Clarke,
at ten years old, hadn't known what he was doing to
Derek. He had never needed to feel guilt at all.

Secure in that knowledge, he remembered at last why he
had. He'd sat on the outside toilet, hearing the screams.
Very gradually, a sly grin had spread across his mouth. It
served Derek right. Someone had played a trick on him,
for a change. He wouldn't be able to pass it back. Clarke
had hugged himself, rocking on the seat, giggling silently,
starting guiltily when a soft unidentified thumping at the
door had threatened him.

He gazed at the memory. It no longer made him writhe;
after all, he had been only a child. He would be able to tell
Edna at last. That was what had disturbed him most that
evening in the park: it hadn't seemed right that he couldn't
tell her. That injustice had lurked deep within their marriage.
He smiled broadly. "I didn't know what I was doing," he
told himself again, aloud.

"But you know now," said a muffled voice behind
him.

He sprang to his feet. He had been dozing. Behind him,
of course, there was only the window and the unhurried
mist. He glanced at his watch. He was to talk to his
sixth-form class about ethics: he felt he would enjoy the
subject even more than usual. As he closed his door he
glimpsed something moving in the indistinct depths of the
trees beyond the playing field, like a fading trace of a
memory: a tree, no doubt.

When the class had sat down again he waited for a
moment, hoping they might question the ethics of the
detention he'd ordered. They should be men enough to ask

him. But they only gazed, and he began to discuss the relationship between laws and morality. A Christian country. The individual's debt to society. Our common duty to help the law. The administration of justice. Justice.

He'd waxed passionate, striding the aisles, when he happened to look out of the window. A man dressed in drab shapeless clothes was standing at the edge of the trees. In the almost burnt-out sunlight his face shone dully, featurelessly. Shadows or mist made the gray mass of his face seem to flutter.

The janitor was skulking distantly in the bottom corner of the pane, like a detail squeezed in by a painter. He was pretending to weed the flowerbeds. "Who is that man?" Clarke called angrily. "He has no right to be here." But there was nobody except the janitor in sight.

Clarke groped for his interrupted theme. The age of culpability: one of the class must have asked about that— he remembered having heard a voice. The age of legal responsibility. Must not be used as an excuse. Conscience cannot be silenced for ever. The law cannot absolve. One does not feel guilt without being guilty. Someone was standing outside the window.

As Clarke whirled to look, something, perhaps the tic that was plucking at his eye, made the man's face seem the color of mist, and quaking. But when he looked there was nothing but the field and the mist and the twilight, running together darkly like a drowned painting.

"Who was that?" Clarke demanded. "Did anyone see?"

"A man," said Paul Hammond, a sensitive boy. "He looked as if he was going to have a fit." Nobody else had seen anything.

"Do your job properly," Clarke shouted at the janitor. "Keep your eyes open. He's gone round there, round the corner." The afternoon had crept surreptitiously by; he had almost reached the end of school. He searched for a phrase to sum up the lesson. "Remember, you cannot call yourself a man unless you face your conscience." On the last words he had to outshout the bell.

He strode to Elland's classroom, his gown rising and sailing behind him. The man was chatting to a group of his boys. "Will you come to my office when you've finished, please," Clarke said, leaning in.

Waiting in his office, he felt calm as the plane of mist before him. It reminded him of a still pool; a pool whose opaque stillness hid its depths; an unnaturally still and opaque pool; a pool from whose depths a figure was rising, about to shatter the surface. It must be the janitor, searching behind the mist. Clarke shook himself angrily and turned as Elland came in.

"Have you been questioning my authority in front of your class?"

"Not exactly, no. I answered a question."

"Don't quibble. You are perfectly aware of what I mean. I will not have the discipline of my school undermined in this way."

"Boys of that age can see straight through hypocrisy, you know," the teacher said, interrupting the opening remarks of Clarke's lecture. "I was asked what I thought. I'm not a convincing liar, and I shouldn't have thought you'd want me to be. I'm sure they would have found my lying more disturbing than the truth. And that wouldn't have helped the discipline, now would it?"

"Don't interrogate me. Don't you realize what you said in front of my son? Does that mean nothing to you?"

"It was your son who asked me what I thought."

Clarke stared at him, hoping for signs of a lie. But at last he had to dismiss him. "I'll speak to you more tomorrow," he said vaguely. The man had been telling the truth; he had clearly been surprised even to have to tell it. But that meant Peter had lied to his father.

Clarke threw the draft of the letter into his briefcase. There was no time to be lost. He must follow Peter home immediately and set the boy back on the right path. A boy who was capable of one lie was capable of many.

Far down the corridor boys shouted, the wooden echoes of their footsteps fading. At the door to the mist Clarke hesitated. Perhaps Peter found it difficult to talk to him at school. He would ask him about the incident again at home, to give him a last chance. Perhaps it was partly Clarke's fault, for not making it clear how the boy should address him at school. He must make sure Edna didn't intervene, gently, anxiously. He would insist that she leave them alone.

The fog pretended to defer to him as he strode. It was fog now: trees developed from it, black and glistening, then dissolved again. One tree rustled as he passed. But surely it had no leaves? He hadn't time to go back and look. The sound must have been the rattling of the tree's wire cage, muffled and distorted by the fog.

Home was half a mile away, along three main roads. Peter would already have arrived there, with a group of friends; Clarke hoped he hadn't invited them in. No matter; they would certainly leave when they saw their headmaster.

Buses groped along the dual carriageway, their engines subdued and hoarse. The sketch of a lamp post bobbed up from the fog, filling out and darkening; another, another. On the central reservation, beyond the fog, a faint persistent rustling seemed to be pacing Clarke. This was always an untidy street. But there was no wind to stir the litter, no wind to cause the sound that was creeping patiently and purposefully along just behind him, coming abreast of him as he halted, growing louder. He flinched from the dark shape that swam up beside him, but it was a car. And of course it must have been disturbing the litter on the road. He let the car pass, and the rustling faded ahead.

As he neared the second road the white glare of mercury-vapor lamps was gradually mixed with the warmer orange of sodium, contradicted by the chill of the fog. Cars passed like stealthy hearses. The fog sopped up the sodium glow; the orange fog hung thickly around him, like a billowing sack. He felt suffocated. Of course he did, for heaven's sake. The fog was clogging his lungs. He would soon be home.

He strode into the third road, where home was. The

orange sack glided with him, over the whitening pavement. The fog seemed too thick, almost a liquid from which lamp posts sailed up slowly, trailing orange streaks. Striding through the suppressed quiet, he realized he had encountered nobody on the roads. All at once he was glad: he could see a figure surfacing darkly before him, fog streaming from it, its blank face looming forward to meet him. He could see nothing of the kind. He was home.

As he fumbled for his keys, the nearby streetlamp blazed through a passing rift in the fog. The lamp was dazzling; its light penetrated the thickset curtains Edna had hung in the front rooms; and it showed a man standing at its root. He was dressed like a tramp, in ancient clothes, and his face gleamed dully in the orange light, like bronze. As Clarke glanced away to help his hands find his elusive keys he realized that the man seemed to have no face, only the gleaming, almost immobile surface. He glared back at the pavement, but there was nobody. The fog, which must have obscured the man's face, closed again.

One room was lighted: the kitchen, at the far end of the hall. Edna and Peter must be in there. Since the house was silent, the boy could not have invited in his friends. Clarke closed the front door, glad to see the last of the fog, and hurried down the hall. He had taken three steps when something slithered beneath his feet. He peered at it, on the faint edge of light from the kitchen. It was a plastic bag.

In a moment, during which his head seemed to clench and grow lightless as he hastily straightened up, he realized that it was one of the bags Edna used to protect food. Several were scattered along the hall. She must have dropped them out of the packet, she mustn't have noticed. He ran along the hall, toward the light, toward the silent kitchen. The kitchen was empty.

He began to call to Edna and to Peter as he ran back through the house, slipping on the scattered bags, bruising his shoulder against the wall. He pulled open the dining room door, but although the china was chiming from his footsteps, there was nobody within. He ran on, skidding, and wrenched open the door of the living room. The faintest of orange glows had managed to gather in the room. He was groping distractedly for the light switch when he made out Edna and Peter, sitting waiting for him in the dark. Their heads gleamed faintly.

After a very long time he switched on the light.

He switched it off at once. He had seen enough; he had seen their gaping mouths stuffed full of sucked-in plastic. His mind had refused to let him see their eyes. He stood in the orange dark, gazing at the still figures. When he made a sound, it resounded through the house.

At last he stumbled into the hall. He had nowhere else to go. He knew the moment was right. The blur in the lighted kitchen doorway was a figure: a man, vague as fog and very thin. Its stiff arms rose jerkily, perhaps hampered by pain, perhaps savoring the moment. Gray blotches peered from its face. He heard the rustling as it uncovered its head.

# *Conversion*

YOU'RE in sight of home when you know something's wrong. Moonlight shivers gently on the stream beyond the cottage, and trees stand around you like intricate spikes of the darkness mounting within the forest. The cottage is dark, but it isn't that. You emerge into the glade, trying to sense what's troubling you.

You know you shouldn't have stayed out so late, talking to your friend. Your wife must have been worried, perhaps frightened by the night as well. You've never left her alone at night before. But his talk was so engrossing: you feel that in less than a night you've changed from being wary of him to understanding him completely. And his wine was so good, and his open-throated brightly streaming fire so warming, that you can now remember little except a timeless sense of comfortable companionship, of communion that no longer needed words. But you shouldn't have left your wife alone in the forest at night, even behind a barred door. The woodcutter's cottage is nearby;

274

at least you could have had his wife stay with yours. You feel disloyal.

Perhaps that's what has been disturbing you. Always before when you've returned home, light has been pouring from the windows, mellowing the surrounding trunks and including them like a wall around your cottage. Now the cottage reminds you of winter nights long ago in your childhood, when you lay listening to a wolf's cry like the slow plummeting of ice into a gorge, and felt the mountains and forests huge around you, raked by the wind. The cottage feels like that: cold and hollow and unwelcoming. For a moment you wonder if you're simply anticipating your wife's blame, but you're sure it's more than that.

In any case you'll have to knock and awaken her. First you go to the window and look in. She's lying in bed, her face open as if to the sky. Moonlight eases darkness from her face, but leaves her throat and the rest of her in shadow. Tears have gathered in her eyes, sparkling. No doubt she has been crying in memory of her sister, a sketch of whom gazes across the bed from beside a glass of water. As you look in you're reminded of your childhood fancy that angels watched over you at night, not at the end of the bed but outside the window; for a second you feel like your wife's angel. But as you gaze in, discomfort grows in your throat and stomach. You remember how your fancy somehow turned into a terror of glimpsing a white face peering in. You draw back quickly in case you should frighten her.

But you have to knock. You don't understand why you've been delaying. You stride to the door and your fist halts in midair, as if impaled by lightning. Suddenly the vague threats and unease you've been feeling seem to rush together and gather on the other side of the door. You know that beyond the door something is waiting for you, ready to pounce.

You feel as if terror has pinned you through your stomach, helpless. You're almost ready to flee into the woods, to free yourself from the skewer of your panic. Sweat pricks you like red-hot ash scattered on your skin. But you can't leave your wife in there with it, whatever nightmare it is, rising out of the tales you've heard told of the forest. You force yourself to be still if not calm, and listen for some hint of what it might be.

All you can hear is the slow sleepy breathing of the wind in the trees. Your panic rises, for you can feel it beyond the door, perfectly poised and waiting easily for you to betray yourself. You hurry back to the window, but it's impossible for you to squeeze yourself in far enough to make out anything within the door. This time a stench rises from the room to meet you, trickling into your nostrils. It's so thickly unpleasant that you refuse to think what it might resemble. You edge back, terrified now of awakening your wife, for it can only be her immobility that's protecting her from whatever's in the room.

But you can't coax yourself back to the door. You've allowed your panic to spread out from it, warding you farther from the cottage. Your mind fills with your wife, lying unaware of her plight. Furious with yourself, you compel your body forward against the gale of your panic. You reach the door and struggle to touch it. If you can't do that, you tell yourself, you're a coward, a soft scrabbling thing afraid of the light. Your hand presses against the door as if proving itself against a live coal, and the door swings inward.

You should have realized that your foe might have entered the cottage through the doorway. You flinch back instinctively, but as the swift fear fades the panic seeps back. You can feel it hanging like a spider just inside the doorway, waiting for you to pass beneath: a huge heavy black spider, ready to plump on your face. You try to shake your panic out of you with the knowledge that it's probably nothing like that, that you're giving in to fancy. But whatever it is, it's oozing a stench that claws its way into your throat and begins to squeeze out your stomach. You fall back, weakened and baffled.

Then you see the rake. It's resting against the corner of

the cottage, where you left it after trying to clear a space
for a garden. You carry it to the door, thinking. It could be
more than a weapon, even though you don't know what
you're fighting. If your wife doesn't awaken and draw its
attention to her, if your foe isn't intelligent enough to see
what you're planning, if your absolute conviction of where
it's lurking above the door isn't false— You almost throw
away the rake, but you can't bear the sense of your wife's
peril any longer. You inch the door open. You're sure you
have only one chance.

You reach stealthily into the space above the door with
the teeth of the rake, then you grind them into your prey
and drag it out into the open. It's a dark tangled mass, but
you hurl it away into the forest without looking closer, for
some of it has fallen into the doorway and lies dimly there,
its stench welling up. You pin it with the teeth and fling it
into the trees.

Then you realize there's more, hanging and skulking
around the side of the door frame. You grab it with the
rake and hurl it against a trunk. Then you let your breath
roar out. You're weak and dizzy, but you stagger through
the doorway. There are smears of the thing around the
frame and you sway back, retching. You close your mouth
and nostrils and you're past, safe.

You lean on the rake and gaze down at your wife.
There's a faint stench clinging to the rake, and you push it
away from you, against the wall. She's still asleep, no
doubt because you were mourning her sister all last night.
Your memory's blurring; you must be exhausted too, because you can remember hardly anything before the battle
you've just fought. You're simply grateful that no harm
has befallen her. If she'd come with you to visit your
friend none of this would have happened. You hope you
can recapture the sense of communion you had with him,
to pass on to your wife. Through your blurring consciousness you feel an enormous yearning for her.

Then you jerk alert, for there's still something in the
room. You glance about wildly and see beneath the win-

dow more of what you destroyed, lying like a tattered snake. You manage to scoop it up in one piece this time, and you throw the rake out with it. Then you turn back to your wife. You've disturbed her; she has moved in her sleep. And fear advances on you from the bed like a spreading stain pumped out by a heart, because now you can see what's nestling at her throat.

You don't know what it is; your terror blurs it and crowds out your memories until it looks like nothing you've ever seen. It rests in the hollow of her throat like a dormant bat, and indeed it seems to have stubby protruding wings. Its shape expands within your head until it is a slow explosion of pure hostility, growing and erasing you. You turn away, blinded.

It's far worse than what you threw into the forest. Even then, if you hadn't been fighting for your wife you would have been paralyzed by superstition. Now you can hardly turn your head back to look. The stain of the thing is crawling over your wife, blotting out her face and all your sense of her. But you open your eyes an agonized slit and see it couched in her throat as if it lives there. Your rage floods up, and you start forward.

But even with your eyes closed you can't gain on it, because a great cold inhuman power closes about you, crushing you like a moth in a fist. You mustn't cry out, because if your wife awakens it may turn on her. But the struggle crushes a wordless roar from you, and you hear her awake.

Your seared eyes make out her face, dimmed by the force of the thing at her neck. Perhaps her gathered tears are dislodged, or perhaps these are new, wrung out by the terror in her eyes. Your head is a shell full of fire, your eyes feel as though turning to ash, but you battle forward. Then you realize she's shrinking back. She isn't terrified of the thing at her throat at all, she's terrified of you. She's completely in its power.

You're still straining against the force, wondering whether it must divert some of its power from you in order to

control her, when she grabs the glass from beside the bed.
For a moment you can't imagine what she wants with a
glass of water. But it isn't water. It's vitriol, and she
throws it in your face.

Your face bursts into pain. Howling, you rush to the
mirror.

You're still searching for yourself in the mirror when
the woodcutter appears in the doorway, grim-faced. At
once, like an eye in the whirlwind of your confusion and
pain, you remember that you asked his wife to stay with
yours, yesterday afternoon when he wasn't home to dis-
suade you from what you had to do. And you know why
you can't see yourself, only the room and the doorway
through which you threw the garlic, your sobbing wife
clutching the cross at her throat, the glass empty now of
the holy water you brought home before setting out to
avenge her sister's death at Castle Dracula.

# The Chimney

MAYBE most of it was only fear. But not the last thing, not that. To blame my fear for that would be worst of all.

I was twelve years old and beginning to conquer my fears. I even went upstairs to do my homework, and managed to ignore the chimney. I had to be brave, because of my parents—because of my mother.

She had always been afraid for me. The very first day I had gone to school I'd seen her watching. Her expression had reminded me of the face of a girl I'd glimpsed on television, watching men lock her husband behind bars; I was frightened all that first day. And when children had hysterics or began to bully me, or the teacher lost her temper, these things only confirmed my fears—and my mother's, when I told her what had happened each day.

Now I was at grammar school. I had been there for much of a year. I'd felt awkward in my new uniform and old shoes; the building seemed enormous, crowded with too many strange children and teachers. I'd felt I was an outsider; friendly approaches made me nervous and sullen, when people laughed and I didn't know why I was sure they were laughing at me. After a while the other boys treated me as I seemed to want to be treated: the lads from the poorer districts mocked my suburban accent, the suburban boys sneered at my old shoes.

Often I'd sat praying that the teacher wouldn't ask me a question I couldn't answer, sat paralyzed by my dread of having to stand up in the waiting watchful silence. If a teacher shouted at someone my heart jumped painfully; once I'd felt the stain of my shock creeping insidiously down my thigh. Yet I did well in the end-of-term examinations, because I was terrified of failing; for nights afterward they were another reason why I couldn't sleep.

My mother read the signs of all this on my face. More and more, once I'd told her what was wrong, I had to persuade her there was nothing worse that I'd kept back. Some mornings as I lay in bed, trying to hold back half-past seven, I'd be sick; I would grope miserably downstairs, white-faced, and my mother would keep me home. Once or twice, when my fear wasn't quite enough, I made myself sick. "Look at him. You can't expect him to go like that"—but my father would only shake his head and grunt, dismissing us both.

I knew my father found me embarrassing. This year he'd had less time for me than usual; his shop—The Anything Shop, nearby in the suburbanized village—was failing to compete with the new supermarket. But before that trouble I'd often seen him staring up at my mother and me: both of us taller than him, his eyes said, yet both scared of our own shadows. At those times I glimpsed his despair.

So my parents weren't reassuring. Yet at night I tried to stay with them as long as I could—for my worst fears were upstairs, in my room.

It was a large room, two rooms knocked into one by the previous owner. It overlooked the small back gardens. The smaller of the fireplaces had been bricked up; in winter, the larger held a fire, which my mother always feared would set fire to the room—but she let it alone, for I'd screamed when I thought she was going to take that light away: even though the firelight only added to the terrors of the room.

The shadows moved things. The mesh of the fireguard fluttered enlarged on the wall; sometimes, at the edge of sleep, it became a swaying web, and its spinner came sidling down from a corner of the ceiling. Everything was unstable; walls shifted, my clothes crawled on the back of the chair. Once, when I'd left my jacket slumped over the chair, the collar's dark upturned lack of a face began to nod forward stealthily; the holes at the ends of the sleeves worked like mouths, and I didn't dare get up to hang the jacket properly. The room grew in the dark: sounds outside, footsteps and laughter, dogs encouraging each other to bark, only emphasized the size of my trap of darkness, how distant everything else was. And there was a dimmer room, in the mirror of the wardrobe beyond the foot of the bed. There was a bed in that room, and beside it a dim nightlight in a plastic lantern. Once I'd awakened to see a face staring dimly at me from the mirror; a figure had sat up when I had, and I'd almost cried out. Often I'd stared at the dim staring face, until I'd had to hide beneath the sheets.

Of course this couldn't go on for the rest of my life. On my twelfth birthday I set about the conquest of my room.

I was happy amid my presents. I had a jigsaw, a box of colored pencils, a book of space stories. They had come from my father's shop, but they were mine now. Because I was relaxed, no doubt because she wished I could always be so, my mother said, "Would you be happier if you went to another school?"

It was Saturday; I wanted to forget Monday. Besides, I imagined all schools were as frightening. "No, I'm all right," I said.

"Are you happy at school now?" she said incredulously.

"Yes, it's all right."

"Are you sure?"

"Yes, really, it's all right. I mean, I'm happy now."

The snap of the letter slot saved me from further lying. Three birthday cards: two from neighbors who talked to me when I served them in the shop—an old lady who always carried a poodle, our next-door neighbor Dr. Flynn— and a card from my parents. I'd seen all three cards in the shop, which spoiled them somehow.

As I stood in the hall I heard my father. "You've got to control yourself," he was saying. "You only upset the child. If you didn't go on at him he wouldn't be half so bad."

It infuriated me to be called a child. "But I worry so," my mother said brokenly. "He can't look after himself."

"You don't let him try. You'll have him afraid to go up to bed next."

But I already was. Was that my mother's fault? I remembered her putting the nightlight by my bed when I was very young, checking the flex and the bulb each night— I'd taken to lying awake, dreading that one or the other would fail. Standing in the hall, I saw dimly that my mother and I encouraged each other's fears. One of us had to stop. I had to stop. Even when I was frightened, I mustn't let her see. It wouldn't be the first time I'd hidden my feelings from her. In the living room I said, "I'm going upstairs to play."

Sometimes in summer I didn't mind playing there—but this was March, and a dark day. Still, I could switch the light on. And my room contained the only table I could have to myself and my jigsaw.

I spilled the jigsaw onto the table. The chair sat with its back to the dark yawn of the fireplace; I moved it hastily to the foot of the bed, facing the door. I spread the jigsaw. There was a piece of the edge, another. By lunchtime I'd assembled the edge. "You look pleased with yourself," my father said.

I didn't notice the approach of night. I was fitting together my own blue sky, above fragmented cottages. After dinner I hurried to put in the pieces I'd placed

mentally while eating. I hesitated outside my room. I
should have to reach into the dark for the light switch.
When I did, the wallpaper filled with bright multiplied
airplanes and engines. I wished we could afford to redeco-
rate my room, it seemed childish now.

The fireplace gaped. I retrieved the fireguard from the
cupboard under the stairs, where my father had stored it
now the nights were a little warmer. It covered the soot-
encrusted yawn. The room felt comfortable now. I'd never
seen before how much space it gave me for play.

I even felt safe in bed. I switched out the nightlight—
but that was too much; I grabbed the light. I didn't mind
its glow on its own, without the jagged lurid jig of the
shadows. And the fireguard was comforting. It made me
feel that nothing could emerge from the chimney.

On Monday I took my space stories to school. People
asked to look at them; eventually they lent me books. In
the following weeks some of my fears began to fade.
Questions darting from desk to desk still made me uneasy,
but if I had to stand up without the answer at least I knew
the other boys weren't sneering at me, not all of them; I
was beginning to have friends. I started to sympathize with
their own ignorant silences. In the July examinations I was
more relaxed, and scored more marks. I was even sorry to
leave my friends for the summer; I invited some of them
home.

I felt triumphant. I'd calmed my mother and my room
all by myself, just by realizing what had to be done. I
suppose that sense of triumph helped me. It must have
given me a little strength with which to face the real terror.

It was early August, the week before our holiday. My
mother was worrying over the luggage, my father was
trying to calculate his accounts; they were beginning to
chafe against each other. I went to my room, to stay out of
their way.

I was halfway through a jigsaw, which one of my
friends had swapped for mine. People sat in back gardens,
letting the evening settle on them; between the houses the

sky was pale yellow. I inserted pieces easily, relaxed by
the nearness of our holiday. I listened to the slowing of the
city, a radio fluttering along a street, something moving
behind the fireguard, in the chimney.

No. It was my mother in the next room, moving luggage.
It was someone dragging, dragging something, anything,
outside. But I couldn't deceive my ears. In the chimney
something large had moved.

It might have been a bird, stunned or dying, struggling
feebly—except that a bird would have sounded wilder. It
could have been a mouse, even a rat, if such things are
found in chimneys. But it sounded like a large body,
groping stealthily in the dark: something large that didn't
want me to hear it. It sounded like the worst terror of my
infancy.

I'd almost forgotten that. When I was three years old
my mother had let me watch television; it was bad for my
eyes, but just this once, near Christmas—I'd seen two
children asleep in bed, an enormous crimson man emerging from the fireplace, creeping toward them. They weren't
going to wake up! "Burglar! Burglar!" I'd screamed,
beginning to cry. "No, dear, it's Father Christmas," my
mother said, hastily switching off the television. "He
always comes out of the chimney."

Perhaps if she'd said "down" rather than "out of" . . .
For months after that, and in the weeks before several
Christmases, I lay awake listening fearfully for movement
in the chimney: I was sure a fat grinning figure would
creep upon me if I slept. My mother had told me the
presents that appeared at the end of my bed were left by
Father Christmas, but now the mysterious visitor had a
face and a huge body, squeezed into the dark chimney
among the soot. When I heard the wind breathing in the
chimney I had to trap my screams between my lips.

Of course at last I began to suspect there was no Father
Christmas: how did he manage to steal into my father's
shop for my presents? He was a childish idea, I was almost
sure—but I was too embarrassed to ask my parents or my

friends. But I wanted not to believe in him, that silent lurker in the chimney; and now I didn't, not really. Except that something large was moving softly behind the fireguard.

It had stopped. I stared at the wire mesh, half-expecting a fat pale face to stare out of the grate. There was nothing but the fenced dark. Cats were moaning in a garden, an ice-cream van wandered brightly. After a while I forced myself to pull the fireguard away.

I was taller than the fireplace now. But I had to stoop to peer up the dark, soot-ridged throat, and then it loomed over me, darkness full of menace, of the threat of a huge figure bursting out at me, its red mouth crammed with sparkling teeth. As I peered up, trembling a little, and tried to persuade myself that what I'd heard had flown away or scurried back into its hole, soot came trickling down from the dark—and I heard the sound of a huge body squeezed into the sooty passage, settling itself carefully, more comfortably in its burrow.

I slammed the guard into place, and fled. I had to gulp to breathe. I ran onto the landing, trying to catch my breath so as to cry for help. Downstairs my mother was nervously asking whether she should pack another of my father's shirts. "Yes, if you like," he said irritably.

No, I mustn't cry out. I'd vowed not to upset her. But how could I go back into my room? Suddenly I had a thought that seemed to help. At school we'd learned how sweeps had used to send small boys up chimneys. There had hardly been room for the boys to climb. How could a large man fit in there?

He couldn't. Gradually I managed to persuade myself. At last I opened the door of my room. The chimney was silent; there was no wind. I tried not to think that he was holding himself still, waiting to squeeze out stealthily, waiting for the dark. Later, lying in the steady glow from my plastic lantern, I tried to hold onto the silence, tried to believe there was nothing near me to shatter it. There was nothing except, eventually, sleep.

Perhaps if I'd cried out on the landing I would have

been saved from my fear. But I was happy with my
rationality. Only once, nearly asleep, I wished the fire
were lit, because it would burn anything that might be
hiding in the chimney; that had never occurred to me
before. But it didn't matter, for the next day we went on
holiday.

My parents liked to sleep in the sunlight, beneath
newspaper masks; in the evenings they liked to stroll along
the wide sandy streets. I didn't, and befriended Nigel, the
son of another family who were staying in the boardinghouse. My mother encouraged the friendship: such a nice
boy, two years older than me; he'd look after me. He had
money, and the hope of a moustache shadowing his pim-
ply upper lip. One evening he took me to the fairground,
where we met two girls; he and the older girl went to buy
ice creams while her young friend and I stared at each
other timidly. I couldn't believe the young girl didn't like
jigsaws. Later, while I was contradicting her, Nigel and
his companion disappeared behind the Ghost Train—but
Nigel reappeared almost at once, red-faced, his left cheek
redder. "Where's Rose?" I asked, bewildered.

"She had to go." He seemed furious that I'd asked.

"Isn't she coming back?"

"No." He was glancing irritably about for a change of
subject. "What a super bike," he said, pointing as it
glided between the stalls. "Have you got a bike?"

"No," I said. "I keep asking Father Christmas, but—"
I wished that hadn't got past me, for he was staring at me,
winking at the young girl.

"Do you still believe in him?" he demanded scornfully.

"No, of course I don't. I was only kidding." Did he
believe me? He was edging toward the young girl now,
putting his arm around her; soon she excused herself, and
didn't come back—I never knew her name. I was annoyed
he'd made her run away. "Where did Rose go?" I said
persistently.

He didn't tell me. But perhaps he resented my insistence,
for as the family left the boardinghouse I heard him say

loudly to his mother: "He still believes in Father Christmas."
My mother heard that too, and glanced anxiously at me.

Well, I didn't. There was nobody in the chimney, waiting for me to come home. I didn't care that we were going home the next day. That night I pulled away the fireguard and saw a fat pale face hanging down into the fireplace, like an underbelly, upside down and smiling. But I managed to wake, and eventually the sea lulled me back to sleep.

As soon as we reached home I ran upstairs. I uncovered the fireplace and stood staring, to discover what I felt. Gradually I filled with the scorn Nigel would have felt, had he known of my fear. How could I have been so childish? The chimney was only a passage for smoke, a hole into which the wind wandered sometimes. That night, exhausted by the journey home, I slept at once.

The nights darkened into October; the darkness behind the mesh grew thicker. I'd used to feel, as summer waned, that the chimney was insinuating its darkness into my room. Now the sight only reminded me I'd have a fire soon. The fire would be comforting.

It was October when my father's Christmas cards arrived, on a Saturday; I was working in the shop. It annoyed him to have to anticipate Christmas so much, to compete with the supermarket. I hardly noticed the cards: my head felt muffled, my body cold—perhaps it was the weather's sudden hint of winter.

My mother came to the shop that afternoon. I watched her pretend not to have seen the cards. When I looked away she began to pick them up timidly, as if they were unfaithful letters, glancing anxiously at me. I didn't know what was in her mind. My head was throbbing. I wasn't going home sick; I earned pocket money in the shop. Besides, I didn't want my father to think I was still weak.

Nor did I want my mother to worry. That night I lay slumped in a chair, pretending to read. Words trickled down the page; I felt like dirty clothes someone had thrown on the chair. My father was at the shop taking stock. My mother sat gazing at me. I pretended harder; the words waltzed slowly. At last she said, "Are you listening?"

I was now, though I didn't look up. "Yes," I said hoarsely, unplugging my throat with a roar.

"Do you remember when you were a baby? There was a film you saw, of Father Christmas coming out of the chimney." Her voice sounded bravely careless, falsely light, as if she were determined to make some awful revelation. I couldn't look up. "Yes," I said.

Her silence made me glance up. She looked as she had on my first day at school: full of loss, of despair. Perhaps she was realizing I had to grow up, but to my throbbing head her look suggested only terror—as if she were about to deliver me up as a sacrifice. "I couldn't tell you the truth then," she said. "You were too young."

The truth was terror; her expression promised that. "Father Christmas isn't really like that," she said.

My illness must have shown by then. She gazed at me; her lips trembled. "I can't," she said, turning her face away. "Your father must tell you.'

But that left me poised on the edge of terror. I felt unnerved, rustily tense. I wanted very much to lie down. "I'm going to my room," I said. I stumbled upstairs, hardly aware of doing so. As much as anything I was fleeing her unease. The stairs swayed a little, they felt unnaturally soft underfoot. I hurried dully into my room. I slapped the light switch and missed. I was walking uncontrollably forward into blinding dark. A figure came to meet me, soft and huge in the dark of my room.

I cried out. I managed to stagger back onto the landing, grabbing the light switch as I went. The lighted room was empty. My mother came running upstairs, almost falling. "What is it, what is it?" she cried.

I mustn't say. "I'm ill. I feel sick." I did, and a minute later I was. She patted my back as I knelt by the toilet. When she'd put me to bed she made to go next door, for the doctor. "Don't leave me," I pleaded. The walls of the room swayed as if tugged by firelight; the fireplace was huge and very dark. As soon as my father opened the front door she ran downstairs, crying, "He's ill, he's ill! Go for the doctor!"

The doctor came and prescribed for my fever. My mother sat up beside me. Eventually my father came to suggest it was time she went to bed. They were going to leave me alone in my room. "Make a fire," I pleaded.

My mother touched my forehead. "But you're burning," she said.

"No, I'm cold! I want a fire! Please!" So she made one, tired as she was. I saw my father's disgust as he watched me use her worry against her to get what I wanted, his disgust with her for letting herself be used.

I didn't care. My mother's halting words had overgrown my mind. What had she been unable to tell me? Had it to do with the sounds I'd heard in the chimney? The room lolled around me; nothing was sure. But the fire would make sure for me. Nothing in the chimney could survive it.

I made my mother stay until the fire was blazing. Suppose a huge shape burst forth from the hearth, dripping fire? When at last I let her go I lay lapped by the firelight and meshy shadows, which seemed lulling now, in my warm room.

I felt feverish, but not unpleasantly. I was content to voyage on my rocking bed; the ceiling swayed past above me. While I slept the fire went out. My fever kept me warm; I slid out of bed and, pulling away the fireguard, reached up the chimney. At the length of my arms I touched something heavy, hanging down in the dark; it yielded, then soft fat fingers groped down and closed on my wrist. My mother was holding my wrist as she washed my hands. "You mustn't get out of bed," she said when she realized I was awake.

I stared stupidly at her. "You'd got out of bed. You were sleepwalking," she explained. "You had your hands right up the chimney." I saw now that she was washing caked soot from my hands; tracks of ash led toward the bed.

It had been only a dream. One moment the fat hand had been gripping my wrist, the next it was my mother's cool slim fingers. My mother played word games and timid chess with me while I stayed in bed, that day and the next.

The third night I felt better. The fire fluttered gently; I felt comfortably warm. Tomorrow I'd get up. I should have to go back to school soon, but I didn't mind that unduly. I lay and listened to the breathing of the wind in the chimney.

When I awoke the fire had gone out. The room was full of darkness. The wind still breathed, but it seemed somehow closer. It was above me. Someone was standing over me. It couldn't be either of my parents, not in the sightless darkness.

I lay rigid. Most of all I wished that I hadn't let Nigel's imagined contempt persuade me to do without a nightlight. The breathing was slow, irregular; it sounded clogged and feeble. As I tried to inch silently toward the far side of the bed, the source of the breathing stooped toward me. I felt its breath waver on my face, and the breath sprinkled me with something like dry rain.

When I had lain paralyzed for what felt like blind hours, the breathing went away. It was in the chimney, dislodging soot; it might be the wind. But I knew it had come out to let me know that whatever the fire had done to it, it hadn't been killed. It had emerged to tell me it would come for me on Christmas Eve. I began to scream.

I wouldn't tell my mother why. She washed my face, which was freckled with soot. "You've been sleepwalking again," she tried to reassure me, but I wouldn't let her leave me until daylight. When she'd gone I saw the ashy tracks leading from the chimney to the bed.

Perhaps I had been sleepwalking and dreaming. I searched vainly for my nightlight. I would have been ashamed to ask for a new one, and that helped me to feel I could do

without. At dinner I felt secure enough to say I didn't
know why I had screamed.

"But you must remember. You sounded so frightened.
You upset me."

My father was folding the evening paper into a thick
wad the size of a pocketbook, which he could read beside
his plate. "Leave the boy alone," he said. "You imagine
all sorts of things when you're feverish. I did when I was
his age."

It was the first time he'd admitted anything like weakness to me. If he'd managed to survive his nightmares,
why should mine disturb me more? Tired out by the
demands of my fever, I slept soundly that night. The
chimney was silent except for the flapping of flames.

But my father didn't help me again. One November
afternoon I was standing behind the counter, hoping for
customers. My father pottered, grumpily fingering packets
of nylons, tins of pet food, Dinky toys, baby's rattles,
cards, searching for signs of theft. Suddenly he snatched a
Christmas card and strode to the counter. "Sit down," he
said grimly.

He was waving the card at me, like evidence. I sat down
on a shelf, but then a lady came into the shop; the bell
thumped. I stood up to sell her nylons. When she'd gone I
gazed at my father, anxious to hear the worst. "Just sit
down," he said.

He couldn't stand my being taller than he was. His size
embarrassed him, but he wouldn't let me see that; he
pretended I had to sit down out of respect. "Your mother
says she tried to tell you about Father Christmas," he said.

She must have told him that weeks earlier. He'd put
off talking to me—because we'd never been close, and now
we were growing farther apart. "I don't know why she
couldn't tell you," he said.

But he wasn't telling me either. He was looking at me
as if I were a stranger he had to chat to. I felt uneasy,
unsure now that I wanted to hear what he had to say. A

man was approaching the shop. I stood up, hoping he'd interrupt.

He did, and I served him. Then, to delay my father's revelation, I adjusted stacks of tins. My father stared at me in disgust. "If you don't watch out you'll be as bad as your mother."

I found the idea of being like my mother strange, indefinably disturbing. But he wouldn't let me be like him, wouldn't let me near. All right, I'd be brave, I'd listen to what he had to say. But he said, "Oh, it's not worth me trying to tell you. You'll find out."

He meant I must find out for myself that Father Christmas was a childish fantasy. He didn't mean he wanted the thing from the chimney to come for me, the disgust in his eyes didn't mean that, it didn't. He meant that I had to behave like a man.

And I could. I'd show him. The chimney was silent. I needn't worry until Christmas Eve. Nor then. There was nothing to come out.

One evening as I walked home I saw Dr. Flynn in his front room. He was standing before a mirror, gazing at his red fur-trimmed hooded suit; he stooped to pick up his beard. My mother told me that he was going to act Father Christmas at the children's hospital. She seemed on the whole glad that I'd seen. So was I: it proved the pretense was only for children.

Except that the glimpse reminded me how near Christmas was. As the nights closed on the days, and the days rushed by—the end-of-term party, the turkey, decorations in the house—I grew tense, trying to prepare myself. For what? For nothing, nothing at all. Well, I would know soon—for suddenly it was Christmas Eve.

I was busy all day. I washed up as my mother prepared Christmas dinner. I brought her ingredients, and hurried to buy some she'd used up. I stuck the day's cards to tapes above the mantelpiece. I carried home a tinsel tree which nobody had bought. But being busy only made the day move faster. Before I knew it the windows were full of night.

Christmas Eve. Well, it didn't worry me. I was too old for that sort of thing. The tinsel tree rustled when anyone passed it, light rolled in tinsel globes, streamers flinched back when doors opened. Swinging restlessly on tapes above the mantelpiece were half a dozen red-cheeked, smiling bearded faces.

The night piled against the windows. I chattered to my mother about her shouting father, her elder sisters, the time her sisters had locked her in a cellar. My father grunted occasionally—even when I'd run out of subjects to discuss with my mother, and tried to talk to him about the shop. At least he hadn't noticed how late I was staying up. But he had. "It's about time everyone was in bed," he said with a kind of suppressed fury.

"Can I have some more coal?" My mother would never let me have a coal scuttle in the bedroom—she didn't want me going near the fire. "To put on now," I said. Surely she must say yes. "It'll be cold in the morning," I said.

"Yes, you take some. You don't want to be cold when you're looking at what Father—at your presents."

I hurried upstairs with the scuttle. Over its clatter I heard my father say, "Are you still at that? Can't you let him grow up?"

I almost emptied the scuttle into the fire, which rose roaring and crackling. My father's voice was an angry mumble, seeping through the floor. When I carried the scuttle down my mother's eyes were red, my father looked furiously determined. I'd always found their arguments frightening; I was glad to hurry to my room.

It seemed welcoming. The fire was bright within the mesh. I heard my mother come upstairs. That was comforting too: she was nearer now. I heard my father go next door—to wish the doctor Happy Christmas, I supposed. I didn't mind the reminder. There was nothing of Christmas Eve in my room, except the pillowcase waiting to be filled with presents on the floor at the foot of the bed. I pushed it aside with one foot, the better to ignore it.

I slid into bed. My father came upstairs; I heard further mumblings of argument through the bedroom wall. At last they stopped, and I tried to relax. I lay, glad of the silence.

A wind was rushing the house. It puffed down the chimney; smoke trickled through the fireguard. Now the wind was breathing brokenly. It was only the wind. It didn't bother me.

Perhaps I'd put too much coal on the fire. The room was hot; I was sweating. I felt almost feverish. The huge mesh flicked over the wall repeatedly, nervously, like a rapid net. Within the mirror the dimmer room danced.

Suddenly I was a little afraid. Not that something would come out of the chimney, that was stupid: afraid that my feeling of fever would make me delirious again. It seemed years since I'd been disturbed by the sight of the room in the mirror, but I was disturbed now. There was something wrong with that dim jerking room.

The wind breathed. Only the wind, I couldn't hear it changing. A fat billow of smoke squeezed through the mesh. The room seemed more oppressive now, and smelled of smoke. It didn't smell entirely like coal smoke, but I couldn't tell what else was burning. I didn't want to get up to find out.

I must lie still. Otherwise I'd be writhing about trying to clutch at sleep, as I had the second night of my fever, and sometimes in summer. I must sleep before the room grew too hot. I must keep my eyes shut. I mustn't be distracted by the faint trickling of soot, nor the panting of the wind, nor the shadows and orange light that snatched at my eyes through my eyelids.

I woke in darkness. The fire had gone out. No, it was still there when I opened my eyes: subdued orange crawled on embers, a few weak flames leaped repetitively. The room was moving more slowly now. The dim room in the mirror, the face peering out at me, jerked faintly, as if almost dead.

I couldn't look at that. I slid farther down the bed, dragging the pillow into my nest. I was too hot, but at least beneath the sheets I felt safe. I began to relax. Then I realized what I'd seen. The light had been dim, but I was almost sure the fireguard was standing away from the hearth.

I must have mistaken that, in the dim light. I wasn't feverish, I couldn't have sleepwalked again. There was no need for me to look, I was comfortable. But I was beginning to admit that I had better look when I heard the slithering in the chimney.

Something large was coming down. A fall of soot: I could hear the scattering pats of soot in the grate, thrown down by the harsh halting wind. But the wind was emerging from the fireplace, into the room. It was above me, panting through its obstructed throat.

I lay staring up at the mask of my sheets. I trembled from holding myself immobile. My held breath filled me painfully as lumps of rock. I had only to lie there until whatever was above me went away. It couldn't touch me.

The clogged breath bent nearer; I could hear its dry rattling. Then something began to fumble at the sheets over my face. It plucked feebly at them, trying to grasp them, as if it had hardly anything to grasp with. My own hands clutched at the sheets from within, but couldn't hold them down entirely. The sheets were being tugged from me, a fraction at a time. Soon I would be face to face with my visitor.

I was lying there with my eyes squeezed tight when it let go of the sheets and went away. My throbbing lungs had forced me to take shallow breaths; now I breathed silently open-mouthed, though that filled my mouth with fluff. The tolling of my ears subsided, and I realized the thing had not returned to the chimney. It was still in the room.

I couldn't hear its breathing; it couldn't be near me. Only that thought allowed me to look—that, and the desperate hope that I might escape, since it moved so slowly.

I peeled the sheets down from my face slowly, stealthily, until my eyes were bare. My heartbeats shook me. In the sluggishly shifting light I saw a figure at the foot of the bed.

Its red costume was thickly furred with soot. It had its back to me; its breathing was muffled by the hood. What shocked me most was its size. It occurred to me, somewhere amid my engulfing terror, that burning shrivels things. The figure stood in the mirror as well, in the dim twitching room. A face peered out of the hood in the mirror, like a charred turnip carved with a rigid grin.

The stunted figure was still moving painfully. It edged round the foot of the bed and stooped to my pillowcase. I saw it draw the pillowcase up over itself and sink down. As it sank its hood fell back, and I saw the charred turnip roll about in the hood, as if there were almost nothing left to support it.

I should have had to pass the pillowcase to reach the door. I couldn't move. The room seemed enormous, and was growing darker; my parents were far away. At last I managed to drag the sheets over my face, and pulled the pillow, like muffs, around my ears.

I had lain sleeplessly for hours when I heard movement at the foot of the bed. The thing had got out of its sack again. It was coming toward me. It was tugging at the sheets, more strongly now. Before I could catch hold of the sheets I glimpsed a red fur-trimmed sleeve, and was screaming.

"Let go, will you," my father said irritably. "Good God, it's only me."

He was wearing Dr. Flynn's disguise, which flapped about him—the jacket, at least; his pajama cuffs peeked beneath it. I stopped screaming and began to giggle hysterically. I think he would have struck me, but my mother ran in. "It's all right. All right," she reassured me, and explained to him, "It's the shock."

He was making angrily for the door when she said, "Oh, don't go yet, Albert. Stay while he opens his presents,'' and, lifting the bulging pillowcase from the floor, dumped it beside me.

I couldn't push it away, I couldn't let her see my terror. I made myself pull out my presents into the daylight, books, sweets, ballpoints; as I groped deeper I wondered whether the charred face would crumble when I touched it. Sweat pricked my hands; they shook with horror—they could, because my mother couldn't see them.

The pillowcase contained nothing but presents and a pinch of soot. When I was sure it was empty I slumped against the headboard, panting. "He's tired," my mother said, in defense of my ingratitude. "He was up very late last night.''

Later I managed an accident, dropping the pillowcase on the fire downstairs. I managed to eat Christmas dinner, and to go to bed that night. I lay awake, even though I was sure nothing would come out of the chimney now. Later I realized why my father had come to my room in the morning dressed like that; he'd intended me to catch him, to cure me of the pretense. But it was many years before I enjoyed Christmas very much.

When I left school I went to work in libraries. Ten years later I married. My wife and I crossed town weekly to visit my parents. My mother chattered, my father was taciturn. I don't think he ever quite forgave me for laughing at him.

One winter night our telephone rang. I answered it, hoping it wasn't the police. My library was then suffering from robberies. All I wanted was to sit before the fire and imagine the glittering cold outside. But it was Dr. Flynn.

"Your parents' house is on fire," he told me. "Your father's trapped in there. Your mother needs you.''

They'd had a friend to stay. My mother had lit the fire in the guest room, my old bedroom. A spark had eluded the fireguard; the carpet had caught fire. Impatient for the fire engine, my father had run back into the house to put the fire out, but had been overcome. All this I learned later. Now I drove coldly across town, toward the glow in the sky.

The glow was doused by the time I arrived. Smoke scrolled over the roof. But my mother had found a coal sack and was struggling still to run into the house, to beat out the fire; her friend and Dr. Flynn held her back. She dropped the sack and ran to me. "Oh, it's your father. It's Albert," she repeated through her weeping.

The firemen withdrew their hose. The ambulance stood winking. I saw the front door open, and a stretcher carried out. The path was wet and frosty. One stretcher-bearer slipped, and the contents of the stretcher spilled over the path.

I saw Dr. Flynn glance at my mother. Only the fear that she might turn caused him to act. He grabbed the sack and, running to the path, scooped up what lay scattered there. I saw the charred head roll on the lip of the sack before it dropped within. I had seen that already, years ago.

My mother came to live with us, but we could see she was pining; my parents must have loved each other, in their way. She died a year later. Perhaps I killed them both. I know that what emerged from the chimney was in some sense my father. But surely that was a premonition. Surely my fear could never have reached out to make him die that way.

# Call First

IT was the other porters who made Ned determined to know who answered the phone in the old man's house.

Not that he hadn't wanted to know before. He'd felt it was his right almost as soon as the whole thing had begun, months ago. He'd been sitting behind his desk in the library entrance, waiting for someone to try to take a bag into the library so he could shout after them that they couldn't, when the reference librarian ushered the old man up to Ned's desk and said, "Let this gentleman use your phone." Maybe he hadn't meant every time the old man came to the library, but then he should have said so. The old man used to talk to the librarian and tell him things about books even he didn't know, which was why he let him phone. All Ned could do was feel resentful. People weren't supposed to use his phone, and even he wasn't allowed to phone outside the building. And it wasn't as if the old man's calls were interesting. Ned wouldn't have minded if they'd been worth hearing.

"I'm coming home now." That was all he ever said;

then he'd put down the receiver and hurry away. It was the way he said it that made Ned wonder. There was no feeling behind the words; they sounded as if he were saying them only because he had to, perhaps wishing he needn't. Ned knew people talked like that: his parents did in church, and most of the time at home. He wondered if the old man was calling his wife, because he wore a ring on his wedding finger, although in the claw where a stone should be was what looked like a piece of yellow fingernail. But Ned didn't think it could be his wife; each day the old man came he left the library at the same time, so why would he bother to phone?

Then there was the way the old man looked at Ned when he phoned: as if he didn't matter and couldn't understand, the way most of the porters looked at him. That was the look that swelled up inside Ned one day and made him persuade one of the other porters to take charge of his desk while Ned waited to listen in on the old man's call. The girl who always smiled at Ned was on the switchboard, and they listened together. They heard the phone in the house ringing then lifted, and the old man's call and his receiver going down: nothing else, not even breathing apart from the old man's. "Who do you think it is?" the girl said, but Ned thought she'd laugh if he said he didn't know. He shrugged extravagantly and left.

Now he was determined. The next time the old man came to the library Ned phoned his house, having read what the old man dialed. When the ringing began its pulse sounded deliberately slow, and Ned felt the pumping of his blood rushing ahead. Seven trills and the phone in the house opened with a violent click. Ned held his breath, but all he could hear was his blood thumping his ears. "Hello," he said and after a silence, clearing his throat, "Hello!" Perhaps it was one of those answering machines people in films used in the office. He felt foolish and uneasy greeting the wide silent metal ear, and put down the receiver. He was in bed and falling asleep before he wondered why the old man should tell an answering machine that he was coming home.

The following day, in the bar where all the porters went at lunchtime, Ned told them about the silently listening phone. "He's weird, that old man," he said, but now the others had finished joking with him they no longer seemed interested, and he had to make a grab for the conversation. "He reads weird books," he said. "All about witches and magic. Real ones, not stories."

"Now tell us something we didn't know," someone said, and the conversation turned its back on Ned. His attention began to wander, he lost his hold on what was being said, he had to smile and nod as usual when they looked at him, and he was thinking: they're looking at me like the old man does. I'll show them. I'll go in his house and see who's there. Maybe I'll take something that'll show I've been there. Then they'll have to listen.

But next day at lunchtime, when he arrived at the address he'd seen on the old man's library card, Ned felt more like knocking at the front door and running away. The house was menacingly big, the end house of a street whose other windows were brightly bricked up. Exposed foundations like broken teeth protruded from the mud that surrounded the street, while the mud was walled in by a five-story crescent of flats that looked as if it had been designed in sections to be fitted together by a two-year-old. Ned tried to keep the house between him and the flats, even though they were hundreds of yards away, as he peered in the windows.

All he could see through the grimy front window was bare floorboards; when he coaxed himself to look through the side window, the same. He dreaded being caught by the old man, even though he'd seen him sitting behind a pile of books ten minutes ago. It had taken Ned that long to walk here; the old man couldn't walk so fast, and there wasn't a bus he could catch. At last he dodged round the back and peered into the kitchen: a few plates in the sink, some tins of food, an old cooker. Nobody to be seen. He returned to the front, wondering what to do. Maybe he'd knock after all. He took hold of the bar of the knocker, trying to think what he'd say, and the door opened.

The hall leading back to the kitchen was long and dim. Ned stood shuffling indecisively on the step. He would have to decide soon, for his lunch hour was dwindling. It was like one of the empty houses he'd used to play in with the other children, daring each other to go up the tottering stairs. Even the things in the kitchen didn't make it seem lived in. He'd show them all. He went in. Acknowledging a vague idea that the old man's companion was out, he closed the door to hear if they returned.

On his right was the front room; on his left, past the stairs and the phone, another of the bare rooms he'd seen. He tiptoed upstairs. The stairs creaked and swayed a little, perhaps unused to anyone of Ned's weight. He reached the landing, breathing heavily, feeling dust chafe his throat. Stairs led up to a closed attic door, but he looked in the rooms off the landing.

Two of the doors which he opened stealthily showed him nothing but boards and flurries of floating dust. The landing in front of the third looked cleaner, as if the door were often opened. He pulled it toward him, holding it up all the way so it didn't scrape the floor, and went in.

Most of it didn't seem to make sense. There was a single bed with faded sheets. Against the walls were tables and piles of old books. Even some of the books looked disused. There were black candles and racks of small cardboard boxes. On one of the tables lay a single book. Ned padded across the fragments of carpet and opened the book in a thin path of sunlight through the shutters.

Inside the sagging covers was a page which Ned slowly realized had been ripped from the Bible. It was the story of Lazarus. Scribbles that might be letters filled the margins, and at the bottom of the page: "p. 491." Suddenly inspired, Ned turned to that page in the book. It showed a drawing of a corpse sitting up in his coffin, but the book was all in the language they sometimes used in church: Latin. He thought of asking one of the librarians what it meant. Then he remembered that he needed proof he'd been in the house. He stuffed the page from the Bible into his pocket.

As he crept swiftly downstairs, something was troubling him. He reached the hall and thought he knew what it was. He still didn't know who lived in the house with the old man. If they lived in the back perhaps there would be signs in the kitchen. Though if it was his wife, Ned thought as he hurried down the hall, she couldn't be like Ned's mother, who would never have left torn strips of wallpaper hanging at shoulder height from both walls. He'd reached the kitchen door when he realized what had been bothering him. When he'd emerged from the bedroom, the attic door had been open.

He looked back involuntarily, and saw a woman walking away from him down the hall.

He was behind the closed kitchen door before he had time to feel fear. That came only when he saw that the back door was nailed rustily shut. Then he controlled himself. She was only a woman, she couldn't do much if she found him. He opened the door minutely. The hall was empty.

Halfway down the hall he had to slip into the side room, heart punching his chest, for she'd appeared again from between the stairs and the front door. He felt the beginnings of anger and recklessness, and they grew faster when he opened the door and had to flinch back as he saw her hand passing. The fingers looked famished, the color of old lard, with long yellow cracked nails. There was no nail on her wedding finger, which wore a plain ring. She was returning from the direction of the kitchen, which was why Ned hadn't expected her.

Through the opening of the door he heard her padding upstairs. She sounded barefoot. He waited until he couldn't hear her, then edged out into the hall. The door began to swing open behind him with a faint creak, and he drew it stealthily closed. He paced toward the front door. If he

hadn't seen her shadow creeping down the stairs he would
have come face to face with her.

He'd retreated to the kitchen, and was near to panic,
when he realized she knew he was in the house. She was
playing a game with him. At once he was furious. She was
only an old woman, her body beneath the long white dress
was sure to be as thin as her hands, she could only shout
when she saw him, she couldn't stop him leaving. In a
minute he'd be late for work. He threw open the kitchen
door and swaggered down the hall.

The sight of her lifting the phone receiver broke his
stride for a moment. Perhaps she was phoning the police.
He hadn't done anything, she could have her Bible page
back. But she laid the receiver beside the phone. Why?
Was she making sure the old man couldn't ring?

As she unbent from stooping to the phone she grasped
two uprights of the banisters to support herself. They gave
a loud splintering creak and bent together. Ned halted,
confused. He was still struggling to react when she turned
toward him, and he saw her face. Part of it was still on the
bone.

He didn't back away until she began to advance on him,
her nails tearing new strips from both walls. All he could
see was her protruding eyes, unsupported by flesh. His
mind was backing away faster than he was, but it had
come up against a terrible insight. He even knew why
she'd made sure the old man couldn't interrupt until she'd
finished. His calls weren't like speaking to an answering
machine at all. They were exactly like switching off a
burglar alarm.

# The
# Companion

WHEN Stone reached the fairground, having been misdirected twice, he thought it looked more like a gigantic amusement arcade. A couple of paper cups tumbled and rattled on the shore beneath the promenade, and the cold insinuating October wind scooped the Mersey across the slabs of red rock that formed the beach, across the broken bottles and abandoned tires. Beneath the stubby white mock turrets of the long fairground facade, shops displayed souvenirs and fish and chips. Among them, in the fairground entrances, scraps of paper whirled.

Stone almost walked away. This wasn't his best holiday. One fairground in Wales had been closed, and this one certainly wasn't what he'd expected. The guidebook had made it sound like a genuine fairground, sideshows you must stride among not looking in case their barkers lured you in, the sudden shock of waterfalls cascading down what looked like painted cardboard, the shots and bells and wooden concussions of target galleries, the girls' shrieks overhead, the slippery armor and juicy crunch of toffee-apples, the illuminations springing alight against a darkening sky. But at least, he thought, he had chosen his time well. If he went in now he might have the fairground almost to himself.

As he reached an entrance, he saw his mother eating fish and chips from a paper tray. What nonsense! She would never have eaten standing up in public—"like a horse," as she'd used to say. But he watched as she hurried out of the shop, face averted from him and the wind. Of course, it had been the way she ate, with little snatching motions of her fork and mouth. He pushed the incident to the side of his mind in the hope that it would fall away, and hurried through the entrance, into the clamor of color and noise.

The high roof with its bare iron griders reminded him at once of a railway station, but the place was noisier still. The uproar—the echoing sirens and jets and dangerous groaning of metal—was trapped, and was deafening. It was so overwhelming that he had to remind himself he could see, even if he couldn't hear.

But there wasn't much to see. The machines looked faded and dusty. Cars like huge armchairs were lurching and spinning helplessly along a switchback, a canvas canopy was closing over an endless parade of seats, a great disc tasselled with seats was lifting toward the roof, dangling a lone couple over its gears. With so few people in sight it seemed almost that the machines, frustrated by inaction, were operating themselves. For a moment Stone had the impression of being shut in a dusty room where the toys, as in childhood tales, had come to life.

He shrugged vaguely and turned to leave. Perhaps he could drive to the fairground at Southport, though it was a good few miles across the Mersey. His holiday was dwindling rapidly. He wondered how they were managing at the tax office in his absence. Slower than usual, no doubt.

Then he saw the merry-go-round. It was like a toy forgotten by another child and left here, or handed down the generations. Beneath its ornate scrolled canopy the horses rode on poles toward their reflections in a ring of mirrors. The horses were white wood or wood painted white, their bodies dappled with purple, red, and green, and some of their sketched faces too. On the hub, above a notice MADE IN AMSTERDAM, an organ piped to itself. Around it, Stone saw carved fish, mermen, zephyrs, a head and shoulders smoking a pipe in a frame, a landscape of hills and lake and unfurling perched hawk. "Oh, yes," Stone said.

As he clambered onto the platform he felt a hint of embarrassment, but nobody seemed to be watching. "Can you pay me," said the head in the frame. "My boy's gone for a minute."

The man's hair was the color of the smoke from his pipe. His lips puckered on the stem and smiled. "It's a good merry-go-round," Stone said.

"You know about them, do you?"

"Well, a little." The man looked disappointed, and Stone hurried on. "I know a lot of fairgrounds. They're my holiday, you see, every year. Each year I cover a different area. I may write a book." The idea had occasionally tempted him—but he hadn't taken notes, and he still had ten years to retirement, for which the book had suggested itself as an activity.

"You go alone every year?"

"It has its merits. Less expensive, for one thing. Helps me save. Before I retire I mean to see Disneyland and Vienna." He thought of the Big Wheel, Harry Lime, the earth falling away beneath. "I'll get on," he said.

He patted the unyielding shoulders of the horse, and remembered a childhood friend who'd had a rocking horse in his bedroom. Stone had ridden it a few times, more and more wildly when it was nearly time to go home; his friend's bedroom was brighter than his, and as he clung to the wooden shoulders he was clutching the friendly room too. Funny thinking of that now, he thought. Because I haven't been on a merry-go-round for years, I suppose.

The merry-go-round stirred; the horse lifted him, let him

sink. As they moved forward, slowly gathering momentum, Stone saw a crowd surging through one of the entrances and spreading through the funfair. He grimaced: it had been his fairground for a little while, they needn't have arrived just as he was enjoying his merry-go-round.

The crowd swung away. A jangle of pinball machines sailed by. Amid the Dodgems a giant with a barrel body was spinning, flapping its limp arms, a red electric cigar thrust in its blank grin and throbbing in time with its slow thick laughter. A tinny voice read Bingo numbers, buzzing indistinctly. Perhaps it was because he hadn't eaten for a while, saving himself for the toffee-apples, but he was growing dizzy—it felt like the whirling blurred shot of the fair in *Saturday Night and Sunday Morning*, a fair he hadn't liked because it was too grim. Give him *Strangers on a Train*, *Some Came Running*, *The Third Man*, even the fairground murder in *Horrors of the Black Museum*. He shook his head to try to control his pouring thoughts.

But the fair was spinning faster. The Ghost Train's station raced by, howling and screaming. People strolling past the merry-go-round looked jerky as drawings in a thaumatrope. Here came the Ghost Train once more, and Stone glimpsed the queue beneath the beckoning green corpse. They were staring at him. No, he realized next time round, they were staring at the merry-go-round. He was just something that kept appearing as they watched. At the end of the queue, staring and poking around inside his nostrils, stood Stone's father.

Stone gripped the horse's neck as he began to fall. The man was already wandering away toward the Dodgems. Why was his mind so traitorous today? It wouldn't be so bad if the comparisons it made weren't so repulsive. Why, he'd never met a man or woman to compare with his parents. Admired people, yes, but not in the same way. Not since the two polished boxes had been lowered into holes and hidden. Noise and color spun about him and inside him. Why wasn't he allowing himself to think about his parents' death? He knew why he was blocking, and that should be his salvation: at the age of ten he'd suffered death and hell every night.

He clung to the wood in the whirlpool and remembered. His father had denied him a nightlight and his mother had nodded, saying, "Yes, I think it's time." He'd lain in bed, terrified to move in case he betrayed his presence to the darkness, mouthing "Please God don't let it" over and over. He lay so that he could see the faint gray vertical line of the window between the curtains in the far distance, but even that light seemed to be receding. He knew that death and hell would be like this. Sometimes, as he began to blur with sleep and the room grew larger and the shapes dark against the darkness awoke, he couldn't tell that he hadn't already died.

He sat back as the horse slowed and he began to slip forward across its neck. What then? Eventually he'd seen through the self-perpetuating trap of religious guilt, of hell, of not daring to believe in it because then it would get you. For a while he'd been vaguely uneasy in dark places, but not sufficiently so to track down the feeling and conquer it. After a while it had dissipated, along with his parents' overt disapproval of his atheism. Yes, he thought as his memories and the merry-go-round slowed, I was happiest then, lying in bed hearing and feeling them and the house around me. Then, when he was thirty, a telephone call had summoned him to the hole in the road, to the sight of the car like a dead black beetle protruding from the hole. There had been a moment of sheer vertiginous terror, and then it was over. His parents had gone into darkness. That was enough. It was the one almost religious observance he imposed on himself: think no more.

And there was no reason to do so now. He staggered away from the merry-go-round, toward the pinball arcade that occupied most of one side of the funfair. He remembered how, when he lay mouthing soundless pleas in bed, he would sometimes stop and think of what he'd read about dreams: that they might last for hours but in reality occupied only a split second. Was the same true of thoughts?

And prayers, when you had nothing but darkness by which to tell the time? Besides defending him, his prayers were counting off the moments before dawn. Perhaps he had used up only a minute, only a second of darkness. Death and hell—what strange ideas I used to have, he thought. Especially for a ten-year-old. I wonder where they went. Away with short trousers and pimples and everything else I grew out of, of course.

Three boys of about twelve were crowded around a pinball machine. As they moved apart momentarily he saw that they were trying to start it with a coin on a piece of wire. He took a stride toward them and opened his mouth— but suppose they turned on him? If they set about him, pulled him down and kicked him, his shouts would never be heard for the uproar.

There was no sign of an attendant. Stone hurried back to the merry-go-round, where several little girls were mounting horses. "Those boys are up to no good," he complained to the man in the frame.

"You! Yes, you! I've seen you before. Don't let me see you again," the man shouted. They dispersed, swaggering.

"Things didn't use to be like this," Stone said, breathing hard with relief. "I suppose your merry-go-round is all that's left of the old fairground."

"The old one? No, this didn't come from there."

"I thought the old one must have been taken over."

"No, it's still there, what's left of it," the man said. "I don't know what you'd find there now. Through that exit is the quickest way. You'll come to the side entrance in five minutes, if it's still open."

The moon had risen. It glided along the rooftops as Stone emerged from the back of the funfair and hurried along the terraced street. Its light lingered on the tips of chimneys and the peaks of roofs. Inside the houses, above slivers of earth or stone that passed for front gardens, Stone saw faces silvered by television.

At the end of the terrace, beyond a wider road, he saw an identical street paralleled by an alley. Just keep going.

The moon cleared the roofs as he crossed the intersection, and left a whitish patch on his vision. He was trying to blink it away as he reached the street, and so he wasn't certain if he glimpsed a group of boys emerging from the street he'd just left and running into the alley.

Anxiety hurried him onward while he wondered if he should turn back. His car was on the promenade; he could reach it in five minutes. They must be the boys he had seen in the pinball arcade, out for revenge. Quite possibly they had knives or broken bottles; no doubt they knew how to use them from the television. His heels clacked in the silence. Dark exits from the alley gaped between the houses. He tried to set his feet down gently as he ran. The boys were making no sound at all, at least none that reached him. If they managed to overbalance him they could smash his bones while he struggled to rise. At his age that could be worse than dangerous. Another exit lurked between the houses, which looked threatening in their weight and impassivity. He must stay on his feet whatever happened. If the boys got hold of his arms he could only shout for help. The houses fell back as the street curved, their opposite numbers loomed closer. In front of him, beyond a wall of corrugated tin, lay the old fairground.

He halted panting, trying to quell his breath before it blotted out any sounds in the alley. Where he had hoped to find a well-lit road to the promenade, both sides of the street ended as if lopped, and the way was blocked by the wall of tin. In the middle, however, the tin had been prised back like a lid, and a jagged entrance yawned among the sharp shadows and moonlit inscriptions. The fairground was closed and deserted.

As he realized that the last exit was back beyond the curve of the street, Stone stepped through the gap in the tin. He stared down the street, which was empty but for scattered fragments of brick and glass. It occurred to him that they might not have been the same boys after all. He pulled the tin to, behind him, and looked around.

The circular booths, the long target galleries, the low

roller coaster, the ark and the crazy house draped shadow over each other and merged with the dimness of the paths between. Even the merry-go-round was hooded by darkness hanging from its canopy. Such wood as he could see in the moonlight looked ragged, the paint patchy. But between the silent machines and stalls one ride was faintly illuminated: the Ghost Train.

He walked toward it. Its front was emitting a pale green glow which at first sight looked like moonlight, but which was brighter than the white tinge the moon imparted to the adjoining rides. Stone could see one car on the rails, close to the entrance to the ride. As he approached, he glimpsed from the corner of his eye a group of men, stallholders presumably, talking and gesticulating in the shadows between two stalls. So the fairground wasn't entirely deserted. They might be about to close, but perhaps they would allow him one ride, seeing that the Ghost Train was still lit. He hoped they hadn't seen him using the vandals' entrance.

As he reached the ride and realized that the glow came from a coat of luminous paint, liberally applied but now rather dull and threadbare, he heard a loud clang from the tin wall. It might have been someone throwing a brick, or someone reopening the torn door; the stalls obstructed his view. He glanced quickly about for another exit, but found none. He might run into a dead end. It was best to stay where he was. He couldn't trust the stallholders; they might live nearby, they might know the boys or even be their parents. As a child he'd once run to someone who had proved to be his attacker's unhelpful father. He climbed into the Ghost Train car.

Nothing happened. Nobody was attending the ride. Stone strained his ears. Neither the boys, if they were there, nor the attendant seemed to be approaching. If he called out the boys would hear him. Instead, frustrated and furious, he began to kick the metal inside the nose of the car.

Immediately the car trundled forward over the lip of an

incline in the track and plunged through the Ghost Train
doors into darkness.

As he swung round an unseen clattering curve, surrounded by noise and the dark, Stone felt as if he had
suddenly become the victim of delirium. He remembered
his storm-wracked childhood bed and the teeming darkness
pouring into him. Why on earth had he come on this ride?
He'd never liked ghost trains as a child, and as he grew up
he had instinctively avoided them. He'd allowed his panic
to trap him. The boys might be waiting when he emerged.
Well, in that case he would appeal to whoever was operating the ride. He sat back, gripping the wooden seat
beneath him with both hands, and gave himself up to the
straining of metal, the abrupt swoops of the car, and the
darkness.

Then, as his anxiety about the outcome of the ride
diminished, another impression began to trickle back. As
the car had swung around the first curve he'd glimpsed an
illuminated shape, two illuminated shapes, withdrawn so
swiftly that he'd had no time to glance up at them. He had
the impression that they had been the faces of a man and a
woman, gazing down at him. At once they had vanished
into the darkness or been swept away by it. It seemed to
him for some reason very important to remember their
expressions.

Before he could pursue this, he saw a grayish glow
ahead of him. He felt an unreasoning hope that it would be
a window, which might give him an idea of the extent of
the darkness. But already he could see that its shape was
too irregular. A little closer and he could make it out. It
was a large stuffed gray rabbit with huge glass or plastic
eyes, squatting upright in an alcove with its front paws
extended before it. Not a dead rabbit, of course: a toy.
Beneath him the car was clattering and shaking, yet he had
the odd notion that this was a deliberate effect, that in fact
the car had halted and the rabbit was approaching or
growing. Rubbish, he thought. It was a pretty feeble ghost,
anyway. Childish. His hands pulled at splinters on the

wooden seat beneath him. The rabbit rushed toward him as the track descended a slight slope. One of its eyes was loose, and whitish stuffing hung down its cheek from the hole. The rabbit was at least four feet tall. As the car almost collided with it before whipping away around a curve, the rabbit toppled toward him and the light which illuminated it went out.

Stone gasped and clutched his chest. He'd twisted round to look behind him at the darkness where he judged the rabbit to have been, until a spasm wrenched him frontward again. Light tickling drifted over his face. He shuddered, then relaxed. Of course they always had threads hanging down for cobwebs, his friends had told him that. But no wonder the fairground was deserted, if this was the best they could do. Giant toys lit up, indeed. Not only cheap but liable to give children nightmares.

The car coursed up a slight incline and down again before shaking itself in a frenzy around several curves. Trying to soften you up before the next shock, Stone thought. Not me, thank you very much. He lay back in his seat and sighed loudly with boredom. The sound hung on his ears like muffs. Why did I do that? he wondered. It's not as if the operator can hear me. Then who can?

Having spent its energy on the curves, the car was slowing. Stone peered ahead, tryng to anticipate. Obviously he was meant to relax before the car startled him with a sudden jerk. As he peered, he found his eyes were adjusting to the darkness. At least he could make out a few feet ahead, at the side of the track, a squat and bulky gray shape. He squinted as the car coasted toward it. It was a large armchair.

The car came abreast of it and halted. Stone peered at the chair. In the dim hectic flecked light, which seemed to attract and outline all the restless discs on his eyes, the chair somehow looked larger than he. Perhaps it was farther away than he'd thought. Some clothes thrown over the back of the chair looked diminished by it, but they could be a child's clothes. If nothing else, Stone thought, it's instructive to watch my mind working. Now let's get on.

Then he noticed that the almost invisible light was flickering. Either that, which was possible although he couldn't determine the source of the light, or the clothes were shifting; very gradually but nonetheless definitely, as if something hidden by them were lifting them to peer out, perhaps preparatory to emerging. Stone leaned toward the chair. Let's see what it is, let's get it over with. But the light was far too dim, the chair too distant. Probably he would be unable to see it even when it emerged, the way the light had been allowed to run down, unless he left the car and went closer.

He had one hand on the side of the car when he realized that if the car moved off while he was out of it he would be left to grope his way through the darkness. He slumped back, and as he did so he glimpsed a violent movement among the clothes near the seat of the chair. He glanced toward it. Before his eyes could focus, the dim gray light was extinguished.

Stone sat for a moment, all of him concentrating on the silence, the blind darkness. Then he began to kick frantically at the nose of the car. The car shook a little with his attack, but stayed where it was. By the time it decided to move forward, the pressure of his blood seemed to be turning the darkness red.

When the car nosed its way around the next curve, slowing as if sniffing the track ahead, Stone heard a muted thud and creak of wood above the noise of the wheels. It came from in front of him. The sort of thing you hear in a house at night, he thought. Soon be out now.

Without warning a face came rushing toward him out of the darkness a few feet ahead. It jerked forward as he did. Of course it would, he thought with a grimace, sinking back and watching his face sink briefly into the mirror. Now he could see that he and the car were surrounded by a faint light which extended as far as the wooden frame of the mirror. Must be the end of the ride. They can't get any more obvious than that. Effective in its way, I suppose.

He watched himself in the mirror as the car followed the curve past. His silhouette loomed on the grayish light, which had fallen behind. Suddenly he frowned. His silhouette was moving independent of the movement of the car. It was beginning to swing out of the limits of the mirror. Then he remembered the wardrobe that had stood at the foot of his childhood bed, and realized what was happening. The mirror was set in a door, which was opening.

Stone pressed himself against the opposite side of the car, which had slowed almost to a halt. No no, he thought, it mustn't. Don't. He heard a grinding of gears beneath him; unmeshed metal shrieked. He threw his body forward, against the nose of the car. In the darkness to his left he heard the creak of the door and a soft thud. The car moved a little, then caught the gears and ground forward.

As the light went out behind him, Stone felt a weight fall beside him on the seat.

He cried out. Or tried to, for as he gulped in air it seemed to draw darkness into his lungs, darkness that swelled and poured into his heart and brain. There was a moment in which he knew nothing, as if he'd become darkness and silence and the memory of suffering. Then the car was rattling on, the darkness was sweeping over him and by, and the nose of the car banged open the doors and plunged out into the night.

As the car swung onto the length of track outside the Ghost Train, Stone caught sight of the gap between the stalls where he had thought he'd seen the stallholders. A welling moonlight showed him that between the stalls stood a pile of sacks, nodding and gesticulating in the wind. Then the seat beside him emerged from the shadow, and he looked down.

Next to him on the seat was a shrunken hooded figure. It wore a faded jacket and trousers striped and patched in various colors, indistinguishable in the receding moonlight. The head almost reached his shoulder. Its arms hung slack at its sides, and its feet drummed laxly on the metal beneath the seat. Shrinking away, Stone reached for the front of the car to pull himself to his feet, and the figure's head fell back.

Stone closed his eyes. When he opened them he saw within the hood an oval of white cloth upon which—black crosses for eyes, a barred crescent for a mouth—a grinning face was stitched.

As he had suddenly realized that the car hadn't halted nor even slowed before plunging down the incline back into the Ghost Train, Stone did not immediately notice that the figure had taken his hand.

## MORE BESTSELLERS FROM TOR